THE ALPHA

A BLACK ARROWHEAD NOVEL

USA TODAY BESTSELLING AUTHOR
DANNIKA DARK

All Rights Reserved
Copyright © 2021 Dannika Dark
First Edition: 2021

First Print Edition
ISBN-13: 979-8532-666-48-1

Formatting: Streetlight Graphics

No part of this book may be reproduced, distributed, transmitted in any form or by any means, or stored in a database retrieval system without the prior written permission of the author. You must not circulate this book in any format. Thank you for respecting the rights of the author.

This is a work of fiction. Any resemblance of characters to actual persons, living or dead, is purely coincidental.

Edited by Victory Editing and Red Adept. Cover design by Dannika Dark. All stock purchased.

www.dannikadark.net
Fan page located on Facebook

Also By Dannika Dark:

THE MAGERI SERIES
Sterling
Twist
Impulse
Gravity
Shine
The Gift (Novella)

MAGERI WORLD
Risk

NOVELLAS
Closer

THE SEVEN SERIES
Seven Years
Six Months
Five Weeks
Four Days
Three Hours
Two Minutes
One Second
Winter Moon (Novella)

SEVEN WORLD
Charming

THE CROSSBREED SERIES
Keystone
Ravenheart
Deathtrap
Gaslight
Blackout

Nevermore
Moonstruck
Spellbound
Heartless
Afterlife

THE BLACK ARROWHEAD SERIES
The Vow
The Alpha

Chapter 1

I rapped my knuckles against Melody and Lakota's bedroom door. "Wake up, lazybones. You're working the early shift today, remember?"

"I'm coming, I'm coming," Melody grumbled.

I drifted down the hall toward the kitchen to see if the coffee was ready.

"Hope!"

I whirled around. When Lakota poked his head into the hall, I giggled. His hair looked like it had been through a wind tunnel.

He squinted from the light in the living room behind me. "What time do you get off tonight?"

"Nine at the latest. It depends on how busy we get."

He eased into the hall and shut the door behind him, his red shirt halfway tucked into his boxers. "We need to do something about those hours. It'll be fall soon, and I'm not having you two working after dark."

I snorted. "You're my brother, but remember that I'm not someone you can order around. Be sure to let me know when you break the news to Melody that you're deciding our business hours, because I'm *dying* to see her reaction."

"Hire the twins. They could use some part-time work."

I loved Melody's younger brothers, but that wasn't going to happen. "You don't think it's inappropriate to ask two alpha males to work beneath me in a low-paying position? How will that groom them for a leadership role in a pack? They have their own destiny to follow."

He rubbed his face. "Just be sure to come straight home instead of going to see Mother."

Lakota and Melody had recently formed a fast and permanent relationship, and shortly afterward, Lakota had moved in with us. It was wonderful having my older brother around, but the apartment was quaint, and a couple needed privacy that the thin walls couldn't provide. I respected their needs and occasionally went straight from work to visit with my old pack, which my father led. I loved having wolves around me, but Lakota and I weren't a pack, and hearing the carnal cries of my best friend and brother wasn't my idea of a fun Friday night.

Or almost every other night of the week for that matter.

"I planned to visit with Mother before they left town in the morning, but if you insist, I'll be here. Now dress yourself. A sister shouldn't have to see such things." I smiled, shading my eyes as I turned on my heel.

He chuckled before closing the door.

Lakota was my half brother but my whole heart. We hadn't grown up in the same house, but he'd always been my protector, and we visited every chance we got. For the past few years, he'd taken on a job as a bounty hunter, and that meant seeing him less often. But after mating with my best friend, Lakota was in search of a new beginning. No rush. He had plenty of money saved and wanted to extend his honeymoon with Melody for as long as possible before figuring out his life. Even though we occasionally bickered, I loved having my big brother around. He was a good man who took care of those he loved.

If only he took care of his dirty laundry instead of tossing it on the bathroom floor.

I swept my long hair behind my shoulders and padded down the hall, the wood floor chilling the soles of my bare feet. When I reached the living room, I swung right toward the kitchen. I loved early morning regardless of the weather. There was something spiritual about the start of a new day—a time when I felt the most connected to my wolf.

Since our apartment building had interior halls and elevators, it was safer than most places in the Breed district. A beautiful row of tall windows spanned the living room on my left, all the way to the kitchen. I approached the short pony wall that separated the two rooms and poured a leftover bottle of water into one of the houseplants on the ledge. Mel and I had different tastes when it came to decorating, so she claimed the living room, and I had dominion over the kitchen. I'd selected every dish, and the trivets and pot holders were handmade by members of my former pack as going-away gifts when I moved out. Melody's grey room and hot-pink couch might have clashed with my earthy tones, but I loved the visual contrast between our personalities.

Melody strolled into the room in her favorite patchwork jeans and a cotton shirt. She yawned noisily and plopped down on a barstool, yesterday's makeup smeared beneath her heavy-lidded eyes.

"Did you at least brush your teeth?" I asked.

Mel scratched at her messy ponytail. "I'll brush them after breakfast. I don't know why you bother waking up this early when you don't have to work until the afternoon."

I smiled and slouched on the stool across from her. "Do you really need to ask? I've always liked getting up with the sun."

"Maybe we should have called our store Sunbeam instead of Moonglow."

I chuckled softly and gazed at the suncatcher in the window. Because we managed the business together, we had the luxury of managing our schedules. We could have made them fixed, but we'd decided it wouldn't be fair for one person to always work the late shift and miss the opportunity to go out on dates.

Not that I went out on dates, but Mel and Lakota enjoyed having drinks at Howlers or seeing a late show at the Alamo Drafthouse.

When the coffeepot beeped, I set the carafe on a trivet between us and retrieved buttermilk biscuits and bacon from the warming oven. Mel poured coffee into a mug she'd bought as a souvenir on her last trip to Dallas.

Lakota appeared, scratching the scar on his bare chest before hiking up his loose jeans. He leaned on the island and swung his keys around his index finger. "I'll drive you to work."

Mel chomped on her biscuit, crumbs showering her plate. "Think again."

He peered behind him at the red scooter leaning against the wall by the front door. "Maybe it's time for you to buy a car like a real adult, *wife*."

She narrowed her green eyes at him. "I like the exercise and the wind in my hair, *husband*."

He chewed off a piece of bacon, which was no longer crispy after spending an hour in the warming oven. "No worries. Something tells me you'll be changing your tune when it's forty degrees outside and raining."

"This is Austin, not Cognito. It's not like we're going to get buried in twelve feet of snow. A few chilly days out of the year won't stop me. Besides, I own a raincoat."

He kissed her temple before swaggering off. "We'll see, Freckles."

She glared at me with a look of annoyance. "He thinks he knows everything. I'm not a girly-girl. A little rain never hurt anyone." After taking a quick sip of coffee, she wiped her finger beneath her eye and stared at the dark smudge on her fingertip. "I need to take a shower and get ready. Are we putting out your new line of earrings today?"

I cast my eyes down at my grey harem pants, which looked more like a skirt since the legs were so wide. "Maybe."

I was proud of my jewelry, but launching a new line gave

me butterflies. I'd spent weeks with my assistant on these earrings, and I wasn't sure how they would sell since they were comprised of feathers and small beads. Most of my other pieces were quality gemstones, but what set these apart were the feathers, which had once belonged to Shifters. Would customers be willing to pay the asking price? Would they laugh?

"Not to hassle you, but I need to know whether to put them out or not," Melody continued. "We've had that empty case on reserve for the past week, and people are excited to see what's coming."

I squared my shoulders and tamped down the urge to chicken out. "Go ahead and put them out if you want."

"Well, gee... don't get all happy on me now. Nervous?"

"Guilty as charged."

She smiled warmly. "The mind boggles. You're going to sell the heck out of those earrings, and you know it. Nobody else around here is selling feathers, and people will love the Shifter connection. It was such a good idea."

I took her empty plate and turned away to rinse it in the sink. "Did you two finish packing for your trip?"

"I think so. Do you want to help me dye my hair tonight?"

I peered over my shoulder at her. "Since when do you need my help? You've been dying your hair since you were what... thirteen?"

She twisted her mouth to the side. "Because I'm dying it brown."

My jaw slackened, and I shut off the water. I hadn't seen Melody's natural hair color in more than a decade, not unless you counted her roots showing in the past few weeks. "What do you mean you're dying it brown?"

Mel broke apart a piece of bacon and gave me a sheepish look. "I'm about to formally meet his adoptive family, and I'm afraid I'll embarrass him. They know all about me, but seeing me in the flesh with purple hair? They'll think I'm immature and not serious about our relationship."

"Then maybe you should dye it back to blue."

She glared.

I dried my hands on a dish towel. "Mel, you have to be true to yourself. Don't pretend to be someone you're not. If you dye your hair and change your clothes, who will it be that they're accepting? You or an impostor?"

She twirled a lock of loose hair around her finger. "It's not just his parents I'm meeting. It's everyone. Uncles, friends, cousins... I just want to make a good impression. All his uncles will be there, and I'm afraid of making Lakota look like a fool."

"Who looks like a fool?" Lakota boomed from across the living room.

I nodded at Mel. "Your mate wants to dye her hair brown before the trip."

He reached the end of the kitchen island and rested his elbows on it. His hair hung past his shoulders, shielding the edges of his face, but I could still see him giving Melody a pointed stare. "What's she talking about?"

Melody's right shoulder lifted in a subtle shrug, but she didn't answer. Normally Mel didn't care what the world thought about her. But she loved Lakota deeply, and family acceptance was everything among Shifters.

"Tell you what," he said. "*I'll* help you dye it. We'll swing by the drugstore after you get off work and pick up some purple dye. Your roots are showing."

Mel raised her eyes toward him, tears glittering in the corners. "Don't make this into a joke. Meeting your parents as your mate is a big deal. We mated without telling anyone, and that's already left a bad impression with the whole family. Now they're going to take one look at me and—"

"Understand why you're the woman of my dreams." Lakota reached out and captured a tress between his fingers. "Do you think my parents are superficial? Have you seen my wardrobe? You've got moxie, and I'd be embarrassed as hell if you went to see them with your tail tucked between your legs. Be yourself. I want them to meet the woman I fell in love with, the woman who stole my heart."

She slapped his shoulder and stormed off. "Why do you always have to be so romantic? I can't even argue with you anymore."

Lakota rocked with laughter and winked at me. "She's got her mother's fire in her. Thanks for breakfast, little sis. I'm heading out to the Weston house in about an hour to talk with Reno."

"Is my brother going to be a private instigator?" I quipped.

"*Investigator*," he corrected. "You're too sassy for your own good." He gobbled up another piece of bacon, speaking with his mouth full. "I'm still undecided, but since I have plenty of money in reserve, there's no rush. I've worked my tail off these past few years, so it's nice to have a little vacation."

"Any more time off and our sofa will have a permanent impression of your backside."

He snorted. "You want to ride with me? I won't be gone long."

"I can't."

His brows furrowed. "Why not?"

"I'm heading out to a cast."

Lakota stood up straight. "As in... a cast of hawks? Do I know them?"

"Well, I don't think they're all hawks, so I'm not exactly sure what to call them."

Not all Shifters lived in the same animal group. Some wildcats lived together, but many were loners by nature. Other races banded together for security, such as birds. I'd recently heard about a cast of hawks living nearby, which had planted the idea of feather jewelry. Sure, I could have bought a bunch of feathers off the internet, but I wouldn't know anything about their origin. The personal connection between my jewelry and the Shifters was essential since most of my customers were Breed.

"Shifter feathers aren't easy to come by, not unless they're voluntarily given up or found," I informed him. "The lady I spoke with seemed willing to provide a limited supply."

"So they don't mind you plucking them bald?"

I poked his arm. "They lose feathers during a shift. My contact has access to different species, everything from pheasants to peacocks. When I offered to pay her money for something that was going into the trash anyway, we struck a bargain. Out of respect, I agreed not to discount her pieces like I do with some of my other merchandise."

Lakota stared at me, unblinking.

"They're a respectable group of Shifters," I said, reassuring him. Lakota could be overprotective to a fault. "They're all women, in case you're concerned about a male performing a dance of seduction in front of me."

His shoulders sagged. "All women? That's fine then."

"You're so silly."

"No way in hell is my sister gonna be wooed by a flamingo."

"Aw, but you know how I love skinny legs."

As I steered around him, he caught my wrist. "Be careful, little sister."

"Always am."

Chapter 2

I parked my green Toyota sedan next to a pickup truck with so many hood ornaments affixed to the exterior that I couldn't even see the paint. I'd seen all kinds of unusual cars in Austin, so nothing surprised me. When I got out, a gentle breeze lifted a few strands of my hair. I smoothed them back in place before tightening the knot at the bottom of my white button-up shirt.

When Melody and I had dreamed up the idea of Moonglow, I'd never imagined our job would include anything other than working in the store and designing the merchandise. But here I was, scheduling meetings and learning how to negotiate contracts.

The lady I'd spoken to regarding the feathers lived in a quaint house by Shifter standards. It reminded me of a Spanish villa—stucco exterior, clay-tile roof, and archways at the entrance. Wind chimes hanging from a nearby tree sounded like tiny bells playing a nonsensical tune. Tall trees bordered the property, and giant pink crepe myrtles added a splash of color to each corner of the house, front and back. The houses in the neighborhood were spaced generously apart, and most of the homes had paved driveways. I walked around the circular driveway, admiring the fountain in the middle.

When I rang the bell, no one answered.

"Are you Hope?" a woman yelled from above.

I backed up several steps and swung my gaze to the upper balcony.

A lady in a floral shirt pointed to my right. "Asia's in the backyard. You can walk around."

I waved and followed the narrow sidewalk around the side of the house, careful to avoid a large ant mound that had taken over some of the concrete. When I reached the back, the first thing that entered my mind was that they didn't have a pool, something I often saw in Shifter homes. They had plenty of room, but maybe bird Shifters weren't big fans of water. Instead, they had a tiled patio with a fire pit. The sheer number of beautiful plants around the yard and in planters made it a horticulturist's dream.

Asia stood in front of a large cactus, spraying water on a cluster of aloe vera plants with a green hose. She glanced up at me and flashed a bright smile. "You're early!" The water splattered on the patio when she turned around, some of it spraying onto her beige shorts and white tank top. "Hold on. Let me shut the water off."

I strolled over to a glider bench near the house and took a seat in the shade. I'd never asked Asia about her name, but I found it curious since she was Asian. Either her parents had a sense of humor or it was a nickname. Most Shifters gave little consideration to social norms.

The faucet squeaked as she shut off the water. Asia strode toward me, leaving behind a trail of wet footprints. "Do you want something to drink?"

"No, I'm fine," I said. "Don't trouble yourself."

She took a seat and fanned her face with her hand. Loose strands of hair floated free from the messy knot on top of her head. "It's hot today." She kicked the rocker to set it in motion and straightened her legs as a child might. "We need a cool breeze. Why doesn't Mother Nature understand that we are delicate women? This sun is no good for my skin," she said, holding out her arm. "You see? I already have a burn."

I laughed. "There's always sunscreen."

She waved her hand and wrinkled her nose. "I don't trust what those humans put in bottles. All those chemicals. It's a conspiracy. Their food and products make you sick, and then the doctors and pharmaceutical companies swoop in to make a fortune selling you drugs to get well. We don't get cancer or things like that, but I still don't trust them. One day they might end up making something that actually *does* make us sick. You know… there could be one of us working in their labs. Someone who wants to discover a chemical that'll destroy Shifters."

I smiled inwardly, the glider giving me a taste of wind against my face. I hadn't pegged Asia as a conspiracy theorist, so I decided to switch topics before she got on a soapbox. "We're launching the new jewelry today. I wanted to stop by and give you the news but also speak to you about a contract."

Her thin brows arched. "Contract?"

"I know we talked about it, but if sales go well with this first batch, I'd like to work exclusively with you. It's not fair for either of us to go into business together without working out the details. I'm still uncertain how they'll sell, but I think it would be wise to create a short-term contract in case I need immediate supplies, and then we can negotiate for something more long-term. This is a great opportunity for both of us."

Asia drew up her slim legs and gripped her knees. "Does that mean I have to make a contract with my suppliers? Or do you just want one with me? I don't know. This sounds too complicated."

"That would be up to you," I said, praying she wouldn't find this too overwhelming. "If I were in your shoes, I'd create a basic contract with everyone I obtained feathers from. It's really easy. There's nothing to it. I know someone who can draw up the paperwork and go over it with you. A contract is just peace of mind so that no one leaves you hanging, especially if you're paying them a cut. I had issues with my old gemstone supplier, and right before our store launched, he tried to swindle me out of money and then backed out when I refused to pay."

"What an asshole."

"It almost ruined our launch. A good contract would have made him keep his end of the bargain until the renewal period, and by then, I could have found a replacement without putting my business in jeopardy. You're someone I trust enough to work with, but I don't want either of us in a vulnerable position."

She reclined her head. "Contracts sound like a *lot* of work. We have girls in the house who make lots of money. I just water the plants."

Asia was no different from low-ranking packmates who didn't have an important job. Sometimes their duties were around the house, allowing other Shifters to shine and bring in the big money.

"This is a chance for you to show those women how important you are in this community," I continued. "Think about it. All these feathers you have lying around are worth something. I think you'll enjoy the responsibility. I'll need quality feathers, and I'm sure you have ideas on the best way to acquire those. Everything starts small at first, but you might come up with some great ideas to expand the variety. As for negotiating with outside Shifters, it's better to pay them a flat fee than give them a percentage of your cut. Don't let a supplier talk you into a royalty share. All *you* have to do is clean and package everything for me. We'll touch base every now and again to discuss pricing strategies based on sales. If the demand goes up, then so will the price. You'll get a percentage, and that's not a deal I'd normally make with anyone. But I like you, Asia, and you deserve to be a part of this venture. You can either keep the money for yourself or share it with the house; it's up to you."

Asia tilted her head to the side. "Me… a businesswoman. You would laugh if you knew about my humble beginnings." She patted my hand. "You are a good speaker, Hope. Very smart girl. Send me the paperwork and make sure to put down how long the contract is for so I can estimate how many feathers I'm able to give you."

I smiled and tried to hide my relief. "We'll work it out. Why don't you run an estimate on how many you can provide me per week, and we'll go from there?"

"Oh, I'm good with math," she boasted. "But I need to think about what to do when my housemates are away on a job and they won't have anything to contribute."

"Understood. I wouldn't want you to go around plucking their feathers out in the middle of the night to make up for the loss."

She laughed melodically and got up. Then she bent forward and spoke in a hushed voice. "You know I laugh, but there's one girl I would do that with. She always puts out her cigarettes in my plants. I'd like to pluck the feathers right off her bird's little ass."

I snorted and tried not to laugh. I liked Asia's bluntness. She spoke in an animated voice that was endearing, none of her emotions veiled. "I hope you don't mind my coming out here this morning on short notice. I prefer having these kinds of discussions face-to-face." Knowing someone might be listening in, I lowered my voice. "Also, if you don't trust the leader of your house to have your back, you should consider creating separate contracts with everyone."

She wrinkled her nose. "Why?"

I wasn't sure how to put it delicately, but sometimes the people you trusted most were the ones who made your life hell. "Since they're also supplying the goods individually, you'll want to make sure no one is going to change their mind one day and put you in a tight spot. They need to know their roles are important even if they're not doing any work. They should always have an option to quit, but a contract will make sure they finish out the time frame set in the terms so none of us get screwed. I can't involve myself since it's more of a family meeting. Make sure everyone is okay with you collecting their fallen feathers. If you plan to keep the money for yourself, they'll need to know. That might change how they feel about giving you their feathers. They might not care, but people can be funny about certain things."

"Some people are so funny that they like putting out their nasty cigarettes in *my* plants. They say birds of a feather flock together, but they don't tell you the part about how some people have a big beak and poop all over your garden. Do you want to stay for lunch?"

I stood up. "I'd love to, but I need to work on a few pieces before my afternoon shift. Maybe next time?"

She held up her finger. "I'll hold you to that. I make good food, the best you've ever had. You come by next time, and I'll make tempura, miso soup and… Do you like Japanese food? I can cook anything. You've never had my barbecue!"

I chuckled and tucked my long hair behind my ears. "Call me after your family meeting, and we can get together. If I don't hear from you by, say Tuesday, I'll call and fill you in on how it's going with sales."

Asia clapped her hands together. "Okay! Sounds like a plan. I have to finish watering my plants," she said, heading toward a watering can. "Nobody around here cares. If it were up to them, they would just let them wither and die." Asia turned her gaze to the upper balcony and shouted, "Unless they burned the house down with their cigarettes!"

I waved goodbye and headed back to my car. My gosh, that girl was a riot! She and Mel would get along famously. I only hoped she could convince the others in the house. Otherwise, our new line would be nothing more than a limited edition. Not a big deal since my gemstones brought in a lot of business, but I hungered for more than just money. The dreamer in me wanted to test my creative boundaries.

After I started the car, I rolled down the window and circled the fountain on my way back to the main road. The wind cooled my skin, and I leaned my head out to savor the feel of it combing through my hair. Teased by the beautiful weather, my wolf paced beneath my skin, itching to go for a run.

The downside of living in an apartment in a congested city was not having enough space for our wolves to stretch their legs. They couldn't smell pine and earth or feel cold water splashing beneath their paws as they crossed a stream. Wolves weren't meant to be confined, and I wondered how much longer I could survive in an apartment. The human side of me loved the convenience, but my animal paid the price. She only got to enjoy the outdoors on scheduled trips to my father's house, where he lived on the outskirts of Austin. And how long did I really want to keep that up?

I steered left, remembering a nice patch of land on the way back owned by the Shifter Council. They'd bought up a lot of land in the early days to keep it in reserve. No one ever went out there. My wolf was smart enough not to cross any boundaries that would lead to occupied territory, and it wouldn't be the first time I had run wild on land the Council owned.

When I reached the stretch of land, I pulled my car off the road and parked near a short barbed wire fence with sunflowers clustered around it. To keep thieves and nosy people away, I lifted the hood and left it open using the rod. Then I locked my purse in the trunk and hid the keys inside a cooler in the back seat. A giant oak tree shaded half my car, and after a quick glance around, I stripped out of my clothes and folded them neatly in the passenger seat. A mockingbird sang from a branch overhead before diving at a squirrel that scurried into the high grass. My wolf wanted to chase it too, so I gripped the fencepost and hopped over, careful not to catch myself on the barbed wire.

A jackrabbit sprang out of his hiding spot near my feet, his strong legs jarring loose the white florets from dandelions as he trampled them. A blue jay squawked overhead, alerting all to my presence. Wild animals could sense a Shifter. We weren't like them, so predators ignored us, and prey fled for their lives. I waited patiently as my spirit wolf prepared to come out. Overhead, miles of blue sky washed over me like an ocean.

I closed my eyes, arms spread wide, as my wolf emerged in pursuit of the rabbit.

Chapter 3

By the sun's high position in the sky, I guessed it to be around noon. I stood up and brushed the dirt off my naked body, relieved that I had plenty of time to shower before going to work. My leg muscles ached, a typical side effect whenever my wolf had a good run.

With my car still parked in the same spot, I stole a quick glance at the empty road before springing over the barbed fence, which was designed to mark territory rather than keep people out. Nothing would startle a human more than seeing a naked woman walking around in the woods.

When I opened the passenger door, I gaped at the empty seat.

"Where are my clothes?"

Had I remembered it wrong? Maybe I hadn't put them in plain sight this time. I felt beneath the seat and searched in the back.

Nothing.

They're gone! This can't be happening.

My heart raced as I looked underneath the car and even inside the engine. The rational side of my brain knew that I would have never placed them by the fence, but I checked anyhow before returning to the car.

What an absolute nightmare!

After grabbing my keys from the cooler, I searched the

trunk only to find my purse and a spare tire. Flustered, I tossed my purse in the back seat and looked around once more.

"What am I going to do?" I cupped my cheeks in my trembling hands, the gravity of the situation sinking in as my shoulders and chest burned from the blazing sun. Sweat trickled down my nape, and I wiped away the beads of sweat forming on my upper lip.

Had we lived in a rural area outside city limits, it wouldn't have been a big deal. I could have shifted and let my wolf guide me home. But driving into the city naked? Not an option.

When I heard the sound of an engine picking up speed, I ducked behind my car until it sped by.

Crouching in the dirt, I stared at my blurry reflection on the door. "You are in so much trouble."

There was no possible way I could drive naked into the city without a cop pulling me over or someone taking a picture on their phone. And riding up the elevator into our apartment? Forget it! Mel was at work, and I would rather live in the woods as a wild woman than call Lakota. He'd deliver a lecture for the ages about trespassing on private land, even though I'd seen him do it once or twice. Calling my family was out of the question. It would disappoint them that I couldn't live independently without asking for their help. Aside from that, my father would shoot me if he knew I was standing naked on the side of a public road, and Lorenzo Church was a force to be reckoned with. Nothing would embarrass a Packmaster more than word getting out that his daughter went for a joyrun on private land.

The thought crossed my mind to call Asia, but that wasn't exactly the best way to secure a contract. I needed to keep things professional with her, not give her any reason to doubt my abilities.

My eyebrows pinched together when I heard another vehicle slowing down. The motor thrummed, and the windows must have been down because some rock band was screaming the phrase "head like a hole."

I waited for the music to fade as the car passed, but the volume never changed. Curious, I peered through the window at a big white truck with red mud caked on the bottom. The incline placed his truck higher, preventing me from seeing the driver.

"Is someone out there?" a voice boomed.

I froze.

"Please leave, please leave," I whispered. The last thing I needed was for my wolf to get spooked and jump out.

The music abruptly shut off with the engine. When a door clicked open, my pulse skyrocketed.

"Stay where you are!" I shouted.

The man chuckled, his deep voice a rich timbre. "And why's that?"

As his heavy footsteps drew closer, every hair on my body stood on end. This situation had just escalated from bad to worse because the mysterious stranger on the other side of the car was undoubtedly an alpha. His power rippled through the air like an electrical storm.

By the time he rounded the front of my car, it was too late to argue. He glimpsed me and immediately turned on his heel, rocking with laughter. The long braid down his back made me wonder if he belonged to a pack or a tribe.

Though crouched low with my long hair concealing some of my profile, I knew he'd gotten more than an eyeful of my backside. "Stand down, alpha. An exposed female is present."

He bent over in stitches, and his sonorous laugh made me want to find the nearest stick and poke his eyes out. Instead, I tossed a small rock at the back of his head.

"Ow!" His shoulders hunched, and he rubbed at his scalp. "I've never met such a bashful Shifter. I can't help it. So, uh… car trouble?" He erupted in another fit of laughter.

I sprang to my feet and snatched the sunshade from inside my car, using it to shield myself. I had no qualms about nudity during a shift, but I didn't make a habit of parading around naked in front of strangers while having a conversation. Especially not alphas. "You can turn around now."

When he peered over his right shoulder, I glimpsed his face. He had a strong jaw and masculine features—very much Native American. I'd never seen a man with such broad shoulders and a heavy brow. He was a beast of a man, like a barbarian in modern clothing.

When his eyes traveled down to the sunshade, he choked with laughter and bent over again. "I'm going to piss myself."

I glanced down at the Daffy Duck sunshade and didn't see the humor. "You might be an alpha, but you must not hold a Packmaster's rank."

The laughter died in his throat, and he straightened. "I thought someone needed my help. I must have thought wrong." He slid on his dark shades and headed to his truck without looking back.

I jogged after him, but he'd already reached the road. "Wait! Please… I do need your help. My clothes are gone."

The alpha stopped short but didn't turn around. His sleeveless black shirt revealed beefy arms that were perfectly sculpted but not grotesquely muscular. Though his cargo pants hung a little loose, I could easily see how built he was beneath them, and he carried himself like a man who feared nothing. I guessed him to be around six and a half feet or more, excluding the extra lift his boots provided. His deep, commanding voice had a luscious undercurrent that changed the texture in an indefinable way.

"Where are your clothes?" he asked.

"If I knew that, I wouldn't be standing naked on the side of the road."

A car flew by and honked.

"Did your car break down?"

"No, my car is fine. I just…" *Out with it, Hope. Fess up.* "I was joyrunning on private property. I don't have a pack, so before you question me about why I didn't shift on my own land—"

"I don't really care what you do out here," he said matter-of-factly. "It's not my business. Do you live close by?"

"No. I'm from the heart of Austin."

His lips thinned. "This isn't Austin?"

"This is Greater Austin."

A gust of wind cooled my bare back, reminding me of my dire situation.

He opened the passenger door of his truck and reached inside, whistling the whole time. A few moments later, the man turned, and I took three steps back.

I'd never seen anyone with permanent ink on his face. A tribal design covered the entire left side, and though his eyes remained hidden behind black shades, I could feel them all over me.

He tilted his head to the side. "My name's Tak, and I'm visiting from Oklahoma. I won't eat your face off."

My feet rooted in place as he approached, a masculine swing in his step, his face sculpted like a warrior's. This was a man who could easily deliver a deathblow with one swing.

Tak offered me a handful of garments and flashed his teeth. "They won't fit, but they'll get you home. You needn't worry. I'm only dangerous when provoked."

I held the shade against me with one hand and gathered the clothes in my free arm. "Thank you, sir. Are you attached to a pack or are you a… maverick?"

"Maverick? That's an interesting but polite way to put it. I'm not a rogue, and my Packmaster doesn't need to know about my chivalrous deed. I won't receive any medals for doing what any decent man would do. I'd get a lashing if I left you as I found you."

I inclined my head and stepped back. Kind or not, I didn't trust outsiders and wanted to put distance between us.

He started to turn away and then snapped his fingers. "Actually, there *is* one favor you can do for me."

I mashed my lips together at his roguish grin.

"I'm lost," he explained, rocking on his heels. "Men aren't

supposed to ask for directions, so I'm entrusting you with my little secret. The city is… confusing, and I need to find a gas station to buy a map of Austin."

My eyes flicked back to his truck, which faced right. "You're going the wrong way. This road eventually leads to a lake. Turn around, and after a mile or two, you'll hit a major intersection. Go right until you reach the big gas station on the left. You can't miss it, and they'll have whatever you need."

"Do they have a sunshade like yours?" He winked and circled around to the driver's side.

Thank the fates for sending a man generous enough to offer me his clothes. Just the fact that he had a spare outfit was a good omen. It could have been so much worse had the cops thrown me in a human jail for public indecency. I had no pack, and breaking Council laws could tarnish my reputation.

When he got in the truck and started it, the music blared. Before he took off, I rushed toward the open passenger window, stopping short of the fiery hot asphalt.

"Something else?" the alpha asked, turning down the radio.

"I… I appreciate your kindness."

He grinned. "Anytime, Duckie."

The back tires spun, and I stepped aside as he lurched forward and made a U-turn. A red car suddenly raced by so quickly that a gust of wind ripped the shade right out of my hand. It spun in the air like a butterfly, and I stood naked on the side of the road, listening to my rescuer's laughter as he sped away.

Chapter 4

At least I'll never see *him again*, I thought, waiting for the elevator to reach my floor. My least dignified moment would just have to be getting caught naked on the side of the road while joyrunning, wouldn't it?

Especially by an alpha.

While his name sounded vaguely familiar, it was a relief to discover he wasn't a local Packmaster but a visitor from out of town. Gossip traveled fast among Shifters, and a rumor like that might affect our business sales. Moonglow was not only my venture but also Mel's. This was our security deposit on our future—a sustainable income that would be an attractive asset for a Packmaster accepting new additions. In an ideal world, Melody and I would join the same pack. But even if we didn't, creating separate business accounts wouldn't be terribly difficult. Yet careless stunts could jeopardize not only our business but also our chances of joining a reputable pack in the territory. It hadn't sunk in until the moment I was caught.

I gripped the waistband of the baggy jeans the stranger had given me and headed down the hallway toward my apartment. What kind of world did we live in where people freely stole clothing without regard? Thank the fates they hadn't found my keys and taken off with the car.

As soon as I opened the door, Lakota materialized in front of me.

"Didn't you get my messages?"

I set my keys on the accent table. "No. Was there an emergency?"

Lakota's cross look made me shrink with guilt. He must have left the messages when I was out on my run, and I hadn't bothered to check my phone on the way home.

"I have to get ready for work."

Lakota folded his arms. "Where have you been all this time? When you didn't answer, I came back home to see if you left your phone behind. Needless to say, I've been worrying my ass off. This is what happens when you don't tell me where you're—" His eyes skated down and narrowed. "Why are you wearing men's clothes?"

I swung a left, the long pants dragging beneath my feet as I shuffled down the hall.

"Where have you been?" he said sharply.

"You're not my keeper!"

Lakota seized my arm. "Don't play these games, Hope. I'm not your Packmaster or even an alpha, but I'm your brother. I'm family. That should count for something. Family looks out for each other, and maybe I'm concerned that my little sister was incommunicado for the past six hours and then shows up in men's clothes."

I sighed and turned to face him. "Must I always explain everything I do and everywhere I go? Don't you trust me?"

"Ask me how much I trust some of the jokers in this town who would like nothing more than to bang Lorenzo Church's only daughter. You're a trophy to half the men around here."

Still gripping the jeans with one hand, I gently pulled my arm out of his grasp. "You have nothing to be concerned about. I'm a woman of twenty-four, Lakota. I would never pair up with an unworthy man, especially behind your back. I have too many good things in my life to throw it all away for a wolf who doesn't respect me enough to meet my family. Will you trust me on this?"

He lowered his head and sighed. "Come home as soon as you lock up the store. We're still planning to leave tonight."

"Most people begin trips in the morning."

He lifted his head and flashed a bright smile. "I'm not most people. Traffic is better at night, and Mel will sleep until morning. Then we'll switch so we can drive straight through. Promise me you'll be here? I can't leave without knowing you're home safe."

"I promise."

I reached for the doorknob.

"Good. And Hope? I trust you. But someday soon, you're going to tell me why you're wearing those clothes."

When I closed the door to my room, I let the jeans drop to the floor. I hated lying to Lakota, but even worse, I hated his criticism. Shifting on private property owned by the Council was wrong, but what choice did I have? We didn't own land, and if I hadn't let my spirit wolf go for a run, there could have been consequences. I was still learning to find harmony with my animal, so I had to release her lest she decide to shift at an inopportune time, like at work later this afternoon.

I reached across the bed and closed the blinds. Because we had a corner unit, plenty of light poured into the bedrooms as well as the living room and kitchen. Both bedrooms were on the right side of the hall and the bathroom at the end. To give myself room to work, I'd purchased a twin bed for the right-hand corner. Against the left wall was a desk my mother had built. Wide drawers framed each side, and she'd built a back shelf with small drawers and hooks to hold my stones, beading, and accessories. Shikoba sent me gemstones in large shipments, and the boxes easily fit beneath the desk until I could sort through them. It was a beautiful thing to be able to wake up each morning and look at my dreams.

I removed my sandals and placed them on the shoe rack inside my closet, which was filled to the brim with some of Melody's fabrics. We were running out of room, especially since Lakota moved in and they bought a larger bed. She had a sewing machine in there, and though she outsourced labor to a local pack, she still worked for hours at a time, creating new designs. His clothes filled all the empty spaces in their closet, so she used mine for overflow. We could have moved our work into the living room, but we agreed long ago to keep that space separate from our work life. On top of that, our things would just clutter up the apartment and make it feel less like a home.

I closed the closet door, my thoughts drifting back to a question that often kept me awake at night. Lakota would never ask me to leave, but what if he wanted me gone and was too ashamed to say anything?

I folded the jeans and then slipped out of the baggy T-shirt the stranger had given me. Before folding it, I held the garment to my nose and drew in a deep breath. It hadn't been worn recently; I could smell the laundry detergent. But there was another distinct smell clinging to it—a pleasant one. It had a woodsy fragrance with a hint of musk. I folded up the black shirt, wondering what to do with his clothes. When the memory of his laughter as he sped away entered my mind, I considered setting them ablaze. It wasn't my nature to cower before a man the way I had, but I'd never seen anyone quite like Tak.

I placed the garments on the bed and then appraised myself in the full-length mirror. Tak's indifference made me wonder if he found me undesirable. The men in this town knew who I was, so their perception of me was shaped by my father. Having a stranger assess me based on looks alone was humbling. Was my long hair not pleasing? Granted, it was a plain color. Not silken black like my father's or even mahogany brown like my mother's, but closer to the color of potting soil. I'd always been told that I had the dark eyes of an old soul. I frowned, a tiny line appearing between my eyebrows. Since going through the change, I'd put on weight. My breasts had always been full, and though I had a narrow waist, my hips and backside were full of curves—another reason I preferred baggy pants. Shifter men liked curves, so the less attention I drew to myself the better. But what could have made that stranger run away so fast? Were my features displeasing?

And why was I spending so much time thinking about it? I'd never cared before if men found me desirable.

I inched closer to the mirror and touched the left side of my face. My fingers traced across the puncture scars on my lower jaw and temple where a rogue wolf had savagely bitten me. The white marks had grown more noticeable over the years, especially since I didn't cover them with makeup. They could have been a whole lot worse had a Relic not treated me. Shifters considered scars on women a sign of weakness. Scars from bicycles or other mishaps were easily distinguishable from the telltale marks of a wolf's fangs. It was common to see young men instigating fights before their first change, and those scars implied a lot of things. Maybe that person was a troublemaker, maybe they'd displeased their Packmaster, maybe they weren't a good fit for a pack. Men were aggressors, so scars were par for the course. But for someone to attack a woman, it must have been a serious event. It was a double standard, but the truth rarely mattered. If there were two things I'd learned, it was that life isn't fair, and assumptions always prevail.

The fates had marked me for a reason.

"Are you sure you don't have any in the back?" the gentleman asked, his gold ring tapping against the glass counter. It was a gaudy ring of a bear's head, which made me curious why he would take an interest in my jewelry.

I pushed a clipboard toward him. "Write down your name and number if you want to go on the waiting list. We sold out this morning."

"I've seen three women wearing them today," he went on.

"Everyone's talking about them." He pointed at the feather earrings dangling from my ears. "Are those them?"

"Yes, but these aren't for sale. These were the prototype, and they're sentimental. Is there a special lady you want to buy something for? We have a lovely collection of necklaces that might interest you."

He released a controlled sigh as if calming his growing impatience. I quickly assessed his wealth by his designer watch and the BMW parked out front. My earrings weren't comparable to a diamond necklace, but people were funny about desiring items that were unique.

I glanced up at the wolf clock on the wall that ticked one minute past nine in the evening. "You'll be the first one I call when the next shipment arrives."

He leaned against the counter, his blue eyes twinkling. "I'll pay you five hundred for the ones you're wearing."

Yeesh. What an unforeseen turn of events. I expected curious customers to come in and check the jewelry out, but I would never have imagined that my earrings would sell out by noon. "Tell you what, I'll put a star by your name and make sure you get first choice. I can't guarantee I'll have the design you're looking for, and I don't make custom pieces on request. I use different kinds of feathers, but each set is certified Shifter-authentic."

He licked his lips and looked around. I couldn't help but notice how smooth his shave was, how strong his cologne, how stylish his button-up and slacks. He emulated a male model like those in magazine ads. Every strand of his blond hair was perfectly combed back, and his eyes were a crisp blue. There was nothing boyish about his features; he looked like a sophisticated man who knew how to get what he wanted in every situation.

He scribbled his name on the form. "This is my phone number. If I don't answer, leave a message." He put a giant asterisk next to his name. "I'm Dutch. What's your name?"

"Hope Church."

He tilted his head to the side, his eyes narrowing. "You're Lorenzo's little girl, aren't you?"

I lifted my chin. "I'm only little to those who look down on me."

Humor danced in his eyes, and he set down the pen. "I've seen you walking along the streets every so often, but I didn't know you were related to the Church pack."

I smothered a laugh and collected the clipboard before glancing at his name. "You're probably the only one in this city who doesn't know me by sight. Do you live around here?"

He studied the expensive pieces inside the counter. "I own a fine jewelry store two streets over."

"Ah. So you're my competition. Did you come here to spy on my wares?"

He barked out a laugh. "You're not even in the same ballpark."

I folded my arms and shifted my weight to one leg. "I charge what's fair. Maybe it's you who is overpriced."

He leaned on his elbows. "Give me your number."

My cheeks burned hot.

Dutch gave me a playful wink. "A woman who blushes. Be still my heart."

Flustered, I set the clipboard in a drawer, and the pen went rolling beneath the counter. "I need to close up the store now."

He snatched a business card from the holder on the counter and tapped it against his nose. "This'll do. Promise you'll call when you get the next shipment?"

"You have my word. Have a wonderful night, Mr. Day."

Dutch snorted as he pivoted around and headed out. "You do the same."

I removed the drawer from the register and locked it in the safe under the counter. As I reached into a cabinet to retrieve my purse, a peculiar noise made me perk up my ears. It sounded like the squeaking my paper towel made when I washed the front windows.

I stood up and looked across the empty store.

Odd.

Since I'd already locked the display counters a short time ago, I grabbed my keys and flipped off the lights. When I crossed the room and took another look around, my phone rang.

"Are you locking up?" Mel asked.

"I had a last-minute customer, so I'm running a little late. Do you want me to bring you two something to eat for your trip? I can swing by the sandwich shop before they close. You can pack them in a cooler if you're not hungry."

I stepped outside and locked the door, my phone pinned between my shoulder and ear.

"No, you don't have to bother," she said. "I ate that leftover burger in the fridge, and Lakota wants to have a midnight dinner in Dallas at this taco place that's open late. I'll probably nod off by the time we get to Waco, so he'll just have to go inside and eat a chimichanga all by himself. Road trips at night have a narcotic effect on me. I just wish he had a bigger truck so I could stretch out."

"Well, you could always put a mattress in the back," I quipped.

Melody laughed and relayed the joke to Lakota.

Before turning away, I noticed a white letter envelope taped to the window. I peeled it off the glass and turned it over. There wasn't a label, but Breed messengers relayed notices all the time on behalf of others. In a hurry to get home, I tucked it in my purse. "Be sure you take all the water bottles in the fridge. That'll save you from having to make any unnecessary stops. Don't worry about leaving me any; you know I prefer tea."

"Lakota! Can you grab the water out of the fridge?" she yelled in my ear. "Sorry."

"That's okay," I said, getting in the car. Once the door closed, I turned the key and tossed my purse in the passenger seat. "Did you pack your favorite pillow?"

"Lakota!"

I laughed. "I should let you go before you forget something else. I'll be home in just a few minutes."

"Awesome! See you then." Melody hung up, and I slipped my phone in my purse.

A thrill raced through me while I admired our store through the windshield, the headlights spotlighting the mannequins in the window display. Everything was falling into place. We had regular customers, and if I could secure a deal with Asia, we'd have something unique to offer the Breed community.

Some immortals considered Shifters to be at the bottom of the totem pole—hate spawned out of jealousy for our gift of transformation. After slavery was abolished, Shifters no longer hid in the shadows. Even though I was a wolf, the feather earrings instilled a sense of culture and respect for all. My jewelry connected the wearer with Breed life—a visible badge of sorts. Mel called it Shifter pride, but many of the customers asking for them weren't Shifters at all. Maybe they were supporters and wanted a way to show others, or maybe having a small piece of our power felt like magic in their hands. In any case, each pair of earrings came with a certificate of authenticity, which also included a brief history about the type of bird Shifter they were derived from and the meaning behind any stones that might be part of the piece. It was the best way to honor the avian community.

What I'd already accomplished was more than I ever dreamed possible.

And now, after trying something risky and new, I finally believed that my life wasn't about luck or timing. Maybe the fates were watching over me and I'd finally gotten into their good graces again.

One could only hope.

I glanced at the envelope poking out of my purse and wondered, *Why wait?*

Chapter 5

"Where have you been?" Mel blocked the entrance to the apartment, leaving me standing in the hall. "I thought you'd be here thirty minutes ago."

"I wish you hadn't waited for me."

"*When* we leave is no biggie. I just didn't want to send out a search party."

I worried my lip, not mentioning the envelope taped to our store. I'd opened it before leaving, and it left me so shaken that I'd thought long and hard about the right thing to do. This trip was important to Melody and Lakota, and they'd been planning it for a long time. Chances were the letter was nothing more than a prank.

I noticed her freshly dyed hair—a deep shade of purple. "Your hair looks good. Did Lakota help?"

She pulled a strand in front of her face. "I *told* him to wear gloves. Were you daydreaming again? Lakota almost went looking for you."

"I'm surprised he didn't."

Then I heard people talking from inside the apartment. I tried to peer around her, but Melody eclipsed my view. "Who's in there?"

She twirled her hair with her finger, her voice barely above a whisper. "That's a long story. He's not staying, and Lakota's trying to get rid of him so we can leave. Our things are already in the truck. We were just waiting on you to get home. Are you okay?"

I shook my head. "I'm fine. Why?"

"You look pale."

I smiled and held my arm next to hers. "Compared to whom, Casper?"

Mel was certainly dressed for a road trip. Sweatpants, one of Lakota's wolf T-shirts, and a pair of fuzzy slippers.

"I hope you're not getting out of the truck to eat tacos in Dallas," I said.

She glanced down at her casual attire. "This is the style these days. Haven't you seen what humans are wearing to the grocery store? Nobody cares anymore." Melody backed away from the door to let me in.

I set my keys on the small table beside the door and swung my eyes up to Lakota, who was sitting on the pink sofa against the far left wall. But that wasn't what held my attention. It was the stranger sitting across from him. All I could make out were his massive arms stretched along the back of the grey sofa and a braid pinned between his back and the cushion.

Lakota swung his eyes sharply over to me. "Where have you been? I thought we had an agreement."

I dropped my purse on the floor and held out my hands. "I apologize for my tardiness, but I'm here now."

The visitor turned his head, revealing a tattooed profile. When his smoldering eyes locked on mine, my heart slammed against my rib cage.

It's him! The man who'd seen me naked on the side of the road. The man whose clothes were neatly folded in my bedroom. The man I thought I'd never have to see again.

The man who was giving me a wolfish grin from the back of our sofa.

"Tak, this is my sister. Hope, meet Tak. He's leaving."

Tak turned to Lakota. "You didn't tell me you had a sister. In fact, you didn't tell me a lot of things."

Lakota stood up and glared down at him. "That's something we're going to have to discuss another time. We really have to leave. It's a long drive, and people are expecting us."

"You two have a good trip," I said, darting toward the hall to get as far away from the stranger as possible before he decided to tell Lakota about what had happened earlier. "Unless there's something important you want to talk to me about, I'm going to bed."

"You're leaving her here alone?" I heard Tak ask as I walked briskly down the hall.

Lakota jogged up behind me and captured my arm. "I wanted to talk to you before we left."

I turned to give him my attention.

"I know we spoke about this before, but I'm asking you to close up the shop before dark. Just for the week."

"Lakota, that's a lot of business we'll lose. Mel's already given you the figures of how much we make from people who shop after work. Plus tomorrow is Saturday, and that's our biggest sales day of the week."

"It's not safe for you to be out at night alone. Everyone's heading up to Cognito with us."

He had a point. Melody's parents and brothers were driving up separately, and my family was heading out at first light. Mating ceremonies weren't required among Shifters. Most just made it official by going to the local Council and signing paperwork. But it was a show of respect for both sides to celebrate afterward with a dinner or peace party. Because of the unique circumstances of Mel and Lakota's secret ceremony, they felt it was in everyone's best interest to bring all the families together so no one had any bad feelings about the union. Since our store was new, we couldn't afford to shut it down for a week. So I'd volunteered to stay behind. I already knew his adoptive parents; I'd visited them many times when we were younger.

Worry flickered in Lakota's eyes, so I decided to put his

mind at ease. "If it makes you happy, I'll close the shop at eight."

"Seven."

"No, we have daylight until eight."

"By the time you finish cleaning and locking up, it'll be dark."

"There will still be plenty of people out shopping, and we live so close. I'll park my car right in front of the door so I won't have to walk far. Don't worry, brother. Not all villains come out with the moon. Some walk in the daylight with the rest of us."

He propped his arm against the wall and glowered. "Is that supposed to make me feel better?"

"I could always stay with Father's pack."

"Hell no," he fired back. "Look, I know you grew up with them, but you and I both know that's not an option. There are still a lot of single wolves in the Church pack who would like nothing more than to mount my sister."

"You're disgusting. Nobody is going to mount me."

"I'm serious," he continued. "You're a prize to them. I know how young wolves are, and a few in this town bed every Packmaster's daughter as a competitive sport. I don't want you sleeping there. End of discussion."

"Who is that man?" I whispered, peering around him. I couldn't see the guest from the hall, but I wanted to make sure he wasn't listening.

"Tak's an old acquaintance."

"Friend?"

Lakota lowered his arm and scratched his forehead with his purple hand. "I'm not sure. It doesn't matter anyhow. He's leaving."

"Good. He frightens me."

Lakota smirked. "He frightens a lot of women. So we're good on you closing the shop at seven?"

"Eight."

He shook his head. "I'll call you when we get there. And

by the way, there's a small canister of mace on the kitchen island. Put it on your keychain."

I wanted to laugh, but Lakota was just being a big brother. "Have a safe drive."

He patted my head. "Stay out of trouble."

⟶

Hours Earlier

Shortly after Tak's strange run-in with the stunning woman on the side of the road, he located a gas station, purchased a map, and wound up even more lost than when he'd started. Somehow, he'd left Austin, and he almost ended up in San Antonio before realizing his mistake and turning the truck around.

Cities were confusing as hell. Too much traffic, misleading signs, and so many distractions.

Tak was born and raised on tribal land in Oklahoma, far from town. Everything his people needed to survive was on their land: food, herbs, meat, and weapons. They even made their own furniture and tools. But some liked gathering in the local bar or going to the grocery store to purchase luxury items. He'd even bought his truck directly from a local Shifter instead of a dealership. Tak's tribe owned a television, so his exposure to the outside world was primarily through the news. But nothing had prepared him for the reality. The drive down to Austin was unmemorable until he reached Dallas. Panic raced through him each time the highway branched, and the locals were batshit crazy! They weaved in and out of traffic like angry little hornets.

Tak witnessed things he'd never seen before, like sexy women on giant billboards and vagrants begging for money on street corners.

He obeyed traffic signs and drove slow since patrol cars were pulling people over. The last thing he needed was the police locking him up for doing something wrong. Like every Shifter, Tak had a fake license, but he didn't know much about human laws or which ones landed a person in jail.

After exiting the highway, he took his time searching for Melody's apartment. The sun had set by the time he found the damn street. When he approached the front entrance, he waited by the locked doors until a resident came out. Tak sensed the man was Breed, so he gave him a friendly nod and slipped in through the door.

The elevator closed in around him like a metal coffin, and sweat beaded on his brow as he paced back and forth until the doors finally opened on the fifth floor. Once he located apartment 509, he pounded his fist against the door.

"Did you forget your key?" a woman called. When the door swung open, Melody dragged her gaze up and stared at him with wide green eyes. "Tak? What are you doing here?"

Melody looked just as he remembered, except her hair was a darker shade of purple, and her clothes were something a man would wear. Women in his tribe certainly didn't dress in baggy sweats and oversized T-shirts.

She gave him a guarded look and turned her head away. "Lakota?"

Tak quietly waited in the hall, his hands clasped in front of him. Poor Melody was caught in the middle. Tak had nothing against her and had even given her a ring as a peace offering. The mating ceremony on his father's land between Lakota and Melody had been a ruse, but their affection for one another was undeniable.

After Lakota had left the state, Tak thought he could move on and forget they ever knew each other. It was hard to forgive a man he trusted as a brother—one who'd tried to pin a murder on him. But there were too many unanswered questions. When Tak later found out that Lakota was a bounty hunter, it should have put his mind at ease.

But it hadn't. The truth burrowed in him like a thorn. Lakota had completed his job investigating a murder but deceived Tak in the process, forging a fake friendship in order to infiltrate the tribe. Tak had never bonded with another male as he had with Lakota, and the betrayal haunted his dreams.

Melody stepped back when Lakota approached the door.

"Uh... H-hey, Tak," he stammered. Lakota's blue eyes searched his, no doubt deciphering if this was a friendly visit or one that would end in bloodshed. He probably wondered how much Tak knew about his current living situation.

Tak put his weight on the doorjamb. "Hey, *brother*. Aren't you going to invite me in?"

"*Lakota*," Melody hissed.

Lakota looked over his shoulder at her, his voice stern. "Can you give us a minute?"

She flounced off to the left and out of sight.

Lakota stepped back and gave an imperceptible nod. "Come inside."

Tak swaggered into the apartment and widened his eyes at the décor. "You have a pink couch," he said, gravitating toward the kitchen, which made him feel more at ease.

Lakota strode ahead of him and reached inside the fridge. "How did you know I was here?"

"My father has Melody's address. You know that."

Lakota kicked the fridge shut with his heel, a bottle in each hand. "And you came all this way to see my mate?" he asked, his tone laced with suspicion.

When Lakota set the bottle of beer on the island, Tak sputtered with laughter. Tears wetted his eyes, and he wiped them away. Lakota's hands were purple—the same color as Melody's hair.

"Something funny?" Lakota gave him a blank stare, which made it even funnier.

Tak snorted and grabbed his beer. "Not at all. But I hope you didn't take a piss right after you played hairdresser. Your woman might be frightened to see an eggplant coming at her in the bedroom."

Lakota shook his head and strode into the living room. "Still the same old ham."

All humor erased from Tak's expression as he followed. "Not quite the same old Lakota I remember. Is there something you want to tell me about why you're living here?"

Lakota set his bottle on the side table and sat on the pink couch, his hands resting on his thighs.

Tak circled around the light-grey sofa across from Lakota and plopped down. He flicked a glance up to an abstract painting of grey wolves and wondered if this was typical of how all city Shifters lived.

"Don't bullshit me," Lakota began. "You're not here to see if Melody and I are together. You found out I'm a bounty hunter, and that's what this is about."

Tak slid his beer bottle between his legs and stretched his arms over the back of the sofa. He hadn't known for certain that Lakota was living here, but he'd had a strong feeling these two wolves had settled down for real. "Why didn't you tell me who you were from the beginning?"

"And put my job in jeopardy? I can't afford to trust anyone when I'm working undercover."

"So our friendship *was* a lie."

Lakota raked his hair back as if he was going to tie it up. "No. I never lied to you. Yeah, I needed to get my foot in the door with your tribe, and you were my way in, but I only lied about my job. I was never fake around you. Maybe I tweaked my accent a little bit, but I saw you as the brother I never had. Don't you think it bothered me when all the evidence pointed at you? And don't forget, *you* lied to *me*."

"That was different. I couldn't tell anyone I was feeding those people."

Tak's empathy for destitute rogues living between territories had been a source of pride and shame. Shifters were too proud to beg, and he couldn't stomach watching them die of starvation. Family always came first, and Tak broke that loyalty by stealing from his own people.

Lakota stared down at his discolored hands. "That was your alibi, Tak. If you had trusted me with that information, I wouldn't have accused you. I would have understood, even if your tribe wouldn't have. I'm not trying to play the sympathy card, but you weren't the only victim in this friendship."

"Lakota, we need to go," Mel urged from the hall. "She should be here any minute, and it's almost ten."

Lakota cursed under his breath and leaned forward. Before he opened his mouth, the sound of keys jingled in the outside hall.

Melody rushed to open it, and Tak heard her ask, "Where have you been? I thought you'd be here thirty minutes ago."

The chatter quieted to an inaudible level.

"This isn't a good time," Lakota said quietly. "Did you drive all the way down here just to see me?"

"Why else would I come to a city where the highways are stacked on top of each other?"

Lakota rubbed his stained palms. "Bad timing. We're going out of town for a week, and we're already behind schedule. I want to talk this over with you, but your timing is shit. It's going to take more than a few minutes for us to sort through what happened. I'm sorry you came all this way for nothing, but you're gonna have to come back another time. If you have our number, call ahead, and I'll make sure I'm here."

"Too busy for an old friend," Tak murmured.

"It's *family*," Lakota stressed. "You should know more than anyone that family comes first. Mel and I are mated for real. It wasn't just a show to secure a deal with your father. Maybe that's how it started, but it's not how it ended. Now we've got to make amends with the family since we did it behind their backs. This is an important trip that we can't postpone."

Tak could appreciate how awkward it must have been for them to return home and confess the truth. It made him wonder why they'd bothered admitting anything at all. If they really loved each other, why not just go through a ceremony again in front of the Council and pretend as though nothing had ever happened?

Too many questions. Not enough time for answers.

"I want to settle what's between us once and for all," Tak said decidedly. "If not now, then another time. I'll go and leave you to your family gathering."

Lakota snapped his attention toward the door. "Where have you been? I thought we had an agreement."

Tak heard the sound of keys hitting a table.

"I apologize for my tardiness, but I'm here now," a woman replied.

Every hair on Tak's body stood on end. He recognized that voice. It was the beautiful woman from earlier, the one who'd crouched naked behind her car on the side of the road. Tak hadn't been able to get her out of his head all day, especially not after a gust of wind had blown away her Daffy Duck sunshade, unveiling a body that made him hungry with need.

Damn. Meeting a woman of her caliber was like glimpsing a shooting star. Her long mane looked spun from silk, an earthy brown that put his dark color to shame. He admired the way she'd confronted an alpha male, and the fire that sparked in her eyes when she spoke. Had she a stitch of clothing on, Tak's tongue would have been hanging out of his mouth like a cartoon character. But he'd fall on a sword before making an undressed woman feel fear, even though he could do little about his looks. The situation had gone from awkward to downright hilarious when she held that damn sunshade in front of her and made him erupt with laughter. It couldn't be helped, especially since he'd always been a man easily amused.

However, there was a moment when he'd revealed his face and she recoiled. Tak was used to that reaction from some of the townies, but they were white women. Never once had his appearance startled a woman who shared the same skin color as him, and it troubled his mind for most of the day. Women in his tribe were used to his tattoo, and they all knew who he was, even if they came from another territory and had never met him before. His reputation definitely preceded him. But this woman's reaction reminded Tak that he was an interloper in the outside world.

He slowly turned his head and looked over his shoulder at her. She didn't give any indication that she knew him, but when he saw a startled look in her eyes, it made him grin.

"Tak, this is my sister. Hope, meet Tak. He's leaving."

Tak shifted in his seat. He sure as hell wasn't about to admit to Lakota that he'd seen his sister naked. There were certain lines you didn't cross with a man, and even though they needed to have a conversation and settle their dispute, Tak played dumb. "You didn't tell me you had a sister. In fact, you didn't tell me a lot of things."

Lakota rose to his feet, and Tak could sense his annoyance. "That's something we're going to have to discuss another time. We really have to leave. It's a long drive, and people are expecting us."

Hope stood motionless, like a deer in the headlights. "You two have a good trip. Unless there's something important you want to talk about, I'm going to bed." As if lightning had struck her in the backside, she took off down the hallway like an arrow.

Tak couldn't believe his ears. Did she just wish her brother a good trip? The apartment didn't appear big enough to house any other Shifters. "You're leaving her here alone?"

Without answering, Lakota disappeared down the hall to speak with his sister.

Melody grabbed the untouched beer from between Tak's legs. "You probably shouldn't drink and drive. This isn't the country, and you might end up hitting a pedestrian. Lakota doesn't think sometimes." She headed into the kitchen behind him, and Tak listened to the sound of wasted beer gurgling down the sink drain.

He rubbed his eyes, exhausted after a long day on the open road. There was no way he could drive all the way home at this late hour. Tak needed to find a motel and get some shut-eye before his wolf grew any more restless at the idea of Lakota leaving his sister behind. Hope wasn't his concern, and for all he knew, she had a mate who would be home at any moment.

Tak stood up and approached the scenic windows. They had a nice view from the fifth floor. "Are there any Breed motels around here?"

Melody dropped the empty bottle in the trash, unaware that Tak hadn't touched a single drop. "Um, I'm sure there are. Usually they're alongside the highway. I bet if you head back the way you came, you'll hit a few. I don't know anything about the rates around here."

A door closed in the hall.

"What are you two talking about?" Lakota asked.

Tak watched his reflection in the glass. "I've been driving all day, and I'm beat. I thought it would just be a day trip. I didn't bring much cash with me, so I need a cheap place to stay for the night."

Lakota scratched his jaw. "Let me see… The cheapest Breed motel I know of around here is a couple of miles north." He pulled open a drawer and scribbled something on a small piece of paper. "The owner doesn't care if you shift, but you'll pay for any damages, so it's better if you don't."

Melody switched off the kitchen light. "And how exactly would you know *that*, husband?"

"A friend told me, wife."

Tak chuckled to himself. He'd been around enough mated couples to know that these two were life mates—souls destined to be together.

Lakota ripped off the paper and extended his arm. "Here. Follow these directions."

Tak turned and glanced at the paper. "I remember seeing this place." He tucked the paper in his pants pocket and looked between them. "I guess I'll be on my way."

Lakota shook his head, eyes downcast. "I want to make this right between us, for better or worse. But you have a shitty sense of timing. Call me in a week. Maybe I'll save you the drive and come up there instead."

Tak arched an eyebrow. "You might get skinned alive. I have a few packmates who didn't appreciate you skipping town so quickly."

Lakota held his hands out. "I can't make it right with the whole tribe, and my bet is you're talking about Kaota. Your people took me under their wing, and I'll always appreciate it. But you and I had a friendship, and now it's fucked up."

Tak flicked his eyes over to Melody, who was staring at the clock on the microwave. "I don't want to hold you and your woman up. I'm guessing you have a long drive, so I'll be on my way. Apologies for the intrusion."

As he neared the door, Lakota called out, "Tak!"

He half turned, not making eye contact.

Lakota heaved a sigh, and Tak guessed there were a whole bunch of words that he wanted to say but wouldn't. "Have a safe drive."

Chapter 6

The next morning, I woke up early and prepared for the long day ahead. Hopefully I wouldn't fall apart working alone on our busiest day of the week. At around ten, Melody called to tell me the whole story about the hair-dye fiasco. Since Lakota had fallen asleep beside her in the passenger seat, she spoke freely about his fear that his beloved uncles would have a field day cracking jokes about his purple hands.

Men were silly about such things.

After we hung up, I called my assistant to see if she wanted to earn extra money helping me out at the store, but as expected, she declined. Alice was supremely shy and worked from home. She used to come over on the rare occasion when Melody was at work, but after Lakota moved in, all that changed. I wasn't sure what Alice's animal was, but she didn't put out the wolf vibe at all. Sometimes a person's physical appearance hinted toward their animal, but she didn't have excessively furry arms or anything like that. Her delicate features were beguiling even if she wasn't conventionally attractive. It must have been the red hair. Redheads were coveted in the Breed world, especially by Shifters. But her introverted personality didn't make it likely she'd ever find a mate. Because of that, I'd generously offered her more opportunities to earn money helping us out. She was clever and quick to learn my designs, but unfortunately, she had no interest in working inside our busy store.

Luckily one of Melody's aunts had free time on Sunday to watch the store for half a day. I figured she could work the morning shift and that would allow me some time to sleep in since I'd have a long week ahead.

"These pants are so unique," a woman gushed. "I don't normally wear slacks; I'm from a different generation. But these are marvelous and so feminine. They almost look like a dress."

I rang up the price of the olive-green slacks with the wide legs. "If you like these, my partner plans to have more color options available soon. They're popular, and we've had a number of requests for blue and salmon."

She adjusted her gold-rimmed sunglasses. "I'll be sure to stop in again and look for them."

"Is this your first time at Moonglow?"

"Yes." Then the lady cupped her hand around her mouth and whispered, "I'm a Mage."

I smiled and touched her hand. "We welcome everyone here. My partner and I are Shifters, but we have friends and family who are other Breeds. Nothing pleases us more than to see people of all races wearing our merchandise."

She respectfully inclined her head. "I'll definitely be coming back. You can count on it."

I closed her bag and slid it forward. "We also don't tolerate discrimination, so if anyone ever gives you a hard time in here, let me know. I slipped a coupon in the bag for fifty percent off on your next visit. Have a wonderful afternoon."

She turned away with a jaunty step and pranced out the door. I knew it was excessively idealistic, but nothing made me happier than thinking that maybe in some small way, we were bringing people together. So much division existed in our world that it was nice to have a safe place where people could put aside their differences.

As the woman exited the shop, a tall man held the door open for her.

My breath caught.

Tak filled the doorway, his brown skin and ropes of muscle caught in the afternoon sunlight. By the looks of his cargo pants and black muscle shirt, he hadn't changed clothes. But he'd taken the time to neatly braid his hair. His eyes lingered on one of the mannequins in the window that wore a sneak peek of a new clothing line coming next month. He gravitated toward the Native American artwork on the wall and didn't notice me as he sauntered in. A blonde sidestepped to avoid running into him.

"How much are these?" a young girl asked, pointing at my beaded bracelets on the revolving display.

"Twenty dollars."

She grimaced. "Got anything cheaper?"

I recognized this girl from one of the local packs and knew she didn't have much money to spend. Teens in the Breed world didn't have credit cards, and most didn't have jobs until they became independent.

I gestured to a tall display in the corner. "We have a few pretty rings for as low as fifteen dollars over there. These are special stones, so no two pieces are alike. That's as low as I can price them, but it's totally worth it. Everything you see in this store was mined, sold, and created by Shifters. Try finding that at Walmart."

She grinned blithely and hurried off to check them out.

Why on earth had I made that promise to Lakota about closing early? Especially when there were more buyers than browsers today.

A man slapped his plastic bag on the counter. "Are you the manager? I need to speak to the manager."

I flicked a glance at his hairy arms, immediately put off by his surly demeanor. "That would be me. Can I help you with something?"

"You sure as hell can. You sold me a piece-of-shit purse. I gave it to my mate, and it had a broken strap."

I furrowed my brow. "We don't have a return policy for damages."

"It came that way."

I pulled the purse out of the bag and examined the strap. It looked as though it had been ripped off, threads hanging loose. Melody's purses could survive an attempted burglary, so it didn't make sense. "This purse was damaged after it left our shop."

"Are you calling me a liar?"

I squared my shoulders. "My partner and I inspect each piece of merchandise before we wrap it. There's not a chance we would have sold you a five-hundred-dollar bag with a broken strap. Do you have the receipt, Mister…?"

"Dumont." He angrily reached in the bag and waved the paper in front of my face. Mr. Dumont stared daggers at me with his beady eyes—the only feature on his face I could see behind his bushy beard. He didn't strike me as the type who would buy an expensive handbag for a mate, but I had to put aside speculation and focus on the facts. He didn't look familiar, so Melody must have been the one to ring up his order.

I took the receipt and reviewed the information. "You've had this purse for over three weeks?"

"Her birthday was yesterday," he fired back. "As soon as she tried it on, the flimsy strap broke. It's ruined."

Human stores had a policy that the customer was always right. Breed shops didn't work that way. The price of the purse was five hundred dollars, and because it was a one of a kind, it was one of Melody's favorites. If she were here, she would probably flip her lid.

"For a fee, we can repair the damages," I offered.

"No," he said, speaking to me as if I were a child. "You're going to give me a refund, and I want an extra five hundred for the way you're treating me."

Tak eased into view, admiring a display of necklaces inside the glass counter.

"Sir, it's clear that your mate damaged the purse. Had it been a small tear inside, it's possible we could have overlooked that flaw. But this," I said, shaking the strap at him, "shows me that your mate doesn't know how to take care of nice things. You can either pay for the repairs or stand here and argue with me. But I promise that if you choose to go to battle with me on this, I'm going to cut off the rest of this strap and whip you right out of my store."

Tak snickered and pivoted away.

Dumont pointed his finger in my face. "What gives you the right to speak to me like that? I'll be sure to let your Council know about this."

I gave him a mechanical smile. "Do so. I'm sure the Shifter Council has nothing better to do than worry about a purse."

His eyes narrowed. "Then maybe the public should know that you sell junk," he said, turning away. He raised his voice. "This place is a junkyard filled with worthless secondhand trash, just like the owners. It's all fake! You dirty Indians need to go back to living in the woods."

Incensed, I grabbed the purse and circled the counter as fast as my feet would allow.

"Don't waste your money here," he continued. "This place is nothing more than a—"

Snap!

Before he could finish his sentence, I whipped him on the ass with the strap of that broken purse. Not my most professional moment, but I saw red. Nobody, but *nobody*, came into my shop and smeared our reputation with lies.

People around us looked confused and drifted away from the crazy shopkeeper who was beating her customer.

I lifted my chin, my hands shaking. Regaining my composure, I lowered my voice. "If you open your mouth again, I'll raise charges of slander."

When he inched forward, a mountain moved between us.

"Got a problem with Natives?" Tak said, his voice low and dangerous. "Because if you do, I'm about to get real uncivilized."

The man stalked off, the bell jingling noisily as he flung the door open and left.

I glanced up at the giant before me. "Who asked you to intervene?"

Tak peered over his shoulder at me, his eyebrows sloping down in the middle. "What was your plan if he had attacked you?"

With the purse still in hand, I returned to the register. "He wouldn't have tried. This isn't a bar."

Tak followed me, and when he reached the counter, he tapped his finger against the hand-carved wolf statue Lakota had given us. "Funny running into you here. Everywhere I go, there you are."

I placed the purse inside a drawer for safekeeping. "Exactly why are you here?"

Tak shrugged. "Thought I'd check out the famous Moonglow. So you're *the* Miss Church? Melody's partner? I didn't make the connection since Lakota doesn't share the same name. Your business brings my father good money."

My jaw slackened. "Your father is... Shikoba?"

Tak gave a mirthless smile but didn't answer. Instead, he steered his attention to the items beneath the counter on his left. The quiet way he examined each item in the display made it feel as though he was judging me. Shikoba was our gemstone supplier, but he'd never seen my designs. Had he sent Tak to spy on our business? Would this man return home and tell his father that my jewelry was unworthy of his stones?

Tak rested his forearms on the glass and held a pensive look on his face that left me curious as to what he was thinking. His handsome mane reached the center of his back, the braid secured by a leather hair tie with tiny turquoise stones on the tasseled ends. I imagined he was a formidable leader in his tribe. But why would a man permanently mark his face?

"Let me see this one," he said, tapping the glass with his index finger.

I looked down and raised my brows. Most men wanted to see the chokers, but none had ever asked to see my most cherished piece—a squash blossom necklace with a downturned crescent at the bottom. I had chosen only the most beautiful turquoise stones to pair with the silver, and though I knew the necklace would be too conspicuous for most Shifters, it spoke to my heart. That piece was the only item I'd made by hand that was still in the glass display from day one, and I guessed it would remain there for many years to come. It was flashy, big, and priced high.

"You don't want to see this piece," I said. "That choker looks more your style."

His thick eyebrows gathered in a frown when he looked at the bone choker adorned with silver and black beads. "I don't want to see that one. I want to see *this* one."

"This is for serious buyers only."

Tak opened his wallet, and when I glimpsed a few twenty-dollar bills, I decided to save him the embarrassment.

I touched his hand. "It's fifteen thousand."

Tak stilled, staring at his insufficient funds. He retracted his arm and tucked his wallet back in his pocket. "For that kind of profit, I hope you're paying my father well for his stones."

"Rest assured we have a fair contract. I don't base prices on the blue book value; it's about the time put into crafting each one and choosing the right stones that fit together. There's love in every piece I make, but some are more valuable than others."

"I can buy a car for that much."

Insulted, I went back to the register. "Then perhaps you should. My father says only laborers drive white trucks."

A chuckle rumbled deep in his chest. "Does your father not labor?"

"My father is one of the most respected Packmasters in the

territory, so tread carefully when deciding whom you choose to insult in this town. If one of his packmates had overheard that remark, they would have drawn blood."

He tilted his head to one side, his dark eyes lit with interest. "How long have you been living apart from a pack? What do they call it? Rogue?"

"Independent." I moved a jar of mints aside. "Tell me, how is it you know my brother and yet you didn't know about me?"

Tak rubbed the tattooed side of his face and looked away. "If Lakota hasn't mentioned me, then I'm not sure I want to answer that."

The clock on the wall reminded me of how many tasks I needed to complete before closing up the store. "Weren't you supposed to be leaving town?"

"I couldn't leave without swinging by the store." He rested his hands on the counter, arms straight and shoulders broad. "My father will want a full report."

Sweat touched my brow.

Tak smiled invitingly, his voice sweet like honey. "I don't think I've ever met a woman quite like you."

When his eyes settled on the scar on my forehead, I looked away and moved our wolf totem to a new spot. "I'll be sure to let Lakota know you stopped by."

"Does your brother usually leave you unguarded for days at a time? Do you have a mate, or is it just you in that apartment?"

Butterflies flitted in my stomach. At five eight, I'd never felt small around anyone until now. I wished Lakota hadn't told this guy they were going on a trip. He probably hadn't thought it mattered since Tak was leaving town.

But Tak was still here.

Standing in my shop.

Tak snatched a peppermint from the bowl by the register and grinned as he twisted open the clear wrapper. Chomping on the candy, he swaggered toward the door, and even walking away, he looked fierce. I'd never seen such a dominant alpha, one who didn't need to summon his wolf to win a fight.

When he opened the door, a burst of sunshine enveloped him. "See you around, Duckie."

Chapter 7

After locking up the display cases, I scanned the room one last time and went down my mental checklist of everything that needed to be done before leaving. I'd already locked the register drawer in the safe along with our most expensive jewelry. The books and inventory were up to date, the floor was swept, and the counters had been cleaned. I'd also mopped up a spill I'd made in the break room earlier that day.

Lakota had no idea how long it took for one person to wrap things up, especially when customers were still standing in line past closing. He'd hung around the shop before, but Mel and I had a system when working together that made it easy to finish quickly and get out of there. Without her, it had taken me until after dark.

Just as I flipped off the lights, I realized I'd forgotten to empty the wastebaskets. *Dang it!* We had one behind the counter, one in the break room, two in the bathroom, and one near the register.

"Oh, it's always something," I huffed, tossing my purse on the counter.

For a moment, I considered leaving it for the morning, but trash didn't take long to stink up a room. After stuffing the small plastic bags into the larger black one in the break room, I gathered up the rest in the bathroom. Mel and I tried to keep it clean, but sometimes people left a mess or threw out food they had brought in with them. Once I tied off the bag, I headed to the back door and shouldered it open.

Our trash bin was in the alley just to the right of the door, lit by a caged bulb affixed to the building. While every shopkeeper had a dumpster assigned to them, sometimes the delis behind us got overloaded, and they snuck over and used ours. I hated that because it stank up the back of our store. I hurled the bags through the opening and stilled when I heard a loud crash.

That was close.

The thought crossed my mind that there might have been a serious accident out front, so I dashed inside to see if I could help. When I circled the counter and ran toward the front door, I skidded on something hard and caught myself on a rack before falling. The floor twinkled, drawing my attention. As I looked closer, I realized pieces of glass were scattered across the room. I swung my gaze up to a massive hole in the right-hand window, large shards hanging precariously from the top.

There were no men outside swinging at each other, nor were there signs that a car had jumped the curb. Too stunned to come up with any ideas, I was drifting toward the wall when something caught my eye. Glass crunched beneath my feet as I moved closer and stared down at a black bowling ball.

I sighed at the mess. "Can't you kids find something better to do on the weekend? Pizza? A movie? A slumber party? Not destroying someone's property?"

As if the humans weren't bad enough, it was a common rite of passage among young Shifter males to initiate asinine dares. They usually did it after their first change, and it wasn't uncommon for them to do something extreme.

I turned on the dimmer lights and surveyed the damage. Our poor mannequin. It looked like someone had thrown her to the ground and beat her with her own arm. Even worse, tiny pieces of glass sparkled against folded clothes on one of the freestanding shelves. No sense in worrying about damages. I needed to fix the window first and foremost.

I hurried to the counter and searched through our address book. One of Mel's aunts had given us a list of Breed repairmen in case of an emergency. They didn't have set working hours, which made them some of the best.

I cleared my throat. "Hi, is this Mr. Mo Franklin?"

"It is," the man replied, a TV blaring in the background.

"My name is Hope Church, and I'm the co-owner of a shop on Starlight Road."

"Moonbeam? Yeah, I know it," he said, his Texas drawl unhurried and friendly.

"Moonglow, actually. Someone referred you, and I have a situation."

He sniffed and turned down the TV. "Gimme the details."

"Our front window is broken."

I could hear him grumbling as he must have been sitting up from a lying down position. "What are the measurements?"

I rummaged through our drawer until I found a small book with miscellaneous notes. I gave him the information. "I'm not sure what to do. I have all this merchandise and can't leave the store open like it is. Do you think you can board it up or something?"

"If it comes to that, I can. But let's see if we can't find you a window replacement first. I'll need to send one of my boys to the warehouse to check the inventory. I think I had an order for that place years ago, but most of the stores along the strip are standard. Shouldn't take more than a few hours to find a match. As long as we have the window, I can repair it by the morning. For an extra fee, I'll send one of my boys out to guard your store if you need to go home. Otherwise, your merchandise is open to the public."

Something outside caught my attention. "That sounds great, Mr. Franklin. I really appreciate your doing this on short notice. I thought I was going to have to hang a tarp over it for the next two weeks."

He chuckled. "No, y'all don't have to worry. We run a tight ship, and since our clients are limited to Breed, we can usually swing emergency calls. Don't worry about cleaning up; we'll do that. Just move your merchandise away from the window."

"Perfect."

"You want to pay extra for the guard? My son can be there in ten minutes. Maybe less."

It seemed like a sound idea. "Yes, please."

"Joe's a bear, so you're in good hands. He drives a red truck."

As soon as Mo hung up, I sent a message to Melody's aunt and told her she was off the hook for coming in on Sunday. I didn't give her details, only that I had business matters to attend to and had decided it was a better idea to close the shop. She replied to call if I changed my mind, but Naya led a busy life and shouldn't have been our backup in the first place.

I dragged a small display shelf to the center of the store and then moved a few racks away from the window. Just when I set the mannequin down by the counter, an odd noise made me spin on my heel. "Hello?"

I dropped the mannequin's broken arm and grabbed my keys, the small canister of mace dangling from one of the rings. Deciding not to make the suicidal move of poking my head through the hole in the glass, I opened the front door and peered outside. Two lovebirds were sharing a cigarette across the street and down a ways, but other than that, not a soul in sight.

There it was again!

I crossed the sidewalk and circled my car to the passenger side. The moment I caught sight of fur, my heart skidded to a stop. It might have been a stray animal, but my gut told me it was a Shifter.

"Come out from behind there. I can see you!"

I squinted, trying to discern if that was a black tail peeking out from behind my front tire. A tail of *what*?

"I have a weapon, and backup is on the way."

My finger rested nervously on the mace release lever. I wasn't certain how to use it since I'd never owned one before.

When I stepped back for a better look, a wolf came into view. His hind quarters protruded from beneath my car, and part of me wanted to run. But where would I go? The store had a gaping hole in the window, and I needed my car.

"Are you the one who broke my window? Come out from there before I call the Council."

A guttural whimper came from the shadows—like a wolf in pain. What if a car had struck him?

No way was I going to reach under the car, so I grabbed his hind legs and dragged him out. I knew a lot of wolves in the territory by sight, and hopefully this one belonged to a familiar pack so I could call his alpha to pick him up. When his head came into view, his tongue was hanging out and his eyes were closed. Was he dead?

I cautiously knelt and ran my hands across his thick coat. No blood coated my palms, but an injured wolf was a dangerous one, so I kept a close watch while I examined him. When I touched the side of his head, broken pieces of skull shifted beneath the skin.

I grimaced. "Oh my God." Whoever this guy was, he needed immediate help. "Shift," I said firmly. When he didn't respond, I prodded his side with a finger in hopes the pain would rouse him. "Shift!"

He growled weakly, his eyelids fluttering.

I repeated my less than gentle approach at waking him. "Shift before you die!"

Though facing away from me, he bared his fangs. Normally that aggressive type of gesture would have sent me running, but instead, I stood up and frantically searched for help. The two people across the street had left, and I hesitated about calling over a random stranger. What if they were a human and called animal control? That was a Shifter's worst nightmare.

Squatting, I readied myself to run. Poking a wolf was

about as effective as killing an elephant with a flyswatter, so I needed to resort to extreme measures. With a quick swing of my arm, I smacked his hindquarters. "Shift!"

He rolled as if to flip over, and in a swift movement of magic and shadows, the creature shifted from wolf to man.

I scarcely breathed when I gazed upon his tattooed face. He lay naked on his right side, his long hair unbound. What on earth was Tak doing out here at this hour? How long had he been lying by my car? Blood still trickled from the partially healed wound on his head, wetting the concrete.

I patted his thigh. "You need to shift again. Do you hear me? If you fall asleep, you might not wake up. Tak?"

He groaned, his eyes still closed.

Shikoba led one of the largest Shifter tribes in Oklahoma. If I let his son die in front of my store, I was certain I could kiss my career goodbye.

I pinched Tak's brawny thigh, but he lay motionless.

"If you don't shift, I'm going to take a belt to you!" I slapped him hard on the ass, and his eyes popped wide open.

He pushed himself up and scowled. As if caught in a dream, I watched his brown eyes connect with mine while his body slowly morphed. Usually the process of shifting went fast, but fur grew from his skin like magic. His limbs changed shape, and his stern jaw stretched into the toothy mouth of a wolf. It was a beautiful and intimate thing to watch, but when his wolf rose to his feet, I held up my can of mace in terror. Was Tak still awake in there, or would his animal rip me to pieces?

The wolf staggered toward me and then collapsed at my side.

I catapulted to my feet and backed away from the unconscious animal, my heart racing. His skull appeared mended, but there was no telling if he had suffered brain damage. Based on his incessant laughter earlier that day, odds were he was already afflicted.

A horn honked twice, making me jump and drop my keys.

I quickly gathered them up and looked at the red truck that had stopped behind my car.

A shadowy figure leaned out of the window. "Are you Miss Church?"

"Yes?"

"I'm Joe." He backed into the parking space on the other side of my car before shutting off his engine.

I dusted off my hands while the young man got out and rounded the front end of my car.

"What kind of trouble you got going on?" He knelt down in front of Tak and then peered up at me with a quizzical stare. "Is he the one who broke your window? Remind me never to piss you off."

"No. At least, I don't think so. I know him. He's not from around here, so there's no one I can call to collect him off the street. Will you help me put him into the car?"

Joe stood up. He was a lanky guy with dark-rimmed glasses, but you couldn't judge a book by its cover. Bears—especially grizzlies—were dangerous, regardless of their human appearance. "Are you sure you want to do that?"

"I can't leave him here."

"You should probably call the Council and let them take care of it."

Tak couldn't have damaged my window. Committing an offense against someone who shared a contract with his tribe would shame his father. I wasn't sure what Tak's relationship was with Lakota, but turning him in didn't seem right.

"Help me," I pleaded, unlocking the door with my key. "I still have to run inside and lock the back entrance. Do you need me to leave you the key to the store?"

Joe scratched his chin. "You have a hole the size of Jamaica in that window. I shouldn't have any trouble getting in. Don't worry. We'll take care of everything. Believe it or not, this kind of thing happens all the time. Immortals have a lot of enemies, but mostly it's just a bunch of rowdy kids running off the leash. I'll keep a lookout. My father will call when the job's done, so make sure you keep your phone turned on." Joe heaved the large black-and-grey wolf in his arms and scooted him into the back seat. He didn't recoil in fear but neither did he handle him gently. Had Tak tried to snap at Joe, I might have had to deal with a pissed-off grizzly on top of everything else, and they were known to kill our kind.

I slammed the door. "You're a lifesaver."

Joe brushed the fur off his shirt. "You might change your mind after you get the bill. Guarding property costs more than labor."

"You can't put a price on peace of mind. Can you do me a favor?"

"What's that?"

I looked left and right. "If you see anything suspicious, can you let me know? You're probably right about it being a bunch of kids horsing around. You know how mischievous boys are."

"I sure do. Just last week, a couple of shitheads who belong to a den of lions took a baseball bat and smashed out a few windshields, including mine. They think because there isn't a juvie for Shifters, they can do whatever they want. Nobody goes to jail for vandalism, but that doesn't mean they'll get off scot-free. Karma has a way of bitch-slapping the wicked, especially when you fuck with an immortal who has nothing but eons of time to plot his revenge."

If what Joe said was true, I wondered what I'd done to anger the spirits. Perhaps I hadn't yet paid the price in full for the sins of my past.

Chapter 8

Dragging a humongous wolf from the parking garage to my apartment building took a Herculean effort, and while I hoped that someone would walk by and volunteer to help, the only person I passed was a Mage who gave me the evil eye before getting in his Porsche.

Not everyone liked Shifters.

And as it so happened, not everyone liked pinheads who drove sports cars either.

Tak wouldn't wake up—probably for the best. His wolf weighed a ton, but not nearly as much as his human counterpart. I could never have dragged Tak to the apartment all by myself.

Once the elevator reached our floor, I grabbed his hind legs and pulled him down the hall. Sweat beaded on my brow and behind my neck.

"Why did you have to be the biggest wolf in all the land? What do they feed you guys up in Oklahoma? Buffalo?" Tak was a mighty wolf, and my legs were about to buckle from the whole affair. "Don't you dare make me regret this."

"You need help?" a man called out.

I glanced over my shoulder at Nash, the pizza delivery guy and also a hero in the making.

He set down his red thermal bag and jogged over. "Is this Melody?"

My eyes settled on the red sauce stain on his white shirt. "Don't trouble yourself. You have food to deliver," I said, out of breath.

He lifted the hind legs and took over. "A little hair never hurt anyone."

"Thanks." I wiped my forehead and stole a second to catch my breath.

When we reached my apartment, he set the wolf down while I unlocked the door and switched on the light.

"Right there is fine." I stepped aside to let Nash drag the wolf inside.

Nash could have easily lifted Tak's wolf, but I sensed his trepidation. A person took risks when handling a wounded Shifter in animal form, and surely Nash had sensed Tak's alpha power. Nash had never disclosed what his animal was, nor had we ever asked. We ordered pizza or lasagna at least twice a week since the shop was on the same street as ours. Nash was our regular delivery guy, and by the muscles on his arms, he must have delivered a lot of large orders.

I set down my purse and frowned at the blood streaks on the wood floor leading out to the hall.

Nash returned to the doorway. "I'm guessing by the big willy that this isn't your purple-haired friend."

"No, it's not Mel. It's someone my brother knows."

"That's a relief. Hold on." Nash turned down the hall, and I hurried to the kitchen to wash my hands and get a drink of water. "I'll just leave this here," he said.

Grabbing a dish towel, I turned around to see what he was doing. Nash stepped over the wolf and presented me with a box of pizza.

"No, really," I insisted. "I can't take someone else's dinner."

"It's not a real order, so you're in luck." He set the box on the island and patted it. "We don't have online ordering or deal with credit cards, so we get a lot of pranksters ordering pizza for strangers. Kids think it's funny. Sometimes the person being pranked feels guilty and pays me anyhow, but the asshole down the hall slammed the door in my face. It's all yours if you don't mind olives. I know how you guys like pizza, and this one is super tasty. It's the thick crust with garlic sauce."

I opened a drawer to pay him.

"Don't even try," he said, strutting into the living room. Nash flipped his red baseball cap backward, which hid his curly blond hair.

"Thanks, Nash. I owe you."

I ran an empty glass underneath the tap. While I quenched my thirst, I wondered what I should do about Tak.

Nash looked around the apartment. "I only ever see this place from the doorway. Is this a corner unit?"

I rounded the island with a damp dish towel in my hand. "Yes. We got lucky. The best part is all the light we get since we have windows on two different walls." I knelt to wipe up the blood. "Corner units aren't easy to come by, and the layout feels more spacious than the other apartments."

"So you have windows in the rooms?" he asked, pointing at the hall.

"Yes. It's just a two bedroom, but you'd be shocked how high the rent is."

"Sweet. I practically live in a dungeon with only two windows." He hopped left to right and averted his eyes. "Mind if I use your bathroom real quick? Usually I pull over at a gas station or McDonald's. I wouldn't normally ask, but I don't think I can hold it any—"

"Go right ahead," I said, saving him the embarrassment. "It's the last door at the end of the hall."

Nash hurried around the corner and slammed the door.

After cleaning up all the blood in the outside hall, I crawled into the living room and soaked up the rest. What in the world had Tak's wolf been doing beneath my car in his condition? Had he lost control and shifted on the street? Maybe his wolf had escaped the motel and somehow remembered my store. Or maybe Tak opened his big mouth and pissed off a local.

He must have crawled beneath the car to protect himself since injured animals in the open are vulnerable. I could have accidentally backed over him. I shuddered at the thought of it.

I sat there for a moment and wondered if I should call Melody. It would either ruin their trip or make them worry needlessly, and this gathering was important to both families. I could only imagine the bountiful meals and conversations uniting both sides. It was tough missing out on all that fun, but I'd promised Melody that I'd go up with them next time.

When I stood up, Nash emerged with a more relaxed look on his face.

He brushed his wet hands over his T-shirt, his eyes soaking in the spacious apartment windows. "Would you mind putting in a good word for me with the landlord? I've been waiting for something to come up in this building. It's close to my job, and I like that it has garage parking. The place where I'm staying now doesn't even have covered parking. My car got pummeled in the last hailstorm. Man, I'd *love* a corner unit."

"I'll put in a word, but I can't promise anything. The manager's a tough guy to deal with."

Nash stepped around the wolf and into the hall. "If I were you, I'd lock him in the bathroom. He's not lucid, and if he wakes up and gets confused, he'll attack you. Maybe you should let Lakota decide what to do with him."

I stared down at the wolf, realizing the danger. "Lakota's not here, so I'll probably shut him up like you suggested. His family can come get him if he doesn't shift back."

"You do that." Nash glanced at his watch. "I better run before my orders get cold. Take a load off and eat that pizza while it's still hot. You look beat. I don't usually give away my food, so don't tell anyone. If word gets back to my boss, he'll fire me."

"Thanks again for the help," I said. "I really appreciate it. See you next time." I locked the door and then backed up against it.

Tak's wolf was a handsome blend. His ebony coat had grey patches, but I'd never seen anything more striking than his face. It reminded me of his human one, with the left side grey and the other half black. Had he tattooed his face to match the division in his wolf's features?

I knelt down and wiped the dried blood from his temple, but his fur was too dense for me to examine his injuries. Nash was right. Leaving Tak's wolf in an open room in this condition created a potentially deadly situation, so I carefully dragged him down the hall and into my bedroom. Mel's room was out of the question. I'd never forgive myself if Tak's wolf tore up any of her designs.

No sense in lifting him onto the bed; I'd barely gotten him out of the car without breaking my back. Too much solid muscle for me to attempt such a feat.

What an impressive creature, I thought.

I retrieved an old blanket from the closet and spread it out on the floor. Tucking one edge beneath his back, I held his hind legs and twisted his body toward the blanket, doing the same with his front legs until he rolled over on top of it.

"There," I breathed, collapsing on the floor. My arms and back were as sore as the dickens. I pinched one of the fat pads on his paw. "You need to wake up and shift. I can't have a wolf in my house."

When he didn't respond, I decided on another tactic. It didn't seem right to keep pinching and prodding him, so I crawled up behind the wolf and ran my fingers up his soft belly. Sometimes alphas responded to the sound of a woman's voice, and I hoped he was lucid enough to hear me. My face brushed against his soft fur until my lips reached his pointy ears.

"Are you awake in there, alpha male? *Shift.*"

His wolf eloquently transformed to a human so fast that I didn't have time to move away. I lay against his back, my arm wrapped around him, fingers splayed across his strong chest.

My lips were touching the shell of his ear, my body pressed tight against his.

Tak remained unconscious, so I breathed a sigh of relief and sat up. Checking to see if his skull fracture had healed, I touched his temple and pushed all around his head. His eyes didn't flutter once. Moonlight poured through the window, and up close, the details of his tattoo came to life. It didn't mark his nose, but the sharp design began along his left jaw and went from his chin to his hairline, some of it crossing over his eyelid. I traced my finger over the lines, following the patterns before stroking his thick eyebrows, which arched in the center. Some men's eyebrows went straight across or sat heavy on their eyelids, but not Tak's. It gave him a mischievous look even when sleeping.

He wasn't so scary in this tranquil state.

When his eye blinked open and he seized my wrist, I shrank back in surprise. Tak's grip was iron, but I managed to twist my hand free and scamper away. My heart thudded against my ribs as my back met the wall, and I drew up my knees. I knew better than to trust strangers—especially wolves.

He turned over until his shoulder blades touched the floor, leg bent and concealing his manhood. Tak blinked in confusion at me, then let his gaze travel up to the ceiling. "What happened?"

"You don't remember?"

He touched his crown, his eyes dulled from the trauma. "Did you slap me on the ass?"

"Did you break my store window?"

Tak reached up for my bed and crawled onto it. I swallowed hard, trying to avert my eyes from his backside, and he had a spectacular one. When he collapsed facedown on my green bedspread, I thought about how all his man bits were rubbing against my favorite blanket. It was too late to worry about such silly things, so I collected the one from the floor and used it to cover him up.

"My head," he groaned into the pillow. Then he turned his head to face the window.

"You need to shift again. I can't really assess if you have brain damage or not."

"Were you petting me a minute ago?"

I felt the heat of embarrassment rise in my cheeks. "I'm locking you in here until morning. Then you have to leave." I neared the door and peered over my shoulder at him. "And don't touch anything."

Tak wearily raised his arm and touched the windowsill.

Once in the hall, I shut the door and leaned my back against it. Groans filled the quiet space, but they were the sounds of a man in pain. I didn't like that sound coming from my bedroom, as if it might somehow soak into the walls and live here forever. He could have asked me for an aspirin, but everything about Tak struck me as stubborn. Shifting to heal required a lot of energy, so hopefully he'd be zonked out for the rest of the night. My mind drifted back to that secret moment when I'd held him—what it felt like to have someone that strong in my arms. A secret part of me wondered if that was what life was like for mated couples.

Lakota would kill me if he knew what I was up to, but he'd have to stand in line behind my father, who would probably kill the wolf first. No matter.

What's done is done.

A few minutes later, I grabbed two slices of pizza and devoured them. Hauling a wolf around by the hind legs had given me a voracious appetite. I could have eaten more, but my eyelids grew heavy as if weights were pulling them down. The Tak dilemma would have to wait until morning. I still had the store to worry about. The last thing I remembered was grabbing my phone and collapsing on the couch, my thoughts drifting to the wolf in my bed.

Tak struggled to open his eyes, but his lashes were stuck together. He rubbed his face against a soft pillow and drew in a deep breath, instantly growing hard. Hope's scent was all around him. In the sheets, on the blanket that covered him, and all over the pillowcase. He lay there for a minute just soaking it all in.

Soaking *her* in.

How the hell had she managed to carry him all the way up to her apartment alone? She must have had muscles like a horse. The thought made him grin as he rolled onto his back and stared up at the ceiling.

On top of all that, she had brought him into her bedroom.

Not the hall, not the doorstep, and definitely not the bathroom.

The idea of it nestled in his head and made his wolf stir. The innocuous gesture had layers upon layers of meaning. Women in his tribe didn't bring strange men to their beds, nor did they cozy up behind them while they were in wolf form. And they certainly didn't pet them while doing it. Those acts were reserved for lovers. Was he remembering correctly? Surely Hope wouldn't have been caressing his cheek on the tattooed side of his face. It must have been a nice dream. After all, he'd sustained a near-fatal head injury last night, and he'd be lucky if he could remember how to tie his shoes.

Tak sat up and wiped the sleep from his eyes.

"Shit," he muttered, realizing he didn't have any clothes to change into.

He rubbed his temple, checking for scars. Though the wound had healed, phantom pains still shuddered through him. His bones creaked and muscles ached when he stood up and stretched. Glaring at her closet, he decided not to rummage through her personal things in search of men's clothing. By the looks of her modest room, Tak didn't sense that another male shared her space.

That pleased him more than it should have.

He walked to the foot of the bed and marveled over the

fine craftsmanship of her desk. Someone had put a lot of love into carving that piece, and it was almost as magnificent as the jewelry that filled the shelves and hung from hooks.

Yet as beautiful as they were, all of those trinkets paled in comparison to the squash blossom necklace he'd seen on display in her store. Any man in his tribe would be honored to own something that impressive. Tak regretted thinking he could own it for only one hundred dollars. She must have been insulted. He'd just never seen jewelry marked so high, but maybe she priced important pieces as a test to make sure that only the right person made her an offer—one who deserved to wear it.

Curious how long he'd been asleep, Tak peered into the hall for signs of life. A house this quiet didn't seem right. He lived in a big tribe, and people were always running about doing chores and visiting with packmates. Tak awoke each morning to the sound of birds chirping through open windows, women singing, and children laughing. How could anyone live in a tomb such as this?

Tak silently moved into the living room and spotted Hope curled up on the pink sofa against the left wall. He stood there for a moment and admired her, his fingertips reaching for her silken tresses. Women in his tribe wore theirs braided, so seeing Hope's loose locks tempted him to touch her hair. She looked peaceful lying there with her knees drawn up. Had it been chilly, he would have found a blanket to cover her up.

He glanced down at his naked body and decided to put distance between them in case she opened her eyes. No sense in giving the woman a start with his endowments.

The living room didn't seem at all her style. He still couldn't get over the pink sofa. Tak stopped in front of a short divider wall and admired the houseplants sitting on top. Someone loved and cared for them. Not a single dead leaf, and the dirt was moist to the touch. A suncatcher in the kitchen window caught his attention, the green and yellow bird spraying colors onto the kitchen island. He circled around the wall and gripped the back of a barstool. Hand-stitched pot holders hung from the side of the fridge, and on the freezer door, a wolf magnet pinned a photograph of Hope and Melody in front of their store, big smiles on their faces. The homemade flour and sugar canisters on the counter made him wonder if she'd bought them or someone in her family had made them. There were more crafts in the kitchen, and he instantly liked this room.

Curious, he opened two folding doors to the right of the fridge and peered inside a laundry room. There weren't any clothes, only a folded-up quilt on the dryer and a large piece of fabric draped over a hook. He pulled it free, and when he shook out the thin material—uncertain what it was used for—he decided to wrap it around his waist and tie a knot.

Tak found a bag of thick rubber bands and put one between his teeth while he meticulously braided his hair in the back. He'd done it a million times and could make a perfectly straight braid even in the dark. He had to wrap the band around the end a dozen times, and though it probably wouldn't hold all day, it would suffice. Tying it back wasn't just for the convenience of getting his hair out of his face. It was a symbolic link to his people. His tribe had many traditions, one of them being that both men and women braided their hair in a single braid. The only exception was his father, who wore two. Walking around with unbound hair was like not wearing pants.

He rubbed his chest and then stretched out his arms. The thought of eggs made his stomach growl. Tak opened the fridge and frowned.

No eggs.

"Figures," he muttered.

The one thing in the whole world that would have completely satisfied his craving. Not just any craving, but the food craving all Shifters had after a shift. It had been hours, but the taste for eggs still lingered. He'd never had this problem before since they raised their own chickens. Tak pulled out a package of bacon and shoved away thoughts of scrambled eggs, sunny-side up, poached, over easy, boiled, and even raw.

A casserole would be even better, he thought.

Tak turned around and pressed his back against the fridge, staring across the apartment at the slumbering woman. He should have left town yesterday, but his wolf wouldn't allow it. No matter what resentment he harbored toward Lakota, it had nothing to do with his sister. Hope was just a stranger, but a sense of duty and responsibility came over him—a desire to guard this woman as if she were precious gold. But those feelings conflicted with a voice in his head that reminded him Hope wasn't his concern. Women like her didn't need men like him.

But maybe she could use a blanket.

Chapter 9

The sound of whistling danced in my head, and I sleepily rubbed my eyes. When I opened them, I was lying on the pink sofa with a quilt over me. I had no memory of getting it out, but as groggy as I was feeling, maybe my memory couldn't be trusted.

Startled, I flew up to a sitting position.

What day is this? What time is it?

When I realized I wasn't late for work and the pieces of what had happened the night before fell into place, I breathed a sigh of relief.

Until a second thing startled me—smoke.

Across the living room, Tak was standing in the kitchen in front of my stove.

Shirtless.

A single braid of dark hair ran down his bare back, and he was whistling like a bird set free from its cage. I drew in a breath, the aroma of bacon eclipsed by the white smoke that filled the room like a thin haze.

"Ow!" he hissed, swinging his arm away.

I padded across the living room, still dressed in yesterday's clothes.

"Ouch!" This time, he added a sharp word. I didn't recognize his language, but I guessed I had just learned my first swear word in it.

"What are you doing?" I asked, rubbing the kink in my neck.

He turned around, holding the spatula as if he intended to spank me with it.

Now there was a silly thought.

"Trying to cook bacon."

"You're going to set off the fire alarm." I noticed the red spots on his chest from the bacon grease popping. "Maybe you should put on an apron. Haven't you ever fried bacon before?" Another plume of smoke billowed from the pan. "Turn down the heat before you start a grease fire!"

Tak rotated the dial until the burner clicked off. He scooped up the black pieces of bacon, a scowl on his face as he searched for the trash can.

I went to the island and sat down to watch the giant wandering around my kitchen in my blue sarong.

"I'm a good cook," he insisted, putting a lid over the pan. "I'm just not used to your stove. Something's wrong with it. Fire doesn't come from the burners."

"They're electric. We don't have gas stoves in this building."

After Tak opened the kitchen window, he sat across from me. I couldn't take my eyes off his massive shoulders as he rested his forearms on the countertop and stared at the door.

"Are you expecting someone?" I asked.

"You don't have any eggs. I was craving eggs."

"We have eggs. I keep them in the bottom drawer since Lakota likes easy access to all his meat. We probably eat more processed food than we should."

He kept looking to my right. "Do you want me to make some?"

"You're the guest. It's not right for you to cook anything for me."

He shrugged. "I'm not an invited guest. You saved my wolf. The least I can do is to cook you a meal."

Why wouldn't he look at me? Having a conversation with his profile was awkward and unnecessary, so I stood up and rounded the island. As I passed by him, I gently touched his shoulder. "You don't have to hide your face for my benefit. I've already seen your tattoo."

"I was just saving your appetite."

"It doesn't bother me. Do you want any leftover pizza?"

"I don't eat that stuff."

I dumped the cold pizza into the trash and set the empty box against the wall. All the excitement from the night before must have done a number on me. Maybe a little food in my belly would alleviate my headache. I found the carton of eggs in the fridge and a package of cheese. "Omelets it is."

"Cheese? That's not how you make an omelet." Tak rose from his seat and pulled veggies from the fridge before he took my cutting board hostage. "Set the fire, and I'll do the rest."

I found it curious that Tak couldn't manage something as simple as an electric stove. But from what Melody had told me, Shikoba's people were self-sustaining and had few modern luxuries. They probably canned food, made jerky, and roasted fresh game over an open fire. Just imagining it made me envious.

I put a clean skillet on the stove and moved the dirty bacon pan into the sink.

Butter sizzled when he dropped it into the hot skillet.

"Cast-iron skillets are better," he remarked. "These never last."

I regarded him as he cut into a green bell pepper. Even barefoot he was so much taller than me. "My sarong looks good on you."

Tak had a way of smiling with his eyes that sent goose bumps across my skin. "You think? Maybe I'll start a fashion trend with the warriors in my tribe."

"Are you *sure* you don't have brain damage?" I teased.

Tak finished dicing the peppers and pushed them into a pile. "My head still hurts, but I'll live. Did you see what happened?"

"You don't remember?"

With one hand, he cracked two brown eggs into a bowl. "It's fuzzy. I remember shifting, and then after a while, I got sleepy and let my wolf take over. I shouldn't have, but he's cunning enough to stay out of trouble."

I stared vacantly at the backsplash behind the stove. "Wait a minute. I thought you shifted to protect yourself against an attack."

He didn't reply. He just kept beating those eggs.

I turned to look at him. "Are you telling me you shifted *before* the attack? On purpose? This isn't the country. You can't just let your wolf run out in the open. It's too dangerous. Not just because of the cars, but animal control might capture you."

Tak threw back his head and laughed.

"It's not funny! Every Shifter's worst nightmare is going to the pound."

He set down his knife. "Do you ever laugh?"

"This isn't a laughing matter. What if the cops had arrested you? Who would have bailed you out?"

He flashed a grin, and curse me for thinking him handsome.

Tak jerked his chin toward me. "What's wrong with your neck? You keep rubbing it."

"I slept on it wrong. I just have a crick in it."

When he closed the distance between us, I sucked in a sharp breath.

"Can I do something?"

Wide-eyed, I stared up at him as he reached out and braced his hand where my shoulder and neck met. His thumb pressed deep, and he suddenly gripped the top of my head with his other hand and tilted it. Tak had large hands, and when he began kneading my neck, I had a funny feeling in my stomach. I closed my eyes, and he moved my head again, his other hand sliding down to my shoulder and then working its way back up.

My arousal startled me, and I slapped his hand away. "That'll be enough."

"Better?"

I turned my neck in a slow circle, the pain miraculously gone. "Yes, thank you. Did a healer teach you that trick?"

He studied me for a moment. "Your father must be a serious man. It makes me curious about your mother. Are they opposites or the same?"

Flustered, I grabbed the bowl of chopped vegetables and dumped them into the skillet. Why was he asking about my parents?

Tak suddenly pressed his body against my back and reached around me. I couldn't tell if it was the burner heating me up or his close proximity, but when he grabbed the saltshaker and said, "'Scuse me" in a rough voice against my ear, a flash of heat rippled from my breasts to my lower belly.

I wriggled free. "I need to brush my teeth."

The louder he chuckled, the faster I fled toward the hall. Once I reached the bathroom and slammed the door, I stared at myself in the mirror.

Oh. My. God.

No wonder he kept looking away. It wasn't about hiding his tattoo; it was *me*. I looked like a troll who'd been living between the seat cushions for the past three hundred years. One piece of my ratted hair had stuck to the side of my face where I must have drooled in my sleep. What little eyeliner I'd applied the day before had smeared around my eyes, and red marks that looked like grid lines covered the right side of my neck where the pillow sham must have wrinkled. I cupped my hand in front of my mouth and assessed my breath.

Just as I thought.

I quickly brushed my teeth and then stepped out of my dirty clothes. For a brief moment, I thought about taking a shower, but there was too much to do. Had Mr. Franklin finished repairing the store window? I'd also fallen behind on chores. Like making sure I'd wiped all the blood off the floor in the living room. Not to mention doing a load of laundry, checking the mail, and changing out my sheets and blankets. After I finished combing the tangles out of my hair, I gazed at myself in the mirror and reached for a bottle.

Tak would be out of my life in less than an hour, so why should I care what I looked like? Yet there I was, slathering my naked body with scented oil.

I swung the door open and gasped when I slammed into over two hundred pounds of pure alpha male. The moment Tak's hands rested on my bare shoulders, I panicked, stumbling backward into the bathroom and slamming the door in his face.

No laughter that time.

I wrapped a towel around my naked body and took a deep, calming breath. "He's just a man," I whispered to myself. "It's not like you're entertaining an important Packmaster."

I opened the door, expecting to see him gone. Tak was staring down at his chest, and fire burned my cheeks when I noticed two oily imprints in the shape of my breasts.

"I-I thought I— Th-the eggs are done," he stammered, still staring at his chest, a spatula in his hand.

"Can I get dressed?"

As soon as he stepped aside, I walked coolly into my bedroom and closed the door. The towel dropped, and I glanced at myself in the mirror.

Boy, was I shiny.

After rubbing the oil in, I grabbed my favorite pair of overalls and a white T-shirt. What I really wanted to do was go back to sleep, but someone had to sweep up the store and make sure there weren't any small particles of glass embedded in the fabric of our merchandise.

I finally emerged from my bedroom, fresh-faced and barefoot. Hopefully I could look him in the eye.

Tak was sitting at the kitchen island, watching me. Much to my relief, he'd wiped away the oil marks on his chest.

He cleared his throat. "I hate to ask, but I need to borrow

Lakota's clothes. My truck is at the motel along with my things."

Which meant he'd shifted at his motel. Time for answers. "What was your wolf doing outside my shop at that hour?"

"Sit down and eat," he said, tapping the edge of my plate. "I don't like seeing a woman with an empty stomach."

Tak had plated our breakfast beautifully, and my mouth watered at the sight of the sliced tomatoes.

"This looks delicious."

"Maybe you should take a bite and let me know if it meets your standards."

I arched a brow and sat down. "I'm not going to judge your food."

He sipped his juice. "Shame. It's worth judging."

I cut the egg with the edge of my fork and flashed him a playful smile. "I'll be the judge of that."

"Ah, so she does have a sense of humor after all."

Tak's was the best omelet I'd ever eaten, and I wasn't a huge fan of them. "Not bad."

"Was there a compliment buried in that remark?" Tak chuckled and devoured a large bite. "That's funny."

"What?"

He spoke with his mouth full. "I only see that look on a woman's face when I make her come. If that's the look you make for something that's just okay, I'm tempted to serve you my famous grilled rabbit."

I lowered my eyes. "You shouldn't talk dirty while we're eating."

"I don't mean anything by it. So… Lakota is gone for the entire week?"

I stuffed my cheeks with more of his omelet and didn't answer.

"See, I was thinking about sticking around for a few days," he continued. "I've never been in the city before. Not a big one like Austin. Might as well look around while I'm here."

"Is that the only reason you're staying?"

"No," he said matter-of-factly. "Last night you asked me if I broke your window. Sounds like you've got trouble."

"Just some kids."

"Was it about the same time you found me? My wolf wouldn't have attacked a group of rowdy boys. And I don't think any kid would have the balls to knock an alpha in the head, even on a dare."

I set down my fork. "I thought alphas shared headspace with their wolves? Do you black out like the rest of us?"

"No. But sometimes I get tired and let him take over while I sleep. I trust my wolf. I just wish he'd woken me up when it mattered."

"What time is it?" I peered around Tak, but the microwave clock was showing the remaining seconds of whatever I'd last heated up.

"I guess ten by now."

"Ten?" I exclaimed, jumping to my feet. "It can't be." I cleared the microwave cooking time and stared at the clock display. What if I'd missed the repairman's call? Had Joe locked up the store like he promised? What if they weren't able to replace the pane and all my merchandise was wide open for anyone to steal?

"It's ten fifteen?"

Ignoring me, he continued stuffing his face. "I've never seen a woman sleep in so late. Is that how city wolves live? Instead of waking up when the rooster crows, you wake up at the honk of a horn?" He touched his chin with the prongs of his fork. "I guess if you do all your hunting at the grocery store, there's more time for sleeping in."

"I have to go. *You* have to go."

"You didn't finish your breakfast."

I slipped on a pair of sandals and grabbed my purse. "Come on!"

"I'm wearing a dress," he pointed out.

"I'll drive you back to your motel. Now let's go."

Tak stood up and swaggered toward me, the blue sarong fitting him more like a napkin around his waist. "In this?"

"If you're too good for it, then leave it behind. But I'm not lending you my brother's clothes. It would be disrespectful to him since you're not even supposed to be here. You wouldn't fit in them anyhow."

He smoothed back his hair and locked his fingers behind his head. "Have it your way, Duckie."

I was about to admonish him for giving me that silly nickname, but when I opened the door, the words dissolved on my tongue.

Folded neatly in the hallway at the threshold to my apartment were the clothes I'd worn on the day I went joyrunning.

The ones someone had stolen from my car.

Chapter 10

"What's upset you?" Tak asked for the second time.

Or maybe it was the third.

"My mind is on the store," I said in all honesty.

He rested his elbow on the car window and moved his hand in a serpentine motion against the wind. "Then we go there first."

I decided not to tell him the truth. Alpha wolves could be unpredictable. Some had an innate desire to sniff out trouble and punish the wicked.

Whoever had stolen my clothes knew where I lived. Melody's brothers might have pulled such a prank, but they were out of town along with everyone else I knew. Could it have been Tak? How much did I really know about this guy? He clearly had a sense of humor, and his timing couldn't have been more impeccable when he drove up. Maybe in the middle of the night, he ran out and retrieved the clothes to mess with my head. If he had some kind of vendetta against Lakota, then harassing his sister made sense. But logic went out the window when the ridiculous image of him running down the street naked entered my mind. What would be the point?

The moment the light switched to green, the car behind me held down the horn. I glared in my rearview mirror, wondering why two seconds was too long to wait.

Tak suddenly opened the door and got out.

"Where are you going?" I called out, wide-eyed as he sauntered toward the back.

I turned in my seat, and it was like watching a silent movie. Tak stood in the middle of the street in a sarong. He reached inside the driver's side open window of the car behind us and opened the door.

My breath caught when he leaned inside the car. What was he going to do, kill a human for honking the horn? A dizzying wave of panic swept over me, and the temptation to speed away grew strong. I couldn't get wrapped up in something like this. I'd be an accomplice.

Seconds later, Tak straightened, turned around, and swung his arm like a pitcher. A shiny cluster of keys somersaulted through the air, landing on top of a tire shop across the street.

Through the open door, a swarm of profanities flew at Tak. But he ignored the guy, casually swatting a bug on his neck as he headed back.

When he got in and shut the door, he took his time adjusting the seat to give him more legroom.

Thunderstruck, I kept staring.

He finally noticed. "Something wrong?"

"I… I thought you were going to kill him."

He said something in his language.

"What does that mean?"

Tak's knees came apart as he relaxed, and he turned his head and gave me a tight grin. "There are better ways to piss off a man than to break his nose. My people save their daggers for true enemies. My fists are to protect and serve. But assholes like that don't get my time. People will never trust an alpha with a hot temper."

I wanted to hit the gas, but the light had turned red again. "I need to drop you off at the motel."

"No. You need to take care of business. Family first. Business second. Brain-damaged houseguests third."

I chuckled and shook my head.

"You should do that more often," he said. "You have a nice smile. Laughter is good for the soul."

"I laugh all the time. It's just hard to find humor when my life is falling apart."

Tak suddenly reached over and turned my chin to face him. He brushed his fingers across my jaw and stroked my cheek with a compassionate touch—one that was unexpected and reassuring. The intensity of his gaze was so powerful that I couldn't look anywhere else—it drew me in and held my attention. Within moments, my restless wolf settled, and I realized Tak was using his alpha power to calm me.

"If someone has made you afraid, I'll take care of it," he said, his words inviting no argument.

His promise wrapped around me like a blanket, and as much as I wanted to let him keep touching me, I drew back. I knew better than to let a wolf beguile me. Many were smooth talkers who would do anything to get what they wanted.

I knew all about that game of consequence.

Tak lowered his arm but kept looking at me.

When the light turned green again, I hit the gas. After a few turns, we arrived at my shop and were lucky enough to find an empty spot up front. People were strolling down the sidewalks with shopping bags, and one little girl in a pink dress flew by with an ice cream cone melting down her hand.

I opened my door. "Wait here. I'll just be a few minutes."

To my relief, the store window was miraculously intact as if nothing had occurred. I approached the door, scanning the sidewalk for glittering flecks of glass. Mr. Franklin and his men had done a superb job cleaning up, but I still planned to sweep and mop later on.

I whirled around when I caught Tak's reflection in the window. He stepped up on the curb, and I thought how one strong gust of wind might blow that sarong clear across the street, where a bevy of women were gawking at him.

I quickly unlocked the door. "You're going to ruin my reputation."

He chuckled darkly and held the door open. "That's what I do best."

I rushed to the counter to make sure that all my jewelry was accounted for. I closely examined the locked displays and checked the safe where I hid the more expensive pieces. Everything looked okay, so I headed to the back of the store to make sure the door was locked.

When I returned, Tak was standing in the middle of the store with a bowling ball in his hands.

"Lose something?" he asked, closing the distance between us.

I looked down at his bare feet. "Careful where you step. There might be glass."

He reached the counter and propped the ball against the register. "What happened last night?"

"I don't exactly know. I was taking out the trash and heard a loud noise. By the time I came back inside, they were gone. I found that on the floor by the window."

"Do you have any enemies?"

I repositioned the wolf carving to face the door. "None."

"You hesitated."

"I'm not really sure how to answer that. I'm a Packmaster's daughter, so I guess my father's enemies are my enemies."

Tak rested his palms on the counter and leaned forward. "A woman of your station should be revered and respected by those in the community. No one would dare threaten any of my sisters, even though they're mated."

Dodging his question, I knelt to check the safe again.

Years ago, I brought shame to my family. Only those in close circles knew about the scandal. I had just gone through my first change, and my packmates were looking at me in a different light. I exuded the power of the old world, which was alluring to the opposite sex. An older wolf in our pack seduced me. I wasn't naive about Shifter desires, especially after having gone through heat for the first time. My mother always said that my purity was a gift—one I should give to a chosen life mate. In retrospect, I should have listened to her. I ended up giving my virginity to someone who didn't matter. My father was adept at reading people, and it didn't take him long before he noticed the intimate and familiar way that wolf looked at me. When he found out the truth, he almost killed the wolf. Instead, he disgraced him by kicking him out of the pack. My parents swept it under the rug, but there was no telling who else might have found out about it. That uncertainty made it difficult to look my former packmates in the eye. Did they know my secret? Did my actions make my father an incompetent leader in their eyes?

It made moving out with Melody the sanest thing to do.

There was no shame in having sex outside of marriage, but it was a big no-no to fool around with packmates in secret. Packmasters kept the peace, so it was crucial for them to know about any developing relationships that could jeopardize the harmony of the pack. The alpha might have to make the decision whether to allow that union under his roof or put in a transfer request.

Two or more wolves vying for the same woman can be trouble, which is why children move out when they come of age. Not all packmates are mated, so running a cohesive pack is imperative.

I'd put my father in a difficult situation by keeping my affair a secret. It was deceptive and unworthy of the kind of woman they'd raised.

"You're quiet down there," Tak said. "Are you sure that's all that happened last night?"

I put everything back in the safe and stood, my thumbs hooked behind the straps of my overalls. "It just shook me up. That's all."

He sniffed and turned around. "Maybe the message was meant for Melody or Lakota. That, I could see. Your brother seems to leave a mess wherever he goes."

"Or maybe it was just a prank. At this point, there's nothing I can do about it but speculate. There's no note, no witnesses who came forward, and no reason to worry myself sick. The show must go on."

He folded his arms, his back still to me. "So what are your plans for today?"

I looked around the shop. "It'll take me a while to clean everything to my standards. No sense opening the store today, so I guess when I'm done, I'll go home and do chores. If there's any time left, I might work on some designs."

"Do you make all that jewelry yourself?"

"I used to, but now I just come up with the designs. My assistant assembles the popular items we sell in high volume, which gives me time to focus on the more expensive pieces."

His back muscles flexed when he lowered his arms. "Do you want to go out?"

"I have work to do."

"No, I mean when you're done." His braid rose a little higher on his back when he looked down at his bare feet.

"There's nowhere I need to go."

He peered over his shoulder and stared intensely. "You're going to make this hard for me, aren't you?" Tak slowly turned around and splayed his fingertips on the counter. "Do you... want to go out... with me?"

My stunned gaze traveled from his bare chest to the sarong knotted at his hip.

A smile wound up the tatted side of his face. "I can either change clothes or wear this. Whatever you want."

"You mean a date?"

"I'm not asking to be your life mate. I just thought you could show me around the city. You have the day off, and I'm in no rush to get home. I want to know you, and that means spending time together."

I thought about it. How often did I ever go out with someone other than my best friend and brother? After the stressful night I'd had, maybe a little lunch and sightseeing would put me in a better state of mind. "Are you going to tell me what your relationship is with my brother? It looked like you two wanted to toss each other out the window."

He shook his head. "That's between your brother and me."

I wiped a hair off the counter. "Then you can't ask me out. I could never do anything to dishonor my brother."

Tak steered his attention to the glass counter on my right. "You have a lot in common with your jewelry."

"What do you mean by that?"

He stared vacantly at everything in the store except me. "I guess I have no reason to stay." He backed up a few steps and bowed. "It was a pleasure, Miss Church. I'll be sure to let my father know his gemstones are in good hands."

I opened my mouth to say something, but nothing came out. How could I risk damaging my relationship with my brother when I still didn't know who this man was and why there was animosity between them? They could be sworn enemies.

The bell jingled on the door when he left the shop. Maybe it was all a misunderstanding. Surely Lakota wouldn't have made enemies with the tribe who supplied my gemstones. It was better that Tak leave, but as I watched him standing outside, my wolf howled, calling for his return. I secretly hoped he'd turn around and look at me one last time.

But he didn't.

Two women sauntered past him and turned for a second glance. I laughed when a gust of wind made the sarong open up at the side. The women noticed. No doubt their dirty thoughts would have set a confessional on fire. Tak stood with his face to the wind, unperturbed by his provocative display. The sun shone on his brown skin, and he looked like he should have been in a painting on my wall.

When Tak turned to leave, he bumped right into Dutch—the man who'd come into my store yesterday looking for feather earrings. They stared each other down for a brief moment, each man lifting his chin and not showing a submissive bone in his body. It was a common display among Shifter men, who were always posturing among one another.

Tak finally swaggered off, and I blew out a breath.

Dutch poked his head in the door. "Mind if I intrude? I know you're closed, but I just heard about the trouble you had last night."

"Watch your step," I said, gesturing at his leather shoes. "I don't know how well they cleaned up, and I still have to shake out all the clothes and sweep again."

"Do you have a large box or something wide to catch the glass?"

I thought about his clever idea. "There should be some in the alley."

Dutch disappeared and quickly returned with a cardboard box. "Shake them out in here."

I collected one shirt at a time and thoroughly shook each one out inside the box, carefully inspecting them for glass particles. Dutch did the same, and the conversation dwindled for several minutes.

"Want to tell me about it?" he asked, breaking the silence. "Word spreads fast. When Mo Franklin is around, it's never for a good reason."

"Someone smashed my window. I didn't see it happen, so there's not much to tell."

Dutch shook out another blouse, and I stole a moment to admire him. Not many men I knew wore dress slacks. His pale-blue button-up shirt made his eyes look like multifaceted gemstones, and a leather belt finished off the ensemble. Despite his crisp appearance, I liked that he wasn't afraid to roll up his sleeves.

"Have you had this kind of trouble before?"

"When we first opened up," I admitted. "We had a few obscene words written on the windows, and they even left a flaming bag of manure outside the door. I guess it was the welcoming committee."

"Did you report it to the Council?"

"The Shifter Council? My partner's former Packmaster had a talk with one of them, and he said without evidence, there wasn't anything they could do. There aren't security cameras on this side of town for obvious reasons." I folded another shirt and set it aside. "Even if they did find the culprits, what could they do? A slap on the wrist is all."

After we finished shaking out all the garments from the shelf, Dutch lifted the broken mannequin. "Do you want me to take off her clothes?"

I bubbled with laughter. "You barely know each other."

He gave me a thin-lipped smile. "That's rarely made a difference before."

I dusted off a dress hanging from a rack. As I did so, I couldn't strip my eyes away from the way Dutch's fingers deftly unfastened each button on the back of the blouse. He took his time, and the way he did it was so sensual that I could almost imagine that mannequin was me. He probably took his time seducing women the same way.

Dutch circled the mannequin, his fingertips tracing around her narrow hips, until he faced her. Unable to look away, I watched as he brushed his hand down her shoulders, the delicate straps sliding away and the garment falling to the floor. He stroked one of the smooth breasts with the tips of his fingers.

I swallowed hard, my throat parched.

"Will you look at that," he said, gazing upon her alabaster chest. "I've never seen breasts like these before. Why don't they make them more… realistic?"

When he snapped his gaze in my direction, the shirt slipped out of my hand. "I guess they don't want to sexualize them."

Dutch smiled and circled the box to pick up the shirt I'd dropped. When he stood up, we were a breath apart. His cologne filled my nose, inviting me to lean in. "You might attract more male shoppers. A breast is lovely, but nothing is more titillating than the sight of a woman aroused."

His gaze slipped down to my white T-shirt, and he stared at my overalls as if he had X-ray vision.

"Thanks for helping out," I said, feeling fire in my cheeks. "After I sweep and mop the floors, I plan to go home and rest."

His brow arched, and he glanced at his expensive-looking watch. "Why don't I pick you up at five? We can discuss security and come up with a plan to protect our businesses. We don't need senseless violence in our neighborhood. I'd stay and chat with you longer, but I'm on a short lunch break and need to get back to my store."

"I won't be here that late."

He canted his head and regarded me for a moment. "Let's meet somewhere then. Do you have any suggestions?"

"Howlers?"

"That'll do. We'll talk shop over a glass of wine."

It wouldn't hurt to share a little information. Most owners in the neighborhood didn't like people knowing their business, so they kept to themselves. "Okay. You've talked me into it. Five o'clock at Howlers."

Coins jingled when he put his hands in his pockets and headed toward the door. "If you need anything, do you know where to find me?"

"Two streets over, right? Thank you again."

When he opened the door, his musky cologne wafted across the room. "My name's Dutch, just in case you forgot. See you this evening, Hope."

Once alone, I stared at the hand-carved wolf, completely dumbfounded by the turn of events in just one day. Two complete strangers had entered my life for reasons not yet known—men who couldn't be more opposite. That, combined with the mystery behind the property damage, gave me a strong premonition that the perfect storm was brewing, and I was caught in the eye.

CHAPTER 11

After Tak finished drying off from a quick shower, he tossed the white towel on the motel room floor. "What the hell were you thinking?" he asked his reflection. "You have no business hitting on a woman like that."

Not just because of her lush beauty, but high-ranking women in his tribe were off-limits to that kind of invitation—especially from him. Though Tak was an alpha, he would never attain the rank of a Packmaster within his tribe. That made him less of a catch, but it didn't stop a few of the wild ones from knowing him intimately. He enjoyed the companionship of a woman in bed, but nothing more. Anyhow, Tak didn't know how to impress a woman like Hope. Leaving her shop with his tail between his legs only proved that point.

He grabbed a clean pair of black cargos from his bag and a grey cotton shirt that fit him snugly. While he hadn't bothered to wash his hair, he'd removed the rubber band so that he could braid it again the right way.

"You should have never stuck around," he said, chastising himself. "See what you get? You're lucky her father didn't walk in and see you in that dress." Tak pulled the shirt over his head, wondering why it mattered what her father thought of him.

The more he stopped trying to think about her, the more

she invaded his thoughts. Hope's duality fascinated him, as did her independence. Did a woman like her even require a man in her life? She had her own source of income, and not everyone could be business savvy. Tak had learned by watching his father that it required intelligence, motivation, and a certain kind of decisiveness that not everyone possessed.

Just as she'd been decisive about having the good sense to reject his offer. When he implied she had a lot in common with her jewelry, her befuddled reaction left him wondering if she'd taken it as a compliment or an insult. Her pieces were beautiful, rare, and deserving of a worthy owner. That was the meaning behind his remark, but an explanation would have embarrassed him since it was on the heels of a rejection.

"Jackass," he muttered, relaxing on the edge of the bed.

And worst of all, he liked her. She was the whole package. Her thoughtfulness, sensitivity, and family loyalty were qualities he most admired. There was something about her face that made it difficult to look away. Not overly feminine or traditionally beautiful, but soulful and expressive. Her lips were plump and inviting, and damn if she didn't have the prettiest eyelashes. Hope was the kind of woman he imagined himself with in another life. She made him feel protective. She brought out the warrior in him.

Tak put on his pants and stood up. He lifted his black comb from the nightstand and ran it through his long hair, which was tangled from the night before and still carried a wave. A knot formed in the pit of his stomach when he thought about their interaction in the store.

Did he really believe that Hope would have accepted his offer? No respectable woman would go against the wishes of her blood, and he respected that. Tak wanted resolution with Lakota—he needed to find out how much of that friendship had been genuine. Lakota didn't know about Tak's past, and that made their bond special. It wasn't that Tak didn't have friends; he got along fine with the men in his tribe. But tension existed beneath the surface. In most nontribal packs, one alpha lived under the roof and led the pack. However, the Iwa tribe expanded territories and formed small subpacks. While each Packmaster headed his own group, they worked together as a sort of Council with Shikoba as their leader.

Even though Tak had the power and entitlement of an alpha, he held no rank.

He never would. Not with his tribe. Tak would always be the wayward son to his father and to his people.

That displacement made room for conflict. Betas saw him as weak and often challenged him with words to assert their dominance. It was common behavior for wolves to create a pecking order amongst each other, and Tak was fair game since he'd never hold a Packmaster's rank. It became difficult to control an escalating situation—betas would criticize him or refuse to comply.

Perhaps that was another reason why Texas was a welcome respite. No one knew him here. Men on the streets who sensed his alpha power looked upon him with suspicion and fear. He liked it. Tak had put up with the derision from his own packmates for too many years, and though he was the type of man who got along with everyone, it hadn't dawned on him how much it had beaten down his spirit until this short little trip.

Tak took his time braiding his hair. His tribe was the only home he'd ever known, but it was also a place he didn't belong. When Lakota had left town, Tak fell into a state of depression. He felt trapped again, so maybe this visit meant something more than just mending a friendship. Tak was standing on the precipice of a life-changing decision, and if he wasn't careful, he might wind up choosing the wrong path.

Tak stared down at his callused hands, which ached to have someone to hold. Sometimes the loneliness made him want to turn back to the bottle. As much as he wanted to get shitfaced and forget about his best friend ditching him and a beautiful woman rejecting him, drinking would only make him a weaker man. It had been a long road to recovery—

not just from the emotional trauma of his past but also the stigma of being a recovering alcoholic. They didn't have AA meetings or recovery programs in his tribe. Tak had overcome his demons alone, and sometimes he wondered if the door to his hell was still open just a crack.

Thoughts about his past and future conjured images of the present. After shifting last night for a brief run, his wolf had led him right back to Moonglow. Wolves don't understand pride or honor; they're motivated purely by instinct. He'd skulked in the shadows, watching her. Guarding her. He wasn't convinced that the city offered any measure of safety, especially knowing how rogues preyed upon the weak or unguarded. Females living outside a pack were vulnerable, so Tak had communicated to his wolf that they were staying put until she was safely in her car. At some point, Tak must have grown tired and blacked out. He couldn't remember anything about the lump on his head. One minute he was watching her help a customer, the next he was lying on her bedroom floor.

Tak grabbed the laminated guide from the dresser and scanned through it. He spotted a familiar brand on the leaflet—the universal symbol identifying Breed establishments. He flipped it over and a place called Howlers caught his attention. The last thing he wanted was to stroll into a Vampire bar; he needed to be around his own kind. Maybe find a woman to make him forget the emptiness inside. Tak knew how to make a woman laugh, and he also knew how to make her hot and needy.

The small print said that Howlers had drinks, games, music, and good food.

"Sounds like my kind of place," he said, tossing the guide on the bed. "Might as well see how these city boys like to party."

Chapter 12

"You have an interesting style," Dutch remarked, admiring my maroon palazzo pants, which were wide from top to bottom. My black sleeveless shirt was nothing special, and I hadn't put on any jewelry or perfume after my shower. This wasn't exactly a date, so I didn't want to embarrass myself by overdoing it.

After taking a seat, I handed him a laminated menu so we could order food.

Dutch eyed the alcoholic beverages. "What's the house drink?"

"Devil's Eye, but take my word for it and stick to the bottled drinks."

"You know this place pretty well?"

I smoothed my hand over the table, which had plenty of scratches from bar fights and men showing off their knives. "Howlers is like a second home."

When he arched his eyebrow, it revealed a deep line on his forehead. "A bar is like home?"

"It's not the place that matters but the people you're with."

Melody's uncle Denver was one of the bartenders, and our old packmates came here a lot. I wasn't crazy about the bar scene. I preferred spending my free time at arts festivals or having dessert in a café.

Since it was Sunday evening, there were plenty of empty

tables and booths. The jukebox cranked out one rock song after the next, and though a few raucous men were playing pool to the far right, they didn't bother us since our table was close to the bar.

"True that!" Denver shouted from the hall next to the bar. He stripped out of his black work shirt and waved at the other bartender. "See ya tomorrow. I'm outta here." As he passed by, he took a second glance at me and then backed up a step. "Hey, honeypie. What's a nice girl like you doing in a place like this with a man like that?"

Dutch turned in a way that made me wonder if he was going to get up and start a fight.

"This is Dutch," I said. "He's a shopkeeper in the area, and we're just talking business. Dutch, this is Denver Cole, the bartender here and a friend of mine."

The two men nodded at each other.

Denver rumpled his blond hair and winked. "I'm late, and I hate to keep the little miss waiting."

"Tell everyone hello."

"Will do!" He rushed out the door and did a little spin as someone walked in at the same time.

I turned back to Dutch and wrapped my fingers around my cold glass of tea. "I think you'd like him. I've known Denver my whole life."

Dutch propped his elbows on the table and loosened the top button of his grey shirt. "Do you think I invited you here to talk business?"

"That's what you said earlier."

He moved my glass aside and held my hand. "I just mentioned what we could talk about, and we're done talking business. When a man asks a woman out, it's not because he wants to pick her brain. You have a certain look I find interesting."

I withdrew my hand. "What about intelligence or sensibility? Those aren't desirable traits?"

He shrugged and sat back. "That comes later, if at all. I'm a man who admires beautiful things."

I folded my hands on the table. "Tell me, when one of your diamonds or other pieces has a flaw, does it affect the value?"

"Of course."

"Imperfection *increases* the value of my stones. It's those discolorations and fractures that make a gemstone truly beautiful because it means there is no other like it in the world. It's not a carbon copy of another."

"But you sell costume jewelry. No offense, but you don't deal in precious gems. Your stones are more ubiquitous, and that makes them worth less."

"Why should one type of stone have more value than another? They're just rocks, Dutch. You can shine them up all you want, but they're rocks. Diamonds sparkle, but they have no character or color."

He reached for my hand and lifted it, looking at the stark contrast between his pale skin and my honey-brown. "I don't mind a little color."

"Am I the flawed diamond?"

"We all have flaws," he said, brushing his lips across my knuckles. After a swift kiss, he let go and sat back. "Do you mind if I ask your ethnicity?"

"I'm a mix of tribes."

I was also part Caucasian on my mother's side, but that invited more questions than I was willing to answer.

He steered his gaze away. "Ah."

His enigmatic reaction piqued my curiosity. "That's all you have to say?"

"I thought maybe Spanish. I'm not familiar with Native American Shifter culture." His blue eyes lit up, and he turned the ring on his finger. "Spain is a marvelous country. It's probably in my top five if I had to list them all."

"You like to travel?"

"Immensely. There's so much beauty out there." Dutch

momentarily got lost in his thoughts, and when he returned his attention to me, his eyes were lit with interest. "I'm curious about your animal, but it's rude to ask."

"I don't mind. I'm a proud wolf."

Dutch guzzled his beer and then set down the bottle. "Do you live with a pack or a tribe?"

"Me personally? I'm independent for now. But my people live in both packs and tribes. My father's pack is a blend of cultures, but when you drive out into the country, you'll see more of us living in tribes. I grew up in a pack, so that's the only life I know. What about you?"

He gave a tight-lipped grin. "I'd prefer not to say."

I nodded and looked toward the pool tables. Shouts erupted followed by the sound of pool balls clacking together. It made me wonder if Dutch was a docile animal, such as a deer. I didn't notice any clues in his demeanor, and sometimes herbivores or birds were the least likely to reveal their animal. They believed it put targets on their backs, especially if they had enemies. The bear ring seemed like a ruse, and the style didn't suit him at all.

I wasn't certain what to believe. Dutch certainly didn't strike me as a ferret, though the idea of being able to carry him in my purse tickled me.

"What are you grinning about?" he asked.

That made me smile even wider. "Nothing."

"I'm no pig, but I might be a jackass."

We both chuckled.

But the laughter died in my throat when I glanced up and spotted Tak approaching with a purposeful stride. It caught me so off guard to see him that I sat in stunned disbelief. He wasn't just casually passing by on his way to the exit or even the bathroom; he made direct eye contact and was zeroing in on our table.

Before reaching it, he snagged an empty chair from an adjacent table and dragged it behind him. He then flipped it backward and straddled it in the empty spot to my left.

Dutch gave him a black look. "This is a private conversation. I think you need to move."

"Thinking isn't knowing," Tak pointed out. "Either you *think* you know something, or you know. I remember you. You're the one who wasn't looking where he was going."

My eyes narrowed. "Tak, what are you doing here?"

Wheeler Cole—another of Mel's uncles—suddenly strode up behind Tak and clapped him on the shoulders. "Is *this* who you've been going on about for the past two hours?" he said, briefly flicking a glance at me.

I blanched. Not just at the realization that Tak was still in town and at the very bar I'd come to, but that he'd buddied up with someone I knew. Worst of all, they were talking about me! Had Tak told him all about my taking an unfamiliar wolf into my home? Men revealed secrets when intoxicated.

Wheeler grabbed Tak's braid and jerked him out of the chair. "Come on, sweetheart. We need to go for a little walk." Tak was bigger, but you didn't want to mess with Wheeler. If the tattoos all up and down his arms didn't give it away, then his surly attitude did.

Dutch curled his lip and watched them head over to the bar. "So this is where you like to socialize? Maybe we should go somewhere more private. I don't like crowds."

I pretended to listen, but I could hear Wheeler and Tak arguing. Fights in Breed establishments could get you blacklisted, but they were fairly commonplace in Shifter bars. Certain animals were territorial, packs clashed, and Shifters had chips on their shoulders when it came to how the community treated them.

When I glanced back at the bar, Wheeler had Tak in a chokehold, and Tak was holding the pointy tip of a blade to Wheeler's groin.

I launched to my feet. "I'll be right back."

Dutch didn't have time to answer. I was already at the bar.

"What are you doing?" I hissed. "The two of you are behaving like children."

They both looked up at me, Tak's face a shade of purple and Wheeler grimacing from the pinch of the blade.

"Christ!" Wheeler let go and jumped back a foot.

Tak stood up straight, and his pocketknife closed with a click. "Do that again, and I'll make your woman a new set of earrings out of your testicles."

Wheeler grabbed a random guy's beer and guzzled it. "Put that on my tab and order him another," he said to the bartender while rubbing his crotch.

Tak placed his hand on my back and led me toward the jukebox. Hopefully Wheeler would leave us alone, but he could be as stubborn as a mule.

"You don't have a pack to watch over you," he said, admonishing me with a glance. "Why are you out alone with another Shifter?"

"Why do you care?"

Dumb question. Tak was an alpha, and that meant he was nosy by nature.

Tak rested his arm on the jukebox. "Do you know what his intentions are? Because if you don't, I can fill you in."

"He runs a shop in the area. It's business."

"It didn't look like business to me when he was kissing your fingers."

Hands clenched in fists at my side, I gave him an indignant look.

"You're right," he said, a sudden bend in his voice. "I have no business in your life. But I care about what happens to you."

"You also asked me out. How would that have been any different?"

He straightened up and squared his shoulders. "Because I wouldn't have brought you to a bar—even if it was your idea. My intentions were honorable."

"What makes you think his aren't? You don't even know Dutch. He's a nice man."

Tak's energy prickled against my skin.

Few things were more seductive than the way an alpha could claim a woman with a single word. Their voice resonates in the most primal area of our brains, compelling us to submit whenever they pushed that power into their voices.

With bated breath, I wondered what that word might be. His lips parted, and he held my gaze, fire simmering in his dark eyes. A current of alpha power lapped against my body like waves to a shore, but he never spoke a word. He never gave me that command.

I moved around him, my hands trembling. "I have to go," I whispered, hurrying away. The effect Tak had on me was like nothing I'd ever known, and it went way beyond the fact he was an alpha wolf. Something about being near him was familiar, magnetic, and intoxicating. It frightened me to think that anyone could have that kind of power over me. And he sensed it too, because he didn't wield his power irresponsibly. Tak could have pressed on and made my wolf submit to his command.

But he hadn't.

As I breezed through the bar, a man rose up from his table and jerked his arm at me. Beer splashed in my face, and I blinked in surprise. My feet rooted in place as I looked down at my wet blouse, my mouth agape.

"Fuck you and your cheap-ass purse," the man snarled.

It took me a second to blink away the alcohol and recognize him as the irate customer who had tried to return a damaged handbag in my store.

A few chair legs scraped against the floor as bystanders rose to their feet, and all I heard before the explosion of violence was Wheeler announcing, "And boom goes the dynamite."

Chapter 13

Before I could fully comprehend what had just happened, I slapped Dumont in the face for throwing his drink on me. And then he struck me back.

The sharp sting shocked me so much that I stumbled. People rushed at him from all directions, and out of nowhere, he shifted into a giant grizzly. Grown men backed up when the bear unleashed a monstrous roar that made my hair stand on end.

The sight of him turned my legs to jelly, and I collapsed onto my back. Rarely could a single wolf take down a bear of his size. Several men scattered for the door, but not Wheeler. He shifted into a brown wolf and flanked the bear on the right.

"Take that outside!" the bartender bellowed.

Dutch appeared in my line of vision, holding a chair with the legs pointing out. He reminded me of a circus ringmaster taming the lions.

The bear swiped his enormous claws at me, and Wheeler lunged, biting his leg before scuttling backward.

One minute I was staring at the jaws of death, and the next, Tak's wolf appeared, interposing himself between the bear and me as he dug in his heels and stood over my legs. Pinned to the ground, all I could see of him were his hind legs and low tail. My blood ran cold. Even though Tak was an alpha, there was a chance his wolf could turn on Wheeler in the melee since the two wolves didn't know each other.

"Stay down," Dutch ordered, distracting the animal with the chair.

The bear swung his massive head left and right, looking between the two wolves and a bar full of curious spectators who didn't appear eager to lose their lives over a spilled drink. My feet were within his reach, and I wanted to pull them up but was afraid he'd shred them to pieces with one swipe of his paw.

I can't breathe.

Cold terror washed over me as flashbacks of a childhood attack raced through my head. The wolf lunging and biting my face, my head in his jaws, Melody screaming, the sense of helplessness, the agony, the fear of dying. Even now that I could shift, I was catatonic. My mind flipped between past and present, and I clutched a barstool behind my head and quelled the urge to scream.

The bear's paw batted my foot, but I couldn't see him. Tak was the only thing separating me from certain death, and if he abandoned me, I would undoubtedly meet a gruesome end. He confronted the deadly beast with a savage growl that made my breath hitch. Tak wasn't just guarding me; he was ready to die for me. My wolf could never fight off such a powerful animal, but could Tak's?

Wheeler moved swiftly, commanding the bear's attention. When the grizzly lumbered after Wheeler, Tak snarled and locked his jaws on the animal's neck. The bear swung his head, shaking him off, and swiped his paw—a blow powerful enough to knock a grown man down. But not Tak. His paws barely left the sticky floor.

My wolf fought to break free, and I had to shut my eyes to push her spirit back down. Without a pack—without my family—it would be suicide.

I gripped the barstool, which was bolted to the ground, and dragged my body away.

A shotgun blasted from behind the bar. "Get out, or I'll call the Council and start blacklisting your asses!" the bartender roared. "And if you break that chair, you're paying for it."

I risked a glance.

Rivulets of blood raced down Dutch's arm, dripping from his fingertips. When he steered his gaze to the door behind him, I sensed he wanted to flee. Wheeler's brown wolf had bloodstains on his mouth and neck. Tak faced away from me, and the grizzly appeared more alarmed about him than Wheeler's wolf. Alphas were relentless and less apt to back down than most. They could galvanize a group into action and would fight to the death.

A husky man leapt over the wall and laid his hands on the bear's back, blue light emanating from his palms. The animal jolted, his eyes rolling back, and a broken roar quaked through the room. Did the Mage have enough energy to bring down an animal that size? He did it three more times until the bear finally surrendered.

"All right. Show's over," the bartender announced. "Everyone better start shifting back."

Dutch's injuries looked severe but not grave. Blood saturated his torn shirt, and he needed to shift to heal. When he rushed for the door, I sighed with relief. Shifting in front of wolves with blood in their mouths was suicide.

Wheeler kept his eyes trained on the bear and stood guard while everyone dusted themselves off and headed out.

Tak's wolf turned and gazed down at me. I froze when he craned his neck forward and sniffed my face. After licking my chin, he shifted to human form. His long hair cascaded around me, his fists on either side. But all I could think about was the bear, who let out another pained roar.

"Are you hurt?" Tak brushed my hair away from my eyes.

I wanted to tell him I was okay, but I wasn't.

I was far from okay.

Strong women weren't supposed to cower, and yet I couldn't stop shaking.

After he yanked on his pants and stuffed his feet in his boots, Tak knelt and centered his eyes on mine. "You're coming with me."

He gently lifted me, and I buried my face in his chest. All I could think about were the people in that bar who knew me. Word was going to spread about how Lorenzo Church's only daughter had behaved like a coward in the face of danger. I couldn't stop the flood of tears.

Tak nodded at the bartender. "When that wolf shifts back, tell him Hope is in good hands. He knows where to find me."

Suddenly a wave of dizziness had me trembling. My heart pounded at a frenetic pace, making it difficult to breathe. An impending feeling of doom descended upon me—the feeling of death. My throat closed up, and my chest constricted as if someone had wrapped a belt around it and was tightening one notch at a time.

I writhed in his arms. "I can't breathe. I can't breathe."

Tak changed from a walk to a jog, and I clung to his chest. When my feet abruptly touched the ground, I wobbled for a moment before Tak caught me by the waist.

With his free hand, he opened his truck door and then lifted me into the passenger seat. I pressed two fingers against my neck, my accelerating heartbeat making me feel my own mortality.

After buckling my seat belt, he cradled my head in his hands. "I swear on my life that I'll protect you. You're going to be okay, do you understand?"

His alpha power sedated me like a warm fire on a winter's night. But it was too late. I'd already hyperventilated myself into blacking `.

⫸⎯⎯⎯⟶

Tak sped toward his motel without delay. With Hope passed out, it would give her inner wolf a chance to sleep. Fighting against your animal took its toll, but she'd played it smart back at the bar. That grizzly wouldn't have hesitated to go after an aggressive female wolf.

Some Shifters had no sense of morality.

When Tak had arrived at the bar, he'd bumped into a man who challenged him to a game of pool. They instantly connected because of their tattoos, and after a while, they sat down and talked. The wolf named Wheeler bragged about his mate and was dead set on giving Tak relationship advice. Tak never mentioned Hope by name, but he told Wheeler about the woman who wouldn't give him the time of day. Wheeler informed him that a good woman doesn't give a damn about rank or even a checkered past. He said they were attracted to men willing to show them their Achilles' heel.

Tak couldn't have disagreed more. Tak believed women wanted a strong man who didn't expose his weaknesses or have a dark past.

The two carried on their debate until Tak spotted Hope seated at a table with another man. Tak studied the man's confident demeanor, his expensive watch, and the way he leaned in to give her his undivided attention. It wasn't until the young bartender approached their table that the man turned his head and Tak recognized him.

From that point on, Tak no longer focused on Wheeler. All he could wonder was what that man had said to make her laugh so spiritedly. What sweet words had he uttered that she'd welcome his lips on her hand?

It made his blood boil. Sweet-talkers led wolves astray. They were the scoundrels in the pack you had to keep a close eye on. The guy didn't come across as a wolf, so Tak wondered about his motives.

Tak glanced over to the sleeping princess beside him. He should have left town and gone back to his tribe where he belonged, but an invisible force had tethered him to this woman. Now he couldn't leave—not with all the dangers lurking around every corner. Evil spirits were at work, and Hope was their object of attention.

He pulled into the parking spot outside the motel and got out. Sweat touched his brow as the sun burned like a torch. In a few hours, it would be dark. But in the city, nighttime didn't bring reprieve from the sweltering summer days. The heat that baked into the concrete made the evening breeze barely noticeable.

Nearing the passenger door, he placed his hands on the roof of the truck.

Damn. He needed to control his anger. The scene at the bar flashed through his mind—that motherfucker splashing his drink in Hope's face. Tak had reached for his dagger, but a split second later, she struck the man. When the Shifter hit her back, Tak lost it. Consequences be damned, he had no choice but to intervene.

A lone female stood no chance against a grizzly that size. Tak's knife would have done some serious damage, but at the risk of Hope getting injured in the skirmish. To pin that bear in place and get his sights off Hope, he had to threaten him with a wolf attack. The protective instinct overpowered him, and though Tak's wolf should have gone straight for the jugular, his only thought was to guard Hope with his life. Eye contact from an alpha was intimidating to a weak-minded Shifter, and he counted on the bear backing down.

When he opened the truck door, Hope spilled into his arms.

"Easy now," he murmured, unbuckling her seat belt. "We're almost there."

As soon as he lifted her in his arms, an inexplicable calm came over him, and he kicked the door shut. Hope's eyes opened and closed, but she remained silent.

It wasn't easy for him to unlock the motel door, but once inside, he placed her on the bed and switched on a dim wall lamp. Her beer-stained clothes needed to go, but he didn't dare remove them while she was in this fragile condition. Tak wanted nothing more than to give this woman a hot bath and allay her fears.

She rolled over and faced the bathroom, her arms tucked against her chest. When he circled the bed and knelt beside her, she averted her eyes. Her submissive body language broke his heart. He couldn't imagine the loneliness and hardships these young Shifters experienced without a pack. Living independently wasn't a tradition his tribe practiced, so they never had to worry about fighting battles alone. This custom of moving away from the pack didn't seem natural, but he could see how it would remind them not to take family for granted.

"Do you want to talk about it?" he asked softly.

The frown line between her eyebrows slowly diminished as he brushed the pad of his thumb over it. Her eyelids dropped like anchors, and Hope fell asleep within seconds. This wolf needed rest.

He crossed the room to the table where he'd set down her purse. Maybe he could find Lakota's private number on her phone. Tak was certain he'd come back if he knew about the dangers unfolding in his absence. Hope needed guidance from someone she trusted.

When he opened her purse, a folded envelope caught his attention. He should have left it alone and minded his own business, but suddenly her business had plopped all over his life.

Tak removed the letter and unfolded the paper. The moment he read the sinister words, his wolf tore through his skin and emerged.

CHAPTER 14

I WRINKLED MY NOSE WHEN FUR tickled against it. A familiar smell enveloped me, and I hovered between dreams and wakefulness. Was I on a date with Dutch? Images flashed through my mind of Tak approaching our table. I had gotten up to speak privately to him, and then...

My eyes snapped open at the terrifying image of a grizzly.

The memory frightened me more than the wolf I currently embraced. His ebony coat had familiar grey patches—Tak's wolf. I recognized his scent. Wolves didn't smell like dogs, nor did they even smell like wild wolves. They carried the same scent as their human counterpart, only stronger.

Tak was large and took up half the bed. Belly up, he snoozed, a deep rumble sounding in his chest with every inhale.

Is he snoring?

I gingerly lifted my arm away from his body and drew back, his pointy fangs precariously close to my face.

I'd always been terrified of wolves who were strangers to me. Yet despite my trepidation, something compelled me to stroke the beast's head. Maybe it was my wolf wanting to thank him for having saved my life, but my impulsive need to touch him shocked me.

When he suddenly sneezed, I froze solid. Tak's dark eyes

found mine, and before I could leap off the bed, he licked my arm and then sprang to his feet.

I'd never seen a wolf so big—so formidable. Tak's aura made me want to wrap myself inside it.

The moment he jumped off the bed, he shifted so gracefully—so seamlessly—that it was impossible not to admire.

It was equally hard not to admire his firm, round backside. It drew my attention to the curve in his back that led up to his broad shoulders.

Tak grabbed a pair of pants and put them on, never once making eye contact. "You were asleep a long time," he said. His long hair was unbound. I imagined it normally carried a wave when unbraided, but after a shift, the body usually goes back to its original state.

I rubbed my eyes and sat up. "What happened?"

Tak strode to a travel bag in the corner and pulled out a bottle of water. "Here," he said, offering it to me.

I cracked open the lid and guzzled down half the liquid. Once I quenched my thirst, I screwed the cap back on and looked around the motel room. "Where's Wheeler? Is he hurt?"

"Wheeler's fine." Tak chuckled quietly, as if hiding an inside joke from me. "He stopped by earlier and made the manager open the door. My wolf wouldn't let him in, but he understood that you're under my protection. After a few cuss words, he finally left. Wheeler cares about you. Was he one of your former packmates?"

"No, but he's practically family." I set the bottle on the table, sat up, and put my feet on the floor.

Tak sat down next to me, his imposing height undiminished. "You want to talk about what happened back there?"

Talk about the most embarrassing moment of my life? Not a chance.

"You have nothing to be ashamed of," he continued. "That grizzly had no business shifting in front of a woman after a deserved slap in the face. You had the right to stand your ground, but he had no right to threaten you. Unstable men like that need to be taken into the woods and shot."

Tak's nonjudgmental understanding took me by surprise, and when my lip quivered, I stood up. "I shouldn't be here. I need to go home."

"You've been asleep for hours. Unless you want to walk home in the dark, we wait until morning. You need to rest."

"I can call a cab if you won't drive me. I just feel safer at home."

Tak stood up and erased the distance between us. "When you're with me, you're safe."

I backed up against the door, my hand on the knob.

"I'm not going to hurt you," he promised. "Has that ever happened before? Your episode, I mean."

My episode. How did he know to call it that? Panic attacks weren't common among Shifters, especially since danger often had the reverse effect on wolves. It awakened our animal, and we fed off that power.

I dodged his gaze and weaved around him. "Sometimes it happens when I'm least expecting it, but it's never been that… paralyzing. Not in public where everyone could see me." I sat at the foot of the bed and buried my face in my hands. "Now they're going to know."

"Know what? That you were afraid of a rogue grizzly four times your size?" Tak rocked with laughter. "You and every other man in that bar."

I lowered my arms. "I lack courage."

He folded his arms and leaned against the wall by the door. "You're not weak because you can't take down a grizzly with your purse. How many women your age in this town left their packs and opened up their own store? How many have a contract with a man like Shikoba? He doesn't do business with just anyone, you know. There are prominent tribes in the region he wouldn't close a deal with. Courage comes in many forms."

"People expect more from me. Cowering beneath a bar isn't befitting of a Packmaster's daughter."

He nodded. "I know a little something about that. Maybe we have more in common than I thought."

"I doubt it."

Men like Tak feared nothing. He couldn't possibly understand my shame. I looked down at my bare feet and then noticed my shoes beside the dresser.

"I have a clean shirt if you want to change," he offered. "I always bring extra in case I feel like taking a shift." Tak was holding in a laugh, and I suspected his play on words would have earned him a laugh in the bar.

"I've already taken some of your clothes."

He strode over to his bag. "That's right. Why didn't you offer them to me when I stayed the night?"

"I forgot I had them," I admitted.

He handed me a brown shirt. "You just wanted to see me in a dress. Don't deny it."

I smiled and began to unbutton my blouse, which reeked of beer and cigarette smoke. Tak turned toward the curtain and pretended to be straightening the drapes while I changed.

I pulled his shirt over my head and flipped my hair out from inside the collar. Growing up in a pack, one could hardly be bashful. Aside from that, he'd already seen everything. "Why did you shift?"

"At the bar?"

"No. Here."

Tak remained silent for a few seconds as he stared down at the table beside him. "Who gave you this letter?"

"What letter?"

He turned halfway and glowered. "The one that says: 'I'm going to cut off your head.'"

A chill ran down my spine when I saw him pointing at a piece of paper on the table. "Where did you get that? Were you going through my things? You had no right."

"You were unconscious. I had every right to look for

your phone to get Lakota's number. My apologies for getting distracted by the death threat."

My eyes settled on the torn envelope beside it.

"Well?" he pressed. "Who gave this to you?"

"I don't know. Someone taped it on the window outside our store. We had trouble when we first opened, probably—"

"Kids?" he finished. "No, a boy didn't leave you that note. Were you in the store at the time? Was Melody or anyone else there?"

"It was just me."

"Then it was meant for just you." He turned away and muttered something in his native tongue. Tak must have shifted after reading the threat.

A million things raced through my head, and I stared at the dark television in front of me as the details unfolded like a bad late-night movie. "When we first opened the store, we were prepared for a backlash. There's not much retail real estate left in the Breed district, and most of the owners around here are men. The pranks were juvenile compared to what others had experienced, so we just shrugged them off. There was nothing we could do about a little writing on the windows. They probably thought we'd be embarrassed by it, but it'll take a lot more than name-calling to scare us off." I gazed at the note on the table. "I plan to tell Melody and Lakota when they get back, but I'm not sure there's much we can do about it. I don't have the money to hire a personal bodyguard, and how long can I live my life like that?"

"They broke your window. You're in danger."

"We don't know if it was the same person. A lot of people are jealous of our success." Frustrated, I crawled up the bed and fell to my side, giving him my back. "What should I do?"

"Being a lone wolf makes you an easy target. If you had a Packmaster, this wouldn't be an issue."

"But as it stands, I don't. Nor do I have any desire to join a pack just for protection."

He snorted. "That's what a pack *is*. Protection."

I dipped my nose inside the collar of my shirt, smelling Tak's scent buried in the threads. "Well, my chances of finding a respectable pack just dwindled after that fiasco back there."

Tak circled the room and sat on the edge of the bed. I had a strange compulsion to reach out and touch his hair, but I admired it instead.

"Do you think that bear left the note?"

I thought about it. "No. I found it before the incident in the shop. I'll talk to Lakota about it when he returns. He'll know what to do."

Maybe I didn't have a bodyguard, but Lakota had spent years as a bounty hunter, and that offered me a small measure of comfort.

Tak peered over his shoulder at me with those warm brown eyes. "What about that man you were with tonight?"

"Dutch? He didn't mention murdering me on our date, but who knows what he might have revealed by the time we ordered dessert," I said, hiding a grin.

"I wouldn't put it past a guy like him. Smooth talkers are the ones you have to watch out for."

My smile withered. Tak was right about that one.

His eyes settled on me for a long time. "Where did you get your scars?"

I instinctively reached up and traced my finger across the ones on my jaw. "When I was a girl, a rogue attacked me."

He jerked his neck back. "A wolf did that to you?"

I nodded.

"What happened to him?"

I tucked my hand underneath the pillow. "Ask Wheeler. He's the one who killed him."

"I owe him a beer." Tak furrowed his brow. "Had the wolf gone mad? Sometimes rogues who wander the woods for years lose all sense of morality."

"It happened just before the war started. Mel and I were walking in the field when he came upon us. At first, we thought he belonged to one of the neighboring packs. I don't know why he singled me out, but he knocked me down and…" My eyes squeezed shut, the memories so vivid that it seemed like only yesterday when it happened. I could still feel his front paws punching the air out of my lungs as he knocked me down. I could hear Mel's bloodcurdling scream when his jaws locked around my head. I could still smell the stench of his hot breath and feel the cut of his sharp canines. Unable to look at Tak, I continued. "I was frozen with fear, afraid that if I moved he would rip off my face. I have little memory after that. Mel somehow scared him off, and someone carried me back. That part's a blur, but the attack is so fresh in my mind that sometimes I think my heart will stop beating."

"A crime that unspeakable should have never happened to a child. It makes little ones fear their own kind or even themselves." Tak's hand smoothed my hair, and he kept petting me that way until I felt calm again. "Is that when your panic attacks began?"

I nodded.

"Have you ever talked to anyone about it?"

"My family understands how it changed me, but they don't know how to help. They've done their best to give me advice, but forgetting doesn't stop the nightmares. It doesn't stop the episodes. And it certainly doesn't stop me from becoming a paralyzed mess when my life is in danger."

"You did nothing to be ashamed of back there," he reiterated. "I don't give a damn what anyone in that bar thinks of your reaction, and neither should you. Staying low kept you from becoming that bear's target. You don't have a Packmaster around to tell you that, so maybe you need to hear it from me. I had an uncle killed by a grizzly. One swipe took off half his head. And what you're dealing with—it's no one's place to judge. They don't know what you've been through."

"Easy for you to say."

Tak withdrew his hand, eyes downcast. "I know about trauma. Everyone deals with it differently."

I noticed the bend in his voice and treaded carefully with my question. "What could traumatize an alpha?"

Tak turned away and rested his forearms on his knees. "Killing his mate."

I sat up, my eyes wide. "Say that again?"

After a long stretch of silence, he finally spoke. "Maybe you should call that cab after all."

His admission made my heart drop. Maybe I should have taken him up on the cab, but I had to know more. "On purpose?"

Tak's knuckles turned white as he squeezed his fingers together, and I watched his sculpted features contort. When he tried to speak, he choked on a sob, his body shaking as he buried his face in his hands. I'd rarely seen that depth of sorrow.

When his emotional break subsided, he wiped his face and heaved a sigh. "I'm an alcoholic. I used to be, anyhow."

My heart sank. If this story involved physical abuse, I wouldn't be able to offer him words of comfort. That was where I drew the line. My heart had no room for any man who would strike a woman.

"We weren't actually mated," he continued. "We didn't hide our relationship, and we were as close as any mated couple, except for the living-together part. Her father knew about my problem and wouldn't agree to the pairing. We could have gone behind his back, but she didn't want it that way. His approval meant something to her, and she thought he'd warm up to me in time. My drinking never affected my behavior toward her. I always treated her with love and respect. It was just something that became bigger than me."

"Why did you drink?"

Tak wiped his face again, his voice changed from the pain. "I don't know. Maybe to cope with living in my father's shadow. I could list a million excuses, but none of them matter. I lost control."

My hand slid away from his back when he grabbed the water off the end table and gulped it down. "What happened?"

He set the bottle on the table and turned to face me, his eyes downcast. "I was drinking at the bar one night, and she showed up to bring me home. I made her laugh. Even when she was mad at me, I could make her laugh. She handed my keys to one of my packmates and insisted on driving me home in her car. It wasn't the first time she'd come to my rescue, but maybe it bruised my ego that particular night. Once outside, I snatched the keys away from her and got in the driver's seat. She tried to stop me, but I'm a stubborn wolf. I distracted her with kisses until she laughed. Then I promised to drive slowly. We lived out in the country, and there isn't any traffic late at night. *Why* didn't she get out?"

I shook my head.

"I don't remember the drive or anything else until I woke up to the smell of fuel and pine. We'd hit a tree, and it almost split the car in half. She wasn't wearing a seat belt." Tears filled his eyes so quickly that they spilled down his cheeks before he could blink.

Something dark flickered in his expression, and I drew back.

Tak gripped a pillow and hurled it across the room with such ferocity that it made me jump. He sprang to his feet and punched the wall, his fist leaving a crater. "She suffered because of me. She died because of me. Alone, on the hood of a car! I wasn't awake to hold her, to comfort her, to tell her that I was sorry."

I felt a catch in my throat and stood up. "You don't know what could have been done for her. An alpha's magic doesn't always work. Don't torture yourself over something you can't change. The fates are in control of our lives."

He spun around, his nostrils flaring. "The fates didn't take her out of this world; *I* did. It wasn't her time," he growled. "And I'm the one who had to tell her family. I brought shame to my tribe—to my father. You see an alpha standing before you, but I will never be a Packmaster."

I reached up and touched the dark patterns on his face, tears welling in my eyes. "Is that why they did this? To punish you?"

He shook his head. "I did it after I got sober. Let my sins be a cautionary tale for the younger generations. They need a reminder every single day of the price they'll pay for selfish choices. The symbols show I'm a wolf who strayed from the pack."

I brushed the pad of my thumb across his cheek. "Maybe you were meant to stray for a reason."

He stared at me for a few breathless seconds and then pressed his lips to mine. The kiss was surprisingly gentle at first, and as his arm curved around my back and he pulled me closer, I felt dizzy with the taste of his tears and the scent of him. He claimed me with that kiss, and I stood on my tiptoes, my body melting against his.

When he broke the kiss and backed away, I looked up in confusion.

"It's not right," he said, his voice husky. "I can't take advantage of a virgin."

I blinked at him in surprise before a flurry of laughter escaped. I covered my mouth, unable to process what I'd just heard.

Tak frowned. "I don't understand you city Shifters."

"It's not you," I said, the laughter dying in my throat. "I'm just not sure why you assumed I was a virgin. Are the women in your tribe virgins until they mate? Do you carry them to the bridal suite on a palanquin?"

He twisted his mouth to the side, half amused by my remark but confusion swimming in his eyes. "No, but a woman of your caliber doesn't give it away to just any man."

I spun around and folded my arms. "This one did."

I felt the heat of his body closing in on me.

"I don't believe you."

"Believe it. My ignorant decision almost destroyed my father's pack."

He led me to the mattress to sit and then knelt before me. "There's no sin in bedding a man."

"No, but he was one of my packmates." When Tak grimaced, I wanted to disappear. "People expect more from the Packmaster's daughter. I let an older man seduce me, and part of me wanted to give it away to someone I didn't love."

Tak tilted his head. "Why?"

I'd never shared my reasoning behind it with anyone, and the idea of defending my actions aloud felt freeing. "Because... my father has no sons of his own—no alpha male child to one day align with his pack or even lead it. He loves Lakota, but I'm his only natural child. My dream was to sell jewelry, and his dream for me was to mate with an alpha."

"You didn't want a mate?"

I shrugged. "My father loves me blindly. He never acknowledged my faults—my weaknesses. He just assumed an alpha would find me desirable and I would have my happily-ever-after, but that's not how it works. I wanted to please my father, and I knew he would always worry for me if I never found a strong man to be my life mate. This may sound foolish to you, but I once believed that sex could hold a man—that passion gave you power. Maybe if I had some of that power, it would give me an advantage over other women. What alpha wants an inexperienced virgin? I thought an older wolf could teach me how to be a good lover. It was such a mistake. My mother warned me not to make foolish choices, but did I listen? Lying to my father was one thing, but deceiving a Packmaster is a punishable offense."

"What happened to the man?"

"My father kicked him out of the pack. The confrontation almost ended in bloodshed, but my mother's a skilled mediator and talked sense into him. I don't think the rest of the pack knows what really happened, but *I* know what I did, and that's enough. My father tried to protect my good name, but I don't think he believes I'll ever find a mate."

"And this spineless coward never came for you? He didn't fight for you?"

"He didn't love me. Why would he have?"

Tak cursed under his breath. "What kind of man would sully a woman's reputation?"

"Lakota fears it'll happen again. That's why I'm staying home alone instead of with my old pack while everyone's out of town. I don't know that I'll ever regain their trust." I stared at the empty bottle of water. "All for nothing. The sex wasn't even nice."

His hand felt heavy on my knee. "It rarely is the first couple of times."

"I can't imagine why so many women enjoy it."

Tak's fingers grazed my inside thigh, sending an unexpected flutter of tingles through my core. "Why do you say that?"

"It was painful and rushed. He made me nervous and self-conscious the whole time."

Tak's hand stroked higher, and when his knuckles brushed against the thin fabric between my legs, I trembled. "Do I make you nervous?"

My blood heated from his touch, and everything about him felt so right.

"You chose the wrong man," he said, easing between my legs.

My skin tingled at the touch of his fingers. They explored beneath my shirt and circled over the fabric of my bra.

Tak's eyes drank me in, and his words devoured me. "Will you let me show you how good it can feel?"

"What about my honor? People expect a woman like me to be courted before bedding a man."

He stroked my cheek, and I leaned into him. "The man you gave yourself to didn't realize what a precious jewel you are. Otherwise he wouldn't have made your first time so terrible that you've given up on your desires. He should have pursued you in every way." Tak kissed the corner of my mouth. "I want to show you what a beautiful, sexual wolf you are. As for courtship, you deserve a better man than me, so maybe this is the only honor I can give you."

I wanted him. Yearned to know the feel of his weight. Tak sparked a fire in me, and in his arms, I felt like a woman.

"I have nothing to give you in return."

Tak cradled my neck in his hands, his eyes piercing my soul. For a moment, our spirit wolves danced in the depths of our gaze. "You've already given me what no other woman has."

"What's that?"

"Compassion."

Chapter 15

Tak stripped me out of my shirt and bra before he could bring a blush to my cheeks. He worshipped me with his mouth, drawing in my taut nipple and circling his tongue until I moaned. Tak made me feel like a goddess, as if my curves and imperfections were everything he craved.

I needed to be with this wolf. He awakened a hunger in me that made my heat spells pale in comparison.

When he reached for the lamp, I captured his wrist. "I don't want to be in the dark. I've only ever known the darkness. I want to be in the light. I want to see you."

His breath was hot against my skin as he circled his tongue around my other nipple, his hands unfastening my pants and tugging them free.

Tak pulled me to my feet and then peeled back the comforter. His eyes were ravenous, like a man who hadn't eaten a meal in forty days. "Get in."

Those two words sent a lick of desire through my body, his alpha power pulsing against my skin like a heartbeat. I crawled beneath the covers to the center of the bed while he leisurely stripped out of his pants. Tak struck me as a wolf who took what he wanted, when he wanted, so I couldn't figure out why I was beneath the covers instead of beneath him.

Despite the torment of waiting, I liked the way he took

his time undressing, his smoky eyes trained on me. It gave me a chance to admire his impressive physique—his bronzed body; broad chest; strong legs; and the scars that peppered his knee, shoulder, and torso. Battle scars were common among males, but some of these looked older. I wanted to trace my fingers over each one and learn their stories—offer him the understanding that other women hadn't.

I averted my eyes when he faced me, his impressive erection aimed like an arrow seeking its target.

He eased between the sheets to my right, resting his face on the pillow so our noses touched. "You can look at it if you want."

"Don't be silly. I've seen plenty."

He chuckled, his eyes like crescent moons as he smiled. "There's a difference between seeing packmates naked after a shift and seeing a man who's hard for you. I'm hard for you, and I want you to touch me."

This had always been my worst fear—being with an alpha who would consider me too inexperienced for his needs.

He guided my hand down to his shaft. "Like this."

I'd never touched a man. My previous lover liked me on all fours, and that was as far as we'd ever gotten. Curious, I peered down for a closer look. Tak's wasn't pink and curved like the man I'd slept with years ago. It was thick and enormous up close. I let go, suddenly ashamed for putting him on the spot like that.

Tak caressed my cheek. "I don't think I've ever made a woman blush before."

"Not even your mate?"

A rueful look flickered in his eyes as he brushed my hair away from my shoulder. "We were never intimate. She was twenty but hadn't gone through her first change yet. It's not right to take a woman until she's one with her animal."

It struck me how respectful Tak was to have honored that tradition. While he'd loved her, she still wasn't an adult in his eyes.

"Mood killer," he muttered.

"Not at all. She was an important part of your life. I wouldn't ask if I didn't care." I stroked his cheek, the inked side buried against the pillow. He looked so normal this way, and it bothered me for some reason. "Can we switch sides?"

His eyebrows gathered in a frown. "Why?"

"You're always hiding your face from me. Why do you do that?"

"Because you didn't know the story behind it. Now that you do, it's ugly in a different way. Anyhow, it's not exactly my best asset," he said, humor edging his voice. "Would you like to see what *that* is again?"

When he started to lift the sheet, I playfully slapped his hand. "Switch sides with me."

Tak didn't hop over to the other side; he took his time sliding over me. Our naked bodies brushed together sensually, and I sucked in a sharp breath. My breasts rubbed against his thick chest as he gazed down at me with invitation swimming in his eyes. Tak finally nestled beside me, his unmarred cheek against the pillow.

I rolled on my left side to face him, unable to steer my eyes away from his scars. I traced my finger over one on his left pec. "What are these from?"

His mouth turned down as his chin touched his chest. "Different things. That one's from an enemy tribe when we were battling for land many years ago. The arrow nicked me, and I didn't bother healing it. I've got one on my leg from a snakebite when I was a kid, and another on my hip from falling off my first horse after passing out drunk. The one on my knee and shoulder are from the accident. Same goes with the one in my hairline."

Since his hair was unbound, I reached up and threaded my fingers through it until I found the four-inch scar. I wondered if the reason Tak inked his face had less to do with teaching youngsters a lesson so much as driving women away. Women might sleep with him, but how many would take a mate with such an ominous mark on his face—especially when the symbols identified him as a wolf who had strayed from the pack?

"May I look at yours?" he asked.

I put my hand down.

Tak traced his finger along my temple where the teeth had scraped down until they reached bone. Then he circled over the puncture marks on my lower jaw.

"I wish I could be the warrior people expect me to be," I said quietly.

He lifted my chin with the crook of his finger. "Why do you see yourself as weak?"

"Others have suffered so much more than I have, and they're stronger for it. My tragedy was just a wolf attack, and my scars aren't severe or disabling. Yet I feel disabled."

"It's not the scars on your skin that matter. They're not the ones that do the most damage. You're not weak. You're just on a different path than everyone else, so walk that path with your chin up." He cupped my face, his thumb stroking my cheek. "We're kindred souls, you and I. We both live under the long shadow of great leaders."

I nuzzled against him. Maybe Tak wasn't a notable businessman like his father, but he exuded the tenacity of a fighter and the bravery of a protector. No one else in that bar had shielded me with their body like Tak had. Not once had he left my side—not once! He knew what I needed to feel safe, and that mattered more than dashing into the fray and showing off his prowess. Being around Tak made me feel less crazy and more understood.

He sheltered me with his embrace, his rough hand sliding down my back and putting goose bumps on my arms. I felt so much life when curled up against him. His pounding heart, the breath in his lungs, the warmth of his touch, and the tantalizing scent that lifted off his skin.

"What history do you have with my brother?"

"Do you know about Lakota's job?"

I scooted back to see his face. "A retired bounty hunter? Yes."

His brows arched. "Retired, huh?"

"Is that how you know him?"

"One day I'm up at the bar, and Lakota walks in. We sometimes get people passing through, but not many Natives. We bonded, and I considered him a brother. I didn't know when I invited him onto our land that he was working undercover and using us for information. Then he accused me of murder."

"Why would he do that?"

Tak traced his finger over my shoulder, but his thoughts were distant. "I stole food from my people to feed families living in abject poverty near our land. Since I'd kept it a secret, I didn't have an alibi. And just in case you're wondering, they found the murderer. It wasn't me." He flashed a playful smile, which made me laugh.

I pinched his chin. "I thought as much."

"When my father told me why Lakota was really there, I wanted nothing more to do with him. He left town, and that was that. But the more time that goes by, the more it eats away at me. I don't like unfinished business."

"Lakota is a good man. Friend or not, you can't expect someone working undercover to give up their identity before the case is closed. He took that job seriously, and he didn't even tell his own family where he was from one week to the next. It's not because he didn't trust us. Give him a chance to explain and let him know how it made you feel."

His brown eyes drifted upward. "He knows."

I smoothed my palm down his side. As we held each other and bared our souls, we were more naked inside than out.

He cupped my breast, and I arched into his palm. Tak's callused hands were undeniably strong, and yet his touch was tender. "I don't deserve such beauty."

Stripped by his ardent gaze, I found myself vulnerable.

Tak wasn't rushing into anything, and the foreplay between us was body and soul.

"You think I'm beautiful? I'm all right."

"All right?" He ripped the sheet away with a swift jerk of his arm, the material floating to the floor at the foot of the bed. Tak gripped my backside and then smoothed his hand over my thighs. "You're what men dream about," he said against my lips.

His reverence was something I was unaccustomed to hearing, and I scooted closer until our bodies met. Heat penetrated my skin so exquisitely that I moaned. Tak's blood ran hot—ancient and filled with alpha power. His expressive face could reveal humor or desire in the subtlest shift of his mouth or brow, but there was nothing subtle about the way he looked at me.

I shivered when his fingers danced down my spine, and he squeezed my backside again. I'd always been self-conscious about certain parts of my body, hiding them beneath loose clothing.

But not now.

I draped my leg over his hip, an open invitation.

"I want to kiss your lips," he said gruffly.

When I raised my chin, he put his mouth to my ear and said, "Not those."

The thought of his mouth anywhere on my body made my mind race, but between my legs? I nearly melted in his arms.

Tak kissed the crook of my neck, working his way all around. I nibbled on his earlobe before letting him win.

My God, he was intoxicating.

"Put your mouth on me," he demanded.

I kissed his Adam's apple, and he reclined his head to let me explore every inch of his jaw. His hand grazed my nipple, and I dragged my mouth to his ear and licked the fleshy lobe.

A sharp groan settled in the back of his throat. "I like your mouth on my body."

When I lightly bit his neck, his breath hitched, and he pulled me against him.

My wolf spirit and I converged, her strength mixing with my desire. His skin was so smooth and brown, the taste like summer on my tongue. I kissed his tattoo from the corner of his eye down to the edge of his mouth. The moment our lips met, he scorched me with a deep kiss, his tongue dancing with mine. I was so wet… so ready for him to take me.

The kiss fell apart as he moved down to my breasts. They were pushed together, making it easier for his mouth to travel from one nipple to the other.

"You taste like sweet nectar."

I held the back of his head, my breath heavy. "Don't stop doing that."

He growled, one hand gripping the back of my thigh. I became dizzy from all the sensations. The sharp sting as he sucked on my nipple, the dull scrape of his teeth, the air cooling my skin whenever his mouth pulled away, the hard length of his erection pushing against my thigh, the softness of his hair in my hands.

"I'm going to touch you," he whispered.

Tak slid his hand between my legs, and I jerked in surprise. He lowered his head, his tongue circling my nipple as his fingers slipped inside me.

I stopped worrying about what to do and gave in to the dark hunger of our wolves. I reached down and grabbed hold of his shaft, and I'd never seen him look so startled. It was as if time stopped, and he fell completely still.

"Do you like this?" I asked.

His eyes hooded. "I'm undecided. Keep doing it, and I'll let you know."

When I twisted my wrist, he withdrew his hand and grabbed my ass.

"I like touching you," I whispered.

His lips twitched.

"Is this how you like it?"

Maybe I was being too rough with an alpha—too domineering.

"I don't know, but it feels damn good," he said, kissing my shoulder. "I'm used to doing all the work. That's what women expect with an alpha."

I stroked the length of him faster. His body stiffened like granite, and he made a guttural moan as his fingers bit into my skin.

The urge to turn my back to him became strong. When I moved to roll over, Tak captured my wrist.

"Wait," he said, looking me in the eye. "I want you astride me."

My mind flooded with images of Tak beneath me—a powerful alpha giving me absolute control. It hardly seemed natural, so I hesitated. "Maybe we shouldn't."

"I think we should," he said, his tone raw and needy.

I'd heard stories about alphas taking charge in the bedroom. Tak didn't have a submissive bone in his body, so why would he allow a female wolf to dominate him?

"I thought you were used to doing all the work?"

His roving hand made me forget the question. "Beautiful, I'm tired of rules."

Tak rolled onto his back, taking me with him. He looked at me in awe, excitement stirring in his eyes. My long hair curtained my body like a veil, shading my breasts from his view.

"Touch yourself." He brushed my hair behind my shoulders.

I circled my fingers around my nipples, watching how his eyes hooded and his breath caught in his chest. When I rose up on my knees and allowed my hand to travel between my legs, Tak licked his lips. What did he want to see? How far did he want it to go?

Then I noticed he couldn't move his head since his hair was pinned behind him. "Lean up." When he rose up on his elbows, I pulled his handsome mane free and draped it behind the pillow as he lay back down.

I saw no flaws. Only a selfless man who hid behind humor and a scary tattoo. Tak was the most magnificent alpha male I'd ever laid eyes on, and not just for his physical traits. His character outshone everyone else.

Empowered by my new position, I splayed my fingers across his torso and watched his eyes close. He gripped my thighs, pushing me down his legs until I could see his masculine form.

"You make everything so easy," I whispered.

His eyes remained closed. I had once believed that an experienced man could teach me how to please an alpha. What a foolish notion. I'd never known an alpha could have such patience and understanding. It only fueled the passion between us to know that he was mine to touch, to look upon, to master.

Curious, I looked down at his throbbing erection. The taut skin revealed engorged veins. When I touched the tip, he hissed through his teeth as if I'd hurt him, so I snapped my arm back.

He put his hands beneath his pillow. "Do that again."

I brushed my fingertips over the sloped head and it jerked up.

A sly grin hooked up his cheek, and he made it jerk again. Tak's eyes remained closed, allowing me to admire how amazing he was. Every inch of him.

I gripped his thick shaft in my hand, the skin smooth and warm against my palm. I enjoyed petting him, so I held his erection against my belly and stroked it with my other hand.

Tak's hips surged beneath me, his head thrashing from left to right.

His tortured reaction left me bemused. Maybe he didn't like foreplay half as much as I did. When I rose up on my knees and leaned forward, stroking him against my slick entrance, he nearly bucked me off the bed.

The pillow twisted within Tak's grip as he continued... *not* touching me. And the longer he withheld, the more I craved his hands on my body.

I flattened my palm against his shoulder, using my other hand to position the blunt head of his shaft inside me. Afraid he was silently judging my every move, I anchored both hands on his chest and slowly lowered myself.

Tak looked like a man unraveling at the seams. He turned his head to the side, his teeth biting into his flexed bicep. It was a wild image—one I knew I'd carry in my mind for years to come. When he was deep inside me, all the way to the hilt, I draped myself over his chest like a blanket and nuzzled my face in the crook of his neck. I'd never felt so connected to anyone.

"Is this okay?" I asked, feeling his strong heart beating with mine.

He wrapped his thick arms around me and kissed my forehead. "More than you'll ever know."

Being with Tak was so different from my first lover, who'd criticized me for making noise or not moving the way he wanted. Tak didn't bark orders, and it made me want to take my time and savor him. I kissed his neck, listening to his soft grunts as I worked my way up his jaw.

Tak moved beneath me like a gentle wave, his mouth against my ear. The intonation and dialect was a familiar sister language to my own, and though his words were foreign, my body became the interpreter. He caressed the planes of my back down to the swell of my hips, and when I rocked against him, he growled deep in his chest.

Pleasure spiked through me. I moved to sit up, but he caught my wrists and held me to him.

"I'm not finished." Tak traced his tongue from the base of my neck to my chin before our lips met.

His kiss demanded that I move, riding him fast and hard like a wild mustang. Unable to stop, I placed my hands on his shoulders and pushed myself up.

"That's it," he said. "Let your wolf show you what you need."

A primal urge overtook me, and it felt as though my wolf was about to break free. Heat flooded my veins, my hips rocking so fast that Tak sat up and clutched me. When he pulled my hair, I shattered.

Pleasure hit me in erratic waves.

Before it ended, Tak looked me in the eye. "Do you trust me?"

I nodded.

He lifted me off him and set me down on all fours. My legs parted as he positioned himself behind me. At first he teased me with shallow pumps. My wolf raced beneath my skin as if she were running through the woods on a moonlit night. I felt the heat of her blood pulsing in my veins and the animalistic desires rekindling the inferno within.

Tak grabbed my hips, and the sound of skin slapping together filled the quiet room. When I released a moan, pulsing waves of pleasure filling me up, Tak roared. Each time I cried out, he rewarded me with harder thrusts.

I peered over my shoulder at him, and his eyes went wild. Tak fell across my back, his long hair spilling forward as he found his release. I rocked backward, drawing out more guttural moans until he finally pulled out.

I fell onto my right side, muscles trembling. All the troubles of my past melted away, and I wanted to live in this moment forever. Tak had freed something inside me, and for the first time, there was no guilt. No shame. No insecurities or worries about public opinion. Tenderness and trust had made me a woman, not sex.

Tak made the entire bed bounce when he collapsed beside me.

I stirred with laughter at the serious look on his face.

"So *that's* what it takes to make you laugh?" he asked. "Making love to me? Nothing about that crushes my pride. Nothing at all."

Tak held my hand, and we gazed into each other's eyes. How could I feel so at ease with someone I barely knew? It was as if we'd experienced a lifetime together in the short time that we'd known each other.

"I'm just glad I could make you laugh," he finally said, out of breath. "When I saw you sitting with that man at the bar, I was jealous that he could make you laugh like that."

I thought about Dutch but drew a blank on what he'd said that had me chuckling. "Why should something like that matter?"

Tak wiped his glowing face. "Men are born with a natural ability to make women cry, so every smile is a gift. When you laugh, I can see the very best part of your soul."

My heart clenched, and I squeezed his hand. "Do you talk so sweetly to other women?"

"I speak the truth. Is that sweet talk?"

I tucked his hair behind his ear so I could see his ruggedly handsome face. Behind the strong lines, the ink, his warm gaze, and even the humor he used as a shield, I saw a glimmer of a broken soul. How any woman in his tribe could have not seen his flawed beauty was beyond my understanding. If he were a gemstone, I would have priced him high.

"Do you think you'll travel more, now that you've had a taste of it?" I asked.

"I live in a paradise. What purpose would it serve to look elsewhere?"

I clasped his hand, my thumb brushing over his hard knuckles. "People like seeing the world. There's so much beauty out there."

"You'll never have a content heart until you can see the beauty right in front of you."

Tak had a way of looking into my soul. He possessed so many layers that I couldn't quite figure him out, only that each side of him was honest and true to his character. His words and touch were absent of ambiguity, and perhaps that was what bridged the gap between two strangers.

I wanted to ask about his tribe, his family, his memories, but I was afraid it would remind him of his dark past and conflicts with packmates. This moment between us was too fine to spoil with the wrong words.

"Can I braid your hair?"

When I realized he wasn't joking, I giggled. "Is it blocking your view?"

"No. I... I just want to see what it looks like." He patted my behind. "Come on."

I rolled over and sat up, leaning on my left arm. "I never thought I would be in bed with a man while doing each other's hair. Do you want to have a tea party when we're done?"

"Ah, so you *do* have a sense of humor. I knew it was in there somewhere."

Tak sectioned off my hair and began weaving it together. "This is a sacred tradition among my people. The men in my tribe wear a single braid as a symbol of unity."

"So now I'm just one of the guys?"

He chuckled. "You're a warrior."

"Of what?"

"Your demons."

I glanced up at a cheap picture on the wall. "I'm not doing a very good job."

"Every day you wake up is a battle won." When Tak finished with my hair, he rubbed his hands across my shoulders and then down my back. "You have a fine shape. Why do you hide it?"

"I'm not hiding it."

"I meant with your clothes. Overalls?"

"They're comfortable."

"Hmm." He blew a cool breath against my back.

"Would you rather I wear a low-cut top and tight shorts?"

Tak pulled me against him and softly kissed my nape. "Only for me. No one else." When his kisses tapered off, he ran his fingers through my braid and loosened it. "I like the way you wear it better."

"Do you think I'm a slut?"

Tak's head appeared to my right, and when he spoke, anger clung to his words. "Why would you ask me that?"

I pulled my hair to the front, curtaining my breasts. "When we first opened Moonglow, someone wrote *slut* on the window. Were they just using that word to offend us, or was it meant for me? What if that's how people in this town really see me?"

"Is that how you see yourself?"

I looked up at him. "No. But it doesn't matter how I see myself. People talk, and secrets get out."

Tak caressed my arm. "Keep me warm under the covers. My ass is getting chilly from the air conditioner."

I crawled up to the pillow while Tak pulled the covers over us. His eyes danced with amusement while he tried to find a comfortable snuggling position.

Somehow, even when he wasn't trying, Tak found a way to make me smile.

Our legs tangled and untangled, and no matter what we did, no position was close enough.

"I've never been in bed with a woman," he confessed.

"I find that hard to believe."

Tak kissed my nose. "I meant to sleep."

We turned a few more times and finally cracked up laughing.

"Why don't you spoon me?" I suggested, rolling onto my right side.

"I always did like that utensil best."

Tak pressed up behind me, his mouth against the shell of my ear. "I could get used to this." His arm crossed my chest and gave me something to hold. Now I finally understood why couples enjoyed this position so much.

"Here's something I've learned," he began in earnest. "You can't do anything about gossip. We all make mistakes. It's what you do after that matters. If anyone's to blame, it's the wolf who had the balls to seduce the Packmaster's daughter behind closed doors. Even if you wanted it, you were too young to understand the consequences. He used his position to coerce and mislead you. It's not easy being the Packmaster's child. That much I know. People take advantage and judge you harder for every mistake."

When I shivered, he held me close until the heat from his chest warmed me.

"How old are you?" I asked.

"Fifty or so."

"You look it."

I giggled when he tickled my ribs. Tak appeared in his thirties since wolves age slowly. A number really didn't matter in terms of compatibility in relationships or friendships, but it was a way to find out how seasoned they were. One could tell a lot about a man's life choices based on his age.

"What are you going to tell your father about my store?" I asked.

"I'm going to tell him the truth."

"Which is what?"

"That I've never seen anyone honor his gemstones the way you have. You don't cheapen them. I noticed how you carefully arranged each piece in and around the counter. His name is prominently displayed, and I know that's not in your contract. I'm also going to let him know that you're stingy about who you sell them to."

I laughed. "You didn't really want that necklace."

"Didn't I?"

I traced the lines in his large wrists. He was a giant, and I should have felt small in his arms. But Tak had a way of making me feel important and valued. "Thank you for sharing your story with me," I said respectfully. "It means a lot that you trusted me with the truth."

Tak had probably shared that story a dozen times with his tribe, but something told me he'd never broken down and revealed his suffering. His anguish didn't make him weak in my eyes, and his tears revealed his strength of heart, allowing me to see his courage and fortitude.

Tak didn't answer; he simply hugged me tighter against him and kissed my head. I also appreciated that he'd given me the truth about the conflict between him and Lakota.

"How long are you going to stay in town?" I dared to ask.

"I'll stay until Lakota returns, but only if you scratch my back."

I smiled and didn't give him the satisfaction of an answer.

Though I had only known Tak a short time, I wanted to spend the whole week in his arms… just as we were. But my thoughts were drifting, and I realized I couldn't even stay until dawn. My car was still parked outside Howlers, and I had to open the store early, which meant going home to shower and change.

But for the next few hours, I allowed myself to be a woman held by a man who thought me brave and beautiful.

Chapter 16

After the harrowing ordeal at Howlers two days ago, my life returned to a normal routine. Though Tak had promised to stay in town, I hadn't spoken to him. My hours at the store were long, and by the time I made it home, all I wanted to do was sleep. As much as I missed his company, I needed the space to clear my head. Inviting him to sleep over behind my brother's back would have been a mistake. Maybe Tak understood the position it put me in, or maybe he didn't want to pursue me as anything more than a lover. But either way, he was still around. I'd glimpsed him walking by the window every so often, and I'd spotted his wolf in the shadows last night when I closed the store later than expected.

I slumped down in my chair and admired the view out the living room window. Dusk approached, the colors changing from burnt orange and gold to a hypnotizing shade of indigo.

Instead of sending a message, I found Melody's number in my contact list and only had to wait through two rings. "How's everything going up there?"

Melody sounded like herself again. "We're having a blast. I've never eaten so much food in my life. His dad made the most amazing lemon cake. There must have been some inside joke I didn't get, but the cake was scrumptious. Why didn't you tell me how awesome their home is? I love how they each have their own floor. It's so different from living with a pack of wolves. I practically had to make reservations to use the bathroom at my old place."

I chuckled softly. "Did Lakota's parents have a coronary over your hair?"

She snorted. "Okay, maybe I overreacted just a little bit. They accepted me the second I walked through the door. They're so easy to talk to that it's like having a second family. My parents are impressed with the building and the way they live together like a pack. Did you know his uncle's a Shifter?"

"Of course. Who do you think carved the wolf totem in our store? I knew everything would work out just fine."

"I guess if it wasn't my hair I would have been nervous about something else. Meeting the family and all. By the way, your dad's butting heads with Justus. They were arguing this afternoon. Something about which is faster, a Ferrari or Porsche. Then they both took off in their cars. I thought for sure their mates were going to lock them out for the night." Melody laughed, hinting there was more to the story. "Anyhow, it's not the same here without you."

I steered my gaze up to the heavens. "I wish I could have come, but we'll make the trip another time when things settle down with the store. I'm so glad everyone's getting along and having a good time. That's all I wanted for you. Maybe we can invite everyone down for a peace party."

"How's Moonglow? I didn't think I'd miss work, but I do."

"Nothing to worry about. Sales are up, and Naya volunteered to take over for an afternoon if I need a break."

"That was nice of her. I miss you."

"Me too. Are you still coming home on Friday?"

"Maybe. I'm having such a good time up here, but Lakota's been talking about heading back a little early."

"Why's that?"

"He had a bad dream. I told him that he's worrying over nothing. That's one reason I wanted to call tonight to see how things were going. Maybe it'll put his mind at ease and we can stay."

I didn't mention my own dream about the store in flames. Lakota and I believed dreams were messages, but they weren't literal interpretations. Usually they were metaphors, and the meaning for mine seemed obvious. Someone was trying to shake my confidence.

"Stay as long as you want and tell my brother not to be such a worrywart."

She chortled and repeated my comment, and Lakota said something in the background. Those two really deserved a honeymoon. They'd been cooped up in the house with me since their mating.

Melody cleared her throat. "Did you close that deal with what's-her-face?"

"You mean Asia? Nothing's in writing yet. She's supposed to talk it over with her housemates. We'll see."

"Well, if it falls through, we'll figure something out. Maybe we can just sneak over and pluck them."

I bit back my laughter. "I better let you go. Say hi to everyone for me."

"Will do. Talk to you later."

After I set the phone down, my gaze fixed on the buildings across the street. The light soaked into the brick, amplifying the colors. I loved Texas. Even in the city, the expansive horizon was full of possibilities.

And danger.

Would my stalker ever relent? Some resented that we'd purchased the shop, especially since we were single women. There were people who didn't believe Shifters should own businesses when we had so much land. Maybe someone had targeted me for a specific reason. There were so many angles and no way of knowing the truth.

If only we could set up a security camera, but recorded surveillance wasn't permitted in the Breed district since the

Councils protected the identities of immortals. At least Tak was still around.

When the doorbell rang, I jumped out of my chair. Sometimes our neighbor gave us a heads-up that they were having a party. With Shifters, that could mean a lot of howling. I padded across the floor and looked out the peephole.

"Dutch," I said, opening the door. "How did you get in the building?"

"My charm and good looks?" He gave me a sheepish grin. "I snuck in behind the delivery man. Mind if we talk?"

Impeccable as usual, I thought, admiring his golden hair, which was neatly styled back. Did the man even have whiskers, or did they simply stop growing at his command? Dutch could have been a male model in a cologne ad.

I stepped back to let him inside. "Can I take your jacket? It's a little warm in here."

His sports coat slid off his shoulders, and I hung it up.

"Nice place. It doesn't look anything like what I imagined," he said, staring at the living room.

"I have two roommates, and we have different ideas about interior decorating. Can I get you something to drink? Root beer, tea, water…"

"Wine?" He gestured to the small wine rack in the kitchen.

"Sure. Make yourself comfortable."

While I uncorked the bottle of red and filled our glasses, Dutch strolled around and inspected the apartment. He looked closely at pictures, touched fabric, studied the artwork, and admired the view.

"Do you live nearby?" I asked.

"No." He shook his head. "I don't know how you can tolerate the noise level outside."

Only then did I notice a car alarm going off. "You get used to it. After a while, it's just white noise." I crossed the room and offered him a glass. "I haven't heard from you since that night at Howlers. I've been thinking about you. How have you been?"

He gulped down a large swallow and lingered by the window. "I came by to apologize for abandoning you the other night. It was rude."

"No apology needed. You were injured."

A small drop of wine splashed on his grey button-up, and he brushed it with his hand before setting down his glass. "Rude isn't even sufficient a word. Unforgivable."

"Half the men in that bar took off," I pointed out. "Not everyone's animal can stand up to a grizzly, especially one on a rampage. I'm just sorry that we didn't get to finish our… um… Well, whatever it was."

"Date?"

I furrowed my brow and drifted past him. "I'm still not sure."

After setting my wineglass on the end table, I took a seat on the pink sofa. Dutch remained by the window, gazing down at the street. His pants fit him snugly, as did his shirt, but in an agreeable way. I guessed they were tailored, and I wondered how much money he spent on his wardrobe. Did he have one of those fancy walk-in closets?

Dutch strode over and gestured to the small gap beside me. "Mind if I sit?"

I scooted to the center.

He stretched his arm over the back of the sofa, fingers lightly touching my right shoulder. "Who was that man you were speaking to at the bar?"

"Tak? He knows my brother."

"For a man you're barely acquainted with, he behaved a little possessively. Do you two have something going on?"

Dutch didn't need the full story. I smiled coyly. "It's a wolf thing. We get territorial."

He winked. "Never trust an evasive woman."

I cocked my head and gave him a pointed look. "And never trust a man who doesn't make his intentions clear."

"Touché."

"Could you hand me my wine?"

He reached for the glass. "I couldn't help but notice the ostentatious display of necklaces you had in your counter were priced considerably high. Do you actually sell those, or is it a tactic to make everything else in the store look like a bargain?"

I swallowed a mouthful of heady wine. "Those are harder to sell since my art has to speak to the buyer. Each piece tells a story, each stone unique. Buying a showy piece is a personal decision and rarely has anything to do with the price tag."

When I passed him my glass, it slipped through his fingers and splashed red wine all over his shirt and pants.

Horrified, I fumbled for the stem before it rolled to the floor. "I'm so sorry! I didn't mean to do that."

Dutch stood up and slowly unbuttoned his shirt, working his way from top to bottom before stripping it off. I tried not to stare, but he had a fine physique that resided somewhere in the middle of perfection. It was as if Greek gods had carved him in their likeness, what with his golden locks and aquamarine eyes. He was so different from the men I'd known—men who were physically strong and abrasive. Dutch had clout and a sophisticated aura about him. He walked as if clouds were beneath his feet, and he spoke as if every word would be etched in stone.

"Let me try to clean that," I offered, rising to my feet.

"Don't trouble yourself. It's not worth fussing over." He wadded up the dress shirt and tossed it into a small wastebasket. "So how much do those feather earrings go for?"

I set the glass on the table and strode to the window. "For the opening, we ran them fairly cheap as a test. If I can secure a deal with the seller, I'll have a steady supply. It won't be difficult to move the merchandise. We've never sold such a buzzworthy item. As quickly as they went for a hundred dollars, I'm quite certain a price increase won't impact the demand. You can't buy those anywhere else. That might change if a bird Shifter decides to open up shop, but I have the edge with all the other merchandise we sell. Clothes, shoes, purses—Mel's even thinking about mittens for winter."

He pinched his chin. "You're a clever businesswoman. All that hype over feathers."

I swept my tresses behind my shoulders. "People pay good money for things of monetary value, but you underestimate how much they'll pay for items with a personal connection to something they care about. Customers value my gems because my dealer's tribe handpicks only the best. The feathers connect them with Shifters. Each purchase supports the Breed community. Can you say the same about your collection?"

He shook his head. "Diamonds will always sell, no matter where they came from or who distributes them."

I glanced out the window at a white truck down below. "I suppose. Dutch, you have nothing to worry about. Our customers are entirely different, so it's not like we're hurting your business."

He came up behind me. "Did I say I was worried?"

He didn't have to. Dutch implied my jewelry was not up to par with his and that he'd felt threatened by the new shop in the neighborhood. I wondered if any of his customers had asked him for directions to Moonglow. Did he want to compete by selling similar items? Why else would he have come into the shop to purchase the very earrings that were creating a buzz on the streets? It must have frustrated him to see me profiting from something that wasn't high-end enough to sell in his own store.

When I turned around, Dutch had his hands in his pockets.

"Do you forgive me for running out?" he asked, his expression guarded. "I'm not a man who needs his feelings coddled, so be honest. Let me know what I can do to make it right between us. I don't like making enemies who smile to my face."

"You have a nice smile," I observed, circling around him and collecting our glasses. "What happened back at the bar doesn't bother me. But something else does. Why did you want to purchase my earrings if they're not your style? You don't have a woman or else you wouldn't be here alone in my apartment." I set the glasses in the sink and then turned around, inching up to the edge of the island.

Dutch strolled into the kitchen, chin down but eyes up. "I admire your business tactics."

My brows arched. "Tactics? I love each and every piece I create. There's nothing tactical about that."

He placed his hands on the granite countertop. "Ah, but there is. You could have purchased feathers from any wholesale dealer, but you chose to use Shifter feathers and create letters of authenticity or something along those lines. At least, that's what one woman told me. I wanted to see for myself what came with the purchase."

"You don't provide documents with your precious stones? My intention is to share the history and origin. For many, owning something unique with a history behind it is special. It connects them to the Breed world when so many things in today's culture disconnect us. My mother made this bowl," I said, sliding the fruit bowl toward him. "It's irreplaceable and means more to me than the crystal bowl on top of the fridge."

He leaned forward and tipped his head to the side. "So who's your dealer?"

My lips eased into a grin. "Trying to steal my business?"

"Just curious who would sell you their feathers."

"Why not ask about my gemstone dealer?"

Dutch stood up and waved his hand dismissively. "Everyone knows Shikoba only deals with Natives."

"Ah. So you've tried."

He shrugged. "You have to give the people what they want. But if I can't strike a deal with the most reputable guy in his field, then it's not worth pursuing."

"You spend a lot of time pursuing perfection."

"I'm a man of refined taste."

I tucked my hair behind my ear. "Someday you'll meet a woman so flawed that all you can see is how perfect she is."

Dutch folded his arms. "Doubtful. Women see me as a means to the finer things in life."

"You can't be serious."

He arched an eyebrow. "Can't I? My looks are appealing, but not as much as my money."

I shook my head in disbelief. "If you don't think relationships can be genuine, why do you spend so much time searching for perfection?"

He dropped his arms to his sides. "If a woman stands to gain from a relationship with me, then why should I not have high standards? I'm not cold, Hope. I'm just… practical."

"What about love?"

"Love is irrelevant. One thing you should accept with your success is that you'll never know the genuine affections you call love. Companionship is a suitable compromise. Why should I give my heart away like a commodity?" The light dimmed from his eyes. "I can buy anything I want, but I can't buy love. I can't even earn it. It's the tragic fate of success. You're an ambitious woman, but be careful how well you do in this world. Everyone has ulterior motives, and everything comes at a price."

Despite the niceties, I wasn't Dutch's type. Perhaps he wondered if a woman with equal success could be a suitable match, or maybe asking me out had been a ruse to gain information. The trouble with Dutch was that I couldn't begin to guess his true intentions. I was used to being around people who were straightforward. He danced around words and always left me feeling as though I knew even less about him than what he revealed.

I worried my lip and glanced over at the folded-up paper next to the bowl. I finally gathered the courage to slide it in front of him. "Did you write this?"

His brows knitted together, and he opened the death threat. Dutch quickly shoved it away. "Do you think I would write something so crass?"

"I don't know what you're capable of. We barely know each other. So you didn't leave this outside my shop?"

He gave me an indignant look and wiped at the wine stain that had already set in his pants. "I suppose you also think I'm responsible for breaking your window? Tread carefully, Miss Church. You walk a fine line between curiosity and slander. An unfounded accusation like that could ruin my business and reputation. But I suppose you already know that. Coming here was a mistake."

Maybe it was.

As I saw Dutch to the door and handed him his jacket, I wondered if I'd just made an enemy.

Chapter 17

The next morning was the start of a glorious day. Nothing but miles of blue sky and sunshine. While Naya watched over the store, I decided to pay Asia a visit and find out which way the decision had gone with the household. More importantly, I wanted to make myself available to resolve any unanswered questions.

The wind tunneled through the open windows of my car while an old Tori Amos song played on the radio. When I drove past the spot where I'd first met Tak, I thought of him. I wondered if I should visit his motel room to see if he'd changed his mind and left town. Was he thinking about me? Did he have any desire to pursue me once he settled matters with Lakota? My mother had taught me that a woman shouldn't be too easy—that she should be the ever-elusive catch that every man dreams of, and no great catch pitches herself into the fisherman's boat.

Did I want to be caught?

And more importantly, did I want Tak to be that man? We'd only just met, and yet every time my thoughts drifted to him, I wanted to know more. Did he always braid his hair? Did he like to cook, or was he just trying to impress me? What were his hobbies? How many women had he slept with?

What did he look like in the shower?

I laughed and adjusted my visor. Tak was probably

napping in front of the television without a single thought of me crossing his mind. Once Lakota returned and they settled their dispute, Tak would be out of here. No doubt his wolf was going stir-crazy in the city.

When I reached Asia's homestead, I parked my car in the circular driveway and spied a woman off to the left, chasing a cat with a broom. It must be difficult for a bird Shifter to roam freely without worrying about predators.

Asia rounded the corner on the right side of the house, a straw hat on her head. "Hey, girl!" Her flip-flops slapped against the soles of her feet as she hurried to greet me. "I wasn't expecting you today. Why didn't you call? I would have made lunch."

I raked my fingers through my tangled hair and squinted. "I don't like talking business over the phone if I don't have to. Do you have a few minutes? I have news."

"Oh, I love news! Come inside. We have sweet tea in the fridge. I like hot tea better, but I'm the only one around here who drinks it." She led me through the house. "Go sit out back, and I'll bring it to you."

I ventured out to the back patio, where the overhead ceiling fans spun in lazy circles. The shaded concrete had wet spots that were already drying out, and water glistened on the feathery blades of a hanging fern. I took a seat at the round glass table, the cushioned chair rocking back and forth.

"Here we go," she sang. Asia set down green plastic cups and then wiped the tabletop with a kitchen towel. "So dirty. I clean this table every day, and it still gets a film of green gunk."

"Probably pollen," I said, sipping my drink. "It doesn't bother me."

"Well, it bothers *me*." The rag squeaked against the glass as she polished a dirty spot before finally sitting down. "Whew! I picked some fresh vegetables from my garden this morning, so remind me to send a bag home with you." After a gulp of tea, she tossed her floppy hat on the table and looked at me with excitement stirring in her eyes. "So? What's the big news?"

Condensation dripped down my glass and over my fingers. "Your feathers sold out the first day."

Asia gasped, her mouth agape. "Shut up!"

"We sold everything I had before noon. People were leaving their names and numbers on a waiting list for the next shipment."

She slapped her knee. "Hot diggity! And they're paying full price?"

"Don't be silly. Of course they are."

She traced her finger around her lips, eyes looking upward as if deep in thought. Her shoulder-length hair shone like moonlight over black waters. In normal conversation, I would have complimented it. But not wanting to derail the topic, I stayed focused on my goal.

"You wouldn't happen to have any extra feathers lying around, would you?" I asked hopefully.

"Some aren't good enough to sell. Sometimes they're broken, or the vane separates."

"I'll buy whatever you've got that looks clean. That might take care of those on the waiting list. I hate to pressure you, but you've had a few days to think it over, and I don't want to keep taking preorders if we're not going to do business together. It's not fair to the customers. They're excited about the jewelry, Asia. It's going to be a huge success, and you won't regret it. I need to know by tonight if we can enter a partnership, but I'm not able to draw up a contract unless you can secure the inventory with your suppliers."

"Suppliers," she pondered aloud. The ice clinked in her glass as she gulped down her tea. "These girls… I don't know about them. But I have a few good friends who are interested in selling me their feathers. Doesn't that make me a middleman? How do I know you won't go around me and deal with them directly?"

"Because, Asia, I'm not that kind of person. Sure, it would

cut you out, but that's not how I do business. Do you think they would trust a wolf? It's easier to do business with Shifters who are your own animal; there's a level of trust already established. Aside from that, my guess is you'll have many sources, and that's too much for me to manage. I can't afford to give up more time when I've already got my hands full. That's the same reason I do business with Shikoba instead of traveling the country, negotiating deals. Then I'd have to travel, review the quality, organize shipments—that's not a smart move for me."

"Ahhh. I see now. You send me that contract tonight, and I'll look it over and let you know. Sound good?"

A weight lifted off my shoulders. "There's a lot of Shifter love when people wear those earrings. I'm so glad you confirmed that the avian community wouldn't take offense. It's not the same as the illegal practice of selling pelts or claws, but you never know how people will react. We had several hawks come into the shop, and they were so proud to see people wearing them, especially when we showed them the certificate. I'll give you a copy of one so you can get an idea of how I package everything. Since we have different species contributing feathers, I include basic facts about the type of bird they came from and their traits. It also certifies that the feathers were acquired legally from Shifters, that way nobody thinks there's something malicious going on."

Asia giggled. "We always sweep them up or let the wind take care of them. I never thought anyone would want our old feathers."

I swiveled around in my chair and admired her yard. Despite the Texas heat, she managed to keep all her plants green, and the ones on the patio were overflowing from their planters and pots. Most were annuals, like the purple vincas and green coleus, but the vast majority were perennials. It made me miss having a homestead. Even though I loved living in the city, land was in the heart of every Shifter.

Asia gave me a sly grin. "So what's a nice girl like you doing without a pack?"

"Discovering myself."

She laughed blithely. "Once you find yourself, let me know. Sometimes you just have to settle. That's what I did here. There's safety in numbers. It's not safe for a girl to be out there on her own," she said, wagging her finger. "Too many people want to take advantage, and you don't have a leader to stick up for you. They have legal authority to go after anyone who messes with you. Don't get used to solitary life. You need to find yourself a nice wolf and settle down in a pack. If the business goes under, who will take care of you?"

I gulped down my tea. "You sound like my father."

She lifted her chin. "Smart man."

"Well, this is a rite of passage for wolves who want to find themselves. The modern era has changed the way we live, and most of us want to get out there and prove ourselves before settling down with a pack. It's not forever. Hopefully." I chuckled and watched a butterfly dance on a breeze. "The store is doing well now, and I don't want to jinx it by making any big life decisions."

The hinges creaked when the back door opened, and a grey-haired woman poked her head out. "Asia, I saw that damn wolf again."

Asia crossed her legs and folded her arms. "And what do you want *me* to do about it? I'm not the gatekeeper around here."

"No, but you're the one growing all the damn vegetables that're attracting the rabbits and mice, and they're attracting the cats and wolves."

"Guess you'll have to flap your wings a little faster, Marie."

The door slammed.

"She's so bossy," Asia complained.

"Do you have any hesitations about doing business with a wolf?" I asked. "Be honest."

"It's a perfectly symbiotic relationship. I learned that word today in a crossword puzzle," she added.

I stood up and finished my tea. "Maybe I should go before your roommates chase me off with a broom."

"I'll get your veggies and meet you out front." Asia rushed inside the house, leaving our glasses behind.

Using the stone pathway, I headed around the side of the house, the scent of fresh-cut grass heavy in the air. I waved my hand to break up a cloud of gnats, a soft breeze calling to my wolf. She was restless, and the desire to shift became stronger with each passing minute. I had a feeling coming out to see Asia had something to do with it. The intoxicating scent of green trees and earth called to my animal.

"Not today," I said to her under my breath. "Remember what happened last time? Naked on the side of the road. I bet you think that's funny, don't you?" I plucked a yellow petal off a sunflower and twirled it between my fingers as I neared my car. My thoughts drifted back to when I'd first met Tak by the sunflower patch. Never had I imagined he would be tethered to my memories forever.

Why was I being so coy about visiting him? My mind toiled over consequences more than my heart did. He'd shown me real passion and that sex between unmated couples didn't have to be a shameful act. The least I could do was take him out to lunch. Tak made me want to be open about my sex life, and I couldn't stop thinking about sharing the news with Melody. And why not? I'd learned my lesson about secrets and lies the first time around. Every book has a new chapter, and it was time for me to start mine.

Then again, Tak and Lakota might never mend the rift between them.

Not that it mattered. I leaned against the car and laughed quietly, wondering why I was planning my future with someone I'd only just met, a man who'd revealed his innermost secrets to me but hadn't mentioned anything about staking his claim.

I had too many things on my plate to be worrying about some silly man.

"Your veggies!" Asia cried, jogging out the door with a small paper bag. She reached me, out of breath. "Send me that contract, and we'll talk it over tonight. Don't let my vegetables go to waste."

"Oh, I won't," I promised, hefting the bag. "I'll be enjoying these for dinner."

"Alone?" She cocked her head to the side. "Not to be nosy, but I'm just curious. That's a lot of veggies for one person. Homegrown food is a natural aphrodisiac, you know. That's why I gave you extra."

I snorted. "Bye, Asia."

"I know a nice man," she said as I got in my car. "You like tigers? He's handsome but doesn't have too much going on up here." Asia tapped her finger against her temple. "I can give him your number. I bet he likes big, juicy tomatoes." She waggled her brows and cupped her breasts playfully.

"I don't need a man in my life right now."

She pinched her chin and stared at me through the open window. "I don't know. You kind of have that look I've seen before."

"Of desperation?" I laughed and started the engine.

Asia arched her brows. "No, but if you *were* dating someone, I'd say you looked like a woman in love. Bye now!"

I blinked in surprise as she jogged back to the house.

Love? Impossible. I barely knew Tak, and I'd never been in love to know the feeling.

Yet as my mind began overanalyzing everything, the answer nestled in my heart just as peacefully as the butterfly landing on my shoulder.

CHAPTER 18

Tak strode into his motel room and tossed his keys on the table. Even though it had been a couple of days since he'd last spoken to Hope, he'd taken on the role of her protector. He cared for the woman, and something innate compelled him to look after her—especially after discovering the death threat. Simply walking by her window and knowing he could be there at a moment's notice filled him with immeasurable satisfaction.

There was a decent breakfast bar that offered a bird's-eye view of Moonglow. He'd spent yesterday in there stuffing his face with bagels and watching all the foot traffic outside. Now he barely had two pennies to rub together, so he needed to put a lock on his spending before he wound up trapped in Austin with no gas to get home.

City people were always in a hurry. All they wanted to do was spend money and flaunt it. It showed in the flashy cars parked along the street. Tak was accustomed to a simpler life. People weren't glued to their phones and in search of constant entertainment. Though one thing he did like was how they didn't segregate Natives in Shifter bars like they did in his Podunk town. City people were more accepting of one another. For the most part. He still bumped into a few dickhead Vampires who wanted to start shit because of his tattoos. He didn't trust Vamps. He'd heard stories about how they were secret stealers, so he kept his eyes low and avoided them.

Shifters occupied most of Tak's neck of the woods, and they were highly territorial. A Vampire owned the closest gas station, but he kept to himself. Outside of a Mage or Relic wandering into the stores, Tak rarely interacted with other immortals. Not that he preferred it that way, but he certainly felt like a fish out of water in Austin.

For the past two days, Hope had arrived at the store early, cleaned the windows, and kept herself busy. At noon, she'd turn the sign on the door to CLOSED and disappear into a back room. Today was different. A dark-haired woman in a tight dress showed up to run the store while Hope took off in her car. When Tak followed and realized she was heading out to where they first met, he backed off. Protecting her was one thing, stalking her every move was another.

What a remarkable woman. Tak had never seen anyone more dedicated to the success of their business, and she made him think about things he hadn't pondered in a long time… like forming his own pack. Her ambition inspired him to consider taking risks of his own. He'd thought about breaking away from the tribe, but who would join his pack? No good man or woman would leave the tribe to follow him. And forming a new pack with strangers was just as uncertain. Could he trust someone he hadn't known his whole life, and would they trust a Packmaster who had shamed his family? Tak could easily keep his past a secret, but the truth always comes out. A leader who lied to his pack was not worth following. Aside from all that, would his father see his departure as betrayal to his people?

Tak pulled open the heavy drapes and glared down at the unmade bed. His cock stirred just from his thinking about Hope's soft moans and the way she'd dominated him. Tak had always been gentle with women, but during sex, he was the aggressor. Period. Feeling the heat between her legs as she sat astride him was one of the most powerful experiences of his life. Her consuming gaze, her full breasts, the tantric way she approached sex by taking her time and savoring him. It was what he needed—what his wolf needed. And more importantly, it was what Hope needed.

Tak hadn't changed the sheets in two days.

Two fucking days.

They still carried her sweet scent, and whenever he buried his face in his pillow, it reminded him of her long hair, spirited laugh, and the way she filled his embrace like no woman ever had.

And that was a hell of a realization.

Tak fell backward and hit the mattress, a loud snap sounding from beneath the box spring. He gazed up at a crack in the ceiling and experienced an overwhelming sense of solitude. He missed the comradery with his packmates—the banter and good company. A hunting partner, someone to play games with or laugh over a joke. Kids riding his shoulders. Horseback riding at dawn. Why would anyone choose to be a lone wolf, even for a short time? Lakota's job as a bounty hunter both intrigued and mystified him.

Though he missed country life, Tak could appreciate the city's allure. He'd seen his first coffee shop, and there was so much to see and do. He mostly stayed near Moonglow, the motel, and Hope's apartment, which were all located in the Breed district. He was a stranger in this territory—an alpha without packmates. People didn't trust rogues where he came from, and he suspected it was no different here.

Tak could see himself getting used to city life. Packs here had the best of both worlds—a homestead in the country and plenty of distractions in town. Everything appealed to him but the eateries. Tak grew up hunting and farming, so eating out wasn't something he ever did. He liked knowing where his food came from, which was the only reason he'd eaten the bagels at the café. Bread was a safe bet, and he had watched the man make them from scratch.

Tak squeezed his eyes shut. He hadn't brought enough

cash to afford a motel for a week, and his wolf had already chewed a knob off the dresser. None of his people dealt with bankers, so everyone who worked under Shikoba was paid in cash. Tak made a decent salary for helping his father out with the business, but the money always went back to the tribe for building materials, tools, clothes, and anything else they needed. No one cared about personal accounts since they all had a roof over their head and food to eat. Even in his current predicament, he couldn't bring himself to call his father and ask for money. Then questions would arise, like what the hell was keeping him here?

Hope was keeping him here.

She was the only woman who looked at him as if the marks on his face didn't matter. There was neither scorn nor pity in her eyes. Hope hadn't used him for pleasures of the flesh the way other women had. In her arms, he'd found salvation. In her gaze, Tak felt like an alpha again.

Hope was the first woman who'd made him forget Jenowa. Thirty years had passed since the tragedy, and every woman he'd lain with only reminded him of her absence. Time and loneliness had taught him how to be a good lover—how to worship a woman the way he might have worshipped Jenowa. And with each of them, he always asked himself the same questions. Would she have liked it that way? Would his wolf ever howl for another woman?

None of those questions lingered now.

Tak rubbed his eyes with the heels of his hands, frustrated by his foolishness. He wasn't supposed to love again. That was a vow he'd made a long time ago—one that had always been easy to keep. Tak wasn't fit to love a woman. Jen's death proved that, and he wasn't even worthy enough to say her name out loud.

Why the hell was he even debating the issue—as if he stood a chance with Hope. No woman in her right mind would look at him as a worthy mate, and here he was, fantasizing about the idea of...

Of *what* exactly?

He rubbed his chest when he felt a fire burning deep inside.

"Must be the bagels," he muttered.

Tak kicked off his shoes and stripped out of his clothes. Earlier, the motel manager had caught up with him in the parking lot and warned him that if he didn't pay for that day, he had to be out of the room by three.

Might as well enjoy a hot shower before I have to live in my truck.

Tak moseyed to the bathroom and stepped into the narrow tub. After turning the faucet, he stood beneath the stream of water and unraveled his braid. Large freestanding bathtubs were better, but city folks sure liked their showers. Curious, he looked down at the shampoo bottles that came with the room. It seemed like such a trivial thing, but he'd never used store-bought shampoo before. His tribe made almost everything: soaps, candles, furniture, toys, clothes. They were virtually self-sustainable. Their healers relied on plants like aloe and herbs for treating cuts and burns among the children. They didn't like waste, and all these plastic bottles and packaging were disrespectful to nature.

When he turned a bottle upside down, a dollop appeared in his hand. The pearl-white substance didn't seem like nearly enough for his long hair, so he shook it all out and tossed the empty bottle over the curtain rod. After rubbing the shampoo into his scalp, he held his sudsy hands in front of him. A sonorous laugh escaped.

"What *is* this shit?" He hadn't seen this much lather since the time he'd driven his truck through a car wash.

After he emptied a bottle of soap to slick up his chest and underarms, some of the shampoo slid into his eyes and burned like liquid fire.

Tak growled and squeezed his eyes shut. When water sprayed him in the face, more shampoo got in his eyes and made him back up a step. As he pulled the curtain open, his foot slipped. Tak felt the rod give way before the metal clanked against the tile.

Someone pounded on his motel room door.

"Hold on!" he snarled.

They knocked again, but it sounded more like someone kicking the door.

"Dammit." Still blind, he stepped out of the narrow stall and rubbed his eyes.

Big mistake. He'd forgotten about the soap on his hands, and now his eyeballs felt like someone had torched them with gasoline.

Cursing under his breath, he strode blindly toward the insistent banging, thumping his head on the top of the bathroom doorframe. It was lower than most, and Tak usually dipped his head when walking through doorways. The air conditioner instantly chilled his wet body.

"It's not three yet!" he yelled. What kind of bullshit was this that a man couldn't even take a shower before checking out?

He smacked into the door and then felt around for the knob. Tak was about to get uncivilized if the manager so much as uttered a single complaint about him not leaving fast enough.

He yanked open the door, eyes still squeezed shut. "I'll be out of your hair in a minute!" Tak slammed the door, turned around, and tripped over something on his way back to the bathroom. He was a big man, so when he crashed to the floor, it was like timber falling. As he lay there on his back like a twisted root, he felt the comforter within his grasp and used it to wipe his face.

Unfortunately, it didn't alleviate the searing pain in his eyes.

The knocking sounded again, only this time it was so light that it was like butterfly wings flapping against the door.

Tak lifted his head and pried open his lids just as the door opened… and Hope walked in.

CHAPTER 19

My eyes widened at the display of gratuitous nudity sprawled out on the floor before me. I'd driven straight over from Asia's house, hoping to catch Tak before he went out to the bar or someplace else.

Boy, did I ever catch him.

With the sack of veggies in my arms, I'd knocked on the door with my foot. The third time, I gave up and turned away.

"I'll be out of your hair in a minute!" Tak growled.

I turned around just as he slammed the door in my face. Confused, I shifted the sack in my hand and knocked once more before entering. Nothing could have prepared me for what I found lying on the floor.

Tak's body glistened, suds running down his chest from the ends of his hair. If I hadn't seen his penis before, I sure as heck had a grand view under the spotlight of sun pouring into the room.

"Hope?" he asked, his voice quavering as he looked at me with bloodshot eyes.

I couldn't help myself. I lost it. Completely and utterly lost it. I drew in a vocal breath that sounded like a donkey braying and laughed even harder. When Tak flipped over on his hands and knees, giving me a generous view of his backside as he crawled into the bathroom, I fell to my knees and cradled my aching stomach.

"Finally... she laughs," he grumbled from the other room.

I caught my breath when the laughter began to wane. The visual was too much, and I quickly shut the door behind me before Tak gave the world another peep show. The water ran in the bathroom for a short time, and I wiped my tearstained cheeks as I stared at the wet spot on the carpet.

After a minute or two, Tak sauntered into the room, wearing a pair of jeans. His hands deftly sectioned his wet hair before weaving it into a long braid. "First you laugh when we make love, now it's the sight of my nude body."

I stood up, a laugh still trapped in my throat. "You caught me off guard. I thought I'd find you watching TV or taking a nap. I wasn't expecting full frontal."

While tying off the end of his braid, he jerked his chin at my feet. "What's in the bag?"

"Oh," I said, having forgotten. "Someone gave me their garden vegetables. I didn't want to leave them in the hot car."

Tak smirked and peered inside the bag. "I didn't know you'd planned on staying that long in my room."

My heart did a quickstep, and I set the bag on the table. "What were you saying a moment ago about being out of my hair?"

He flicked a glance at the door. "Oh, that. I thought you were the manager. He's in a hurry to clean the room for the next guest."

I touched the ends of my hair. "Are you leaving?"

He averted his gaze. "This room is too small for me, that's all. I'm not going back on my word. I'll stay until Lakota returns."

I sensed a lie in his explanation but didn't confront him. Aside from the unmade bed, everything looked tidy. No empty water bottles, no food wrappers or other trash. His travel bag on the dresser was zipped up and ready to go.

"Where are you staying?" I asked, wondering if maybe his wolf had caused trouble.

He grabbed his shoes and sat on the bed, facing away from

me. "Someplace bigger. So who gave you all the vegetables? Was it a man?"

"Why would you ask that?"

Tak glanced over his shoulder at me but said nothing. He didn't need to. Shifters hunted for their mates, and though fresh meat was the preferred offering, some wolves took the gesture of providing food very seriously.

"It was a friend," I answered.

"You're good at dodging my questions."

I crossed the room and looked down at him. "I'm not the only one good at being evasive."

He finished lacing up his shoe and hung his head. "I don't mean to insult you with lies. I can't pay for this room anymore, so I'm going to sleep in my truck. It's only for two more days."

"No, you're not."

He looked up at me. "Yes, I am. What other options do I have? None of my people live here."

"You don't have a Breed account?"

"I live on tribal land. What use do I have for credit?"

"Did you ask your father for money? He can wire it to you."

Tak dipped his chin. Yes, I knew that look of being too proud to ask for help. My father had offered many times to pay for our store, and I'd turned him down each time. Children must leave their parents and learn what it means to struggle. Breaking away from the pack is tough, but it's the only way to earn respect. Especially for a young man of fifty.

I chewed on my lip for a moment. "Why don't we work this out later? I have the day off. Would you like to see my city?"

He shook his head. "I'm not into tourist attractions."

"There's more to Austin than that. We'll stay in the Breed district if that makes you comfortable, but I know a few places I think you'll enjoy. If your wolf needs to run, there's a private place I go sometimes."

"Hopefully not that spot by the side of the road."

I laughed and touched his shoulder. "No, that was an emergency stop."

He stood up and towered over me by almost a foot. "You came all this way to be with me?"

My blood warmed as I looked into his soulful eyes. "Is that okay?"

He brushed his thumb along my cheek. "I would be honored if you showed me your city. But I have to warn you—humans make me uncomfortable. In fact, so do Vampires, Chitahs, and—"

"You should give people the benefit of the doubt. When you spend all your time around Shifters, you make the world a smaller place. Come with me, Tak. It'll pass the time and won't cost a penny." I stood on my tiptoes and gave him a hopeful smile. "I have the day off. Please say yes."

He cupped my face in his hands. "For that smile, I'd walk through a firestorm."

His words moved down my body like silk. Tak's feather-soft kiss had me leaning in for more, my hands flattening against his broad chest. The way he tunneled his fingers through my hair and took his time made this kiss entirely different from any other. It lingered, and its lazy course didn't reduce me to a sex-starved animal. All I knew was that kiss—the familiar taste of his lips, the gentle slide of his tongue against mine, the tender way he held me, and most especially the way his heart quickened against my palms when I softly kissed the corner of his mouth as we broke apart.

He gave me an admonishing glance. "You're not thinking about paying for anything, are you?"

"Would you have a problem with a woman paying? Are you *that* old-fashioned about gender rules, or is it because it might bruise your alpha pride?"

A roguish grin appeared, and his eyes danced with amusement. "Duckie, you've got backbone. Anyone ever tell you that?"

"Not often enough."

He tossed his head back and laughed. When his eyes met with mine again, he lifted me into his arms, my feet dangling off the ground. "Show me what I've been missing all my life."

Even though I'd promised to stay in the Breed district, we drove to South Congress so he could see the vendors and eateries, and get a view of the Texas Capitol. Tak turned up his nose at the quirky antique stores and costume shops, and he definitely didn't like that someone had spray-painted the side of Home Slice Pizza and a few other buildings. I tried to explain the eccentricities of the neighborhood, but his naivety was obvious. He'd grown up in a rural Shifter community and probably didn't watch television more than he needed to, if they even owned one.

Tak enjoyed walking, but he kept his fists clenched as if ready for battle. The city must have seemed like a foreign country for a man who had spent his life on tribal land. We stopped in front of a taco bar to listen to a local band playing folk music. The way Tak's nose lifted with every scent in the air hadn't escaped my attention.

"Do you want to see the bats later?" I asked.

His brows furrowed. "Bats?"

I chuckled softly. "Maybe another time. Are you sure you don't want to eat? Nothing goes together like free music and tacos."

Tak waved his hand and continued strolling up the sidewalk. "That's not real food."

"Then what *is* real food?"

"Come with me, and I'll show you." He led me back to his truck, and after a short drive, gestured toward a farmers market.

"*This* is real food," he said, parking up front.

"If you like this, you should see the one they have downtown on Saturday."

Once inside, Tak spoke with a man regarding the price of sausages. When he pried open his wallet and glanced inside, he thanked the man and wandered over to the vegetables. While Tak was distracted, I quickly darted to the counter and asked for the meat. It became a fun game—following him around, adding everything he admired to my basket. When he headed to the bathroom, I seized the chance to make my purchase.

Several minutes later, after I'd memorized all the different cheeses, I swung my head up and saw Tak buying something at the counter. When he turned around, he handed me a giant sunflower.

I twirled it between my fingers. "You shouldn't waste your money on such things."

"Best money I've spent. Are you ready? There's nothing here for me."

I handed him the bags. "I disagree."

Tak's eyes rounded when he looked inside. My lips eased into a grin, and I strutted out the door.

He swiftly caught up and matched my pace. I liked that feeling. Alphas were physical, and their behavior spoke louder than words. He didn't put distance between us or crack a joke after I implied there might be another reason for him to stay in Austin. Instead, he walked so close to me that our arms brushed together.

It was hard to ignore how handsome he looked in his white tank top showing miles of brown skin and muscle. His carved cheekbones and strong features stood apart from other men. He had straight shoulders and a confident stride. People couldn't help but notice him.

I had a terrible feeling he might reconsider leaving after a night of sleeping in his truck, but what could I do? He'd never accept my money for a motel, and staying with me wasn't an option. If only Lakota had stayed a little longer so they could have resolved their differences.

When I glanced at a patio table at the café next door, my

heart went from a flutter to palpitations. It was like seeing a ghost, and I halted in my tracks.

There he was.

River.

The man I'd given my virginity to was eating a burrito. I hadn't seen him in years, and he looked the same, only a little rougher. Same black hair and mustache, but his frame was thinner and he didn't put much effort into shaving anymore. Physically, River looked in his forties. He wasn't handsome, but his appearance wasn't what had attracted me in the first place. While other men were ogling my breasts and backside, River had always complimented my clothes, my eyes, and said I had the most graceful walk.

He wiped his mouth on his arm and glanced over, briefly making eye contact before looking away.

I swallowed hard, no longer aware of Tak's presence.

"Hi, River," I said. When he didn't look back, I moved closer to his table. "River, it's been a long time."

He scooped up the fallen bits of food from his plate and gobbled them up. After wiping his hands on his shirt, he finished off his drink until there was nothing but ice at the bottom.

River didn't recognize me. From his hurried behavior and dirty pants, I guessed he must have been on a short work break and didn't have time to dilly-dally.

I crossed into his line of view to grab his attention. "It's me, Hope. How have you been?"

When River lifted his head and looked around me at a loud motorcycle thundering by, I realized neither his hearing nor his memory were impaired. Even though I had no feelings of love for him, rejection lanced through my heart like a spear. How could he sit there and not even say hello? I'd shared my body with this man, and he ignored me as if I were no better than a stray dog.

Tak approached River from behind, his eyes on me. "Is something wrong?"

River turned around and glared up at him. "A man's trying to enjoy his lunch in peace. Why don't you take your bitch for a walk?"

Tak's expression brimmed with uncertainty. Bitch wasn't a derogatory term in the Shifter world, but he must have sensed there was more going on here than two old friends running into each other.

"River? Why aren't you speaking to me?" I pressed.

He scratched the side of his head with quick movements and stood up. Before I knew it, he'd erased the distance between us and was staring down at me. Hard. I could feel his glare all the way into my soul, as if exposing all my secrets for the world to see. His judgment lashed at me, as did his resentment and cold indifference. Memories of the past swirled in my mind, and when he moved around me and walked off without a word, I broke out in a cold sweat.

Never had one glance made me feel so insignificant.

Tak put his hands on my shoulders. "Who was that?"

My trembling fingers touched the base of my neck. It felt like a heavy man was sitting on my chest and my ribs were about to crack. When I realized what was happening, panic set in, and that was when I lost control. Before I knew it, the world tilted off its axis. I shook my head, that feeling of doom fast approaching. The busy traffic and open sky became a crushing force I couldn't escape.

Not here, I thought. *Please, not now.*

Panic attacks would hit me without warning. They were unpredictable, and sometimes the most unexpected things set them off. Occasionally, I could stop one before it spiraled out of control, but not always. Especially around people I didn't know—people who might judge me for what they were about to witness.

"Hope?" Tak gripped my shoulder with one hand and cupped my cheek with the other. "Look at me." His tone was firm, not at all the way he usually spoke to me.

Backing up a step, I gripped the collar of my brown tunic.

The fear of dying latched on like a nightmare, and my heart raced as if there were sharp talons gripping it tightly. "I can't breathe. I need a Relic." The hair on my nape stood on end, fear lapping against my skin in icy waves. I gulped for air as my heart sped out of control.

Tak backed me up against the building and caged me in tightly until I saw nothing but his chest, shoulders, and pensive gaze. "Look at me."

"I can't," I whispered, shoving against him. "I want to go home. Something's wrong." The words moved so quickly past my lips that I wasn't sure if I was even speaking them aloud. Thinking took a back seat to reacting.

"Nothing's wrong with you," he assured me, his voice like still waters. "You're *safe*. You're healthy. You just need to get out of your head and focus on something. Smell the air, Hope. Take a deep breath and tell me what you smell. Focus."

I tucked my arms against his chest, his voice rumbling through me. Did he know that I couldn't focus on objects? That every car speeding by shook my concentration and spun me around like a top? After drawing in a deep breath, I said, "Your armpit."

He didn't laugh. "That's good. That's real good."

But it wasn't. I had a funny feeling all over, one that made my legs wobble like jelly.

"What else do you smell?"

I shook my head.

"You can do this, Hope. Wolves go by scent. What else?"

"Meat. Grilled meat. Your shampoo. Exhaust fumes."

When Tak put his arm around me, it felt as though he'd glued me to him. "Take another deep breath and try to smell something else. We're going home."

His energy kept my legs moving, but my thoughts were scattered. Tears sprang to my eyes when I remembered my father screaming at River. He'd never taken that anger out on me, but I'd always felt like I deserved it. River had lost his pack and purpose while I lived comfortably with our secret.

Before I knew it, I was leaning away, the urge to flee intensifying.

Tak had awoken my wolf, and now she wanted out.

He hoisted me off the ground and opened the passenger door.

I wanted to explain what was happening, but I was a butterfly caught in a net from which I couldn't escape.

"You're safe with me," Tak whispered in my ear, his arms encasing me. Normally someone pinning me made it worse, but not with Tak. He gently lowered me until my feet touched the ground, never taking his eyes from mine. "I'm going to let go for a second and help you inside the truck. Just don't sit on the tomatoes, or you'll be having pizza for dinner."

I let out a nervous laugh and climbed in. When he shut the door, I pressed my face against the seat and watched him collect the shopping bags from the sidewalk and put them in the back of the truck. The heat from inside the cab melted my skin, the thick air difficult to breathe in.

Tak hopped inside, a light breeze sneaking in through the open door. He brushed my hair away from my sweaty face. "Slow your breathing. Don't worry about leaving your car at the motel; I'll go back for it later. Right now, you're all that matters."

He couldn't have realized how much that meant. My attacks were terrifying and embarrassing, and yet Tak knew all the right things to say.

When he slammed his door, the fear of shifting made me reach for the handle. What if my wolf lost control and attacked him? What if he shifted in self-defense and fought her to the death?

"Stop," he said, capturing my wrist. "Stay right here with me."

"I can't. I need to go. I need to—"

Before I could finish, my skin rippled with magic and unleashed my wolf.

CHAPTER 20

TAK REALIZED THE HOPE SITUATION was quickly escalating. He couldn't be certain if anyone had seen her shift, but a teenager skateboarding down the sidewalk sure noticed the wolf thrashing about in his truck.

Tak held her by the scruff of her neck and channeled his alpha power. "Calm down, beautiful. I'm a friend, and you're safe now."

Though she snarled and fought to escape, he couldn't help but admire Hope's animal. Her dark silver coat looked like someone had sifted powdered sugar on top of her head and shoulders. Among Shifters, nothing compared to a silver wolf. Their unique sheen was unlike anything else, even in the natural world of wild wolves. Hope's front paws looked like she was wearing white slippers, and it made him smile. The Shifters in his tribe were either brown or red coated. Most of the alphas were black.

Her wolf snapped and drew blood from his forearm, but Tak didn't wrench away. That was the dumbest thing you could do with your arm in a wolf's mouth. When the blood of an alpha wetted her tongue, she let go and put her ears back.

"You're a tough girl," he remarked, rubbing her ear. "I know exactly how you feel. You want to protect your mistress because you think she's in trouble. I want to protect her too. We're both on the same side."

Had he not been an alpha, her wolf would have torn him apart by now. She looked conflicted between obeying the voice of reason and protecting herself from a danger that only existed inside Hope's head. He couldn't exactly explain a panic attack to a wolf.

He spoke in his language, saying the words used to calm a temperamental wolf. Physical force would only make the situation worse. Tak had been down this road before. He'd suffered his own nightmares and lapses of sanity. It had taken him many years to conquer his demons, to finally reach a point where he could learn to love life and find happiness again. It splintered his heart to see that despite Hope's success and hard work, her demons had latched on and never let go.

"Shhh." He stroked her ears and centered his eyes on hers. "Nice to meet you. I'm Tak, and you're a pretty girl." Tak wanted to roll his eyes at his cheesy introduction, but she didn't understand what he was saying anyway. Hope was absent in those dark irises, so this was between him and her wolf.

Tak slowly reached into the bag of vegetables and offered her a cucumber.

She groaned and swung her nose away. Tak knew that wolves were easily spooked by sights and sounds, but familiar smells often provided the distraction needed to settle them.

"Picky eater, huh? Do you want to get away from all these humans? Of course you do. They stink of cologne and city smells. I'm going to take you home, so don't chew my face off while I'm driving."

Despite her agitated state, she craned her neck and licked his mouth—an acknowledgment of his dominance.

Now that he'd defused the situation, Tak gingerly started the truck. To his relief, the engine didn't startle her, but the two jovial men walking down the sidewalk did. She launched to her feet and barked at them. Tak wasn't about to shove her onto the floor. Hope's wolf was an impressive creature who could do some serious damage if provoked.

He decided to let her bark.

Before backing out, he noticed the flower he'd given Hope lying on the sidewalk. Maybe he should have left it, but the thought about what Hope had said in the store made his heart clench. Tak hopped out of the truck, shutting the door behind him. A woman like her deserved a lot more than his foolish offering, but the flower reminded him of her.

Wild.

Beautiful.

Dark and colorful.

Perhaps city girls didn't care for perishable gifts, but Tak was a simple man who enjoyed simple things.

Maybe to a fault.

After heading out, it wasn't long before Tak turned down yet another unfamiliar street and decided he was lost. What the hell was he going to do if he couldn't find her apartment? He continued circling the area in hopes of recognizing a street name.

Hope's wolf had sniffed every crevice inside his truck and finally settled in her seat. What could have set off her panic attack? The grizzly at the bar was an obvious trigger, but there was no danger this time. Maybe it was just being out in public, or maybe it had something to do with that man. Tak bristled when he thought about their strange interaction. If they were old acquaintances, then why did he walk off without saying a word to her? Tak wanted to take a belt to the guy, but a confrontation on these busy streets would have been disastrous.

Smart alphas didn't make impulsive decisions, especially ones that would land them in hot water with the higher authority. Sometimes the hardest thing to learn is self-control.

When he spied a familiar landmark, he jerked the wheel to the left and plowed through a red light to make the turn. Cars were honking, but he coolly merged into traffic. At least Hope was smart enough to live in a Breed neighborhood. No one would look twice at a wolf entering an apartment building.

If he could find it.

She must have smelled something good, because she whimpered and kept poking her head in the back seat. He glanced at the bag filled with vegetables that Hope had brought him.

First she brings food to my motel room, and then she buys me more.

Shifters provided for the ones they loved. Surely her people were no different than his in that regard. Was it simple politeness or was there more significance behind it? In any case, it stirred all kinds of primal feelings within him. Just thinking about it made him hard.

Memories of their rapturous embrace tangled in his head but were quickly snuffed out by a brutal truth. His love was a curse, and he cared for her too deeply to bring that kind of pain into her life. She deserved a noble alpha who could provide for her.

Tak couldn't even pay his motel bill.

By some miracle, he finally located her apartment. Uncertain where to park, he pulled up to the front and drove past the signs threatening to tow vehicles until he reached a corner that seemed okay. After collecting the paper sack and her clothes, he glanced out the window and spotted a Sensor performing a sensory exchange with another man on the corner. Where he came from, that kind of transaction went on in private places—not out in the open.

The city was like heaven and hell.

Much like his life.

Tak gave Hope's wolf a long, stern look. "What are the chances you'll bolt as soon as I open that door?"

He was a decent tracker, but not in this concrete jungle. After getting out, he slammed the door and walked to the back to collect the items Hope had bought at the market. Hands full, he circled the front of the vehicle, watching her bounce back and forth excitedly.

"This should be interesting," he said, approaching the door.

Even if he had rope, he wouldn't consider it. You didn't leash a female wolf under any circumstance.

Period.

"Here we go," he muttered, opening the door.

Hope's wolf sat down and tilted her head to the side. She looked too damn sweet to be mad at, especially the way her right ear flopped forward.

"Come on, beautiful. We're home."

She sneezed, but it was a show of resistance.

Tak looked skyward, scheming up another approach. After a thoughtful pause, he pulled the sausage out of the bag and waved it in front of her nose. Because of the plastic seal, she couldn't smell a thing and stared at him as if he were crazy.

"I'm running out of ideas here." Tak held the flower to her nose. "Don't you trust me just a little?"

Her neck craned, and her nostrils flared as she sniffed the petals on the sunflower. Something must have clicked in her memories, because she dove out of the truck and trotted around him, toenails clicking on the concrete.

Sometimes animals made connections with their human counterparts from scents, emotions, and sounds. He wondered if Hope had liked the flower more than she had let on.

Since he had her keys, getting in the building wasn't a problem.

The elevator, on the other hand, spooked Hope enough for her to back up. Tak used the flower to lure her in, and she growled at the man waiting at the doors. He gave Tak a stony look and stayed behind for the next elevator.

As soon as the doors closed, Hope's wolf sniffed the floor and all the buttons. She was a curious thing with a lot of spirit. Once the lingering nervousness had dissipated, she revealed the true nature of her wolf, brave as any by the way she held his gaze. He also noticed how she'd interacted with that stranger. Her posture, the position of her tail, her vocalization—those were all indicators of where a wolf naturally ranked in a pack. Hope was nowhere near the bottom. She carried all the traits of a strong female, and no matter how inferior she might have felt in human form because of her trauma, her wolf was highly intelligent and fearless.

He snorted when she lifted her leg and pissed on the wall by the buttons. It wasn't unusual for dominant females to mark territory, though it didn't always mean they were alphas. Tak adjusted the purse on his shoulder.

As soon as the elevator doors opened, she took off. Tak jogged after her with an armload of groceries and clothes. She skidded to a stop in front of the apartment, her tail wagging excitedly.

Tak fumbled with the keys, and she practically knocked him over while he unlocked the door. Her wolf bounded inside the apartment and danced. He chuckled at the sight of it. A Shifter's animal revealed a lot about their true self. Tak surmised that Hope had her guard up around him, but her wolf revealed that she was vibrant and free-spirited.

After closing the door behind him, he let her shoes fall to the floor and left them there. Tak strolled into the kitchen and set down her purse, clothes, and all the groceries. He put the sausage in the fridge and did a quick scan of the apartment. Everything looked the same as he remembered. Except for one thing—the half-empty bottle of wine and two glasses in the sink.

Not one, but two.

His jaw clenched. When he felt her wolf licking his fingers, it drew his attention away. "Feeling better?"

She sat down and stared up at him, probably wondering what an alpha was doing in her territory.

Tak wondered the same thing. He wasn't her watchdog or packmate. As much as he wanted to stay, it wasn't right for a female to be alone with a wolf who wasn't her packmate. He knew his intentions were honorable, but as far as she was concerned, he was dangerous. Tak would rather die a thousand deaths than bring her harm. She was a queen in his eyes—a noble female who would one day rule a pack.

Doing right by Hope became a moral imperative.

While her wolf was strong and confident, Hope was the one who carried the burden of an evil that happened long before her first change—just a little girl who believed no harm would ever befall her at the hands of her own kind. How could her wolf comprehend the terror she'd survived? An attack that not only marked her face but marked her spirit.

Had they not already killed the monster, Tak would have hunted down the coward and disemboweled him.

Hope's wolf rose up on her hind legs and put her paws on the kitchen island—a polite way of asking him to leave her domain. He didn't belong here, and they both knew it.

Deciding on the best course of action, Tak kissed her wolf on the nose and then walked out the door.

I jolted awake, my heart racing as I sat up and looked around.

Home. *How did I get home?*

The light in my bedroom signaled late afternoon, so not much time had passed since... since what? Waking up from a shift was always disorienting, but the moment I recalled shifting in Tak's truck, I buried my face in my hands.

Oh, no. What have I done?

I remembered biting him, but I'd blacked out soon after and had no memory of what followed. Did he have to subdue me? Had I injured him?

Even worse, what if my wolf had cowered in his presence and fled?

I stood up and took a few deep breaths. I wasn't as shaky as usual, thanks to my wolf taking over and allowing me to rest. During the panic attacks when I hadn't shifted, I didn't feel right for the rest of the day. Weak, jittery hands, exhausted—as if I'd run a marathon. It wasn't the first time I'd lost control of my wolf in a public place, but it had always happened in the Breed district.

That was the second time Tak had seen one of my episodes, and it mortified me. I hadn't gotten a chance to explain that these weren't a common occurrence, but now he must have thought me unstable. A lump formed in my throat as I walked naked through the empty apartment, and his absence made the situation unbearable.

I went back to my bedroom and thought about the sacks of food. Had I gone too far buying him things? It never crossed my mind that it might insult him—me flaunting my money and rubbing his nose in it. I didn't mean it that way and would never intentionally do anything to make him feel inadequate.

I just wanted to do something nice. It was just a paltry sum to spend, but sometimes old-fashioned men could be funny about receiving gifts.

Unable to salvage anything useful by worrying, I decided to work on some jewelry designs. After putting on my dark blue harem pants and a crop top, I sat down at my desk, lining up turquoise stones for a new bracelet design.

What else could I do? Tak had no phone that I was aware of, and he'd already checked out of his motel. By this time, he would be back in Oklahoma, wishing he'd never met me.

Designing jewelry allowed me to forget my troubles and feel centered. The assembly required concentration and a creative eye. Some people meditated or did yoga to find inner peace; I made art.

After a spell, I had two new prototypes. The events of the day had vanished from my thoughts.

Well, except for Tak lying naked on the motel room floor, covered in suds.

I stood up and swiftly left the room, suddenly reminded of my purse, keys, bags, and…

My flower.

When I hurried into the living room, seeing that flower

on my kitchen island made everything okay. I wished I'd never told him it was silly—I loved that he bought me a flower. I just didn't like seeing him waste his money on me when he didn't have any to spend on himself.

The yellow petals had curled a little, but sunflowers were resilient. I filled a narrow vase with water and set it on the kitchen island. After I cut the stem and pulled off a few leaves, I unloaded the groceries. Keeping busy occupied my mind, which had a tendency to overanalyze every little thing, like Tak bailing on me without a word. Perhaps it was unreasonable to expect any man to take on all my emotional baggage.

Nothing cured self-doubt like food, so I fired up a skillet and grabbed the sausage from the fridge. After prepping the green bell peppers, I chopped up the onions and threw them into the skillet. While the onions sautéed, I diced the fresh tomatoes on a chopping board and then pulled out the oregano and other seasonings. Since we had leftover brown rice, I got a little creative with the filling.

Before long, a heavenly aroma filled the apartment. Yet all it did was make me miss my brother sneaking bites of food and Mel singing off-key while setting the table. Food brought wolves together, and lately all these solitary meals were getting to me.

A glint of light caught on the suncatcher, sprinkling colors across the cabinets and floor. Taking the skillet off the burner, I spun around when a peculiar noise snagged my attention. It could have been a neighbor walking by, but it sounded like someone tapping on the door.

Curious, I tiptoed into the living room and peered through the peephole at an empty hallway.

I must be going crazy.

The moment I turned away, the scratching started again.

"Hello?" I called out.

Maybe someone was hurt.

When I reached for the door, I noticed both locks were vertical, meaning Tak had left me alone with the doors unlocked. Anyone could have wandered in! What kind of man would do such a thing? Why didn't he use my keys and leave them with the leasing office? Once again, I'd placed my trust in the wrong man.

Incensed, I opened the door with a hard yank.

I gasped when a massive wolf tackled me, knocking me flat on my back. Tak cleaned my face and neck with his tongue.

"Stop," I said, a giggle rising in my throat. "Stop it, boy. That tickles!"

Was Tak awake in there, or was I alone with his wolf? I looked deep in his eyes, searching for a flicker of the man, but saw none. Bonding with another Shifter's wolf was an honor, because you didn't automatically win over the loyalty of both.

I wrapped my arms around his neck and kissed his furry face. "I missed you," I whispered. "I'm so glad you stayed."

He plopped down next to me, the grey side of his face up. I stroked his beautiful coat, his muscles rippling beneath the surface whenever he moved. Why did he make me feel so at ease—so trusting? I'd rarely felt this safe around another wolf, especially an impressive creature such as this. Tak's animal could kill me with one bite to the neck, yet I drew courage from him as I traced my finger along one of his canines.

And he actually smiled at me.

I laughed and scratched his ear. "You are every bit like Tak. Did you know that? Have you been out there this whole time guarding me? Poor guy."

When I sat up, he sat up with me. His nose twitched, reminding me of dinner.

I sprang to my feet and locked the door before racing into the kitchen to check on my onions. As I scooped them into a bowl, I noticed fur on my fingers. "You wouldn't like this," I called, washing my hands. "It's too spicy."

When I turned around to grab a dishtowel, I jumped with fright. Tak the man was standing on the other side of the kitchen island.

"I like spicy," he said, giving me a wolfish grin.

The height of the island barely covered his black patch of hair down below. I swatted my towel at him. "I just wiped down this counter."

He raised his hands and stepped back. "How long have I been inside?"

"Just a minute or two. You chose to stay?"

Tak furrowed his brow. "What other choice was there?"

My heart melted. His wolf hadn't made the decision to stay—it was Tak. "How long were you in the hall?"

"Long enough to have frightened the pizza man from getting off the elevator. I took a nap after that. What smells so good?" he asked, rubbing his stomach.

I tucked my hair behind my ears. "Nothing fancy. Just some stuffed peppers. I was going to make pinto beans and cornbread, but I couldn't let all this fresh food go to waste. Do you want me to make you one?"

An inscrutable look brimmed in his dark eyes. "You would do that for me?"

"It's no trouble."

He rounded the cabinet and drew close enough that our bodies touched. "It's not a matter of trouble," he said, his voice rough and sexy. "You're asking if you can feed me, Hope. You must know what that does to my wolf."

I knew. A Packmaster accepting food from a stranger was a show of trust. But between an unmated couple—especially when they had already been intimate—there were layers of complexities.

I wanted to look down to avoid his gaze, but Tak was naked and slightly aroused. Instead, I swung my attention toward the window and summoned the courage to apologize. "If I offended you at the market, I'm sorry. I didn't mean to imply you couldn't afford those things."

He put his hand over my lips. "Best gift ever."

"Do you mean it?"

An earnest smile touched his lips. "Not everything I say is a joke."

"Are your clothes in the hall?"

He nodded, hand cupping my shoulder.

"I'll wash them. Go in my room, and you'll find the clothes you lent me the day we met. They're clean and folded up on the closet floor."

He leaned down, his lips brushing against the shell of my ear. "Do they still smell like you?"

I shivered as he slowly turned away and strode off to my bedroom. Tak was a giant, and whenever he entered or left a room, he would dip his head to avoid thumping it on the doorframe. Barefoot, he could easily clear it, but not if he were in his boots.

It was hard not to admire that man's body, but I resisted following him and rinsed off a few more vegetables from Asia's garden while he got dressed.

By the time I finished stuffing four more peppers, Tak returned in jeans and a black T-shirt. He still hadn't tidied his hair in a braid, and it made me feel as though I was seeing a side of him that he didn't show to anyone else.

"I don't want to upset you," he began. "Can I ask you something?"

"Sure."

"Who was that man?"

I stared at the digital screen on the oven, waiting for it to preheat. "That was him. My old packmate."

Tak grew so quiet that it felt as if the air had chilled.

"I feel silly about how I reacted."

"You have nothing to be ashamed of."

My cheeks heated, and it wasn't from the oven. "I let my emotions get the best of me. He's moved on, and I haven't. I should have just kept walking."

I felt myself rambling and fidgeted with a spoon.

"He owes you an apology."

"It's not as if I was a child when it happened. We were two adults who made a mistake."

"Yet you're the only one who carries the burden of guilt.

Do you think there's an age limit on violating someone's trust? Shame and secrecy are the tools of a manipulator. You and I come from different worlds, but the basic law of wolves is the same." Tak brushed my hair away from my shoulder. "I don't wish to make you upset by this conversation, but I want to make sure that you're okay. Are you okay?"

I nodded. "I'm okay."

He pressed a kiss to the top of my head and then gave me some room. "You said someone grew these in their garden?" he asked, his voice more chipper.

"Yes. The woman who sells me feathers loves gardening. She gave me much more than I needed."

"That's the kind of Shifter I'd value in my pack," he said offhandedly.

I quirked a brow and looked at him over my shoulder. "Shall I introduce you two? She's got a sparkling personality and sense of humor… just like you."

"I'll pass. One of me is enough."

"How many of these do you think you can eat?"

He came up behind me and rested his chin on my shoulder. "More than that. How many peppers do you have?"

"Someone has a hearty appetite."

His kiss branded my neck. "Not yet," he replied, mischief in his voice. "Besides, I haven't eaten anything but bagels for the past two days."

I whirled around, horrified that he might be telling the truth.

When he saw the worry in my eyes, he backed up and sat down. "Finish what you're doing," he urged. "There's plenty of time for talk."

I filled an entire baking dish and put it in the oven. After setting the timer, I turned around and folded my arms. "Should I make something else? This won't be enough."

"It'll be plenty."

Unconvinced, I shook my head. "I can cook better meals

than this. It was just the easiest thing to make with our leftovers."

He drew in a deep breath and moaned as he let it out. "Something tells me you could make a tire taste delicious."

I turned away and washed my hands, suds swirling down the sink drain. Why did he make me so nervous? We'd been intimate, and yet Tak had the strangest effect on me. Just knowing he hadn't ditched me but instead spent hours guarding my door had me looking at him differently. He wasn't just sticking around because it was the right thing to do. I'd given him a million reasons to leave, and not once had he left my side.

"Are you this timid around my wolf?" he asked.

After drying my hands, I sat down next to him and crossed my legs. "No. Your wolf's not exactly easy to ignore. He has no qualms about showing his affection."

"What's your craving?"

"You mean after I shift? Oh, it's nothing."

He arched an eyebrow. "We don't ignore cravings in my tribe. It angers the spirits."

I snorted. "You're just saying that to get me to talk."

"Is it something we're about to eat?"

I shook my head.

Tak rubbed his chin and leveled me with his eyes. "I'm not eating your meal until I know what your craving is."

"And what's yours?"

He grinned. "Eggs."

My shoulders sagged. "So that explains the omelets. Would you rather I make one of those instead?"

"It's not about me right now."

He tilted his head to the side. "Tell me what you're craving. Or did you already eat it before letting me in?"

I could have lied, but it wasn't worth the argument. "Bologna."

Most people found that hilarious, but instead of laughing, he got up and opened the fridge.

"Tak, no. It's going to ruin my dinner. And besides, I came out of my shift hours ago. You're the one who should be feeding your wolf's craving."

He turned around, a floppy piece of bologna wiggling between his pinched fingers. His grin was so contagious that I covered my smile and turned away.

"Stop it."

He shut the fridge door and sat down, still wiggling the pale meat. "Take a bite."

"No."

"There's plenty of time before dinner. You know you want it. You have two unopened packages in there."

"I don't want it."

Tak held it with both hands and took a bite, leaving teeth marks around the missing chunk. "Mmm. Processed meat." He grinned, hoping to tempt me, but those pearly whites did little to mask his dislike for bologna.

When he took a second nibble, I had a compulsive urge to snatch it out of his hand like a ravenous wolf and gobble up every scrap. Sometimes the cravings were manageable. Other times, they consumed my thoughts until my hunger was sated.

Hours had passed since my shift. It wasn't as if I *needed* it.

Tak leaned in and tenderly kissed my lips, leaving behind the subtle taste of bologna. Unable to resist any longer, I gave him puppy dog eyes. He chuckled softly and folded the meat before holding it in front of my lips. After a few bites, the only thing left was the juice on his thumb, which I eagerly sucked.

Tak suddenly looked hungry himself, but not for food. He sat back in his chair and took a deep, shaky breath. "So, who came over last night?"

I blinked at the sudden change in topic. "What do you mean?"

He jerked his head toward the sink. "Two empty wineglasses."

"Oh. Dutch came over for a short visit. He wanted to apologize for leaving me at the bar."

"Is that all that happened?"

"I confronted him about the note."

Tak leaned forward. "And?"

"He denied it. I think. Well, he said it was crass. Our conversation left me with a funny feeling. Maybe this isn't something you want to hear, but Dutch led me to believe that he liked me. Now I'm not sure if he was just pretending so he could gather information about my sales. You know that old saying about keeping your enemies close. He's not exactly an equal competitor in terms of the merchandise we sell, but I think he feels threatened that he's not the only jeweler on the block. He seemed a little surprised that I'm also selling high-priced items."

"Maybe you should keep your distance."

"There's something I haven't told you."

Tak's expression hardened, and it made me so nervous that I stood up and went to chop a cucumber.

"When you found me on the side of the road that day, someone had stolen my clothes."

"I know. You mentioned it," he said.

"Yes, but I didn't mention that someone returned them to my doorstep."

Tak appeared at my side and took the knife from my hand. "They *what*?"

"Remember when we left the apartment so I could take you to the motel? The clothes at my doorstep were them. I was in a hurry and had too much on my mind, so I just put them inside and didn't think about it again."

Tak leaned against the counter. "I don't know your customs here or how dry-cleaning works. I should have asked."

"Maybe the person knew me and felt guilty about playing a joke. Do you think I'm paranoid?"

"No, I don't." He reached behind his head and braided his hair as if he were going into battle. "Someone knows you're alone. They're trying to intimidate you. They wouldn't have risked sneaking into your building if your brother and friend were here."

"I know. The bowling ball, the note—all signs point to Dutch, but the clothes don't seem like something he'd do."

"Never underestimate how low a man will stoop to get what he wants."

I turned away and closed the blinds. "And what is it that *you* want?"

"Stuffed peppers. Mind if I have some water?"

"Help yourself."

I usually offered visitors beer or wine, so I had to remind myself that Tak didn't indulge in those vices. I never thought I'd find such a trait so admirable. None of his actions or words were swayed by the influence of a mood-altering substance. His thoughts were pure, and his courage and desires were all his own.

I drifted into the living room and sat on the grey sofa, which faced the wall.

Tak sat down to my left and offered me the bottle. "There was only one."

"No, thanks. I'm not thirsty. Besides, I prefer tea."

He stretched his arm behind me and admired the painting. "You haven't asked, but my guess is you're wondering how your wolf and I got along. Just to allay your concerns—she's not a submissive animal, but she respects the unspoken rules. We came to an understanding."

I grimaced. "But she bit you."

He chuckled and set the water bottle in the crevice beside him. "Your wolf's a fierce protector. A little nip on the arm, but that's to be expected."

Tak's braid had unraveled at the end since he didn't have anything tying it. Part of me wanted to weave my fingers through the twisted locks of hair and let it free, but I ignored the foolish impulse.

He smiled with his eyes and stroked his finger along my cheek and down to my Cupid's bow. "You have pretty lips. You must have gotten those from your mother, but what worries me is that line between your eyebrows."

"What line?" I asked, pretending I didn't know.

He pressed his finger against my forehead. "That one. It makes me intimidated to meet your father."

My heart skipped a beat. "Why would you say something like that?"

"Because if you haven't already noticed, Duckie, I'm falling for you. And I think you might feel something for me too. I see it in your eyes, but maybe I need to hear it from those beautiful lips before I make clear my intent to court you."

My heart flutter was turning into a coronary. "Court me? You can't court me. You and my brother are enemies."

"Lakota has nothing to do with how I feel about you. I want to win your love, and if that means gaining your brother's respect, then that's what I'll do, even if we never resolve what's between us." Tak shifted in his seat to face me and drew closer. "Could you ever love someone like me? Or is Dutch the kind of man you want? I bet he wears white turtleneck sweaters in winter."

As I sat there staring into Tak's chocolaty eyes, I finally saw the light. I used to see my father as a pillar of strength, and I believed that I needed a stoic and formidable man like him to balance out my free spirit. But after meeting Tak, I realized how much like my father I really was. What I needed was a man who could make me laugh, who would protect me with his life—someone who was easy to be with and didn't want to control or fix me. I needed a man to scoop me up in his arms and tell me what he wanted, and that was exactly the kind of man Tak was. Who else would have been so tender and patient with me during a panic attack? Even as an alpha, Tak always put my needs first.

How was it possible to have such a strong emotional connection to someone I'd only just met? No matter how much I wanted to reason it away, the feeling couldn't be ignored. If this was his invitation to courtship, I couldn't take this discussion lightly.

"What can you offer me?" I asked.

Tak stroked my shoulder. "A man like Dutch has money, but can he make you laugh so hard that your soul shines? He probably has a big home, but can he shelter you with his love? His eyes are as blue as the sky, but can he see inside your heart and know your desires? The reason I didn't attack that grizzly is because the only thing that mattered was protecting you. I didn't berate you this afternoon or let you run off, because you needed someone by your side to make you feel safe. I don't know you, Hope Church. I don't know your cherished memories or your favorite pair of shoes, but I know your spirit wolf just as certain as I know my own." His hand slid down and held mine, and I saw something in his eyes I didn't like—doubt. "I'm a fractured man who can only bring you shame for what I've done in my past, and I don't deserve to ask for your heart. But I can't walk away without knowing if you love me. If you think me unworthy, we'll part ways with good memories between us. I just need to know if you love me. Even a little." His downcast eyes shielded the depths of his sorrow. "Maybe that will be enough for me to live the rest of my life alone."

My lip quivered at his brave confession. The two sides of Tak's face didn't represent good and evil as he believed. They were guilt and hope. He wanted to declare love without fighting for it. He wanted me to remind him of what it felt like to be loved, but he still battled with the part of himself that believed he didn't deserve happiness.

"Tak, why do you think you're so undeserving? Charitable love is beneath you. That's not the way I want to love a man, and that's not the way I want a man to accept my love." I stroked his cheek, my fingers running along the dark patterns of ink. "Ask me the question when your heart is whole again, and I'll give you my answer."

It hurt to deny him, but had I said yes, he would have

always regretted the way he offered me his love. If we were meant to be, rejection wouldn't deter him but only make him more determined. For Shifters, half the battle was the chase. Besides, he needed time to consider his options. I wasn't the princess he held me up to be. I was a woman with a checkered past, and he was a man who would never rise to leadership within his tribe.

We were two wrongs, and I wasn't so sure if together we could make it right. Tak needed to be all in, and so did I. We weren't there yet, and I wasn't sure what had to change to make that happen.

"Do you accept my offer?" I asked, unable to read his expression.

When the buzzer went off in the kitchen, Tak howled with laughter. With a wide smile, he rose to his feet. "The fates mock us. Perhaps I should listen to them and accept your peppers first."

Chapter 21

"You are such a cheater!" I cried.

Tak couldn't hide his impish grin, nor did he try. "How can I cheat at dice?"

"That's your third Yahtzee."

"The spirits of my ancestors are watching over me." He penciled in his score. "I like this game. Ours are competitive and not left to chance."

"This is competitive," I argued.

"Yes, but no one loses a finger rolling dice like they do on an axe blade. Is this what people like to play in the city?"

"I don't know what other people do, but we like to have game night. I prefer word games, but I wanted to give you a fair chance, so I picked this one."

I leaned against the couch, my left arm on the cushion. After dinner, we'd moved the coffee table and made ourselves comfortable on the floor with pillows. Tak wanted to stretch out after eating six stuffed peppers. Hours of conversation later, I'd challenged him to a game.

Tak draped his arm across his knee. "Oh, really? Does my vernacular lead you to believe that I'm illiterate?"

"I assumed you only spoke in your native tongue most of the time," I confessed. "Since you live with your tribe, and they're all your people, there's no reason to speak English."

Tak said something in his language that made my toes

curl. He sipped his ice tea and then set the glass down. "My father is adamant about giving his people a solid education. After we teach our children about our own culture and history, they learn about the world. Many of us are multilingual. I'm also fluent in French."

"But why?"

Tak threaded his hair away from his face. "Those who collect gemstones and negotiate with traders have to travel. We interact with many different cultures. My people are fluent in not only the languages of the Breed tribes but also that of the human ones."

"And when do you use French?"

He lowered his eyes to the dice on the floor, which were showing all sixes. "Long ago, my father prepared me for negotiating with traders in Canada. But then I tattooed my face."

Tak didn't finish, nor did he need to explain. A two-faced Shifter wouldn't instill confidence between business partners. He might appear dodgy, especially as the son of the Iwa tribe's great leader. This way, Tak didn't have to deal with outsiders constantly barraging him with questions about his tattoo. He had marked himself for his tribe, but he wasn't obligated to share his story with outsiders. Even without them knowing the meaning behind the tattoo, I noticed the way people on the street looked at him. The cold stares from Shifters who whispered to one another as they passed by. In our territory, alphas commonly inked themselves with memorable tattoos. But on their faces? It raised too many questions.

"I like your face," I blurted out. "And I think you should go to Paris."

Tak howled with laughter and fell onto his back.

"Why are you laughing? I'm serious!"

He wiped his tears away with the heel of his hand. "What would I do with myself in Paris? I can't even navigate through our cities." After a minute, he sat up and collected the dice, dropping them into the cup one at a time. "Is that what you want to do with your life? Save up enough money to travel to distant lands?"

"Not really. Unfamiliar places make me skittish."

"So that's why you didn't go with Lakota and Melody?"

I turned so my back was against the couch. "I've been to Cognito before. I don't understand that city, and I'd never walk in it alone without Lakota by my side. But that's not the reason I didn't go. Someone had to stay and manage the store."

Tak scooted over and sat beside me, his arm around my shoulders. "I saw another woman working in your store today. Couldn't you have hired her for the week?"

"No way! Naya is a busy woman with a full-time job and family. Plus I can't close the store for that long. We're new, and it's important to keep the momentum going. That'll change someday."

"You're smart. You could have figured something out. Isn't family more important?"

I drew my knees up and flicked a small piece of lint off the blue fabric of my pants. "Are you trying to make me feel guilty, or do you just want to get rid of me?"

The warm touch of his fingers on my shoulder made me shiver. "I'm just trying to figure you out."

"Lakota's adoptive parents live up north. I don't know if he told you about that part of his life, but they're not Shifters. This trip was important to them because it's the first time he's presenting Melody as his mate. I've gone up there many times over the years, so it wasn't essential that I be there for this occasion. They really wanted all the parents to come together and celebrate."

Tak looked down. "So Lakota is not your brother?"

"He's my half brother. We have the same mother, but another couple raised him. It's a long story, and it's his to tell."

"Ah. That explains a lot."

"Please don't mention it unless he brings it up. His family history is that of a delicate nature, and—"

"I know about such things," Tak said, giving my shoulder a light squeeze. "You have no other siblings?"

"Lakota's all I have. I'm sure my parents have tried, but since I'm their firstborn, they'll probably never have an alpha. That's not to say it could never happen, but the odds diminish with each child. Maybe that's why they don't talk about it, and it's really not my business to ask. Sometimes you have to accept what the fates give you."

"And what they don't give you." He held my hand.

That one gesture made my heart squeeze tight. A flutter tickled my belly—the kind I usually got before getting on a roller coaster ride. Tak's rough hands revealed that he wasn't afraid of a hard day's work. His dark skin glowed, carrying the light of the summer sun and a scent that was both foreign and familiar.

"What about you?" I asked. "Tell me about your family."

He let go and sat back. "I have five sisters—all mated. No blood brothers. I was my father's only hope to lead the tribe, but that responsibility will go to one of my cousins."

"And your mother?"

He drew in a deep breath and held it for a moment before letting it go. "She died in childbirth. Pregnancy is a vulnerable time since the women don't shift. My little sister almost didn't make it. They had to cut her out. It was a painful decision for my father. Save his mate or save the child. In the end, I think my mother let go of this world so that she could give her baby life."

I shook my head. "I'm so sorry. That must have been incredibly difficult for you all."

"She was a good woman. Kind, always laughing, always in a good mood. She listened. We could talk to her about anything. The house was quiet when her spirit left."

Melody had told me all about Shikoba's serious demeanor. Tak must have favored his mother's personality. I wondered if her absence had wounded him just as much as losing the woman he loved. He had no mother to guide him through his pain and give him unconditional support.

I glanced at my phone.

"Expecting a call?" he asked. "That's the tenth time you've looked at it."

"Asia is supposed to call about our arrangement. I don't have a backup plan, and not many people in the avian community trust wolves enough to do business with them. If she doesn't sign, my feather earrings will just have to be a limited edition. I had a friend draw up a short-term and a long-term contract for her to review. She promised me an answer tonight."

"Give her until tomorrow. She might have asked someone to look over the paperwork. It's better to give a person a full night to review everything. Otherwise they'll feel pressured and back out. My father doesn't handle negotiations lightly and reads all the fine print. If someone tries to rush him, he'll rip up the paperwork and send it back in pieces."

"You're probably right. I hate to be pushy, but we have back orders to fill. When we ran out, I made the mistake of creating a list and promising customers they'd get the next batch. I shouldn't have done that, and now I'm worried I'll lose their respect if we can't deliver."

He squeezed my hand. "My father will hear about the woman he does business with. He'll find your integrity impressive—something he respects far more than success. If this woman backs away from the contract, I'm sure my father will know someone who can help."

While holding his hand, it struck me how thoughtless I'd been. "Stay here. I'll be right back."

I padded down the hall to the bathroom and gathered fresh sheets from the linen closet. When I returned to the living room, Tak was standing in front of the dark windows, looking out. His fervent gaze consumed me through the reflection in the glass as I approached.

"You can help yourself to anything in the kitchen. No

sleeping naked on the pink couch, and try not to drool on the upholstery. Mel wasn't able to find another just like the pink one, so we had to get the grey couch as a companion. I don't have a spare pillow, but you can use the small ones on the sofa."

"Are you asking me to stay the night?"

Tension crackled in the air like wood burning in a hearth. I set the linens on the sofa and felt the heat of his gaze still on me. "If the alternative is you sleeping in your truck, then yes, I'm asking you to stay the night."

"Lakota wouldn't like this."

I squatted and collected the game pieces. "He looks out for me, and that's why he wouldn't approve. But if he were in my shoes, he'd do the same. I don't plan to disrespect him by having sex under our roof."

"You assume I would expect intercourse to be included in your hospitality?"

I set the game box on the grey sofa and stood up. "I can't read minds, so I don't know what you expect from this. All I can give you tonight is a couch."

Tak swaggered toward me and placed his hands on my shoulders. "That's up for debate. You've already given me good company, laughter, and more stuffed peppers than a man could dream of."

I smiled, enjoying the weight of his hands on my shoulders. "They weren't anything special."

He tilted my chin up. "You could have made a cheese sandwich, and I would have savored every bite."

"How about a bologna sandwich instead?"

His eyes twinkled. "Let's not push it. So, no man parts on the couch, no drooling… Any other rules I should know about?"

"No shifting. You've met my wolf, and I've met yours, but our wolves are strangers to each other. Without someone I trust supervising, I don't feel comfortable."

His brows furrowed. "If we're sleeping in separate rooms, why does it matter?"

I shrugged. "Sometimes I shift in the middle of the night in my sleep, so I keep my door cracked. If I don't, my wolf howls until it wakes everyone up. Lakota and Mel are used to it, but I don't want to chance an encounter."

He stroked my cheek with the pad of his thumb. "My wolf would never harm yours. I feel it. I know it."

Part of me wanted to invite him into my bed—to make love and hold each other until dawn—but it would go against the way my pack raised me. I'd made a mistake once before, and even though Lakota, Mel, and I weren't packmates, it was crucial that our wolves trusted one another. Maybe it wasn't a big deal with other Shifter types, but wolves followed rules within a house. Lakota couldn't dictate who courted me, but until he resolved his dispute with Tak, he had every right to forbid intimate relations under our roof. Tak had saved my life, so the couch was a fair compromise.

"Do you trust me to be alone with you?" he asked. "Don't be hospitable if you have a shred of doubt. I can sleep in the outside hall. If that's not far enough, I'll leave."

"I trust you, Tak. If I had a lick of sense, I wouldn't."

He closed his fist over his heart and inclined his head. "I won't betray that trust. You have my word, and my word is my bond."

I placed my hand over his and believed his solemn vow. For the past few hours, Tak had made me forget all my troubles. Not once since dinner had he asked me about River. Nor had he brought up my business or all the happenings of the week. He'd told me stories about living with the tribe, and I realized our experiences weren't so different. I liked imagining him in rolled-up trousers, wading through a stream to sit on his favorite rock and cast his fishing line. I could almost see his packmates gathered near target boards to throw axes and shoot arrows. His tribe was more off the grid than most packs I knew, but we didn't come from completely different worlds.

I traced my finger over his Adam's apple. "I have to leave early for work. You're welcome to stay as long as you want, but if you have somewhere to go, you'll need to wake up early so I can lock the door behind us. There isn't a spare key, and it wouldn't be right to give you mine. If you want to come back here instead of waiting all day for me to get off work, I can drop you off here at lunch. But you'll need to come by the store around eleven." I glanced around the room. "Why don't you just sleep in? There's plenty of food, and we have books to keep you entertained."

"I don't think I can sit on this pink couch for twelve hours."

I inched closer and looked up at him. "Austin is a big city, but alphas don't go unnoticed around here. Howlers is a good place to go if you want to make connections with the local packs. You've already met Wheeler, and it'll pass the time. I probably shouldn't recommend a bar, but roaming the streets isn't really a good idea if people don't know what you're up to. The games are free, and not everyone goes there to drink. It'll give you a chance to get to know some of the local packs. Promise me you won't sit in your truck all day and watch my store."

His lips twitched. "Who says I would watch your store?"

I tickled the stubble beneath his chin. "Don't think I haven't noticed your wolf outside my shop every night."

"You needn't worry," he said, wrapping his arms around me. "I'll find something to keep myself busy."

"Can you say something to me in French?"

Tak looked deep into my eyes. "*Mon coeur ne bat que pour toi.*"

"What does that mean?"

"It means you're terrible at Yahtzee."

"Well, I guess this is good night."

He planted a soft kiss on my mouth. "I'll see you in my dreams."

Chapter 22

Early the next morning, I strode into the kitchen and fried up some bacon and eggs. I'd almost forgotten about my overnight visitor until I glanced at the sunflower in the vase and noticed him across the room. The sun had just pierced the rooftops across the street, its gilded rays slicing through windows like blades forged from fire.

Tak's unbraided hair draped over the armrest, a gold sheet covering the sofa beneath him. He looked like a work of art—a statue dipped in bronze with light playing off the canvas of muscle.

I scooped extra eggs onto his plate along with a thick slice of tomato and the best pieces of bacon. Tak was a large man, and I had my doubts that this was going to be enough to satisfy him. After eating the remaining piece of bacon and a few bites of scrambled egg, I shuffled across the living room to wake him up. When I circled the grey couch, I almost dropped the plate.

What I'd failed to notice from across the room was his enormous erection hiding beneath the top sheet, which covered him to the waist. And it twitched as if it knew I was standing there looking at it.

I dragged my gaze up the length of his body, admiring his handsome physique. Despite his mane, Tak didn't have a lot of body hair. Even his whiskers didn't grow half as fast as Lakota's did.

His nostrils flared when the aroma of bacon and eggs wafted around him. Tak slowly opened his eyes, moaning and stretching like a gentle giant rousing from a thousand-year slumber.

"Morning," he said, peering up, his voice deeper than usual.

I liked the sound of it much more than his daytime voice. "Are you hungry?"

He gave me a wolfish grin and didn't answer.

"I made you eggs. I wasn't sure if you eat them with ketchup or hot sauce, so they're just plain. The bacon isn't crispy. Lakota buys the thick kind that's chewy, but Mel—"

I gasped when Tak wedged his hand between my legs. His fingers played with the fabric of my sleep shorts before traveling up to my panties. My mind whirled, and he stroked me as if he were petting a tame animal.

When I stepped back, he sat up and stripped me bare with one hot look.

"Why did you do that?" I asked on a quick exhale.

He slowly licked his lips and took the plate from my hands. "My wolf wanted to sate your hunger."

I lowered my gaze. "I'm not the one who's hungry."

Tak's eyes hooded. "That's up for debate. I can scent your arousal." He didn't bother using the fork to eat his eggs, and he licked each finger of the same hand he'd used to stroke me. "Satisfying you is my only craving, but the eggs are good."

I swallowed hard; the corner of the sheet barely covered him. "I have to take a shower and get ready. There's juice on the counter, and if you're still hungry, you can help yourself to what's in the kitchen. Just don't eat Mel's peppermints; she hides them in one of the canisters."

Tak cleaned his plate and spoke around the last mouthful of bacon. "We have to pick up your car."

I gave an exasperated sigh. It had totally slipped my mind

that Tak had driven me home. "That's right. I forgot it's at the motel. Maybe I'll just take Mel's scooter."

He glanced over at the scooter parked near the front door and shook his head. "I never imagined Melody living like this."

"What do you mean?"

"She's a warrior. I didn't peg her for a woman who liked loud furniture and tiny pillows."

I collected his empty plate. "Did you think she would mount her bow on the wall next to the pelts of her victims?"

He leaned back and rested his arms on the back of the couch, his erection still in full force. "I'm not sure what I expected from a girl with purple hair and crazy pants. I didn't take her seriously when we first met. She impressed me."

"Is that the kind of woman you want? A warrior?"

He dragged his gaze down my body and back up. "Some women are warriors of the mind, some of the heart, some of the body, and others in bed."

Had Tak witnessed Mel's bravery during her stay with his tribe? Despite her eccentric appearance, Melody embodied a tenacious spirit and unflappable personality that any red-blooded alpha would be proud to have at his side. If those were qualities Tak sought in a woman, where did that leave me?

Tak reached for my free hand. "Did I offend you? Sometimes I stick my foot in my mouth without even knowing."

I tried to pull away, but he held on tightly. "I'm usually quiet in the morning. That's all."

He kissed my knuckles and stood up, the sheet falling away. "I liked having you in the next room."

"Did you sleep well?"

"Sirens woke me up. How do you sleep with all the noise outside?"

"It was hard at first, after living in the country for so long, but you get used to it. We also keep a box of earplugs, but mostly those are for me." As soon as the words left my mouth,

I felt my cheeks flush. I'd once lived in a large pack with plenty of space to give two Shifters privacy during their lovemaking. But around here, I had nowhere to go at three in the morning. I could hear all kinds of curious things from all the way in the kitchen. With anyone else, I wouldn't have minded as much, but I drew the line with family.

Tak gazed at me for what seemed like hours and then collected the plate from my hand. "I'll clean the dishes while you get ready." He leaned down to whisper in my ear, "Let me know if you need any help in there."

A giggle escaped, and I stepped back. "After the condition I found you in on the motel floor yesterday, I might be safer showering alone."

He playfully slapped my ass and strode into the kitchen.

I smiled wistfully. Tak filled a room with his presence and personality. The thought of not having him around made my world emptier than it was before.

Chapter 23

Ten hours into my workday, I was ready to call Melody and beg her to come home. Without backup, I had no time to take a break. I rang up purchases, watched for shoplifters, answered questions, cleaned, processed returns, and answered the phone. I also had to deal with fun moments like my cash register jamming and the little boy who threw up blue ice cream all over the floor.

"Are you sure you don't have this in a size medium?" a woman asked. She sounded like an aristocratic Georgian straight out of *Gone with the Wind*. Her blond hair sagged from the weight of her hairspray, and her gold hoop earrings were so large that they elongated her earlobes. "Maybe over yonder in the back?" she suggested, holding up a black skirt with a bold green pattern at the hem—one of Melody's bestsellers.

"I'm sorry, but all we have is what's on the floor. That skirt in black is hard to keep in stock. Have you looked at the white ones by the front window? I'm pretty sure we have a medium in that color."

She snorted and glanced at the tag. "It don't make no nevermind. Large isn't so bad. A few chocolate pies and I'll fit just as snug as a bug in a rug."

I suppressed a laugh. "If you stop in on the fifteenth, I bet we'll have a fresh supply by then. If not, I'll put you down on our waiting list and give you a call when they're in."

"You're a doll. An absolute living doll. And I'm not just saying that. I'm a Sensor, so I can feel the difference between sincerity and hogwash. Sometimes you go into stores, and the management is snooty. I can't deal with attitude. Puts me in a bad mood."

"Have you browsed through our jewelry? I have a matching bracelet and necklace that'll go with that skirt."

She adjusted her purse strap. "Now you're speaking my language. Lead the way."

Sensors were an interesting group of Breed. They had the ability to feel emotions as well as pass them into others, which is why a lot of them made money by way of sensory exchange. It was recreational for some and an addiction for others. I'd heard stories about mothers who had lost children and wanted Sensors to remove that grief forever. And they could. But everything came at a price.

I led the woman to the glass counter in the back and circled behind the register to point out the jewelry. "It's this one."

She leaned over and drew in an audible breath. "What is that lush stone?"

"Variscite. Some are uniform in color, but I prefer the ones with different shades of milky greens. The imperfections that look like cracks are what make each piece unique, so you won't see anyone else wearing the exact same piece. This is one of my favorites because it looks like a lightning streak. Everything here is custom designed and handcrafted."

She looked up. "By you?"

"The ones here in the case, yes. Nothing you see was made or sold by humans. Everything we offer is high quality and genuine. They each come with a certificate of authenticity."

"Let me try on the bracelet."

I slid the glass door in the back open. Using a cloth, I pulled out the simple bracelet with rounded stones. "The necklace design is pure silver. I also have a silver bracelet with one large stone, but I personally think this one is more elegant and versatile for any occasion."

Instead of putting on the bracelet, she rolled it between her fingers with her eyes closed. A smile touched her lips. "You put a lot of love into these," she said. "I like the way it feels. It has good energy."

I frowned, certain I hadn't touched it with my bare hands when getting it out of the display. "Can you feel my emotions? I made it two weeks ago. I'm so sorry if any emotions were left behind. Maybe I should start wearing gloves when I'm making them."

She laughed. "No, darlin'. Your emotions don't hang around that long. But stones have a way of absorbing energy and keeping it for a while. I suppose they're kinda like me."

I noticed her gold rings. "Maybe you'd like something more refined. I have some pure silver jewelry over by the wall."

"Nonsense. I like to get gussied up now and then, but I'm open to new things. These are just divine. I can't tell you how many of my clients have complimented my blouse. Oh, not this one," she said, noticing my puzzled expression. "I bought another one in here a few weeks ago. Nobody gives my gold watch a second glance, but this"—she tapped the bracelet with one finger—"will catch everyone's eye. You're a talented young lady."

"I can give you a discount."

"Wouldn't dream of it. My compliments are always free of charge. Full price or I walk."

"It's two hundred even for the set. Tax included."

"Sold."

Using the black cloth, I collected the necklace from the display and carefully arranged the pieces in gift boxes. Some Sensors wore gloves in public, but I still tried to be sensitive to their needs. While she browsed the revolving display of rings, I carefully folded the tissue paper to protect the jewelry in the bag. When my cell phone rang, I almost dropped everything.

"Hello?"

"Hi, it's me," Asia said. "Sorry I didn't call last night, but something came up."

"Not a problem. I'm glad to hear from you. I was worried that maybe you didn't receive the contracts, so I was going to send them over again this afternoon."

"I got them."

Asia's terse response left me uncertain. "Is something wrong?" I placed the boxes inside the gift bag, folding more tissue paper on top.

"Okay," she said firmly. "I'm going to tell you the truth."

My stomach did a flip-flop.

"Last night I was reading the paperwork when I suddenly got an email. I don't know who sent it, but they made a counteroffer."

Stunned, I pushed the bag toward the woman, who then handed me a five-hundred-dollar bill. "What do you mean, a counteroffer?"

"They want to pay me more to not make a deal with you."

I slid a clipboard to the customer and pointed to where she needed to write her name and number. "You mean they want to buy your feathers?"

Asia hesitated. "No, they didn't say that. They just wanted to pay me not to sell you anything."

My jaw dropped. "Who?"

"I don't know. They didn't put their name on the email."

I shook my head. "Then you don't know if they were serious."

"Oh, they're very serious. They sent over a deliveryman with an advance."

I slammed the register shut and handed the woman three hundred in change. "Did you accept?"

"Would you be mad? They're offering me a lot of money."

"How much?"

"I can't tell you how many zeros. They said if you matched their offer to stay in our contract, they'll triple the amount."

My hands were shaking. "I understand if you want to take

their deal, and I'll be honest—I can't match their offer. But I have a list of back orders I promised these customers. All I need is one box, and we can go our separate ways."

"They don't want me to give you anything else."

"Who?" I said sharply. "I'm not mad at you, Asia. If this were another legitimate offer, it wouldn't matter. But I want to know who's trying to take my business away. What's their email address? Maybe I can speak to them and sort this all out."

"No, I can't do that."

She sounded torn, and I felt bad for the position she found herself in. Asia and I only had a business relationship, so she had no loyalty to me. Money was important to Shifters. It meant security and taking care of loved ones in the centuries to come. For her, the other offer was easy money. She could just sit back and collect. No work, no negotiations, no contracts, no pressure.

She gave a flustered sigh. "They said if I gave you any information that could lead back to them, they'd withdraw the offer. I'm not allowed to describe the delivery guy or his car, detail the amount of the advance, or anything. I had to sign an NDA to accept the money, which means I can't talk about it. And they said not to forward their email address."

"How long do you have to make up your mind?"

"Tomorrow night. They're sending a contract this afternoon for me to look at. This is so confusing! You didn't tell me I would have to make all these choices."

I touched my forehead when I felt a migraine coming on. "It's not your fault, Asia. If you need the money and it looks like a good deal, you have to do what's best for you. But if you want to do something that's not about money—something you can be proud of—then please keep me in mind. I can't offer you as much as they can, but the reward will be the impact you have on the community. Please let me know when you make your decision. I'm going to hold off on preorders.

If you take their offer, I'll have to tell these people that I can't keep my promise."

"I feel so bad," she mumbled. "I could do a lot with that money. Maybe buy my own house and start a family away from these cuckoo birds. I'm only stuck here because I can't afford to leave. I'm so sorry, Hope. I think I'm going to take their offer. If anything changes, I'll call you. Maybe I can do it for a little while and then we can talk again when I have money saved up. I know you're at work, so I'll let you go. Please don't be mad at me."

I hung up, my hands trembling so much that I almost dropped the phone.

My customer lifted her bag. "Your energy just went from crystal blue to black. Do you want me to take away some of that anger? No charge."

"I'm sorry you had to hear that. I hope you enjoy your purchase and come back again," I said robotically.

She flashed a sympathetic smile. "Whatever it is—it'll pass. These things always do. Here's my card in case you change your mind. My name's Frannie. You can't forget a name that sounds like fanny, now can you?" She chuckled warmly. "Thank you kindly for the gorgeous stones. I'll be back on the fifteenth to check on that skirt!"

After she left, I looked around and saw the store was empty. Sensing my anger, my wolf paced beneath my skin, but this wasn't the time or place to let my primal side take over. I was the only one who could resolve this issue, and that meant confronting the one person who had access to that kind of money—someone with motive.

Dutch.

⟶

Tak sank the last ball into the corner pocket and blew the chalk off the tip of his cue stick as if it were the barrel of a smoking gun.

"Nice shot," Moreland said, his baritone voice so pleasant that he might have had a singing career in another life. "What's your name again?"

"Tak."

The two of them had met a few games ago. It was nice to play with someone who didn't ask a lot of questions and just focused on the game.

"I guess I owe you a beer, Tak."

"I'm a soda man, but I appreciate the offer."

Moreland laughed and propped his cue on the rack. "You're a better man than I. Alcohol has the power to make men weak. Just look around," he said, gesturing toward a drunk lying on the floor and singing along with the music. "That one must have had the Devil's Eye." Moreland led him to a booth, and they took a seat. "What tribe are you from?"

"Iwa."

He nodded and lit up a slim cigar. "I figured you weren't from a pack."

Tak rubbed his chin. "What gave it away—my gorgeous face?"

Moreland puffed on his cigar and let the smoke roll around in his mouth before releasing it in a thick cloud. "Yours is not a face easily forgotten."

"That's what women have told me," Tak replied with a chuckle. "How long does it take you to do your hair that way?"

Moreland touched his braids. "I don't have to style it every day like you do."

"Must be a bitch on shifting days," he said, admiring the tight rows that crossed over the back of Moreland's head. Seemed like a lot of maintenance.

A smile hovered on Moreland's lips. "I only shift when I have to. Never seen a black Shifter with long hair?"

Tak drummed his fingers on the table. "Give me a call the next time you shift. I want to see that shit flying free."

They both laughed hard and eased back in their seats.

Tak had spent most of the morning walking around. He

visited the shops, spoke with the owners, and found a bakery called Sweet Treats where all the food was fresh and made from scratch. Interracial couples passed him on the street, their hands clasped in public displays of affection. People here were more open-minded than those in his hometown, which was populated by old-fashioned Shifters who were still living in the 1800s.

He stumbled upon a theater that only cost a couple of bucks and watched a science fiction movie about aliens attacking the world. Tak kept gazing at the empty chair beside him, wishing he could hear Hope's opinion of the plot, which he found implausible.

The music on the jukebox changed to something bluesy. Tak liked the atmosphere in Howlers compared to the bars in his off-the-map town. They played classic rock instead of country, and people were friendly. It was also nice not having to separate himself from other Shifters. Tak spent so much of his time around members of his own tribe that he sometimes forgot how good it was to talk with strangers and hear their stories. Howlers had a long bar with a low partition wall sectioning off the pool tables and seating area.

It wasn't too busy, and he scanned the room, relieved that Wheeler wasn't there. Even though Wheeler was a tool, Tak appreciated his looking out for Hope. It didn't mean he wanted to have another confrontation with the man, but it was reassuring to know that a lot of men in this town respected Hope.

"Where are you from?" Moreland asked.

Tak folded his arms on the table. "Oklahoma. Tribal land."

"That's far off, and I don't mean by miles. I've been out that way before," he said, assessing Tak more closely. "What brings an alpha all the way down to Austin?"

"Personal matters I need to put to rest with an old friend." Tak leaned forward and lowered his voice. "Do you know a wolf named River?"

Moreland watched the tendril of smoke rising from the

end of his stogie. "There's only one man around here that goes by that name, and he's not welcome in our pack anymore."

Tak's pulse accelerated at the realization that Moreland was Hope's former packmate. Without knowing how frequently city packs kicked out wolves for misconduct or other reasons, he kept his cool and didn't look overly interested. "Why's that?"

Moreland's gaze traveled upward. "Let's just say he stuck his nose where it didn't belong. Men who think they can keep secrets in a pack are fools."

"Did he betray the Packmaster?"

Moreland flagged down a waitress, who gave him a brisk nod before hurrying back to the bar. "Indirectly. What business do you have with River? Because if you're a friend of his, you can get up right now and find another place to sit."

Tak pressed his finger on the table. "That wolf is no friend of mine. I think he offended the woman I was with yesterday."

Moreland looked up and puffed on his stogie. "Now *that* I believe."

"I don't know the ways of city packs, but I'm trying to learn. What do you know of my people?"

Moreland nodded. "I knew someone from your tribe a long time ago. He came from another region out of Arkansas, but they were Iwa."

"Then you understand our word is our bond. I know I'm asking private questions about your pack, but whatever you tell me stays between us. It angers me the way he spoke disrespectfully to my friend, and I want to know what makes him so offensive toward women."

The man set his cigar down and laced his fingers together. "Three can keep a secret if two of them are dead."

"What does that mean?"

Moreland smirked. "Secrets never stay buried as long as the people who keep them are alive. But sometimes... sometimes it's better to shine light on the truth. When you let speculation run wild, you do no service to the victims involved. I'll hold you to your word, Tak of the Iwa tribe, only because I know your people and the value they put on a man's good name. River seduced an important woman in the tribe, a young wolf who was still deciding whether to become independent or join another pack. He besmirched her reputation."

Tak's breath caught. Hearing the story from another party confirmed what must have been Hope's worst fear: that others knew. Quelling his rage, he exhaled and relaxed his shoulders. "And what did the Packmaster do?"

"Lorenzo wanted to end the guy's life, and you don't want to know what that man does with the pelt of his enemies. Enzo's a good leader, but he's not a man you cross. Killing River would have struck fear in the pack and forced him to reveal the truth. But he wanted to protect the woman's reputation, so he allowed River to live under the condition that he leave the pack and never speak ill of them. If that repugnant excuse for a wolf were to ever set foot in this bar, I might lock him in a safe and bury it in the woods."

Moreland was protecting Hope's identity, so Tak treaded carefully. "Was the woman of age?"

Moreland lifted his cigar and studied it for a moment. "I know your tribe breaks off into sections, but a pack is different—especially a large one. If a man wants to court a young woman who's recently gone through her first change, he has to follow the rules. Either wait for her to leave the pack or make the Packmaster aware of his intentions. The alpha decides if the relationship will create conflict within the house. A lot of men were interested in this woman; an open relationship with River would have caused a war."

Tak steepled his fingers and averted his gaze to a table of young women who were laughing. Hope's panic attack at the market had nothing to do with traffic, noise, or even seeing River. It happened because she felt powerless after River treated her with disdain. She'd once trusted the man, and a part of her would always feel connected to him because of the intimacy they'd shared.

If only Tak could go back in time and put that wolf in his place. Had that man ever felt anything true for her, he wouldn't have been so cold.

"Did the wolf not fight for her hand?" Tak wondered aloud.

"All that man wanted was to pick the cherry from the tree. Young women don't realize the power their first lover has over them, but older men are wise to this, and the wrong ones abuse that power. They seduce them with lies and empty promises. That's why they target them before they leave the pack."

"Why should that matter?"

Moreland tapped the long ash off his cigar. "Leaving gives her free will to choose any man she wants, but these men don't want a relationship. So they put them in a position where the affair has to remain a secret. I've seen this happen before. Sometimes they seduce the Packmaster's mate, but usually it's the young ones they target. These wolves are likable guys. Everyone's best friend. The one you least suspect."

Tak took out his warrior's knife and stabbed the table with it. "If I see that rogue again, I'll show him what my tribe does to dogs like him."

Moreland tossed back his head and laughed. "We need more like you in this town."

The waitress appeared and set two beer mugs on the table. Tak pushed his glass toward Moreland, who gladly accepted the gesture.

"Are you a Packmaster?" Moreland asked.

"No."

"That doesn't create problems in your tribe?"

It sometimes did. Dominant alphas butted heads, but usually his tribe would break off into subpacks and move to a different part of the land.

Tak sighed. "My father leads all the packs, so it's not a problem for me."

"I can see that." Moreland gulped down half his drink and wiped his lips with the back of his hand. "I've seen many alphas get too comfortable living the rogue life, and if you live under the power of another alpha, it might weaken you as a leader. Have you thought about starting your own pack… away from the tribe? Don't let time go to waste."

"That's not an option."

Moreland searched his eyes. "A man can do anything he sets his mind to. The only thing stopping him is fear or family. Which governs your decisions?"

"Would you trust a man like River to lead his own pack? There's your answer."

Moreland puffed on his cigar and gazed at Tak earnestly. "If you've committed a grievous offense against your tribe, then make it right. You're still in the tribe, so that tells me it was a forgivable act. But if your packmates refuse to acknowledge your birthright, then maybe it's time for you to take a stand. It won't be long before you begin alienating yourself from the others. Time marches on, and watching young men around you achieve their full potential will eat away at what dignity you have left." Moreland set his cigar in the ashtray. "All men are capable of redemption; few men seek it. I'm not your spirit guide, Tak. I just happen to see a powerful alpha in front of me who has a lot of wolves in this town buzzing with curiosity. Some think you're settling, and a few people are interested in that prospect. There are plenty of Shifters following men they don't believe in for lack of choice. Every so often, there's a peace party, and some trading goes on, but choices get stale. Everyone here knows each other, so when an alpha comes of age, he's already got his buddies picked out. Forming a pack becomes more about favoritism and less about building a strong brotherhood. That's why these numbskulls wind up with so many problems where a mediator is necessary."

Tak was intrigued. "Are you looking to switch packs?"

Moreland offered a smile and looked off toward the bar. "I'm always open to change. If you want my advice, maybe you should extend your vacation a little longer and see what's out there. How about another game? I'll even let you break."

Tak put his knife back in the sheath looped on his belt. "Something tells me I'm being hustled. Did you let me win to boost my confidence?"

Moreland stood up and grabbed the mug with beer still in it. "Call me the hospitality wagon. I like to take it easy on tourists."

Tak remained seated while Moreland moseyed over to the pool tables. A cold chill rinsed over him, the sensation intensifying with each passing second. He brushed his hand over the raised hairs on his arm. He'd never experienced a feeling like this before and wondered if it was what Hope's panic attacks felt like. But Tak didn't suffer from those; something else was wrong. His wolf thrashed beneath his skin, the need to run unbearable.

No, not run. *Chase.*

Chase what?

He couldn't shake the urgency. As he yielded to his animal instincts, his thoughts crystallized. For reasons he couldn't explain, Tak knew with unequivocal certainty that Hope was in danger.

Chapter 24

After Asia's appalling news, I stormed out of Moonglow. Dutch's store was only a few streets over—I'd driven by it the other night on my way home. How could he have gone behind my back and done something so cutthroat? It was one thing to offer a distributor a better deal, but it was something else to bribe them not to do business with me.

Or maybe he hoped I'd outbid him, which would lower my profits.

I'd heard stories about unscrupulous tactics used to drive others out of business, but I never thought it would happen to us. This was something I'd only imagined happening on TV and not in real life.

The late-afternoon sun filtered through the trees along the sidewalk, but the light wasn't responsible for the hot tears welling in my eyes. Every step I took fueled my anger. This was not only about protecting my business but also my family, by whatever means necessary. Every new opportunity was a stepping-stone toward our future, and because we were new, it wouldn't take much to jeopardize our finances.

When I reached his store, I yanked the door open and marched inside. Dutch didn't have a charming bell on the door that jingled, and it was dim inside due to the tinted windows. Glass jewelry counters ran along all walls of the store with the middle area open.

I spied him to my left, helping a customer, and slammed my store keys on the counter to draw his attention. "How *could* you?"

Dutch looked up before smiling at an older lady in a midnight-blue dress. "If you'll excuse me for one moment."

He veered toward the back of the store, and when I realized he was heading for the door to a private room, I jogged after him.

"You can't dodge me! I'll climb over this counter if I have to."

He gave me a baleful look over his shoulder before turning on his heel. When he reached the counter, he placed his palms on it. "What's gotten into you?"

"Besides deception?"

"I'll just come back another day," the woman said, jingling her car keys.

"That's ten thousand dollars walking out the door," he informed me. "Whatever this is, it better be worth it."

I glared at the sparkling diamonds in the display. "I thought someone who ran a prestigious store like this would know about ethics. I've worked so hard—you have no idea. Why are you doing this to me?"

"Is this about the note?"

"First you come into my store to spy on me, and then you pretend to be my friend so you can get inside information. You didn't even care about the feathers; you just wanted to take away a piece of my business. I bet if Shikoba dealt with people outside the tribes, you would have bribed him too."

"Bribe? You've gone mad."

"No, I *am* mad. And if the Council's not going to do anything about it, *I* will."

"Are you threatening me?"

I laughed. "That's a funny thing to say, considering you're the one who's harassing me."

His eyes flicked over to the other customers in the store. "Keep your voice down."

"You don't want your customers knowing you're a crook? We don't even sell the same kind of merchandise. Just because someone spends money in my shop doesn't mean they're going to stop coming into yours."

Dutch folded his arms. "Look, whatever you're talking about, I'm not involved. You're just going to have to take my word at face value."

"I'm not letting you run me out of business. Just because I don't have a Packmaster doesn't mean you can push me around and get away with it. And for your information, it's not going to work."

"Hold your tongue," he said in a caged voice. "Need I remind you about the slander laws? If you ruin my reputation by causing a scene in my place of business, I'll take it to the Council, and *that* might cost you your store."

"How many people can you afford to pay *not* to do business with me? You underestimate my ambition."

Dutch held up his hand. "That'll do. I need you to leave the premises."

"This isn't over," I hissed.

Though I had a million things I wanted to say, all I could do was leave. The fact that Dutch could raise slander charges infuriated me. The Council rarely got involved with business dealings; those matters were handled by the shopkeepers since so many different Breeds were involved. We had no courthouses or judges to impose fines. If I had lived in a pack, the Packmaster would handle something of this magnitude.

But I didn't, so all I could do was flee.

My God, what if I'd fallen into a trap? Had this been his plan all along—to bait me into making a public accusation without hard evidence? And I'd fallen for it. His customers were now witnesses, and people did jail time for slander.

The wind could barely keep up with me as I crossed the street. When a horn honked, I whirled around, slamming my hands on the hood of a car as the driver hit the brakes at the last second.

After crossing the street, I called the only person I could think of who would know what to do.

"It's your dime," Wheeler answered.

"Wheeler, it's Hope."

He cleared his throat. "What's shakin'?"

"Someone's trying to put me out of business."

He chuckled. "That all?"

I stepped onto the curb and quickened my stride. "I know you've got experience dealing with shrewd businessmen. I don't have time to explain all the details over the phone, but I really need your advice. I've just opened a can of worms that I can't close. Can you meet me at Moonglow before I shift and do some real damage to my reputation?"

"Be chill. Are you alone?"

"No, I'm on the street."

"If you feel like you're gonna shift, get the hell inside, lock the doors, and take a deep breath. Gum helps. I'll be there in nothing flat."

After a few minutes, I reached Moonglow. When I tugged at the locked door, I blanched.

My keys.

Flashbacks of leaving them on Dutch's counter came to mind, and I kicked the brick wall. I wasn't in any condition to go back and get them. My hands were shaking, and I couldn't tell if I was on the verge of having a panic attack or shifting in the middle of the street. Neither was an option, especially if one involved my wolf chasing people down the sidewalk.

"Think, think," I whispered.

Maybe I'd accidentally left the back door unlocked. I'd thrown the trash out earlier, so it was worth a shot. Getting off the street might calm my nerves. I headed a few buildings down until I reached a gap that ran between two stores and cut through to the alley. All things considered, at least Melody wasn't here. She would have made it worse by grabbing her bow and standing on Dutch's pristine countertops. I was the levelheaded one, so it upset me that I'd behaved so impulsively.

The alley that divided our street from the one behind us was wide enough to fit the trucks that collected our garbage. Most of the buildings were connected on either side, so that offered a lot of privacy if my wolf decided to burst onto the scene. I stared at the ground, stepping around discarded pieces of trash. Rusty nails, scraps of dirty paper, glass, cigarette butts, pebbles… When I lifted my eyes, I halted in my tracks.

Black smoke billowed from a large trash container ahead on the left. When I looked back and did a mental count of the buildings, I realized it was coming from our store.

I ran, my feet barely touching the ground. The smell of smoke and gas fumes permeated the air. We didn't just throw empty soda cans and paper towels in the bin. All kinds of flammable items were in there, such as flattened cardboard boxes and packing material.

My heart ratcheted in my chest when I reached the fire. A man stepped out from behind the bin, but he didn't notice me since he was searching for something in his pants pocket.

"What do you think you're doing?" I shouted.

I startled him so much that he almost tripped over his own feet while turning to face me. Gas sloshed in the red container he held tightly, and I recognized his bushy beard and beady eyes. Mr. Dumont—the irate customer with the broken purse—was attempting to burn down my store.

Noxious flames licked the outside of the trash bin, black smoke billowing toward the indigo sky.

"Stop what you're doing!"

He took a deliberate step forward, splashing gas on the concrete between us.

"Help!" I screamed. "Someone help! Fire!"

Dumont held up a pack of matches and struck one. Shifting meant watching my dreams go up in flames, so I had to choose between catching Dumont or saving the only thing that mattered.

Dumont made the decision for me when he dropped the lit matchstick on the ground, blocking my access to the door and creating a wall of fire between us.

As Tak neared Starlight Road, he smelled smoke through the open window. It wasn't the rich aroma of a barbecue or a fire pit. The truck jumped the curb as Tak maneuvered around a traffic jam. Black smoke trailed up to the darkening sky, an ominous sight on such a clear day. When he reached the store, his truck screeched to a halt, and he threw open the door, keys still in the ignition. A small crowd gathered in the street, gawking at the sky behind Moonglow. Tak gripped the door handle and jerked, but it didn't budge.

With no sign of anyone inside, he turned left and torpedoed up the sidewalk, knocking a man down and leaping over a dog. Before reaching the end of the street, he glimpsed a gap between two buildings and did a backstep. Tak cut through and wound up in an alleyway. Not wasting time to look around, he veered right and slowed down when he saw the nightmare unfolding.

A short wall of flames stood between Hope and another man. He couldn't tell who it was since the man was facing the other way. If Tak hadn't known it before, he knew now with absolute certainty that he loved Hope. Loved her with a fierceness in his heart he'd never known, and seeing her surrounded by flames made him want to tear the world apart.

If that bastard moved an inch, the savagery Tak would unleash would be legendary.

"Get help!" he boomed, catching Hope's attention. He wanted her out of here, and he knew by the brave look in her eyes that she wanted to save her store.

And so did he.

Her dreams were now his dreams.

In a flash, she turned around and took off like a streak of lightning.

Tak stopped, his shoulders squared and head low. When the bearded man turned around, Tak recognized the grizzly from Hope's store. So much for Breed jail taking care of this guy after the stunt he pulled at Howlers.

Maybe the fates were giving Tak a second chance to give this chickenshit what he deserved.

Tak widened his stance, closing his hands into fists. "You dare attack a Packmaster's daughter?"

"Not your business," Dumont fired back.

"What's going on out here?" someone shouted. But the person was interested in neither Tak nor Dumont, only the intense fire threatening the adjoining shops. Several men sprang into action, fast-moving shadows dancing behind the smoke and flames.

"Stay back," Dumont warned as Tak advanced. "You don't want to mess with me, wolf. My bear will eat you for breakfast and pick his teeth with your bones."

Tak stripped off his shirt and tossed it aside. "Let's get uncivilized."

Damn the consequences—Tak was going to annihilate him.

The two men clashed, each trying to muscle the other down. Tak was over two hundred and fifty pounds of pure ferocity—his moves so raw that he didn't have to think. His knuckles split when they smashed against Dumont's head like a sledgehammer. Tak suddenly lost his footing, and Dumont battered him in the ribs. Adrenaline dulled the pain, and Tak put the guy in a choke hold. Without something to pin him against, it was difficult to keep a grip on him. All he needed was one minute to cut off the circulation and knock this guy out.

Dumont twisted his body and wrenched out of Tak's grip before backing up a few steps. He grimaced, his white teeth smeared with blood. With lightning speed, Tak unsheathed his weapon.

"Big man with the knife," Dumont taunted. "I thought you were an alpha, but all I see now is a pussy. Wouldn't fight me in the bar and won't even fight me now."

Tak's blade was steeped in centuries of valor—a weapon forged for battle and passed down to great warriors. Dumont's words didn't loosen Tak's grip on his weapon. No man with any honor would ask his enemy to give him a fair fight, and as Tak saw it, Dumont had the advantage of being a grizzly.

Flames licked the sky, growing taller and threatening the building as they painted black streaks against the wall. Local shopkeepers splashed buckets of water at the dumpster, attempting to contain the fire.

Dumont stripped off his shirt, his hairy chest the same color as his bear's fur. He unlatched his belt and looped one end around his hand, eyes trained on Tak's knife.

They circled each other, smoke whipping around and showering them with burning embers.

Tak lunged and swiped, his blade leaving an angry red slash across the Shifter's chest.

Dumont swung his arm, and the leather snapped against Tak's hand. Tak wrenched away when the belt came dangerously close to ensnaring his wrist.

A gust of wind tunneled through the alley, the smoke stinging his eyes. He didn't like how the alley boxed them in like two animals caught in a pit.

Body language revealed intent, so Tak focused on every subtle shift of Dumont's eyes, the position of his feet, and the angle of his stance. When the belt lashed him again, he seized it and gave it a hard jerk, pulling Dumont toward him. Knife in hand, Tak aimed for the heart. But before the blade found its home, the Shifter pivoted away.

Dumont circled behind him like a tornado. Tak dropped to one knee and twisted around, making a downward swing with his weapon. The knife plunged into Dumont's leg, but not deep enough to bury the reverse hook, which would have ripped out arteries and flesh. The Shifter jumped back, agony splintering his expression as blood poured from the open wound.

Tak rose to his feet, and their bodies moved like an artistry of war. The furry bastard parried each attack with a blow until he knocked the knife from Tak's hand, the metal skidding across the pavement.

"Tak!" Hope screamed.

"Get out of my way before I unleash the beast," Dumont growled. "Do you really want to die for that cunt?"

Tak leveled him with his eyes. "I will die for love, but you will die for nothing." In a swift moment of magic, he shifted. His wolf rushed headlong and went for the jugular.

Dumont threw up his arm to block the attack. Tak's wolf sank his fangs into the Shifter's arm, and he thrashed wildly, hoping to tear it off. Blood filled his mouth, the sweet promise of death on his tongue. Dumont's hard fist pounded him in the head, forcing him to let go before he suffered a skull fracture.

Dumont moved so fast he blurred, his body rippling as it exploded into an atrocious beast at least three times larger than Tak. The grizzly craned his massive head and roared, the spine-chilling battle cry terrifying enough to make the bravest of men flee.

Tak drew in the bear's scent and searched for weaknesses. Dumont was colossal, his jaws wide and claws long. A lone wolf could easily take on a black bear. But a grizzly? Only if the bear was inexperienced or small, and Dumont was neither. Against a single wolf, odds were always tipped in favor of the bear.

Tak readied himself for what might be his last moments. All warriors wanted their story to be one of legend, and the only way to achieve that was to die a good death.

The bear lumbered forward and swiped with his paw. Tak's wolf dodged his deadly claws and streaked behind him, getting in a bite whenever he could. His goal was to get the bear so agitated that he couldn't think straight. Large predators tired easily.

"Move it! Move it!" a man bellowed.

Tak spotted Wheeler galvanizing the shopkeepers into action with a plan to extinguish the fire. They lined up with buckets of water and a hose.

"Help me pull the damn thing away from the building," Wheeler ordered them. "Hurry up so you can put out the roof fire!"

Hope's voice sounded like an angel amid chaos. "You'll burn yourself! Let it go! It's not worth dying for."

But it *was* worth dying for—*she* was worth dying for. All of Tak's tribulations had led to this one moment.

Despite his size, Dumont's grizzly was surprisingly nimble. When Tak snarled and charged at him, the bear rose up on his hind legs to exaggerate his size. He must have stood eight feet tall. Tak circled around him and nipped at his hind leg so he'd drop down on all fours.

Each time the grizzly faced him, Tak bared his fangs. Sometimes bears got skittish at the sight of a wolf's canines and the whites of his eyes.

Tak yelped when the bear's claws ripped through his shoulder. Swallowing the pain, he lunged forward and locked his jaws around the grizzly's neck. There was no time for mistakes. He angled his body so the bear couldn't bite down, but those large paws battered him mercilessly.

Tak's eyes and mouth filled with a burning stench that forced him to let go. The men finished dragging the trash bin to the center of the alley, and the wind was blowing smoke and charred embers in Tak's face. The grizzly swiped his arm, knocking the wind out of Tak before he slammed against the building and crumpled to the ground.

Tak heaved a sigh, and the concrete became suffused with his blood as it left his body. His eyes burned, and his lungs tightened from smoke inhalation. Through the haze, Dutch appeared out of nowhere, spraying something at the grizzly.

Amid blood and fire, Dutch's fine suit stood out. He held what appeared to be pepper spray on a key ring. Blinded from the mace, Dumont attacked thin air.

Tak watched in horror. Why wasn't Dutch shifting? Was he trying to play hero or commit suicide?

The grizzly charged and threw him to the ground. He raked his claws over flesh, Dutch screaming beneath him. In those grim moments, Tak watched Dutch flop beneath the beast like a rag doll.

"No!" Hope cried, racing into view.

Tak's heart jolted to life as she neared the bear, wielding a piece of lumber like a baseball bat. Her eyes flicked between Tak and Dutch before they sparked like two flames.

The bear lost interest in Dutch and turned around to face the lone woman. No one stood by her side. The men were distracted by the fire, which must have spread. They raced in and out of the shops with buckets of water, a fire alarm chirping from inside a building. Wheeler wasn't anywhere in sight.

Despite searing pain and broken bones, Tak rose to his feet, barking and snarling to draw the grizzly's attention away. Hope stumbled backward, facing a half-ton grizzly with nothing but a plank of wood. Her eyes told the story—that she accepted she was about to meet her death. And when those baby browns swung over to Tak, he knew she was doing it for love.

Fear doesn't define a person; sacrifice does.

The bear's eyes were closed and weeping from the mace. His sense of smell might have also been impaired, but not his hearing. He followed the sound of her voice, her breath, and her footsteps. Tak had once been helpless to save the woman he loved, but not this time.

Half-blind and bleeding, he channeled all his alpha power into a single blow as he crashed into the bear and unleashed his wrath.

Chapter 25

Dumont's grizzly stalked toward me, and though he was blinded from Dutch's heroic act, I couldn't fight him alone. Shifting would get me killed, especially with the chaos, blood, and fire swarming around us. Maybe if I could shove the board down his throat, I'd have a fighting chance.

His jaws opened like a steel trap, saliva dripping in long streams as he craned his neck and roared. My hair stood on end, but thinking about Tak erased my fears. I wanted to go to him—protect him—but I couldn't. The idea that we might never hold each other again filled me with anguish.

Taking advantage of Dumont's blindness, I threw the board a few feet to the side. It clacked against the concrete, diverting his attention.

This bear had blood in his mouth, so I needed to lure him away from Tak. Maybe I could climb onto one of the trash bins and make some noise. When I fell back a step, my foot knocked a pebble across the concrete. The grizzly turned so fast that my wolf rippled beneath my skin.

Seconds before the beast barreled into me, Tak appeared out of nowhere and savagely ripped at the grizzly's throat. Blood poured onto the concrete as skin and fur tore away.

"Hope!" Wheeler shouted. Before I knew it, he hooked his arm around my waist and hauled me back.

The black smoke had changed to pale grey, and voices shouted from behind me. No one cared about Tak. Whether these men were Shifters or otherwise, they had no skin in this game. All they wanted to do was extinguish the fire as they continued hosing down their stores with water. Breed rarely called the fire department because it got humans involved in their business. Dumont had used so much gasoline to set the trash and building ablaze that several people were using fire extinguishers.

Unable to see Tak anymore, I writhed in Wheeler's grip. "Why don't you help him? Let me go! Tak!"

Wheeler set me down and gave me a grievous stare. "If I shift, it'll be bad news. My wolf will turn on your friend."

I spun around when the grizzly roared. It wasn't as ominous this time and sounded like a death knell. I sucked in a sharp breath when he collapsed in a heap of bloody muscle and fur. Somewhere beneath six hundred pounds of bear was Tak, his hind legs thrashing wildly.

When he went still, my heart sank.

This couldn't be happening. My eyes blurred with tears, and my feet rooted in place. The world had just stopped. Maybe if I blinked, I'd wake up, and all of this would have been a dream.

Tak's leg twitched. Moments later, he crawled out from beneath the bear, his dark fur cloaked in blood.

My body sagged with relief. "You're alive," I whispered. "Thank the fates."

Tak stood atop the creature and howled, his face stained with so much blood I didn't recognize him. His victory cry sent chills up my spine.

When I started to run toward them, Wheeler grabbed my arm. "He's got blood in his mouth!"

I wrenched away and kept going despite the danger. Predators who had gotten a taste of blood were geared up for a kill. Often those impulses were so powerful that even the animal's human counterpart surrendered to their primal instincts. The grizzly's eyes were swollen shut, his tongue hanging out. Water flooded beneath my feet as the men washed away the gasoline.

Tak's wolf staggered off the dead animal before collapsing with exhaustion. His injuries weren't grave, but when I looked past him, my eyes widened in horror.

Dumont's grizzly had severely mauled Dutch. The gruesome scene looked fatal, but I could hear him gasping for air.

An older man jogged up and looked between us. "I'm a Relic, but I can only take one."

Dutch choked on his own blood, and I pointed at him. Tak would survive his injuries, but Dutch wouldn't.

"Someone help me put him into my car!" the Relic shouted.

Two men rushed over and carefully lifted Dutch's limp body. There was so much blood that it pained me to think he would probably die. Dutch didn't deserve this ending. I'd been wrong about him all along. He wouldn't have fought the grizzly if they'd been working together. All this time, Dumont was the culprit.

And with Dumont dead, I would never understand why he'd gone to such lengths to ruin me. Maybe he was one of many who'd lost the bid on the property, or maybe he didn't like seeing wolves taking over his town. The packs were strong, and that sparked animosity among local rogues.

It didn't really matter anymore.

"Tak," I cried, falling to my knees.

Wheeler squatted next to him. "We need to get him to shift. I don't like the looks of that wound on his shoulder. It's deep."

Wheeler yelled and shook Tak's haunches, but Tak remained unresponsive. His injuries weren't as grave as Dutch's, but if he didn't wake up and shift, he could wind up disabled. There was also no way to know if he'd sustained any internal injuries.

I smoothed my hand over his ear. "Can you hear me? If you don't shift back, you might die. Please, Tak. Fight harder. You have a purpose in this world—you matter." I stroked his face, wiping at the thick blood.

Wheeler snatched my wrist. "If he wakes up, he'll bite you. I know you care about him, but it's not worth your life."

"Let me go," I bit out.

I'd called to Tak once before as a stranger, and now I called to him with all the love in my heart. Any doubts I'd had about what real love felt like were extinguished the moment I saw him bravely challenge Dumont, turning the threat away from me and onto himself. Tak was a man I could give my whole heart to—someone I wanted by my side as my mate and the protector of our children. Our future flashed before my eyes, and it filled me with a fierce determination to undo this wrong.

"Don't you dare give up," I pleaded, tears blurring my vision. "If you're looking for a reason to stay, then stay for me. Maybe it's not enough, but I love you, Tak. I'll never find anyone else I love as much. You're the bravest man I know, and maybe I don't deserve you, but I can't imagine a life without you in it. Don't break my heart."

One of his brown eyes opened and looked right at me.

In a ripple of magic, Tak transformed into a wounded man. I stared in horror at the claw marks over his shoulder and the lump on his head. Seconds later, Tak fell unconscious again.

"That's a big fucking hematoma," Wheeler remarked. "Help me lift him. I'll take him back to the motel."

"He's not staying there anymore. We're taking him home."

"Home. As in *your* home?" Wheeler stroked his circle beard. "And the plot thickens."

I swung a frosty gaze up at him. "I don't live a pious life, and I don't expect you to treat me like some kind of princess. So you can either help me carry him, or you can move out of my way."

"Take it easy, sweetheart." Wheeler rolled him onto his

back. "Mayhap I was just curious why you'd want to invite a stranger into your home."

I stood up and wiped my bloody hands on my shirt. "He's no stranger. This man has taught me more about love in one week than anyone else has in my entire life. I love him, and you can spread that rumor far and wide if you like, but it's the truth. Maybe he doesn't love me half as much, but that's a chance I'm willing to take."

Wheeler chuckled and shook his head. "If this is a contest on who loves who more, I'm staying out of it." When he stood up again, he raked his fingers through his disheveled hair. "Love is the damnedest thing. Pull your car around, and we'll load him in. He's not riding in my Camaro with all this blood, so I hope you have a roomy back seat."

I'd been standing for ages in my narrow hallway, rubbing missed spots of dried blood off my hands while the Relic treated Tak. This wasn't the same Relic who'd collected Dutch but an old family friend.

What if I lose him? It seemed impossible that I could fall so hard so fast, but now I couldn't imagine a world without him in it. I'd never seen a wolf fight a grizzly before. The local shopkeepers had seen the bear, but not one of them possessed the courage to do anything about it. Shifters didn't usually fight to the death, so it wasn't until Tak took a powerful blow and Dutch went down that I had turned my back on the fire to help.

When the Relic emerged from my bedroom, I lurched forward. "How is he?"

Edward ran his fingers through his dark blond hair. If only the look in his eyes was as reassuring as his British accent. "He's not woken up. I dressed his wounds and have done all I can, but unless he shifts—"

"Will he live?"

"He's an alpha. They're too stubborn to die." Edward led me out of the hallway and into the living room. "It's not grave, but given how close his wounds are to a major artery, I can't say what might have happened had he not shifted. Time will heal his injuries, and he'll keep the scars. There's quicker recovery time if you can get him to shift once or twice more. I'd encourage you to try."

"And the pain?"

Edward reached into his bag and handed me a bottle of pills. "Give him one every six hours. These are strong, so they'll make him sleep for a long time. Only give them as needed. If he's lucid enough to shift, I'd rather him do that a few more times than sedate him. But sometimes they don't have the energy left to shift, or their animal won't wake up."

I held the pills against my chest. "Thank you for coming on short notice. Stay here while I get your money."

Relics had clients they worked with exclusively. For a little extra, you could sometimes find one who was willing to squeeze you into their schedule. Edward had a long history with Melody's old pack, so he was willing to come on short notice.

I padded down the hall to Melody's bedroom. Breed bankers weren't open all hours, so we made deposits twice a month. Every week, one of us would fill a deposit bag with money and take it home to put in the safe, which Lakota had bolted to the floor of Melody's closet. It was convenient to have cash on hand in case of emergencies or large expenses, such as buying a car. But it was too dangerous to keep all your money in your home. Some did, but if word spread, criminals considered it an open invitation.

After opening the closet, I knelt and punched in the code. When the safe door opened, my heart stopped as I stared into an empty box. Had Melody made an early deposit? No... No, I was certain I'd put money in the safe after they left town. I closed the door and examined the hinges, looking for signs of tampering. The empty deposit bag was sitting in its usual place.

A dreadful thought nestled in my head: I'd left Tak unsupervised in my home. If he was in the process of breaking away from his father's tribe, would he have been tempted by a safe full of money? The Tak I knew now wasn't capable of such a devious act, but what were his original intentions? If he wanted to get even with Lakota, it would've been easy to steal from right under our noses. But without the code, how did he get the money out? And why didn't he just leave town afterward?

I refused to believe it.

"Everything okay?" Edward asked, peering into the room.

I sprang to my feet, my cheeks flushed. "I'm so sorry; I thought we had enough cash in the house to cover it. Everything's in the bank. I promise you'll get your money. You know I'm good for it."

"That's fine," he said, glancing at his watch. "I trust you or else I wouldn't have come."

I fought back tears. "Thank you."

"If you need my assistance, just give me a ring. The ointment on the bedside table will speed up the healing process. I'm more concerned about the lump on his head being the reason he won't wake up. He might have suffered a severe concussion, and I'm afraid if that's the case, there's very little I can do. Put ice on it every few hours, and ring me at once if his condition worsens or there's no change in twenty-four hours."

After escorting Edward out, I lumbered into the dark living room and collapsed on the sofa. I needed someone to talk to, so I picked up the phone and called the one person I could count on.

"Hello, sis," Lakota answered.

"Come home."

"Miss me already?"

"I'm so sorry to ruin your trip, but I need your help. Tak's here."

"Tak? Is he harassing you?"

"No, he's injured. The Relic was just here, and I couldn't pay him because someone robbed our safe."

"What the hell?" he growled. "Someone broke in? Were you home?"

I could hear Melody frantically asking him what was going on.

"Lakota, someone set the store on fire. They didn't burn it to the ground, but I don't know how extensive the damage is. There was a grizzly attack and… I just need you to come home so I'm not alone in this."

"Are you safe?"

I stared listlessly at the vacant room. "Yes."

"I'm flying home tonight."

"What?" Melody exclaimed. "Is Hope okay? What's going on?" She must have grabbed the phone from him, because her voice came on next. "Are you all right? What's happening?"

That was when I broke down. "Please don't hate me. I kept secrets from you. Someone's been harassing me and vandalizing the store while you've been gone. I didn't want to worry you because I wasn't sure how serious it was. All that stuff that happened before with the graffiti we ignored, and it was fine."

"Are you hurt?"

"No, but Tak is."

"What the hell is Tak doing there?"

"Mel, I love him. I doubt that's going to make any sense to you right now, but that's how it is. He needs me now, and I have to take care of him. Don't say anything to Lakota. Not yet. I want him to stay focused."

"What happened?"

"Someone set the store on fire, and we need to hire contractors to look at the damages. A Councilman stopped by to question me, and I didn't have anyone to advise me what to say, so I told him the truth. I don't want to be alone anymore."

"What happened to the arsonist?"

I rubbed my forehead. "Tak killed him. I'm also worried about Dutch. He might have lost his life fighting that bear."

"Who the heck is Dutch? I go out of town for a week, and all hell breaks loose. A bear attacked you? Look, we'll be there soon. Lakota's on your dad's phone getting airline tickets."

"What about your truck?"

"The truck is the last thing on my mind right now. We'll have someone take care of that, so don't you worry. Are you sure you're okay? You're not hurt or anything?"

"I'm fine. I'm just shaken up. Make sure you tell my parents I'm not injured. I don't need them worrying for nothing. The money in the safe is gone. I don't know how it happened, Mel. I'm doing everything I can to set things right, and it's falling apart."

"Oh shit," she whispered quietly. "Your father just kicked one of the doors off the hinges. I guess it's safe to say they're coming home early too. How's Tak? Is he there right now?"

"He's unconscious. The Relic couldn't get him to shift, but I'm going to try in a little while. He saved my life, Mel. He really did."

"We'll be there soon. And don't blame yourself, you hear me? Sometimes shit happens, and I've experienced my fair share of it. You shouldn't have to go through it alone. Hang in there. I love you."

"Love you too."

How I'd gotten through this day without having a panic attack was beyond me. I set the phone down and hurried to my bedroom, the bottle of painkillers still in hand. When I entered, Tak was in my bed, the blanket pulled up to his waist. A few puncture wounds had already healed some, but not the claw marks on his right shoulder that stretched down to his chest. They were deep, and the Relic hadn't bandaged them since getting an infection was impossible, and bandaging an unconscious man could cause more damage if he shifted. The towel beneath him collected the blood still seeping from the wound.

I sat down beside him. Only the inked side of his face showed since Edward had draped an ice bag over the right side of his head. I gently lifted it off and examined him closely. His skin was bright red all around the lump, which stretched the skin taut just over his right eye.

"Tak," I whispered. "Can you shift?" I placed my hand on his chest and felt a rumble. "Wake up," I said more loudly. "Wake up or else I'm going to tell everyone the truth."

His left eye popped open, but he didn't say anything.

I had nothing to tell except for how brave he was, but I was willing to try any tactic to get him to listen.

"Please shift for me. You'll scar if you don't."

Tak slowly closed his eye. When his breathing grew heavy, I knew he'd fallen into a deep slumber.

Even though the bed was too small for the both of us, I curled up next to him as close as I could get. Every breath he took was a gift, and just thinking about that split second when I thought I'd lost him made me nuzzle against his shoulder. How had he known to come at the moment I needed him most?

Moonlight poured through the open window and held us together. For the first time, my wolf felt indescribably content. She knew where she wanted to be even if she didn't understand the uncertainties that still lay ahead. What would Lakota say about my devotion to Tak? What would Tak's father say when I called him in the morning to tell him his son was severely injured? How soon would they arrive to take him home where I might never see him again?

How many precious hours did I have left to hold him in my arms?

Chapter 26

When I opened my eyes, I was staring at the ceiling. Tak had his arm draped over my hip, and somehow my legs had wound up beneath the covers. The moon no longer hung in the sky outside my window, but the city lights were bright enough to cast a dim glow in the room. Disoriented, I turned my head to find him asleep. The ice pack must have slipped off, because I could see the shadowy outline of the lump on his head. His wounds were neither better nor worse.

It was the first time I'd ever slept with a man. Truly slept. His breathing was deep and restful, and I didn't want to move an inch. I wondered if our wolves would get along, and the thought of them curled up together warmed my heart.

A sound from another room startled me, and my eyes widened.

What time is it? I thought. *Did I lock the front door?*

In a haze, I slipped out of bed and hurried into the living room. My eyes stung after I switched on a bright lamp.

When the apartment door abruptly swung open, I grabbed a heavy candleholder and held it over my head.

Lakota rushed in like a storm and pulled me into a tight hug. The candleholder fell to the floor with a thud, but I didn't care. As he kissed my head, I felt the protection of family once again. He then held me at arm's length, his blue eyes brimming with concern. "Are you hurt? Do you need a Relic?"

Tak's blood was still all over me, and I realized how shocking it must have looked. "No, I told you I'm fine. I'm sorry about all this."

"Don't be sorry. The son of a bitch who had the audacity to threaten my blood is the one who's going to be sorry."

"He already is."

Mel slung their bags inside. "Why is Wheeler's wolf in the hall?"

I blinked in surprise when I saw a brown wolf scratching his ear. "I don't know. I thought he left. Where's Mother and Father?"

"They came on the same flight but took a different cab from the airport," Lakota said, rubbing his face. "I told him not to trust that driver. He looked like one of those idiots who takes his passengers on the scenic route. Where's Tak?"

When I pointed at the hall, he stormed off.

Mel gave me a quick hug and widened her eyes at my appearance. "I've been worried to death. What can I do? Your mother gave me some kind of herbal sedative to calm me down, so I had plenty of sleep on the plane… and on the cab ride over for that matter."

"Christ!" Lakota boomed. "Tak, wake up."

Melody stepped near the hall. "What's wrong with him?"

I gripped her shirt. "Leave him. He needs rest, not an audience. The Relic said there was nothing more he could do. I haven't had any luck getting him to shift. Maybe Lakota can help."

"Or your father. He's an alpha."

I went to shut the front door. "Once my father sees a strange man lying in my bed, he'll probably pull up a chair and watch him suffer."

"Surely he'll change his mind when you tell him that Tak saved your life."

"He won't see it that way. Once he hears all the facts,

he'll say that all my troubles started the day I met Tak. He's old-fashioned. He'll think that I somehow angered the spirits by inviting him in."

"Well, your mother will talk some sense into him. You can't just let a man suffer like that."

"You don't know my father. He makes blankets out of the pelts of his enemies. That's not a rumor."

Lakota stormed into the room, a swath of hair askew from his topknot. "What happened to him?"

I looked between them and rubbed my eyes. "Why don't you two sit down, and I'll make a pot of coffee. Then I'll tell you the whole story from beginning to end."

One hour and three cups of coffee later, Melody and Lakota were up to speed. I'd told them about the broken window, the death threat, the irate customer, the accusations I made in Dutch's store, how Tak and I came to meet again, the stolen money, and Dumont setting the fire before going feral and trying to kill everyone.

I left out the part about falling in love because Lakota wouldn't be able to focus on anything else. He obviously cared about Tak, but they hadn't resolved their differences, so I didn't know where their relationship stood. It was also premature to reveal my feelings to my brother when I hadn't yet made any declaration to Tak.

Lakota set his empty mug on the kitchen island and turned it in circles. "So that bear was behind it all. You see? This is why you two need a security guard in your store. There are always scammers and extortionists."

"I think I heard about that guy," Melody said, twirling her hair around her finger. "I'd forgotten the story until just now. A couple of months ago, I was talking to a lady who runs an antique store, and she was telling me about some crazy customer who was harassing her, making threats, starting rumors. She even had her windshield busted out, but she had no proof that it was him doing it."

"What happened?" I asked.

Mel's gaze drifted up to the sunflower. "She wound up paying him a big chunk of money to leave her alone, and that was the end of it. It was just one of those cautionary tales we were sharing about bad customers, but maybe he was doing it to other shopkeepers. She thought it was an isolated case, but obviously it wasn't. We should ask around."

"It won't matter to the Council since the case is closed," Lakota pointed out. "From the sound of it, they already ruled in Tak's favor for a justified killing. They're not going to care about all those details since the guy's dead."

Mel tucked her hair behind her ears. "No, but *I* care. Maybe if we had more communication in our neighborhood, we'd know what was going on. We could have stopped it before it landed on our doorstep. I would never have sold him that damn purse." She turned to face me. "And I don't know Dutch, but I hope he's okay. He was the obvious suspect, so you had every right to go in and confront him. I would have done the same."

Lakota chortled. "You would have set his car on fire."

She sipped her coffee. "You underestimate my wrath." Mel set down the cup and tucked her fist beneath her chin. "Maybe we need to create a community watch for store owners. Share information on vandalism and scams. We're always so competitive with one another that maybe we might actually improve business if we worked together."

"I think you're right," I said on a yawn. "If someone is blackmailing one of us for money, then everyone in the area has the right to protect themselves by blacklisting that person. If we can collect enough evidence, maybe the higher authority can lock them up or banish them from the city. No one should have their store burned down, let alone die. It might set an example for others who have the same ideas about messing with Starlight Road. The only challenge is getting others to feel the same way and show up to meetings. You know how people around here are, and they might not trust the new girls, especially the people who are prejudiced against Shifters."

Lakota glanced at the microwave clock. "I should call Mother and see what's holding them up. Maybe they went home first."

All three of us jumped when a fist pounded against the door. "Open up, or I'm knocking it down!" my father demanded.

"The man is psychic," Lakota muttered, hopping out of his seat and jogging toward the door.

Melody and I stood up and wandered into the living room to greet them.

"Where is she?" My father shoved past Lakota.

The moment he laid eyes on me, I felt like a dandelion about to lose all my white florets from an oncoming storm. I straightened my back and lifted my chin, ready for his rebuke as he stalked forward with a menacing stride.

To call my father an intimidating man would be an understatement.

The moment he reached me, he fell to his knees and wrapped his arms around my waist, speaking words of love in his mother tongue. My mother stepped beside him and kissed my cheeks many times, reminding me of her unwavering devotion.

There was no yelling, no anger, no judgment, no withholding of love.

When he finally rose to his feet, he pressed a kiss to my forehead and brushed his fingers across my old scars. It was something he did occasionally in moments of affection. That day had never left his thoughts any more than it had mine. His gaze sharpened when he scanned my body and noticed all the bloodstains.

"I'm fine," I assured him. "It's not my blood."

His eyes narrowed. "What happened?"

"We think the man who tried to burn down our store was

an extortionist. It happened so fast. He was threatening to splash me with gasoline when Tak showed up and—"

"Who's Tak?"

"An old acquaintance of mine," Lakota interjected. "He's from the Iwa tribe."

My father held my gaze. "Go on."

"Tak challenged him, and the man shifted into a grizzly. Everyone was still trying to put out the fire." My head spun just thinking about it, and I rubbed my forehead. "He's hurt, Father. I need you to make him shift. You're the only one here who can. Will you do it, no questions asked? Can you trust me for once?"

He lifted my chin with the crook of his finger. "I trust you always. Everything I do is to protect you, Hope. *Everything*. If that feels like punishment, it was never my intention."

"I thought it was to protect *you*?"

Suddenly we were talking about something else. Melody and Lakota veered into the living room to give us privacy.

My father shook his head, his long hair framing his rigid expression. "Tell me why it is you think I care more about myself than my own flesh and blood?"

"You're a Packmaster. Every decision you make is to secure that position."

"Fair enough. But consider this: if the truth had come out all those years ago and I lost packmates as a result, it would only prove that they weren't worthy enough to live under my rule. River shamed *me* with his lies, not you. He abused his position, and you were young and naive, even if you don't see it that way. You weren't a child, but old wolves are persuasive. He should have never led you to believe that breaking pack rules was acceptable. I kept the secret to protect your honor— to protect your future."

I looked down at a smear of dried blood on my arm. "You've taught me so much, but you also taught me silence. Someday when I join a pack, I want to teach them the consequences of betraying the Packmaster and how it affects everyone's lives.

Secrets tear away trust. I never loved River, and that's why I didn't want to tell you about my intentions. I had none. I wanted to know what it felt like to have a man hold me in his arms, and I stupidly believed his lies."

My father drew in a deep breath. "I should have killed him."

"To what avail? He didn't deserve a death sentence. You would have had to explain it to the pack and to the Council, and that would have meant giving up my shameful secret."

"I'm not ashamed of you."

"But that's how I've felt all this time. Don't you understand? This secret has made me afraid of ever having a relationship or joining a pack. What Packmaster is going to trust a woman who kept secrets? These scars on my face have never gone away. I still have panic attacks, and that's something I'll have to work through. But it's the trauma of what happened in my adult life that's scarred me the most. I don't want you to protect me, Father. I want you to accept my mistakes and love me. Anything else feels like shame."

The light in his eyes grew dimmer. "What can I do to make it right?"

I took his wrist. "Heal Tak. Make him shift."

Without a word, my father bowed and headed down the hallway. Wheeler's wolf trotted in and looked between all of us.

Melody reached in her purse. "I better call my dad to come pick up my uncle before he pees on the floor."

I gave Lakota an apologetic smile as he strolled toward me. "So, how did the get-together go?"

He shook his head and put his arm around me. "Everything's going to be all right, little sister."

My mother collected their bags from the hall and set them inside. "We're staying the night," she said, inviting no argument. "My daughter needs me more than the pack." When she shut the door, she tapped her cane against the floor and looked at the kitchen. My mother was a beautiful woman who still looked in her twenties, but her wisdom somehow made her seem older. "I'll make breakfast. The sun will be up in a few hours, and you'll need your energy. There's much to be done, like assessing the damage at the store and organizing repairs. Try to get some rest, and change out of those clothes. Goodness! All that blood."

Melody leaned over the kitchen island, her feet in the air while talking on the phone. Lakota ambled up behind her and playfully slapped her ass. My mother shooed him out and began pulling food out of the fridge.

Thus ended all my fears that my family wouldn't stand by my decisions and forgive my mistakes. The house felt full again, as did my heart.

Minutes later, my father reappeared with a bemused look on his face.

I met him at the hall entrance. "Well?"

He shook his head. "He wouldn't shift."

I jerked my head back. "You couldn't get him to wake up? Did you use your alpha voice?"

My father pulled out a hard pack of smokes from his shirt pocket, and even though the cigarette was bent, he lit up and took a drag. He held a look I couldn't discern as he released the smoke in a cloudy breath. "Your friend woke up, but he refused to heal."

"Why? I don't understand."

He squinted as if he were trying to read something written on my forehead in small print. "When a Shifter goes to battle for something he believes in, it's his right to keep the scars. I can't force a man to heal if his life is not in danger. It's his choice, and he chose to keep his scars for honor."

"Honor? Who cares about honor? He might have brain damage!"

When a distant chuckle sounded from my bedroom, I knew right then and there that Tak was going to be okay.

CHAPTER 27

TAK GRIMACED WHEN HE TURNED his head and something ice-cold flopped onto his shoulder. Eyes still closed, he grabbed the ice pack and pitched it across the room, embarrassed by all the coddling.

Can't a man suffer in peace?

He'd woken up twice before. Once when Hope had snuggled up next to him, which was a slice of heaven. And the other time, he awoke to some asshole barking orders at him. Not someone from Tak's tribe—this guy had a skull-and-crossbones tattoo on his arm. Tak had a vague memory of telling the man to fuck off.

A bitter taste settled in his mouth, and he slowly opened his eyes to a bright room. A suncatcher of a hummingbird hung high in the window to his right, and Tak furrowed his brow, certain it used to hang in the kitchen.

What time was it? What day?

"Sleep well?"

Startled, Tak snapped his gaze to a man sitting by the door in Hope's working chair. He looked as though he'd been there for a long while—slouched low, legs wide, a short cigarette between two fingers. Tak noticed his skull-and-crossbones tattoo. This guy was also Native American, but not from the Iwa tribe, based on his features. In fact, he kind of looked like…

"You've been asleep for twelve hours," the man said. "Hope crushed up one of those little pain pills by hand and sprinkled it into your mouth like feeding a baby bird. Said she couldn't stand to see you suffer. Before I ask you why Hope is so concerned about your well-being, let's first address your having the balls to tell me to fuck off."

Tak tried to sit up but fell back when a sharp pain lanced through his shoulder. "Who are you?"

"Lorenzo Church," he replied, taking a slow drag from his cigarette. "Friends call me Enzo, but you can call me sir."

Just like Hope, he had long straight hair. They also shared the same frown line between their eyes, only his was deeper and menacing. Alpha power rippled off him in waves, so Tak threw a little of his own back.

Lorenzo's eyebrows popped up. "You're brazen to do that, considering your condition. I'm well aware that you're an alpha."

Tak closed his eyes, trying to focus on anything but the pain searing through his neck and shoulder like fiery claws.

"Maybe what concerns me most is the necklace that you're wearing," Lorenzo added.

The man must be crazy.

"My daughter's had that necklace for a long time—longer than the store has been around. It was how she first became familiar with Shikoba's stones. They were a gift from her mother to do with what she wanted. Hope made that necklace and told me it was for her mate. When I saw her put it up in the store, I assumed she'd given up on finding one. No father wants to believe that his child has chosen a loveless life, so maybe I'm curious as to why I came in this morning and found that necklace around your neck."

Tak's eyes snapped open, and he looked down in surprise. He hadn't even noticed the weight of it. Lorenzo had distracted him so much that Tak hadn't realized the squash blossom necklace he'd admired in her store was around his neck.

Damn if his wolf didn't want to howl.

He reached up with his left hand and touched the turquoise stones. It was a handsome piece, and he wished he could stand in front of a mirror and admire how it looked on him. But his right shoulder was on fire all the way down to his fingertips. Aside from that, he was certain his head might explode if he so much as sat up.

"Anything you want to say to me?" Lorenzo asked.

Tak turned his head to meet his gaze. "I love your daughter. I'd die for her. And when I'm strong enough to stand, I'll get down on one knee and ask for your blessing."

Lorenzo stared at his cigarette. "What's the point if you've already courted her?"

"She doesn't know how I feel," Tak quickly said, his throat parched. "Not really."

"You killed a bear for her. I think she knows."

"What I meant to say is I'm not courting her. Not yet. I don't think she'd accept." Tak's eyes blurred, and he struggled to keep them open.

"And why is that? Have you offended her in some way?" Lorenzo's sharp tone raised the hair on Tak's arms.

"My past might offend her," he replied wearily. "Or it might offend you, and your opinion is what she cares about most."

Lorenzo put out his cigarette in a paper cup and set it on the floor beside him. "I know what the markings on your face mean. You dishonored your tribe."

"I would never dishonor Hope."

"How can I accept that promise when I don't know what you've done?"

Tak couldn't stop touching the necklace as he stared at the ceiling. "I used to drink a lot. I'm not proud of it, but I was young and foolish—a spoiled son living in his father's long shadow. One night, I drove drunk and crashed my car. It should have been me who died, but it was the woman I loved."

His admission was met with silence.

"In the human world, I would have served time. But it

doesn't work that way with us. I've had to live with the guilt. When my tribe stopped reminding me of it, I got the tattoo. I understand if you don't trust me with your only daughter," Tak continued. "But I'm not that same man anymore. I changed my ways a long time ago, but Hope is the one who's changed me the most."

"How?"

"I took responsibility for my actions, but I never forgave myself. I thought avoiding my vices made me a strong man, but I was wrong. Love made me a warrior."

Lorenzo looked away and shook his head. "What do you know of love?"

Incensed, Tak leaned up on his left elbow and settled his weight on it. He gave Lorenzo a good look at the raw wound across his shoulder and chest. "You can take off a necklace, but you can't erase scars. I've chosen to wear these for the rest of my life as a warning. Every man should know what I'm willing to do for someone I love. My wolf called me to her. I can't explain it, but my people believe in soul mates. Our wolves can sense when the other is in danger. That's why I showed up when I did. Had I not loved her, I would have played another game of pool while your daughter confronted a man holding a can of gasoline and a match. Maybe Wheeler would have fought for her, but would he have died for her? A man with his own family thinks twice about such sacrifices." Tak fell onto his pillow and almost passed out from the pain as it burrowed into his flesh and hollowed him out.

Lorenzo sighed and leaned forward on his elbows. "Why don't you put yourself out of your misery?"

Tak couldn't help but laugh. "If you think I'm going to eat a bottle of pills, think again."

Hope's father stood up and approached the bed, a small purple bottle between his fingers. "It's liquid fire. End your suffering and shift. An injury like that requires more than two more shifts to heal completely, so don't worry about losing the marks. When your wolf shifts back, put some of this on the scars you wish to keep. It'll hurt like hell, but it'll do the job. I know it's not something your people traditionally use, but my stomach turns every time I look at that baseball on your forehead. If you don't do as I say, it might become a permanent attraction."

Lorenzo dropped the bottle into Tak's left hand. "I'm not giving you my approval," he clarified. "I'm only giving you liquid fire. You sacrificed yourself for my daughter, and for that, I'm grateful. But you still need to earn my respect. You might want to start by not telling me to fuck off so much."

The two shared a smile before Lorenzo turned away. Tak briefly wondered if this man walked around with liquid fire in his pocket. But Tak had been knocked out for a while, and Lorenzo could have easily acquired some from a neighbor in the building.

"Sir?"

Lorenzo peered over his shoulder, amusement dancing in his eyes. "Yes, boy?"

Tak wanted to fire a comeback, but not as much as he wanted to know that Hope was okay. "Can you send her in?"

"She's gone at my insistence. There's work to be done. Lakota photographed the damages at the store, and they're calling around for repair estimates. Part of the roof caught on fire." Lorenzo stood still and centered his eyes on Tak. "If the fates brought you here to save my daughter, then you have my gratitude. But careful not to mistake that for entitlement. No man deserves my daughter. She is more precious and unique than any gem she sells in her store. The man who wants her heart must honor her in every way. How he speaks to her, provides for her, cherishes and loves her. He must be willing to give her as much love as I do, and that is a high bar to reach."

When Lorenzo gripped the doorknob to leave, Tak chuckled. "I'm a good jumper."

Lorenzo turned around. "I'm going to give you a piece of advice. Not because I like you, but because every man should know this before he starts thinking about a family. It's easy to fall in love; the hard part is being worthy of that love. It's work… every day… for the rest of your life. Some people give up, and they lose everything—even themselves. I can see you're not a young wolf, and maybe that's why I want you to tread carefully. An old wolf misled Hope to betray her Packmaster. She's a stronger woman for it, and I'll not see her weakened by another man again." He held his fist to his chest. "On my word, I'll put that man in the ground."

"So will I," Tak said. "So will I."

CHAPTER 28

AFTER THE CONTRACTORS SURVEYED THE damage, they told us to shut down the store so they could make repairs and bring it up to code. The fire had infiltrated an opening and spread to the shop next door, taking out a larger section of the roof than I'd first thought. Smoke had poured in and left black soot on the walls, which had to be cleaned and repainted—especially in the break room. We also had no electricity, so we hired an additional team to handle that repair.

I leaned back against the counter and stared blankly at our empty store. The front and back doors had been open all morning while we boxed up the merchandise. Some of Mel's outfits were unsalvageable. "I think I'm going to be sick."

Melody put her arm around me. "Just think of it as a vacation while they're doing repairs. When's the last time we had one?"

"We can't afford to close. What if we put some tables and racks on the street?" I suggested, resting my head on her shoulder. "Most of our customers pay cash anyhow, so it wouldn't be difficult to manage. The weather's nice in the mornings. Maybe we can find one of those giant umbrella tables and put our merchandise in three of those parking spaces."

Melody circled around to face me. "That's not a bad idea.

When people see something going on outside, they slow down to check it out. They'll think it's a big sale or something." She glanced at her pale arm. "I could use a little sun. Why don't we spread the word to our neighbors at the ice cream shop and bakery? They had to close down too, but I'm sure they'd join us if we made it into a big block party. We could have fashion, food, and lemonade."

Austin appeared in the doorway, Jericho behind him. "You two should come out of here. We can't do anything else until you get the repairs done."

After hearing about the fire, Melody's former Packmaster offered to help. He brought over box fans and a generator to air out the shop, and Mel's parents hauled all the clothes to the dry cleaner. Lakota and my mother were out back with the contractors, who were still surveying the damage and making plans.

Melody lifted a box of scarves and headed to the door. "I'm going to take this last batch over to the cleaners and tell them we want everything ready by tomorrow."

"We'll give you a lift," Jericho said, putting his arm around her. "It'll be all right, girl. At least the asshat who did this is pushing up daisies."

She scrunched her nose and wriggled free. "You stink."

He shook his sweaty hair away from his face. "You're not exactly smelling wonderlicious yourself." After sniffing his armpit, he stripped out of his concert shirt and draped it over his shoulder. "I'll drive. Hand me the keys."

Austin tossed him the keys and stood outside the door while Jericho strutted off.

Melody looked at me and wiped the sweat from her forehead. "Do you want me to stop off and pick up some fried chicken for later?"

"None for me. The stench in here has killed my appetite. I need to call my father and see how Tak's doing. I'm not certain leaving those two together was the best idea."

Mel blew her purple hair away from her eyes. "Maybe they'll duke it out."

"Don't say that."

She laughed brightly. "You know I'm only teasing. I'm sure everything's fine and we'll discover them playing checkers and drinking tea."

I gave her a peevish glance as I tossed another dirty paper towel into the wastebasket. "I'm going to walk over and visit the banker before he goes home. I still need to pay Edward."

"Do you want to ride with us? I'm sure my uncle won't mind sitting in the back," she said, a mischievous smile on her face as she peered over her shoulder at Austin.

"No, that's okay. It's in the opposite direction from the cleaners and not worth the trouble. After spending all day in here, I need some fresh air. I feel like a zombie."

She gave me a jaunty smile and crossed her eyes. "Tell me about it. I don't even know what time zone I'm in."

"You've had way too many sugary drinks." I glanced around the empty shop. "I wonder if my mom is still out back."

"Last I checked, she was spraying blood off the concrete. Something about bad omens. Lakota bought a long hose they hooked up to the building behind us. You know… it never occurred to me that we don't have a fire extinguisher. I'll pick up a few while I'm out. Hopefully our neighbors will replace the ones they used. Dodging fire inspections and city rules is great, but on the other hand, it makes people irresponsible. Maybe we can think about installing a sprinkler system. Anyhow, I'll go tell everyone we're running errands. Meet you back here in an hour."

The sound of hammering on the roof started up again as the workers continued gutting some of the roof and placing a temporary cover over the holes. We were so lucky that it hadn't gotten out of control and burned the entire building down. While Melody hurried into the back, I grabbed my purse and drifted out into the hot sun. As I cruised by Austin,

I squeezed his arm and smiled humbly. It meant the world to have help from our old packs, but it also made me realize how we shouldn't have to depend on them anymore. They had their own set of issues. Family or not, it wasn't fair to burden them with our problems.

A little girl dashed by me with a balloon in her hand, her mother chasing after her. As I passed in front of a shoe store, a tall Chitah strolled out and stopped to let me pass. It was surreal how life went on as normal, like tornado survivors salvaging what's left of their lives on a beautiful day.

My feet dragged as I replayed every moment of the past week in my head. When I finally looked up, I was standing in front of Dutch's jewelry store. With a heavy heart, I cupped my hands around my eyes and peered inside the empty shop. The lights were still on in the display cases. Dutch must have locked up in a hurry to return my keys.

I wanted to travel back in time and stop myself from going to his store in the first place. Had I never gone, he wouldn't have come after me. My anger had led him into the mouth of danger, and yet it had also saved my life. While I could brush off these events and call them a coincidence, my heart knew otherwise. Everything we do in life is a link in the chain.

I prayed he was all right. Each time I called the number he'd left on my waiting list, it went straight to voice mail. The Relic who had taken him must have been a passerby. I'd never seen him before, and no one knew him based on my vague description.

If Dutch was still alive, I wanted to apologize and find a way to make it right between us. He might never forgive me, but I owed him a favor, and I would remain in his debt until the day he collected.

———⟶

After a leisurely walk, I visited our banker and withdrew

enough funds to cover Edward's services. I took out extra, just in case we needed to pay one of the contractors a deposit.

Large grackles gathered on the sidewalk outside the front door, dining on a pizza crust that someone had discarded. These blackbirds were a nuisance, especially during migration when they flocked in large numbers and drove people crazy at night with all the noise. During the walk back to my shop, I read text messages my father had sent. Tak was awake, so Lakota had gone home to speak with him. If things didn't go well between them, Tak might leave town without a goodbye. Melody's uncle had driven Tak's truck back to the apartment earlier, so all he needed was a reason to leave.

Or a reason to stay.

I hoped leaving the necklace with him would give him reason enough, but now I wasn't so sure.

"Is everything cool?"

I glanced up at Nash pulling up alongside me in his pizza delivery van. I approached the open passenger window and rested my arms on it. "Hi, Nash. How are you doing?"

"I should ask you," he said, a somber look on his face. "I drove by your shop earlier and noticed all the action. I tried to steer down the alley to see what was going on, but they had it blocked off. Word spreads fast around here. The lady at the shoe store made it sound like the whole place burned down."

"No, just some damage in the back. Don't you have air-conditioning in here?" I asked, waving my hand in front of the vent.

"I just dropped off a huge delivery to a pack of three hundred, so I'm airing out the van. It's not good to run the air conditioner with the windows down." He took off his red baseball hat and wiped his fingers through his curly hair, his blond locks sweaty from the heat. Then he put his hat on backward. "Are you going somewhere?"

"No. I just stopped off at the bank, and now I'm heading back." As much as I wanted to go home, my mother didn't have a spare set of keys to lock up, and I had no idea if Melody had returned or gone back to the apartment. "I have to finish up some work at the store," I said, resting my chin on my arm.

"You look beat. Hop in. It's just around the corner."

"What about your orders?"

He laughed. "I've only got two more stops, and you're on the way to one."

Thank the fates for men like Nash. The last thing I needed was a mugger snatching my purse and making off with our money. I climbed inside the hot van. "It smells good in here. I bet it makes you hungry all the time."

The motor rumbled as he merged back into traffic. "I don't eat the stuff myself. I stick to a high-protein diet." He flexed his arm. "Plus when you smell pizza every day, you get sick of it. I go home stinking of sausages. Sometimes they have me chopping vegetables, and I can never get the smell of onions off my hands. Not exactly a turn-on for the ladies."

He slowed at the light and turned the cold air on full blast. Nash had all the qualities a Packmaster looked for, and I was grateful for his kindness. While I stared at the dark circles under my eyes in the visor mirror, he reached for something in the back.

"Here," he said, offering me a slice of pizza. "You look like you've been busting your ass all day. When's the last time you ate anything?"

"I don't remember."

"This one's on the house."

I took the slice. "Isn't this someone's dinner?"

He shook his head. "The last time I delivered to this customer, he didn't tip me. I live off tips, so he can kiss my ass if he has a problem with it."

I took a big bite, gobbling up the stringy cheese. Seemed I was hungrier than I first thought. "I hope this doesn't get you in trouble."

"My boss makes too much money from large orders to give a rat's ass about one customer's complaint. Anyhow, friends don't let friends starve to death."

When I finished eating it all the way up to the crust, I tossed the remaining bread out the window and into a trash bin on the curb.

"Nice shot," he said. "So what happened at the store? I hate to rely on rumors."

I wiped my mouth. "The arsonist is dead. Not much to gossip about anymore."

"Dead?" His eyebrows arched as we turned the corner. "That's some swift justice."

"There was a brawl out back that escalated."

"Why would anyone want to burn down your store?"

"I think he was targeting me for extortion. He's been doing all kinds of things to undermine my business." I rubbed my eyes and reclined my head against the seat. "Now we just have a big mess to clean up."

"Sleepy?" Nash rolled up his window, making the van a little cooler. "It usually doesn't take long for it to kick in."

"What? The cold air?"

"The sedative."

I snorted and looked over at him. "That's not the best joke after the week I've had."

Nash smiled and turned on the radio. An old song by James Taylor played like a distant dream.

I *was* feeling kind of loopy, but I'd been up since before dawn and hardly slept the night before. I glanced in the back to get another slice of pizza when I noticed a black bag next to the open box. Curious, I touched the zipper and realized it was an empty bowling bag.

A sinking feeling formed in the pit of my stomach. "Where's your bowling ball?" I asked, slurring my words.

Nash reached over and patted my head. "Nighty night."

Chapter 29

After he'd shifted to wolf form and back, the deep gashes on Tak's shoulder fused enough for him to seal it permanently. He went into the bathroom and prepared for the painful process. In his tribe, warriors who kept battle scars rarely used liquid fire. Not shifting to heal was a show of bravery, and the elders insisted suffering was the only way to honor their ancestors. But they used liquid fire for tattoos, and Tak knew firsthand about the excruciating process.

They didn't call it liquid fire for nothing. It wasn't an actual liquid; that would be a dangerous weapon. It came in a grease form—like ointment—and it only required a small amount to do the job.

"Do it fast," he muttered, psyching himself up for it.

He gripped the basin with one hand and gritted his teeth as he smeared the liquid fire across each scar, his skin searing as the potion performed its magic. He left alone the parts of the wound that were still open. He'd have to wait for those to naturally seal before he repeated the process to make a more uniform scar.

Tak bellowed in pain, his teeth clenched in a futile attempt to keep quiet. Four claw marks ran from the back of his shoulder right over the front—one precariously close to his neck. Just an inch higher and it would have sliced his head halfway off.

A knock sounded on the bathroom door. "Are you in pain?" Lakota asked.

Tak grimaced as he wiped the residual ointment away with a rag. "What gave it away? The screams?" He glanced in the mirror at the lump on his head, which wasn't as ominous as it had been earlier that morning. The shifting helped, so he didn't bother worrying about it.

Tak couldn't braid his hair with the fire still shooting down his arm and chest, so he left it free. At least he had his own clothes, the ones he'd left behind while guarding Hope's front door. She'd washed and folded them. Damn if she wasn't the most thoughtful woman, even in times of crisis.

Tak opened the door, his white muscle shirt in hand.

Lakota glanced down at it. "Need help?"

"Are you my nurse?"

Lakota grabbed the shirt. "For the right price. Raise your good arm, Your Highness."

Tak put his good arm through the sleeve hole while Lakota looped the shirt over his head. He needed help with his right arm since his muscles were sore and it was excruciating to lift it. Another shift would do him some good, but he wanted to stay lucid for a little while and find out what was going on.

"I'm sorry I left Oklahoma without talking to you," Lakota said, straightening the shirt before stepping back. "I tried, but you're a stubborn asshole, and maybe I didn't try hard enough. I was afraid if you knew the truth about why I was there, you'd think I lied to you on purpose. Our friendship was real. You were like a brother to me. In the end, it was easier to just leave without explanation."

"Why was it so easy for you to doubt my word?"

Lakota held on to the doorjamb. "Because in my line of work, a man's word isn't good enough. Bounty hunters lose their lives for placing their trust in the wrong men. Under any other circumstances, we would have been fast friends. But I still had a job to do. I couldn't tell them you were innocent because you said so. I've got to rule out everyone and make a strong case. I insulted you under your own roof, but you walked away from our friendship without looking back long before I did. I'm telling you, man, I never intended to take advantage of the trust and kindness your tribe gave to me. I didn't know walking in what it was like behind those walls. I've been undercover before and lived with packs, but all of them were involved in criminal activities, and none of them felt like a home. It wasn't easy to leave, but what choice did I have? Your father practically shoved me down the aisle with Mel."

Tak tossed back his head and laughed. Lakota joined in, and just like that, the rift between them mended. They no longer spoke of forgiveness or blame. Tak trusted Lakota, and so did his wolf. Yes, he'd felt betrayed, but now he understood why Lakota had done what he'd done. It wasn't an apology he needed so much as finding out if the bond they shared was real. It was an unconventional way to form a friendship, but Lakota was a strong wolf whom Tak respected. Maybe one reason Tak liked him was that he could envisage a future where Lakota was his second-in-command. Tak hadn't made any concrete plans about leaving the tribe, but maybe he'd thought about it enough that it was time to give it some real consideration.

"Now that we're good, I should probably ask why you're still in town, hanging around my baby sister."

"All I wanted to do was protect her. I know you do things differently in the city, but I couldn't in good conscience leave her alone. Especially a woman inexperienced with weapons. Didn't your father teach her how to use a knife?"

"Hope had her own interests, and they didn't involve hunting deer. Besides, most of us city wolves don't need weapons. We're civilized, remember?" Lakota gripped Tak's good shoulder and led him down the hall. "Let me get you a beer."

Tak chuckled. "I should probably mention I'm a recovering alcoholic."

Lakota stopped cold and searched his eyes. "*No wonder* you never drank the beers I bought you. All this time I thought you were just being an asshole."

Tak winced when another streak of pain lanced through his shoulder. "If I'd told you I was an alcoholic, I would have had to tell you my story. The two go hand in hand, and I didn't want you to know."

"What story? You mean the one about you getting into the accident and the woman dying?"

Tak could scarcely breathe. "You knew?"

"Your packmates like to gossip. They didn't mention alcohol, only that you got the tattoo after the accident. Why didn't you just tell me?"

"You were the only one who didn't see me with tainted eyes. You would have treated me differently."

Lakota turned his mouth to the side, and they resumed their pace. "I had a feeling there was more to the story; the accident was mentioned in passing one night at the bar. Some men have loose lips when they drink."

"I'd like to know which man was flapping his gums about my business to outsiders."

"Outsiders?" Lakota pretended to be insulted.

Tak put his hand on Lakota's shoulder. "Before we go any further, you should know I'm in love with Hope."

Lakota's jaw set. "You better mean hope in the philosophical sense and not my baby sister."

Tak gave his shoulder a squeeze and mashed his lips together to keep from smiling. "She's no baby."

"Let me know when that shoulder of yours is healed so I can kill you."

Tak let go. "So that's all it takes for you to hate me again?"

"A good brother doesn't make it easy for a man to put a claim on his sister."

"I'm not asking your permission," Tak said matter-of-factly. "I just want you to know where I stand. Nothing's decided. She might not even choose me. I already asked her once, and she turned me down."

Lakota's eyes lit up. "Really?"

"Don't look so thrilled."

"She's a smart female. Hope isn't looking for a mate, and she's not the kind of woman who would accept the first offer."

When they entered the main room, Lorenzo was pacing back and forth like a windup toy, his eyes fixed on his phone.

"Have you heard from your sister?" he asked Lakota. "Melody said she's not back."

Tak glowered. "Back from where? I thought she was at the store?"

Lakota glanced at the message before checking his own phone. He didn't seem too concerned. "Did anyone call her? Sometimes she takes long walks."

Lorenzo dialed a number. "It keeps going to voice mail." Then he looked up at Tak as if searching for an answer.

Perhaps he was wondering if Tak had a sixth sense that Hope was in danger, but Tak didn't feel anything was amiss. He adjusted his muscle shirt away from his wound and looked at Lakota, who was reading a message. "Well?"

Lakota blanched. "Austin and Jericho searched the route she would have walked and didn't find anything. The banker said she left."

"When?" Lorenzo asked.

After a pregnant pause, Lakota lifted his gaze. "An hour ago."

⟶

"What the hell were you thinking?" a man roared. "Did I tell you to kidnap her? Did I?"

"You didn't say *not* to kidnap her," I heard Nash reply. "She waltzed out of the bank with a lumpy purse. Look at all that money."

"Yeah, look at all that money," the man parroted. I recognized the voice but couldn't place it. "Do you realize the shitstorm you just opened up?"

"I don't give a damn," Nash retorted. "You promised me more money."

"Wasn't the cash from the safe enough?"

"A drop in the bucket. If she keeps that much in the safe, just imagine how much they have in total. That's a lot of dough."

As I became more lucid, I peered through my lashes. The seat belt still held me up, and the van reeked of pizza. Through the windshield, Nash's red baseball cap came into focus first. I looked at the other man. Messy black hair, mustache… *Wait a minute.* The longer I stared, the more I realized it was River.

My head pounded, and a bitter taste settled in my mouth. I closed my eyes, listening to as much of the conversation as I could through the open window.

"Are you so stupid that you think she's just going to walk into the bank and close her account because you asked her to?" River said, scraping his shoe on the asphalt. "What part of discreet do you not understand?"

I chanced another look. We were parked alongside a road, no buildings or telephone poles within view.

"You need to take her back. *Now*, before she wakes up," River ordered. "This wasn't part of the deal."

"I'm not taking her anywhere until I get more money. I've done a lot of dirty shit for you. Wrote on their windows, delivered your note, threw my bowling ball into the store—and that was my best ball. Played delivery boy so you could pay off that Japanese woman. Is that what you did with your share of the money? You need to get a life. At least I'm not living in the woods."

"How many sedatives did you give her?"

"Same amount I put on that pizza when I broke into her apartment and robbed the safe. Look, I left that life behind a long time ago, so you better believe it's going to take a lot of money for me to put my ass on the line. And by the way, she had a wolf in one of the bedrooms, so I think I deserve a bonus."

"Same wolf you supposedly killed at the shop?"

"He came at me, so I knocked him out with a tire iron. He should be dead."

"But he's not," River pointed out. I heard him drumming his fingers on the hood of the van.

"He must have nine lives. I heard that crazy bear almost killed him."

"Maybe that's who I should have hired."

"Fuck you, River. Those scam artists are unprofessional douchebags. Hope never had a clue what I was doing. That's the way you con someone. Nobody gets hurt."

"This isn't going to work. You need to take her back before she wakes up. You have *no* idea who you're dealing with."

"I'm not afraid of you."

"Maybe not, but if she wakes up, you're going to have Lorenzo Church to deal with, and if he becomes your problem, then that means he's my problem. I don't feel like spending my life on the run."

"You should have thought of that before."

"Goddammit, take her back!"

When I heard a skirmish, I peered through my lashes at them throwing punches. While they were distracted in a testosterone war, I unlatched my seat belt, horrified to discover that the keys weren't in the ignition.

I can't believe this!

All this time, River was the one terrorizing me into quitting the store. Not Dutch, not even the grizzly.

Tire iron. Nash mentioned a tire iron.

When the two men fell out of sight, I quickly reached beneath the seats. Still groggy, I did my best to search the immediate area behind me. A bottle of powder sat inside the open pizza box, the contents spilled carelessly. If Tak's wolf had chased Nash outside my store, Nash wouldn't have had time to reach far inside the van. It had to be around here somewhere! When my fingers touched metal behind the seat, I got a firm grip of the rod and sat up. With one end of the tool bent, I wasn't certain which was the best way to hold it.

River sprang into sight and spat out a mouthful of blood. "I should have handled everything on my own."

"Maybe you should have," Nash fired back from somewhere out of view. "I don't exactly like stalking and harassing women. I thought you partnered up with me because I had easy access to her building, but it sounds to me like you're just too chickenshit about her father to do the work yourself." Nash howled with laughter as he stood up, gripping the van to steady himself.

"You won't be laughing when Church's pack is hunting your ass down. I lived with them for a long time, and they'll skin you alive. Church won't kill you fast; he'll take his time and pour salt on your wounds. You'll beg for mercy. And do you think he'll give two shits that I'm the one who put you up to it?"

"I'm tired of delivering pizzas," Nash said, his tone flat. "I don't want to go back to burglary either. Cracking a safe is easy. But when people start hiring private investigators to track you down, it loses its appeal. If I had enough money, I could figure my shit out and find a real job. Look, I don't want to hurt her; I just want what you promised me. There's no dignity in driving a van around and groveling for tips. I make good money, but it's not enough to live on for the next few centuries."

"That's not my problem."

Nash pounded his fist against the van. "I just made it your problem! What if I sent her father a letter and told him everything?"

"You wouldn't *dare*."

"How much is my silence worth to you?"

"Her seat belt's off," River said, his voice quiet.

With lightning speed, I threw open the door and fled.

When I put enough distance between us, I turned around, the tire iron raised high and ready to strike. "Stay back, or I'll knock your head off!"

Both men slowed their pace, River holding his hands up.

"I'm not going to hurt you," he said. "Your friend made a wrong turn, and I'm helping him take you back home."

Was he delusional? Obviously he hadn't a clue how much I'd heard, but the least he could do was fabricate a good lie.

"You're a better liar than that, River. Remember?"

When he took a step forward, I angled my body, ready to strike.

"I never lied to you," he said.

"You're the one who convinced me that no alpha would want an inexperienced woman. I didn't come up with that all on my own, but you made me believe it was my idea. Months and months of grooming me. You said I was special. You said no one would find out, and my father wouldn't care."

"Your stupidity isn't my fault."

"You were a seasoned wolf with years of experience living in a pack. My father trusted you, and so did I."

His lip curled. "Do you think I care that your feelings are hurt?"

"Why are you doing this? Were you the one who stole my clothes and put them on my doorstep?"

"No, that was *him*," he said, jerking a thumb at Nash.

Nash turned to face River. "You told me to do whatever it took to humiliate or scare her. Don't act all innocent."

I scowled at Nash. "I never would have expected this from you. We've always been good to you. Lakota tips double, and I could have gotten you an apartment in our building like you wanted."

"I made that up so you'd trust me to use your bathroom. I needed to scope out the rooms and unlock a window."

I furrowed my brow. "A window?"

He flapped his arms. "You have a double deadbolt, so it was easier to fly up. Brought my tools inside a bag. I had to ride naked down the elevator since the bag was too heavy with cash for my bird to haul out. Going out the way I came would have also meant leaving your window open, and that would've narrowed down suspects to avian Shifters or Superman. You should get a better safe. That's a crap model you can open with a special magnet. Nothing personal, but a man's gotta eat." He jerked his thumb at River. "This guy paid me to do all those things. Am I sorry? Only that I didn't put enough sedatives in your pizza slice earlier so you didn't have to see this. I've incurred a lot of debt over the years paying off bounty hunters, and I'm trying to get ahead in life. You can't blame me for making a living."

"Hurting someone isn't how you make a living," I fired back.

"Not everyone has the luxury of joining a pack," River said. "Some of us have to fend for ourselves."

His words were weapons intended to inflict guilt and pain.

River branched to the right, closing in on me. "Put that down, and we'll talk. I don't want trouble any more than you do. Drugging you wasn't my idea."

"But threatening me and vandalizing the store was. Don't pretend like you have a moral compass. Did you hire that grizzly to burn down my store?"

"I had nothing to do with the fire. It seems like you're good at making enemies without my help. You see how dangerous it is for a little girl to own a business? Without a pack, you're nothing but a walking target."

"So you were just trying to show me the light?"

When I glimpsed Nash coming at me, I swung the weapon and struck him in the head. His eyes widened for a moment before he swayed and hit the ground like a slow-falling tree.

"Why the animosity?" I asked River, trying to steady my shaking hands. "Why do you hate me so much that you want to destroy my life?"

His lips thinned below his mustache. When he finally spoke, his words dripped with anger and pain. "No pack would take me in. When Lorenzo Church boots you out, people don't need to know the reason. I'm forced to live like an animal, stealing uneaten food from tables and living in the woods so I can save what little cash I have. Then I saw you opened up a business. Well, *good for you*," he sneered. "The Packmaster's princess can do no wrong. We were both guilty, but I took the punishment while you reaped the rewards."

"Do you think it's been easy for me to carry the guilt?"

"There you go again, talking about feelings while one of us is sleeping in a ditch between a cast of hawks and a herd of deer."

"I didn't get a free ride. Nobody gave me anything I didn't earn myself. I worked hard for this business, and I chose to become independent so I could succeed on my own. You don't need a pack to do well in life. I blamed myself for a long time, but you took advantage of a young girl who wanted to feel special. I take responsibility for the choices I made, but I've always felt bad about what happened to you. Did you ever *once* regret the choice you made, and not because of the struggles you've endured but because of how it might have hurt me? Your honeyed words convinced me to lie to my father and deceive him. And not just my father, but my Packmaster. Why couldn't you have waited until I left the pack to be my lover?"

"Then I wouldn't have been the first."

Lakota was right. I was just a trophy to some of these men. I knew River had never loved me, but I wanted to believe that he'd felt something for a young woman he'd spent countless hours giving special attention to. Had everything he said been a lie, all just so he could claim my virginity? Had he done that with other young women in the pack?

Believing that hurt more than anything.

In the distance, an engine roared in our direction. I stepped onto the road and away from River to get a better look at the truck gunning toward us, a mirage of heat fluttering behind it.

"Someone's coming," I said, warning him.

He stepped onto the road, forcing me to turn my back

to the oncoming vehicle. "Humans don't get involved, remember?"

The truck horn blared incessantly.

River reached for the tire iron, and I swung it at him.

"You're going to get yourself run over!" he yelled.

I spun around, startled by screeching tires directly behind me. The white truck came to a hard stop. When my eyes rose from the grill to the windshield, I recognized Tak in the driver's seat. My father and Lakota sat next to him. A gunmetal-grey Camaro eased up behind them. Inside were Wheeler, Jericho, Austin, my mother...

Oh my God.

They emerged from their vehicles.

Slowly. As if to make a point that the cavalry had arrived. Every last one of those Shifters looked prepared to shed blood.

"Wait," I pleaded.

Tak didn't stop. His eyes were on the bloody tire iron in my hand.

I held my left arm in front of my father to stop him from going after River. He dragged his gaze toward me, fire burning in his eyes.

More cars appeared. Melody and members of my old pack formed a wide ring around us. I expected to see River running off, but another car stopped in the opposite direction, more men getting out.

"What *right* have you to take my child?" my father snarled at River.

I blocked his view before he charged. "Father, wait."

Tak approached and swept my hair back. "She's been drugged. Look at her eyes."

"Your scars," I whispered, staring at the red claw marks down his shoulder.

Tak stripped out of his tank top. "He's mine."

"Neither of you will do anything," I declared, dropping the tire iron. It clanged on the concrete and drew everyone's attention. "That man shamed me a long time ago, but he'll shame me no more. He's responsible for everything, Tak. The stolen money, the broken window, the note—he paid off that man to do his dirty work," I said, pointing at Nash. "He's offended me in the worst way by coming after my business and the people I love. I won't have you put one finger on him."

My father's lips peeled back in displeasure. "Why?"

"Because he's mine to challenge."

CHAPTER 30

IF THERE'S ONE THING A pack understands, it's honor.

Tak had already fought one enemy of mine, but this was a battle no man could fight for me, nor would I let him. This had nothing to do with my past with River. He'd threatened my livelihood, stolen our hard-earned money, and hired someone to stalk me. I would never be able to hold my head up if I didn't challenge the adversary who conspired to ruin my life.

My fate was not for him to decide.

I exchanged a meaningful glance with Tak, and he made no further attempt to intervene. That meant more to me than he could possibly imagine. He inclined his head and veered left while my father went right. Challenging River was about salvaging my honor and standing up for my convictions. And yet it was more than that. River suddenly became the wolf who'd attacked me all those years ago. He became the judgmental eyes of my peers. Facing him gave me just enough hope and courage to believe that I might one day become a stronger person.

River's fingers twitched as his gaze flicked back and forth between the Shifters who encircled us. But when his eyes steadied on mine, he showed no sign of fear. I knew in that moment he wasn't afraid of losing—he was afraid of winning.

I'd never fought anyone before, but I could feel my wolf

lending me her courage. This was a challenge between wolves, so I waited for him to make the first shift.

River put his hands on his hips and lowered his head. "I don't want to hurt your daughter. This is a misunderstanding."

"You hurt my little girl a long time ago," my father said, his voice controlled and dangerous. "The only misunderstanding is that you thought you could do it again."

I snatched a rock off the ground and threw it at River to get his attention. It bounced off his head, drawing laughter from the crowd. "Are you going to shift or stick your nose farther up my father's ass?"

There were raised eyebrows and a couple of oohs.

My mother struck the ground with her cane and silenced everyone.

Tak moved behind River and, with a hard shove, pushed him toward me. "A warrior doesn't beg for his life."

I kicked off my shoes, and when I saw a hint of a smile touch River's lips, I gracefully shifted. I only had a few minutes before blacking out. My wolf stalked toward him, head low and teeth bared. I savored the fear in his eyes, and when he stumbled backward, Tak shoved him into the center again.

"Fine," he growled, tearing off his shirt. "Have it your way." Clothes fell away as River transformed into a dirty-brown wolf. His size was unremarkable in comparison to other males, but strength and agility counted more in a fight.

The concrete heated the pads of my paws, and energy from the crowd buzzed against my fur like static electricity. I relinquished all control to my wolf, trusting her instincts as the quiet voice within me rose to a thundering roar.

River's wolf pulled in a scent and hesitated. Seizing the opportunity, my wolf lunged and went for his throat. He dodged the attack and tried to scuttle behind me, but I snapped around and sank my teeth into his back.

River yelped and pivoted around so fast that he bit my muzzle before I knew what was happening. I reared up and knocked him to the ground. He was bigger and stronger but not half as determined.

Not by a long shot.

We fell into a roll, jaws snapping and puncturing the skin. When he tried to blind me with a savage bite, I drew back and sank my teeth into his leg. They ripped through muscle and bone. River's wolf yelped, and when he tried to escape, I trotted around him, blood dripping from my tongue.

A hot wind blew, scattering dirt across the asphalt. My heart was beating like the drum of my ancestors, filling me with the wisdom of who I was. Not just a woman with dreams but the descendant of wolf warriors.

Words tumbled around me like meaningless noise, and all I could understand was the emotion behind them.

Fight.

Fight.

With all the power I could harness, I crashed into River, my rib cage rattling from impact. The metallic taste of blood was salty on my tongue, and I thirsted for more. His overconfidence made him weak. Because of my size, I could get at his throat more easily than he could mine.

When his fangs tore through my back, I growled as he took the dominant position. Shaken, I looked at my father... my mother... so many of my friends and family.

And then I saw Tak.

He nodded at me once, and I saw everything in that look. But most of all, he looked at me as if he saw no weakness. That stirred a fire in me like nothing else. I scurried backward and charged River again—this time snapping my jaws around the soft part of his throat and eliciting a growl that vibrated in my mouth. I had him in a lock, and the more he squirmed to free himself, the more it ripped his flesh. I tightened my jaws into a steel trap. When he tried to escape, I threw all my weight on him and knocked him to the ground.

I stood astride the wolf, my hold even tighter, until he quit struggling.

As he lay there panting, his eyes closed, and his body stilled. I hadn't severed the artery, but I didn't have to.

River was submitting.

Once he turned up his belly, I released my death grip and shifted.

"I've won the challenge and spared your life," I said, reminding him that I had the authority to make demands. I stood beside River, my hair cascading over my breasts, blood staining my skin. "You'll leave the city tonight. If you ever return, you know what that means."

Death. I didn't have to say it. Everyone standing witness knew what it meant to back out on a demand made by the victor.

My father touched my brow, his dark eyes centered on mine. "You're a warrior now," he said quietly.

It wasn't a compliment—not the way he said it.

He implied my spirit wolf was too powerful and independent to mate. Shifters preferred strong women, but few—if any—would take on a woman willing to challenge and kill a male. It raised questions about stability, even though it was a double standard. Only an alpha could handle a woman that strong, and with my checkered past, that would probably never happen.

My father turned and spat on River. "Get that termite out of here."

River shifted to human form as two men hauled him away.

"What do you want to do with the white man?" my father asked.

I thought about Nash, who was still knocked out cold. "He's a Shifter, so turn him over to the Council. Maybe a few years in jail will give him time to regret his actions and ponder the importance of integrity over money."

My father went to take care of it.

A few men howled, still riled up from the fight. As the crowd dispersed, Tak placed his hands on my shoulders and looked me over with careful measure.

Most of my wounds had healed during the shift, but for the first time, I didn't care about the possibility of more scars. It felt like I'd conquered an old demon. The victory filled an emptiness inside me that I'd carried for so long—a dark corner of my soul that had always doubted my courage.

"We need to get off the street," Tak said, wrapping a thin tribal blanket around me. "Someone's bound to drive by and wonder if we're having a nudist party."

I stared into an open field, overcome with mixed emotions. Now that I'd delivered retribution for the wrong River had committed against me, I wondered if he would obey my demands and stay gone. Despite what he'd done, I didn't want him dead. I pitied the man he'd chosen to become.

Tak lifted me into his arms and carried me as if he felt no pain in his shoulder, but I knew that wasn't true. His wounds were bright red, and some open gaps were still weeping blood.

"Did you see how fast she took him down?" someone remarked. *"Jesus."*

I rested my head against Tak's good shoulder. "How did you find me?"

He continued his leisurely pace. "We knew something had happened when you didn't show up at the store, but I couldn't sense anything. Your family called for backup, and we all drove around… searching. Then all of a sudden, I just knew which way to go. The fates led me here."

"Do you really believe that? The fates have done an awful lot to keep us apart."

"Everyone needs to be tested."

I placed my hand against his necklace.

"Someone special gave this to me," he said, puffing his chest out. "I'm never taking it off."

"It might be difficult to shower with it on."

"At least it'll be clean," he quipped, a smile playing on his lips.

"It might be dangerous in bed. You'll knock someone's tooth out."

Tak rocked with laughter and stopped. The wind blew his handsome mane, and in some indefinable way, he seemed like a different man.

"What happens now?" I asked.

He pursed his lips and gazed off in the distance. "I take you home. Just you and me."

"What about Lakota and Melody?"

"They can get a motel."

"What for?"

Tak turned his head so slowly to look at me that I felt a flutter in my belly. "I'm going to run a hot bath, and we're going to bathe together."

My brows arched. "We can't both fit in that tub."

"We'll find a way to fit."

"Then what?"

Tak continued walking until we reached the truck. I climbed up in the seat and looked through the windshield at my father supervising the cleanup. After they loaded River and Nash into the back of Nash's van, they sped away.

Tak got into the driver's side and shut the door. When he started the engine, he blasted the cold air on me, which felt like bliss. Mel hastily gathered my clothes while two men searched the area for more evidence. One woman unscrewed the cap to a large water bottle and doused a bloodstain on the road.

Tak suddenly reached over and turned my chin to face him. "Don't you want to know what happens next?"

"Animalistic sex? Omelets? A movie? Snuggling? Dinner with my family?"

Tak put the truck in reverse. "All in that order."

"My father will never allow it."

He winked. "That's up for debate." Tak tenderly brushed my hair out of my eyes. "Do you remember everything from the fight?"

I nodded.

"Good."

Tak wasn't subtle with his entries or exits. After he circled around, he hit the gas and we tore off. The fact that no one had questioned my leaving with Tak left me wondering what my family's opinion was of this man.

This *incredible* man who had not only saved my life but helped me reclaim it from the ghosts of my past.

He'd taught me that the truth is the hardest obstacle to face, and because of his bravery and unwavering support, I was no longer afraid.

Chapter 31

I sipped my sweet tea while the waitresses in their Howlers T-shirts were buzzing around us like busy little bees, their trays loaded with hamburgers and beer pitchers. Two weeks had flown by since I'd challenged River, and with him gone, life was finally getting back to the way it used to be.

Except for Tak. He had become my new normal.

Mel raised her glass of beer, her jade eyes glazed after too many drinks. "Here's a toast to air-conditioning. God bless."

A few of us laughed and nodded in agreement. The air-conditioning and electricity were up and running as of two days ago, one reason we were out celebrating. Closing Moonglow hadn't impacted sales as drastically as we initially feared. It turned out that selling merchandise on the sidewalk was a creative way to attract new customers. Some folks had heard about the fire and stopped by to show their support. Despite the heat, we made the best of it with the help of neighboring shops and a supportive community.

"Do you think fly Shifters ever existed?" Mel pondered.

Lennon grinned handsomely. "If they did, we swatted them into extinction."

"Bug Shifters aren't possible," Hendrix said matter-of-factly. "It's physically impossible to get that small."

"What about large predators?" I interjected. "They're bigger than our human form."

"Not the same. They're what... five times our size? Tops. We're like a bazillion times bigger than a fly. My junk can't cram into something that small."

Lakota tipped his head to the side. "What about that time you wore a Speedo to the lake?"

"Don't mention that again," Hendrix said with a straight face.

Mel looked between them. "Why do I have the feeling I'm missing out on all the good stories? One of these days, I'm going to get you guys to talk."

Lakota had always been close with the twins. In some ways, he acted as their big brother. Whenever he was in town, he'd take them fishing or camping.

Tak chuckled and looked between Lakota and Melody. "So you two knew each other since childhood."

Mel batted her eyelashes at Lakota, and they shared a private look that spanned years.

Hendrix rumpled his red hair and jerked his chin at Lakota. "Any updates on what happened to the pizza guy?"

Lakota rested his elbows on the table, his blue eyes narrowing to slivers. "The higher authority went easy on him. Five years. He deserves more than that for stalking and drugging my sister."

Mel frowned. "I actually liked Nash. He always gave us extra pepperoni. Why are all the nice guys psychotic assholes?"

Tak put his arm across the back of my chair. "That's what happens when men are motivated by greed. Let it be a lesson that family and morals come first. One man was driven by animosity and the other by money, and look where it got them."

Mel, Lakota, Hendrix, and Lennon nodded in agreement. Tak had made an indelible impression on everyone over the past few weeks. Lennon and Hendrix were always looking for examples of how to lead, even though Tak wasn't a Packmaster.

I'd noticed a change in them during the past year, and I could see they were yearning for something more. It was the same look a man gets when he's searching for purpose. They weren't yet seasoned enough to form their own packs, but time and experience would change that.

"You should have killed River," Hendrix said to me. "That's what I would have done."

Tak shook his head. "Dying is too swift a punishment. A rival's submission is the sweetest victory."

Lennon gave Hendrix another furtive glance, and the two men drank their beers.

"What's up with you two?" Mel asked, pointing at the twins. One of her shoulder straps on her black tank top slid off, but she ignored it. "You're up to something sneaky. Did you put a skunk in Lakota's truck again? Because that wasn't funny the first time."

Hendrix looked at his twin, who raised his eyebrows. After a few beats, Lennon finally shrugged. Sometimes they carried on entire conversations with their eyes and body language.

Hendrix rubbed his finger beneath his eye and nodded. "Me and Lennon are taking off to Alaska."

Mel gave them a sour look. "And you didn't ask if I wanted to come? I'm down for another vacation."

"It's, uh… not a vacation."

"I don't get it."

Lakota adjusted Mel's tank top and put his arm around her. "I think what your brothers are trying to tell you is that they're ready to leave their footprint in the world. They're ready to take the journey that all alphas take."

Tears sprang to her eyes—mostly drunken tears since Mel wasn't a huge crier. "But you're my baby brothers. You can't leave me."

When she pouted, both men rose from the table. Hendrix knelt to her right, and Lennon stood behind her and clapped his hands on her shoulders.

"Did you think we were going to hang around Austin our

whole lives and work in a bakery?" Hendrix asked. "You knew this day was coming."

It was an emotional moment, and I leaned into Tak. Lennon and Hendrix weren't just going out to find themselves; they were embarking on an adventure that could be dangerous as they would encounter rogues, other alphas, and Breed in unfamiliar terrain. Strong packs required strong leaders, and the only way for an alpha to grow to his potential was to challenge himself.

"But what are you going to do?" she went on, mascara streaking down her ruddy cheeks. "You don't have any money. All you do is spend it."

"Maybe bounty hunting," Lennon said. "We haven't decided, but Alaska calls to our wolves. You know we've wanted to live there since we were boys."

Hendrix put his hand on her knee. "It's our time."

Her mouth turned down, and she touched his forehead with her thumb, tracing it along one of the grooves. "You're not allowed to grow up on me. What if you never come back? What if you decide to live there forever?"

Lennon leaned in. "Good grief. If we'd known you were going to get this emotional, we would have hired a singing telegram to deliver the message once we were already on our way."

She reached back and smacked him on the head.

"I'm actually gonna miss that," he said ruefully, taking his seat again when the waitress set down a plate of fries in front of Melody.

Hendrix did the same. "So what about you?" he asked Tak. "Is Austin starting to grow on you?"

Tak grinned at him before finishing off his glass of lemonade.

While he hadn't made his intentions clear in regards to future plans, Tak had gone home twice, and each time he'd returned with another bag of clothes or other personal items. Though we were in love, Tak refused to move in with me. He said he respected me too much to cheapen our relationship, wherever it was going and however long it took to get there. He'd been staying with Hendrix and Lennon, so I guessed he must have known about their plan.

It made me wonder if they knew about his.

I leaned against his shoulder and peered up at him. Tak smiled with his eyes the way he always did when he didn't feel like saying anything. I wasn't sure what our future held, but one day at a time was all I needed. He belonged to me, and I belonged to him.

An Aerosmith song playing on the jukebox hit a chorus that reminded me of something important I meant to share. I pulled away from Tak and patted the table excitedly. "I have some good news!"

With tears still staining her cheeks, Melody stopped pouring mustard on her fries and glared at me. "You waited this long in the evening to give us breaking news? Why is everyone doing this to me? Did you all plan this?" She suddenly let go of the mustard, her eyes widening as she looked between Tak and me. "Are you… pregnant?"

Tak threw back his head and howled with laughter. He had such an infectious laugh that it made nearby patrons look over with interest.

"It's not *that* kind of news," I ground out. "Asia signed a long-term contract. It looks like the feather collection isn't going to be a limited edition after all."

"That's awesome!" Mel exclaimed. "Those earrings have been selling like crazy. I'm so happy for you!"

After the fire, Asia called to tell me she'd changed her mind about the offer. She'd had no idea what had transpired and was horrified to learn that River had bribed her with money stolen from our safe.

I smiled gleefully. "This is a huge stepping-stone for Moonglow. I just hope my assistant can keep up with all my orders or I might have to hire a second one."

Lakota scratched his chin. He had that look he always got

whenever he was brimming with opinions. "If you were in a pack, finding help wouldn't be a problem." He glanced around at everyone and lifted his glass. "Just pointing out that labor would be a job for the pack. You throw away money hiring assistants." He furrowed his brow at Tak and quickly stood up. "Who wants me to kick their ass at pool?"

Hendrix bolted out of his chair. "Only if you promise not to cry when I win."

"Keep dreaming."

When they swaggered off, I lowered my voice and asked Tak, "What was that about? Lakota's acting strange all of a sudden."

Tak touched his necklace and stared thoughtfully across the room. I was overjoyed to see him in the necklace I'd given him. It was too cumbersome to wear all the time, but the meaning behind it was more valuable to me than anything else in the world.

My heart warmed whenever he attentively tucked a lock of hair behind my ear or kissed my temple while at the table. Nothing about our relationship was a secret from my family, friends, or anyone else.

Tak dropped a lemon wedge into his empty glass of lemonade and looked at Lennon. "You and your brother will be a strong alliance when you become Packmasters. In my tribe, it's rare to see two alpha brothers. They seem to run in your family. I bet you have a lot of young women lining up to warm your bed."

Lennon grinned handsomely, stroking the light dusting of whiskers across his jaw. I'd lost track of their age, but they must have been twenty. You'd never know it to look at them. Lennon and Hendrix were no longer the scrawny little boys I remembered.

Melody scooted over and put her arm around his broad shoulders. "No woman is allowed near my baby brother without *my* permission."

He snorted. "And you're saying this because you love me and not because you're as drunk as a skunk?"

"That's my story, and I'm stickin' to it."

"Coming from the sister who snuck behind my back and got mated. You're lucky I didn't lock Lakota's wolf in a trunk and ship him to France."

She lifted her glass and chortled. "Can you imagine Lakota in a beret?"

Lennon took her beer away. "You're such a lightweight."

"Don't let her drive," Tak warned.

Lennon held a solemn look. "We always have a designated driver. Our uncle works here, and we get dibs on the private room if anyone needs to crash. I've only had the one beer an hour ago."

"I'm not judging you," Tak said. "Just think about your actions. There's nothing wrong with someone having too many spirits, especially in celebration. But they become our responsibility, and we have to look out for them."

I stroked Tak's arm, proud of his commitment to truth.

Tak stood up and straightened his shirt. "There's something I need to do. Be right back."

When he didn't head for the restroom, I got butterflies. He stalked toward Lakota, who was busy racking up pool balls. The dim light made it difficult to see anything in the back except for the overhead lamps shining on the billiard tables.

Lennon glanced in that direction. "Wonder what that was about."

"I bet I know," Melody sang, waggling her brows at me.

Lennon snickered. "Maybe he just needed to borrow a pencil."

"Or a recipe for banana nut bread," Melody said with a snort.

"Or maybe they're discussing quantum physics."

"Or *maybe* he wants to invite my brother into a secret knitting circle."

When I realized what was going on, I sprang out of

my chair while Mel and Lennon carried on with the one-upmanship. My palms grew sweaty, and my heart raced as I neared the back of the room.

After tapping Lakota's shoulder, Tak straightened up.

"What's up?" Lakota asked, pool stick in hand.

Tak wiped his forehead, and before he opened his mouth, I grabbed his thick arm and yanked him away.

"What are you doing?" I hissed.

He gave me a look of reproach. "What I should have done weeks ago. I've been waiting for the right moment."

"For what?"

Sweat touched his brow. "No man should think he has the right to a woman's heart without proving his worth. If your family is the condition, then I must also win *their* hearts."

I took a nervous breath. "Now? In a bar?"

Lakota was giving us a suspicious look as he chalked his stick.

Tak's steadfast loyalty to Lakota was evident, but could he convince Lakota that he was worthy of being his brother? When courtship was involved, it was customary for packmates to decide if an outsider would be divisive or an asset to the pack. Since I didn't have one, much of that decision fell on my family.

Tak shook his head. "Don't look so nervous. You're making *me* nervous, and I haven't even gotten around to the hard part of speaking with your father."

Now I understood why Tak looked especially handsome this evening. Others only saw black cargo pants and a sleeveless shirt, but I saw a man who'd selected clothes that would put those fresh scars on prominent display. Not to mention my necklace. And his perfectly braided hair with the elaborate tie at the end. All the food and drink had gone on his tab, and he'd been cracking more jokes at the table than usual.

"I'll be right back," he informed me.

My feet rooted in place as I watched him pivot around and tap Lakota on the shoulder again. When Lakota turned, he didn't have the same smile stamped on his face as moments earlier. His eyes darted back and forth between us, and then he set his pool stick on the table and folded his arms.

Tak cleared his throat and said something I couldn't hear.

"What?" Lakota asked, straining to hear him over a guitar riff.

"Turn down the music!" Tak boomed. A few seconds later, the volume decreased, and people rubbernecked to see what was happening. "I love your sister," he repeated with perfect clarity. "I'm in love with your sister."

"Yes, and that's what concerns me."

I circled around to watch the conversation from a closer distance—Tak on the right and Lakota backed up against the pool table.

Tak lifted his chin. "I've never disrespected a woman, and you know that. And you can't judge me because I've known other women intimately. I'm a man over fifty; that's a given. I respect Hope. She's a woman no man truly deserves, but I'm willing to prove myself a worthy suitor. I've always seen you as my brother, and no matter what happens, that won't change." Tak clasped his hands behind his back and inclined his head. "I'm asking permission to court your sister."

A thunderstruck silence fell around us. Melody and the twins drew closer, listening with rapt attention.

I couldn't hold my tongue any longer. "I don't want him to court me."

Lakota's brows knitted. Tak turned his head so slowly that I felt his alpha energy skating across my skin when he finally looked at me.

"What are you thinking, Tak?" I asked. "Courtship?"

Lakota grinned and pushed off the pool table. "Well, that takes care of that."

I closed the distance between us and looked into Tak's bewildered eyes. "I want to be mated with you, and I won't accept anything less. There's no need for you to court me." Then I turned my attention to Lakota. "He risked his life to save mine. He loves me unquestionably—without conditions. He's protected me. He's loved me consistently and completely.

He treats me as an equal and is kind to my family. What more could you want for your sister? Is there any other man in this room you'd choose in his stead?" I swung my gaze up to Tak. "And if you're not ready to make this official because you suddenly have doubts—"

Tak pulled me into his arms and kissed me hard. My feet were off the ground, my arms around his neck. Kissing him was like coming home, and the idea of spending the rest of my life with this man filled me with more joy than I'd ever known. He softened the touch of our lips and kissed the corners of my mouth.

"And he makes me laugh," I said quietly, staring into his dark and wondrous eyes.

Tak hugged me hard, and bystanders whistled at us. When he set me down, Lakota approached and clapped him on the shoulder.

"You have my permission." Lakota leaned in tight and said privately, "But good luck with my father. Are you ready to be the son of Lorenzo Church?"

Tak smirked. "I think I'll call him Dad."

I laughed. "I wouldn't do that if I were you. He's not fond of that word. It doesn't hold enough respect in his eyes."

Tak stepped on a chair and climbed on top of a table, pulling me up next to him. He put his arms around my waist as if no one else was there. "Maybe I'll call him Pops."

I held on to his neck. "Don't ever lose your sense of humor. It's the one thing I love most about you."

"Love?" he asked.

I felt proud to be in his arms, despite a few skeptical glances thrown our way. It occurred to me in that moment that I'd never given him true words of love. At least not when he was conscious. But words didn't matter. I'd once heard that there are a thousand ways to tell someone you love them without uttering a single word. I never used to believe it.

Until now.

Chapter 32

Tak closed the door behind him in the private room. "Nice digs," he said, admiring the TV on the opposite wall and the leather furniture in front of it.

Lakota took a seat in one of the chairs on the right and put his feet on the coffee table. "It's small compared to what the bigger clubs offer. It used to be a storage room back in the day, but Howlers is a popular bar, so the owner decided to give it a little paint job and make some money on the side."

Tak knocked on the wall. "Soundproof?"

Lakota arched an eyebrow. "I don't see many Vampires who come back here since we're mostly a Shifter bar. I suppose it's insulated, but I never gave it much thought. What's this about? Something you're trying to keep secret?"

Tak strode over to the sofa across from Lakota and took a seat, his elbows resting on his thighs. "What are your plans for the future?"

Lakota drummed his fingers on the armrests. "Why? Are you gonna ask for my hand in marriage?"

"Kind of."

The startled look on Lakota's face made Tak want to laugh, but he was feeling serious about the moment and didn't want to ruin it with jokes.

"I'm the son of a powerful alpha," Tak began. "A leader among leaders. I've learned many great lessons, sat in on leadership meetings, and had very wise mentors. Even after the accident, my father hoped that time would shape me into a leader. But young alphas in the tribe didn't see it that way. When you don't hold rank, you lose respect. That's why I'll never be what you call a Packmaster among my people."

Lakota put his hands in his lap. "You would have made a good one."

Tak took in a breath. "That's what I'm going to find out. I've come to a decision. I'm breaking away from my tribe and forming a pack. I can't do this alone. I need a beta, and you're the only man I'd want at my side."

Lakota stared for a frozen moment. "You want me as your second-in-command?"

"I'm only surprised you haven't been courted by another alpha. You're a strong beta, and I think you know that. You have presence when you walk into a room, and even though you're batshit crazy, you're the kind of man a pack can trust. You have leadership skills, and your days as a bounty hunter show me you're savvy, patient, and on the right side of the law. But friend, it's more than that. You're like a brother to me. I'm not mating Hope without a plan. We need a pack—our wolves demand it. This isn't the first time the thought has crossed my mind. Remember our talks?"

Lakota leaned forward and lowered his head. "I never thought you would break away from your tribe."

"Neither did I, but this is the path I must take. My pack family is out there somewhere, and I need a good beta to help me find them. Someone to help me build a homestead, establish rules, keep the pack in line, and be a loyal wolf I can confide in. If you want me to hold your hand on bended knee, you can kiss my ass. But I'm asking you, Lakota Cross, if you'll join my family and help me lead."

Lakota covered his nose and mouth with both hands, eyes thoughtfully wide.

"I can make homemade bacon if that sweetens the deal."

Lakota cut him a sharp look, and Tak wondered if he was hiding a smile.

"Where do you plan to settle?" Lakota finally asked.

"Wherever we feel best. I'm willing to go anywhere, but right now, Hope and Melody's store takes precedence. We can see what land is available outside city lines. It might be a commute for them, but in time, someone else can manage the store while they focus on crafting new designs."

Lakota nodded. "If we had a pack, we could assign those jobs to them. Mel works too many hours, and she complains she doesn't have time to do what she really loves—designing all those purses and funky clothes. She's too busy running the shop and looking at numbers. Some nights she's too tired to mate with me."

Tak chuckled. "Maybe you lull her to sleep with your sweet words of nothing."

"I don't have a problem in that department."

"Is that what all your previous lovers told you?"

Lakota leveled him with a single glance. "Melody was my one and only."

Tak's eyes rounded, and then he threw his head back and laughed. Lakota looked annoyed, which made Tak laugh even harder. He finally wiped the tears away and settled down. "That explains *so* much. I have respect, but you have much to learn. Melody is going to be a busy teacher."

"Apparently it all comes naturally."

"If you say so." Tak's chuckle was deep and sonorous. "If you ever need advice in that department, you know where to find me."

"My bad. I thought we were talking about a job offer here." Lakota sat back and put his arms on the armrests, crossing one leg over his knee. "So, what can you offer me that no other alpha can?"

"Friendship. Loyalty. Trust. And sometimes I might let you win at a game of pool in front of the pack."

Lakota rubbed his chin, his face framed by his long hair.

"How much do you have saved up? The Council offers limited acres of land to start. You can buy more land as the pack grows, but it's not cheap, especially if you want something with a house already on it."

"We can build a house."

Lakota snorted.

Tak leaned forward. "How do you think the homes in my tribe were built? Do you think we hired people? We did everything. The electricity, the plumbing, the foundation—everything. The key is making sure you have packmates with desirable skills. Maybe in your world, you prefer a man who's good with numbers. But in mine, we look for wolves who are willing to labor and learn."

Lakota raked his hair back. "Are you bringing in people from your tribe?"

Tak shook his head. "I don't think any would leave their families to follow me. Our tribe has too much history tied to that land. This is my path to walk alone. My people can spread the word to other Packmasters from coast to coast that I'm searching for good candidates."

"You might get a bunch of young wolves leaving a pack or rejects. If people don't know you from Adam, there won't exactly be a waiting list."

"But they will know my father, and maybe that would carry some weight. Do you really want to limit our choices to this town? A wider net catches more fish. I'm looking for more than just good packmates; I'm looking for a new family."

Lakota stood up, his expression unreadable.

Tak rose to his feet and looked down at him.

They stared at each other for a beat, Tak waiting for Lakota's answer. He couldn't say much more to sway him one way or the other. It was up to Lakota to decide which path he wanted to take in life, and a man who had to be convinced wasn't a man worth having.

Lakota bowed. "It would be an honor."

Tak pulled him into a hug. "Forget that bowing shit. You're my brother now."

They gripped tighter, and Tak knew he would remember this moment for the rest of his life. It was a new beginning, and he could finally close a chapter of his life that had held him for so long in the wrong story.

When they finally broke apart, Lakota looked away and wiped his eyes. "So, are we gonna be a tribe or a pack?"

Tak heaved a sigh. "Tribe is too sacred a word and defines my people who are from the same culture and blood. But we will be a pack like no other. With you and Hope by my side to lead, we'll rise to power. We'll form alliances and flourish as a family. I don't want to discriminate against others. This is my second chance in life, and maybe it will be for someone else."

"Seems fitting. Our friendship got a second chance, and look where I am now. Second-in-command." Lakota puffed out his chest. "Think I should get that on a T-shirt?"

Tak patted his cheek and laughed. "Put it on your wish list. We'll see if that fat man who climbs down your chimneys will bring you one this year."

"Fat chance," Lakota said as they strode toward the door. "Mel already said I was on the naughty list."

Tak grinned. "And you think that's a bad thing?"

A light blinked by the door, indicating someone was outside.

"Looks like we're cutting in on someone's time," Lakota said.

Tak hung back. "Tell everyone I'll be out in a bit."

Lakota looked over his shoulder, his blue eyes darkening like storm clouds. "If you think you're going to have sex in here with my sister, you can think again."

When he opened the door, Lorenzo Church was standing on the other side.

Before Lakota left Tak and Lorenzo alone in the room, he shot Tak a look of amusement. Tak slammed the door in his face.

Lorenzo was dressed similarly to Tak, wearing a black sleeveless shirt and cargos, only his pants were camouflage green, as if he were going to war. His glossy hair draped neatly down his back, and he looked more put together than Tak last remembered. The man turned so that the skull-and-crossbones tattoo stared at Tak like an ominous warning.

Tak cleared his throat. "Can I get you a drink?"

Lorenzo gave him a sharp look. "Do you still drink?"

"No."

"Why not?"

"Because it makes men weak."

Lorenzo turned and folded his arms. "Are you trying to make me weak?"

This was going all wrong.

"I haven't touched a drop since the accident," Tak explained.

"And yet you serve it to others."

"I can't control what other people do."

Lorenzo lifted his chin and looked at him for a long time. He was a stern-looking man who clearly liked having the upper hand. Years of leading a pack will do that to an alpha. So Tak waited.

For what seemed like centuries.

Lorenzo widened his stance and tipped his head to the side. "Why did you ask to meet me here? And I don't mean this bar, but this room. You don't think people around here talk when they see a Packmaster going into one of the private rooms? Are you trying to sully my reputation?"

"Just tell them we're lovers."

Tak's joke was met with crickets. So much for warming him up.

"Do you want to sit down?" Lorenzo asked.

Relieved this was finally going somewhere, Tak walked past him and sat down in the leather chair. Lorenzo turned to face him but didn't sit on the sofa. Probably because Tak was taller. Instead, he kept his arms folded and suddenly had the dominant position.

Tak wasn't about to have this conversation sitting, so he rose to his feet and met eyes with Lorenzo. "You already know how I feel about your daughter. Out of respect, I've been staying with Hendrix and Lennon while I settle my affairs at home. My intention was to court your daughter, but she doesn't want that."

A smile curved up Lorenzo's cheek.

"She wants to skip the courtship and mate."

The smile turned into an angry slash across his face.

Tak's heart was hammering against his ribs, so he took a deep breath to calm himself. "It was a difficult decision to leave my tribe. It's the only home I've ever known, and it's where my roots are. My people, my heritage, my land, my memories. But none of that holds any value if I can't be with Hope."

"Is she not good enough to invite to live with your people?"

"That's not it," Tak said, shaking his head. "I'll never be a leader among my own people. They've forgiven my sins but haven't forgotten. There are many alphas there without a dark past like mine whom others would gladly live under. I've never run from my mistakes, but I've done a great job at avoiding my potential. If I invite Hope to live there, I'll never be able to look her in the eye. The men respect me as a packmate, not as an alpha. I suspect many are only courteous because of who my father is. Hope deserves a strong mate, and I deserve a second chance to prove my worth as a leader."

Lorenzo canted his head. "It won't take long before your packmates find out about your past."

"I don't intend to hide it from them," he said matter-of-factly. "Lakota has agreed to be my second."

Lorenzo's eyebrows touched his hairline. "First you want my daughter, and then you take my son?"

"Lakota's a smart wolf who makes his own decisions. He

has a lot of options, and he's overly cautious. I'm sure you know he's not a man who acts impulsively. We have a bond, and he's a loyal wolf."

"That he is."

Arms still folded, Lorenzo lowered his head, his eyes downcast.

"You told me that you were grateful I saved Hope's life but that I still had to earn your respect. Hope loves you, and as much as she loves me too, I wouldn't want to disrespect the one man who's made her into the woman she is today. Brave, loving, intelligent, thoughtful, devoted, free-spirited, and cantankerous."

Lorenzo flashed his eyes up. "Are you trying to provoke me, boy?"

Tak chuckled and clasped his hands in front of him. "Just wanted to make sure you were listening. Maybe I'm not the ideal person you had in mind to mate with your daughter, but I promise to give her the world. She already has my heart."

"And her business? Isn't that a lot of responsibility for a Packmaster's mate?"

Tak's jaw set. "If you think I'm going to ask her to give up her dream, you're mistaken. In time they'll have someone else running the store while they focus on the business side of things, but I'd rather cut off my hands than ask her to let go of the shop. If they want to stay, fine. If they want to relocate or expand, fine. That's good income for the pack and might motivate a few others to start up their own business."

Lorenzo gave an imperceptible nod, indicating that was the only acceptable answer. "Hope's challenge against the wolf who did her wrong should teach you a lesson about betrayal. You should fear her more than you do me."

"At least I know she has the capability to be lenient. Something tells me you wouldn't."

"Fair enough." Lorenzo's shoulders relaxed a little. "Tell me why it is that you didn't fight for her."

"I did."

"Not the bear. I meant River."

"I would have, but that's not what she wanted. It would have taken away her honor."

Lorenzo paced toward the door and then turned. "You let Hope face her enemy, and it shows that you honor her. You and I love strong women, and if they want to fight their own battles, you stand by their side and let them. They'll never respect you if you don't give them that power."

Tak nodded in agreement, all his nerves finally settling.

Lorenzo stepped close and poked Tak's necklace with his finger. "If I ever find out that you laid a hand on her, I'll disembowel you."

"You have my word, Pops."

Lorenzo gave him a cold stare. "Don't push it."

"So we're good?"

"I'm still waiting," Lorenzo said, dropping his arms to his sides.

Confused, Tak wondered if he'd forgotten anything. "May I have permission to mate your daughter?"

The silence cut through the room, and Tak couldn't read the man's expression. He clearly liked torturing people.

"Well?" he pressed.

Lorenzo pursed his lips, his dark eyes glittering. "I'm waiting for you to kneel."

Tak thought back to what he'd said when they first met about getting down on one knee for his blessing. "That was a figure of speech."

"Am I to assume that everything you say is a figure of speech? Why would I allow a man to mate with my daughter if his words mean nothing?"

Fuck. Lorenzo wasn't going to let it go, and Tak toiled over that for a moment. On one hand, it was a shitty way to begin a relationship with his father-in-law. He was the new man in Hope's life, and if he continued to bow down to her father, he'd never be rid of his control. On the other hand...

Tak dropped down on one knee and grasped Lorenzo's

hand, holding it tight. He held it as if he were proposing, and the startled look on Lorenzo's face was worth every penny.

Especially when the door opened and Lorenzo recoiled, but Tak wouldn't let go. Lakota gawked at what could have easily looked like one man proposing to another.

Tak pressed his lips to Lorenzo's hand and kissed it softly, his eyes twinkling with amusement as he looked up at the fire heating Lorenzo's cheeks.

With a hard jerk, Lorenzo wrenched his hand free and stalked toward the door.

Tak stood, a wide grin on his face. But the grin withered when he wondered if he'd pushed the joke too far. Not everyone appreciated a sense of humor, and Tak might have just blown his chance.

When Lorenzo reached the threshold, he looked over his shoulder. "I'm a scotch man." After a beat, he nodded. "For future reference."

That was all the approval Tak needed.

Chapter 33

SHORTLY BEFORE OUR CREW LEFT Howlers, I kissed Tak and asked him once again why he wouldn't stop grinning. Surely the private talk with Lakota couldn't have been that amusing. But there was a sparkle in his eyes I hadn't seen before—a renewed vigor that had him lifting me off the ground and spinning me in a circle as we kissed goodbye in the parking lot. Tak's spirit shone brighter than it ever had, and I basked in the glow as I thought about our future together.

Lakota caved easily, but my father would have words with Tak that would wipe that smile off his face. Probably threats about how far he'd hunt him down if he ever hurt or shamed me.

Mating ceremonies weren't a required ritual since making it official with the Council was how the word spread. But I liked the idea of a private ceremony under the moonlight, even if it was just Tak and me exchanging vows.

After everyone went their separate ways, I asked to borrow Lakota's truck. I didn't want unresolved issues in my new life, so that meant learning how Dutch was doing.

A week ago, I'd bumped into the Relic who carried him off that fateful day. It was pure happenstance when he strolled by the store windows, and I dashed outside to gather information about my wounded neighbor. The Relic had taken Dutch to his private clinic and administered what care he could. His words were sobering as he recounted Dutch's four-day coma. In order to survive, his mind had shut down, and that meant he was unable to shift—unable to heal.

The Relic decided against common practice to stitch up the wounds. Dutch had lost so much blood that he had a transfusion. When he finally woke up, he demanded that the Relic take him home. By that point, the damage was done. Shifting would close the existing wounds and speed along the process, but too much time had elapsed to fully heal. The Relic didn't go into detail because of the confidential nature of their relationship, but he implied that Dutch had paid him well for his services. Because I'd witnessed the mauling firsthand, the Relic felt obligated to give me an update. But he asked me to make a solemn promise not to spread rumors about Dutch's condition since it could damage his reputation.

Dutch's store had reopened two days ago. I stopped in, hoping to find him there, but was greeted by a young woman I'd never seen before. She seemed clueless, having never met the man, but explained that Dutch worked from home and had more important things to do than work behind a counter. He must have hired a professional employment agency to find someone trustworthy to fill the position—someone who wouldn't ask questions.

In many ways, she was right. Dutch owned a profitable jewelry store and didn't need to be working retail when there were other business-related duties to attend to. But what bothered me was that I didn't think that was the whole story.

I squinted at the address the Relic had scribbled on a piece of paper. Dutch lived in a prestigious neighborhood on the edge of the city, the large houses spaced apart with an appreciable amount of land between them.

Crickets chirped in the nearby bushes as I rang the bell and waited. All the lights were off, and when no one answered, I knocked. "Dutch? It's me… Hope. Please open up." I rang the bell again and again. Could he hear it in a house this big?

Then I noticed the door knocker and tapped it several times. "Dutch!"

The locks rattled, and I sucked in a sharp breath. When the door eased open, a shadowy figure appeared.

"Dutch? Is that you?"

His hair, which I'd always seen styled back, was now unkempt and covering his left eye. He wore a black mask that shielded his face up to his eyes. The thin material looked breathable and took me off guard.

My voice quavered as I looked into his bright blue eye. "*Oh, Dutch.*"

His gaze lowered.

"I'm so sorry for all this," I said, fighting back tears. "I should have never gone into your shop that day. I want to apologize for the accusations and the way I handled myself. If I hadn't left those keys behind—"

"I smelled the smoke," he began, his voice raspier than I remembered. "When I followed it to the back of your store, I saw the bear. I couldn't run away like before, and shifting... Well, that wasn't an option with a grizzly. My animal instincts aren't to fight."

"It's okay to run, Dutch. Pride isn't worth your life, but I'm eternally grateful for what you did. You saved our lives. I've never seen such bravery. What can I do?"

When I reached out to pull away his mask, he caught my wrist.

"Don't."

"Let me look at you. Maybe that Relic didn't have the best skills. There's probably someone out there who can help you—someone more qualified. It might not be as bad as you think."

"I can afford the best, but nothing can help me now. You don't need to see the damage done." He drew back into the shadows. "I'd rather you remember me as I was."

Tears slipped down my cheeks. "Please forgive me. I never meant for this to happen."

"I don't blame you," he said wearily. "I just don't have a place in your world anymore. Isolation is where I belong now. The fates have punished me for my vanity."

No words were sufficient, not even an apology. "The bear's dead. I don't know if that gives you any peace, but you helped save Tak's life. Maybe that doesn't mean much since you two don't know each other, but I love him. I'm in your debt, and you have my word that I'll make good on any favor you ask of me. I mean it, Dutch."

A moth flitted past me and went inside the house. Dutch ignored it.

"You should go," he said.

"Wait." I reached in my purse and retrieved a white box. "These are for you."

Dutch accepted the square gift box. He flicked his eye up to mine before he lifted the lid and revealed a pair of black feather earrings with white tips.

"I don't know why you wanted a pair, maybe just curiosity. But those are very special. I made them especially for you with the rarest feathers I could find. I don't normally work with diamonds, but I affixed small ones at the top. I thought you would appreciate that."

"What am I to do with these?"

Crestfallen, I looked at the box balanced in the palm of his hand. "Keep them. They were blessed by a spiritual leader. The woman who wears these will have your heart."

He snapped the box closed. "I need to rest."

"Of course. Is there anything you need?"

"No." He began to close the door and then hesitated. "There is one thing you can do for me. Don't speak about my condition with anyone. Aside from the Relic, you're the only one who knows what happened. No one else at the scene would have recognized me—not the way I was. My store is all I have to earn a living. It could jeopardize my business if people found out the truth."

"The truth of you being a hero?"

"Don't make this difficult, Hope. You know how damning scars like these are in the immortal world. These aren't the marks of a man who walked away victorious. Shifters will see me as inferior, and immortals are particular when it comes to how they part with their money. No one will wear my necklaces proudly. I'll just become that sad story everyone talks about whenever they mentioned who they got their jewelry from. I don't want their pity. Swear to me."

Without hesitation, I said, "I swear. But Tak knows you were there. I'll talk to him. What's my secret to keep will also be his. You can trust him."

I didn't mention Melody knowing. Dutch didn't need to worry over details. Mel wouldn't tell a soul if I asked, and she'd never met him anyhow. It broke my heart to say goodbye to a man I barely had the pleasure to know. Dutch wouldn't be receiving visitors in the future, of that I was certain. He had chosen to live a reclusive life, and I grieved for the man who loved to travel.

Dutch stepped back. "I wish you two well. May the fates treat you kindly."

"And you," I whispered, placing my hand on the closed door.

CHAPTER 34

Tak spread a blue quilt across a grassy spot in the shade beneath a maple tree. "Sit," he said.

I watched with amusement while he walked back to his truck and pulled a large picnic basket out of the bed. He looked good in his loose-fitting jeans and white tank top. It drew my attention to his sexy arms and broad chest. I took in a deep breath, enjoying the fragrant scent of summer and the way Tak swaggered back to the blanket. He had a slow and easy walk, the kind that promised he was worth the wait.

After he set the basket down on the grass, he sat on the blanket and pulled out two bottles of sweet tea. "I would have brought wine, but I didn't want to taste it on your lips."

"I prefer tea."

It was late morning—still cool enough to enjoy the weather. A few puffy clouds swiftly moved in front of the sun, casting a dark shadow across the landscape before the sun broke out again.

I yawned, still tired after a night of tossing and turning. My visit with Dutch had left me unsettled, so when Tak called after breakfast and invited me out, I was grateful for the respite. Mel volunteered to watch the store the whole day to give us some private time together.

Tak stood up and towered over me. "Lie down," he said, his hot gaze traveling down the length of my body.

A ripple of excitement zinged through me, and I scooted onto my back so I was staring up at him. "I thought we were eating?"

He swiped his tongue across his bottom lip. "We are."

My breath caught as he went down on his knees. He softly kissed around my navel, and his warm body heated my inner thighs. Tak untied the bottom of my button-up shirt, his eyes locked on mine. When he stroked my sex, I moaned and arched my back.

"Music to my ears," he murmured, doing it again.

The kisses on my inner thigh were pure torture, and when I felt his tongue slide across my skin, I reached for his braid and gripped it hard.

He chuckled deep in his throat and crawled on top of me. Something seemed different about him—that same look I'd noticed before parting ways last night. Maybe it was just the look of my future in his eyes. He kissed me passionately, his tongue thrusting against mine before he quickly withdrew and left me panting for more.

Tak unfastened the buttons on my blouse. When he finished, he slowly opened each side and admired my bare breasts. How could one man fill me with so much desire? His gaze, his touch, his words—all brushstrokes blending our love into one masterpiece. I shivered when he licked his fingertip and then circled it around my nipple, his eyes on mine the whole time. The skin swelled and pebbled at the tips, responding eagerly to his touch.

"I'm going to make you feel good." His voice was smoky, and his words were a promise. Tak slid his hands down my shorts and beneath my panties.

I let out a whimpering moan.

His touch was so intimate—so sensual. I wrapped my arms around him and gently kissed his scars. Tak's breathing became shaky, but his fingers never lost their rhythm.

His forever. Those words burned in my thoughts, and I lifted my hips, craving more.

His lips were mine, and I kissed them.

The branches swayed overhead, leaves whispering their secrets.

Beneath the azure sky, Tak adored me with his hands. My body hummed with desire as I opened my legs and rocked in the waves of exquisite pleasure, abandoning all inhibitions. Those didn't exist with Tak.

He bent down and drew my nipple into his mouth, sucking hard. I gasped and moaned, his soft strokes quickening with my every breath. There was something about being out in the open that heightened my arousal. No doors. No walls. Anyone could see. Anyone could hear. No secrets.

I closed my eyes and writhed beneath him.

His mouth branded me with a penetrating kiss, and I felt myself trembling.

Tak moved his lips to my ear. "Do you want me to stop?"

"No," I whispered, clawing his back.

Tak was a gentle giant, but there was nothing gentle about the hungry look in his eyes.

"If you come for me, I'm going to press your back against that tree and claim you."

The visual entered my mind, and I moaned. "Please, Tak. I need it."

He trembled, shifting his body weight off me and to the side. "You make it so hard for me."

"I make it hard?"

He growled.

"I need more of you. It's not enough."

He pulled my gaze toward him. "Don't. Move."

"What?" I whimpered.

I panicked at first, thinking a bee had landed on my head.

"You're too worked up, and that's my fault," he said. "Lie still. Don't move."

Tak gripped both sides of my shorts as if they were the enemy and stripped them off so I was bare to him.

He nestled his head between my legs, and a tremor of

anticipation rolled through me. The way he gripped my thighs and hooked them over his shoulders made me break out in a sweat. I'd never been so exposed to a man, and a flush of embarrassment heated my cheeks.

"I'm gonna kiss you, Hope. I'm gonna kiss you deep."

When his tongue slid along my wet crease, I nearly kicked him away. He lapped me as if I were honey, and it was more than I could take.

So intimate.

So unbelievably provocative.

And I was so, *so* close.

"You're beautiful when you come," he said. "*Show me.*"

He greedily sucked and twirled his tongue before driving it home. As my breath hitched, I began chasing my release.

Tak growled deep, and the vibration shattered me. Sharp pulses hit me in waves as his alpha power licked across my skin.

"More," he demanded.

"No, I can't."

He rose up onto his hands and lay next to me, his fingers working me over in soft, teasing strokes. "I want your needy cries in my fantasies at night."

My back arched when he hit the right spot.

Tak drew my nipple into his mouth. "Not yet," he said, teeth nipping lightly.

He was using his alpha command, and my body reluctantly submitted. I was right on the cusp—so close to another orgasm and yet unable to reach it.

Tak's hard erection pressed against my thigh. The more I whimpered, the stronger he leaned into me as if his willpower was crumbling.

My fingers dove inside his jeans, sliding over the head.

"Oh, fuck... *Now*," he commanded, alpha power shimmering across my body. "Come *now*."

I squeezed his erection and cried out, my body clenching

beneath his gaze. Tak watched me with ravenous eyes as the last remaining waves of pleasure left me boneless.

He moved my hand out of his jeans and smiled. "You're just full of surprises, aren't you?"

Breathless, I touched his cheek. "Why not let me pleasure you?"

Tak dropped his head on my shoulder, his breathing just as heavy as mine. "I like the feeling of wanting you."

"Then have me. My pleasure shouldn't be your punishment."

Tak chuckled. "We're gonna have a great sex life." He perked his head up and waggled his brows. "Not many couples can say that, you know. They fall in love, but they struggle to know each other in bed. Tomorrow you can sit astride me and face the other way. I want to try that."

I thought about the complicated position. "Wouldn't you rather have me on my hands and knees?"

After all, that was the most desirous position for male Shifters.

He pursed his lips. "I want to do things with you that I've never tried. My hands on your backside as you rock those luscious hips at your own sweet rhythm, the look you throw me over your shoulder as I beg you to go faster. The best of both worlds."

"Then why wait?"

Tak kissed my nose. "Today is about you."

I furrowed my brow when he closed my shirt and fastened two buttons. The man possessed more restraint than I'd ever understand. With flushed cheeks, he sat back and put my panties and shorts back on. I didn't usually wear such revealing clothes, but Tak brought out the woman in me. He made it clear he loved every curve on my body, and seeing the way he kept looking at my thighs made me appreciate why differences mattered.

After I sat up, Tak put a bottle of cold tea in my hand.

I pressed the glass against my neck and sighed. "So which tree are you pinning me against?"

He winked. "That comes after."

"After what?"

"You ask too many questions."

Still breathless and post-orgasm, I soaked in the beautiful morning.

Tak cleaned up with a napkin and then pulled out plastic bags filled with cheese, summer sausage, and fruit. "Do you want to tell me what's bothering you?"

I gulped down my tea and screwed the cap back on. "I went to see Dutch last night."

He ate a handful of cheese cubes and gave me a pensive stare. "What for?"

"Because I owe him my gratitude. He blinded that bear and risked his life to help someone who'd insulted his integrity. He's hurt, Tak. I didn't see all the scars, but he's hurt bad."

"I didn't think he'd survive. I guess the fates aren't done with him."

After eating a few grapes, I tossed the stem in the grass. "He made me promise not to tell anyone about his scars or what happened. I want you to do the same. I already talked to Mel, and she gave me her word."

Tak nodded. "Needn't ask me twice."

"I can't help but feel responsible."

He bent his knee and gulped down half his drink. Then he wiped his mouth with the back of his hand and set the bottle against the basket. "You had nothing to do with it. Men have to stand by their decisions, and what kind of man would he be had he done nothing? Warriors don't let fear hold them back."

"Dutch said he doesn't blame me, but he's bitter about what happened. I don't think he has anyone to look after him. He hired someone to run the store, and I have a feeling he's never going back."

Tak touched his bottom lip, his eyes pensive. "Promise me you won't go see him again."

I frowned. "Why?"

He gazed at something in the distance. "A reclusive man with anger in his heart becomes filled with his own poison. His heart grows bitter. You don't know this man well enough to save him from that dark place. If he ever had feelings for you, he wouldn't want to see you again. Especially now that I've got claim on you."

I stood up and strode off. I knew Tak was right, but it still felt like I wasn't doing enough. Dutch needed a miracle to bring him back, and I didn't have the power to be that miracle.

Tak caught up and turned me around. "Don't be angry with me. I don't want to spoil this day."

"What's so special about today?"

He looked down sheepishly and kicked at the dirt. "I was going to wait until after lunch and after we made love."

I backed up against the tree. "It's not too late."

Tak flashed his teeth and looked like a wolf grinning. The smile faded, and he plucked a small leaf out of my hair. "I was never meant to love a woman."

"That's a silly thing to believe."

He pointed at his tattoo. "My wolf was born with two faces. It raised a lot of concern within my tribe. The elders spoke of it as a bad omen—that I would never find a true mate because my spirit could only love her halfway. Maybe I should have heeded their warning. After the accident, I chose to ink my face to match my spirit wolf and accept my fate. No woman would ever want a man this way. Then I met you, and you loved both halves."

I caressed his cheek. "How could I not love a man who left me on the side of the road with nothing but a sunshade?"

"And how could I not love a woman who laughs after we make love?"

His arm snaked around my waist, and despite our playful banter, neither of us smiled.

I glanced around. "Someone might catch us if we fool around again. This is private property."

"You're right." He placed a chaste kiss to my lips. "I bought it from the Council."

My heart quickened. "You bought this?"

"I wanted to give you proof that I'm staying. Telling you I love you isn't enough. Making promises to your brother isn't enough." Tak bent down and scooped up a handful of dirt, showing it to me. "I want to plant roots with you. We can build a pack on this land, or we can relocate wherever you want to go. Maybe you just want to pass it down to our children and tell them the story about the day their father gave his mother a handful of dirt and promised her the future."

He let the dirt fall into the palm of my hand.

"What about your tribe? Your father? I thought you'd want to live with them."

"Why would you think that?"

"Because they're your people."

Tak closed his fingers around my hand. "*You* are my people. My father carved aside a piece of land for me, but that's never been my destiny. That's why the fates marked my wolf. I've always felt like an outsider, and maybe that's why I made poor decisions in my youth. All that's changed. I'm a better man than I once was, and I vow to protect you with my life. I sold that land back to the tribe to use the money here. Starting a pack will take time, but I want Lakota to be my second-in-command."

I could hardly contain my exuberance. "Really?"

"Something clicked between us from the start," he said. "I already asked, by the way. And he said yes. I haven't figured out all the rules yet, but maybe we'll do something nontraditional like the tribes."

"What about my father? He'll never approve of this. It's too fast, and he barely knows you."

"He already did."

I blanched. "What? When?"

"At Howlers. Right after I spoke with Lakota."

"I didn't see him there."

"You were in the back by the pool tables. I'm glad he slipped by you, or that would have ruined the surprise. That's why today is about you, Hope. I wanted to give you all these gifts so you won't have any doubts or fears that something will keep us apart."

My heart was bursting with joy.

"I don't have money to offer you, but I have this," he said, gripping my closed hand filled with dirt.

"What makes you think I need money to be happy? We have Moonglow. Lakota has savings put aside, and he's been taking some jobs in town."

"Bounty hunting?"

I let the dirt fall to our feet and brushed my hand off. "No, just PI stuff. I think he's trying it out to see if he likes it. Maybe he will, and maybe he won't, but it's kept him busy."

Tak folded his arms. "Sounds impressive. I didn't get as far as asking him about his work. Maybe he's not really interested in settling down then."

"Are you kidding? Lakota adores you. Well, as much as one man can adore another."

Tak rocked with laughter and held me in his arms. We did a little sway, and he did that wonderful thing where he smiled at me with his eyes. "It's all ours," he said. "That's why I didn't wear the necklace today. I wanted our wolves to check out their new territory, and I couldn't leave behind something so valuable."

"It's just money. It can be replaced."

He gave me a light squeeze. "That necklace is worth more than money. It's irreplaceable. So… feel like marking territory and making it official?"

I tried not to look amused. "Are you asking me to pee with you?"

Tak barked out a laugh. "Actually, nothing would make me happier than the two of us taking a piss together. Isn't that how all love stories end? My wolf is coming out of his skin to meet his future life mate."

I traced my fingers over the claw marks on his shoulder. "Ask me."

"Ask you what?"

"Ask me to love you."

The last time he tried, it wasn't worthy of him. His soul was still broken. Even though we'd both made our intentions of mating clear, having a second chance at this conversation felt necessary. Tak needed that moment just as much as I did.

He cupped my shoulders and gazed earnestly into my eyes. I could see his spirit wolf looking back at me, searching for answers.

"If any man ever dishonors you, he'll have to answer to me. I promise to protect you with my life, and you have my word on that. I'll be a good lover and a faithful mate. I won't always have the right words, but I promise you'll never feel safer than in my pack. I want to spend the rest of our days making you laugh, because I've never heard a more beautiful sound. I love you, Hope. I would give you my name, but my people don't have surnames. So take my heart instead."

I placed my hand over his heart. "I accept your offer, Tak of the Iwa tribe. But can you love me as I am? I don't know if I'll ever be over the panic attacks—even after challenging River."

He stepped closer. "Someday they'll be a distant memory; I promise you that. I see you getting stronger every day. We'll get through each one together. Your struggles are mine, and should they never go away, I'll still be here by your side."

"I'll try to laugh more at your jokes, and I'll do my best to help our pack grow and thrive... not only financially but as a family. I'll give you the same respect you've given me. And I'll even cook you eggs sometimes."

Tak rubbed his nose against mine. "Admit it. You love me, don't you?"

"Guilty as charged."

He kissed me hard, the way every woman dreams of a man kissing her—with tenderness and force. With arms wrapped around me. With fire in his touch and his hands splayed across my back. With his whole body leaning against mine. With a promise of a bright future and a love that would grow with each passing day.

His lips brushed against my ear, his words soft and jovial. "I love you too, Duckie."

Printed in Great Britain
by Amazon